THE COMPLETE LUCKY O'TOOLE NOVELLA COLLECTION

DEBORAH COONTS

Chestnut
Street
Press

CONTENTS

LUCKY IN LOVE

LUCKY BANG

LUCKY NOW AND THEN

LUCKY FLASH

LUCKY IN LOVE

A LUCKY VEGAS NOVELLA

NATIONAL BESTSELLING AUTHOR

DEBORAH COONTS

CHAPTER ONE

"ID YOU know my wife is seriously into chicks?"
The guy was brave, I'd grant him that. Approaching
a woman in a bar with that line was no small feat, even in Vegas.

Waiting for an answer, the guy looked at me through clear,
intense eyes as he leaned in close and braced himself with an
elbow on the bar. He tipped his almost-empty flute of champagne
at a woman at the end of the bar. "That's her."

He was a handsome man, with reddish-brown hair, a tan,
creased jeans that looked and fit like European, and one of those
new-style shirts with the subtle embroidery. Well turned-out; hip
but not annoyingly so. "Two's a date, three's a fantasy?"

"Something like that." The guy's eyes settled on his wife with a
warm glow. "She's got the magic touch, if you know what I mean."

His wife, the chick magnet, glanced in our direction and
flipped her highlighted golden hair over her shoulder as she shot
me a come-on look through lowered lashes. She too sipped champagne as she pretended to be interested in the men who swarmed
around her.

"I guess it's great for you—if she shares." Never one to judge, I
kept my tone impassive and my expression bland as I pushed

myself backward off my barstool. Standing, I brushed down my pants. "You two are stunning. And I appreciate the offer. But, as an only child, I never learned to share. I keep what's mine."

"You're missing a good time." The guy's eyes widened a bit as his gaze lazily traveled the length of me.

Most men don't expect a woman over six feet, so I was used to his lingering appraisal—not that I liked it. "I'm sure I am."

"Another time, perhaps?" The guy wasn't going to quit.

I didn't know whether to be flattered or...what? I'd never tried a threesome and I remained confused by the whole appeal of the voyeuristic girl-on-girl men seemed to dig. "Thanks, but not my style."

"Pity," he remarked after taking a sip of champagne, and then once again raking his eyes down the length of me. I hated when guys did that—being very visual myself, I didn't enjoy being the subject of their mental picture show.

I gave him a weak smile. "Sorry, no." Separating sex from emotional attachment sullied both. The only thing those two cared about was how I looked naked—not enough attachment for this gal.

At my sign, the bartender closed out my Diet Coke tab for the evening—I was currently suffering through day twenty-two of the Lucky O'Toole Self-Betterment Program. Unfortunately, this state of austerity severely limited my beverage of choice, Wild Turkey 101, and thus did very little for my overall appreciation of humankind. Turning on my heel, I headed for fresh air to clear my head—before I did something I would be proud of, but would regret in the morning.

As you might have guessed, my name is Lucky O'Toole, and as the Head of Customer Relations for the Babylon, Las Vegas's most over-the-top resort/casino, I hang out in bars. A lot. And, in a city where the action doesn't even pretend to get going until at least ten-thirty—and doesn't really ramp up until the wee hours—I put in twenty-hour days way more than I would like. Today was one of those days. But, as the Chief Problem Solver at the Babylon, I'm in charge of keeping people out of trouble...and staying out of it myself. Tonight, trouble lurked at my shoulder—not good in light of my dangerously low levels of self-control. I could feel bad karma stalking me, ready to sink its teeth into my jugular. And I had no one to blame but myself.

You know how you make a decision to do something months, or even years, in advance, never thinking you would actually have to follow through? Well, over a year ago I mortgaged my soul to the Devil, and now he had come to collect. What did I do that was so bad? I agreed to host the final competition of the reality show *The Forever Game,* where carefully selected couples would vie to win a Las Vegas wedding extravaganza. Had I known that the host, Trey Gold, could inspire women the world over to shoot first and ask questions later, I would have reconsidered. Now it was too late.

After months of auditions around the country, the final four couples were en route to my hotel. The insanity had already begun.

To make matters worse, all of the frivolity would be televised live—reality tv at its finest.

I really hate reality. And, personally, I find putting reality on tv like covering a cockroach in chocolate and calling it a "gourmet experience." But, nobody asked me.

Lost in thought, I didn't notice my mother, Mona, until she caught me at the top of the steps leading from the bar down to the casino floor. "Where have you been?" Her tone was accusatory as usual—a sharp arrow tipped with guilt.

Stumbling on the first step, I grabbed the handrail. "Fielding offers from a couple interested in a threesome. Apparently the wife thinks I'm cute."

That stopped Mother for a moment. Long and lean, her body rippled under a spandex sheath of silver lamé, which was a little looser than her normal painted-on attire. Her bare legs, hinting at an athleticism she didn't have, ended in five-inch stilettos, also silver. Fine bones and a plastic surgeon on speed dial kept her whittled in an envious shape. With her brown hair piled on her head, wispy tendrils tickling her well-kohled eyes, and her lips painted a pouty pink, she was the mother from hell. Beside her, I became interesting scenery on the fringes of her stage, adding color but little substance. Her eyes wide, brown saucers, Mona put a hand on my arm and leaned around me. "Really? A three-some? Are they cute?"

"Mother!"

She chewed on her lip, a hint of mischief in her eyes. "It sounded interesting, that's all. Sue me."

"Convincing District Attorney Lovato to prosecute you would be even better. Come to think of it—he owes me a favor," I groused. Mother had been manageable when she was ensconced at her whorehouse in Pahrump—sixty miles of very uninviting desert between us. But with her in the hotel, perpetually under foot, I lived on the verge of matricide.

"Really, Lucky. You need to get out more. Make more friends." Mona gave me that look that mothers reserve for recalcitrant two-year-olds. "And those clothes, they take boring to a whole new level."

"Silver lamé is frowned upon in the boardroom, Mother, even in Vegas." After successfully navigating the steps, I pulled myself to my full height, brushed down my slacks, hiked up my belt, and took a deep breath.

"Well, I hope you've taken my lingerie advice to heart." She hooked her arm through mine, pulling me close as we ambled across the casino. "Women who say the way to a man's heart is through his stomach aim a few inches too high."

"You should know. But I wouldn't waste your energy worrying about my sex life. Frankly, I don't have the energy."

She leaned in, her mouth close to my ear in order to be heard above the music and laughter of a casino full of gamblers chasing a dream. "How are you going to find Mr. Right if you don't sample the fare?"

"Seriously, you want me to play with a husband pimping his wife to get chicks? I really see a lot of upside there."

"Of course not." Mona shot me a dirty look. "But..."

"And you haven't forgotten Teddie, have you?" I pulled my mother out of the way of a man fist-pumping and bellowing. I couldn't tell if he was happy or not, but since he ordered drinks for everyone, I assumed he was money ahead.

"Teddie wants to be a rock star. He'll break your heart." Mona stated this with certainty, as if the whole world could see the train wreck coming.

"Who'll break your heart?"

The melodious voice set my every nerve afire. I turned to look into the smiling baby blues of the gentleman in question. "You."

"*Moi?*" Teddie fell back, a hand pressed to his heart. "Mona, you wound me to the core. Lucky is my life." He wrapped me in his arms, pulling me to him. Our bodies pressed together and the world fell away. When he captured my lips with his, then deepened the kiss, my heart skipped and then raced, spreading warmth. Too bad he was a budding rock star with a future on the road. Nothing like one huge pothole in the rocky road to love.

When I came up for air, I met the scolding eyes of my mother.

"I may not know much," she whispered as Teddie broke away to greet a fan, "but I do know men."

She *had* made men her life's work. Hopefully the years had taught her a thing or two, but I wasn't going to bank my future on it. Besides, manipulation was Mona's middle name. "This time you're wrong."

Teddie captured my hand as he returned. "You guys don't want to hit the lobby. It's a circus."

"Three rings. I'm the ringmaster," I reminded him.

"Well, there's safety in numbers, right?" He extended an elbow.

I hooked one arm through his and the other through Mona's.

7

Side-by-side, we marched toward the lobby. For some reason I felt like Dorothy skipping toward Oz, full of misplaced confidence.

A wall of energy hit us as we stepped into the lobby, taking my breath away like a punch. Built of marble and multicolored inlaid mosaic, the lobby was a grand cavern invoking a Persian paradise. A flight of blown-glass hummingbirds arced across the ceiling. Fabric in rich hues tented over the reception desk, spanning the length of the far wall. Adjacent to it, behind floor-to-ceiling glass, a mountain of man-made snow beckoned those weary of the heat of the Mojave. For a small ransom, anyone could slap on a pair of K2s and slip down the slope. Angling away from Reception was the opening to the Bazaar, world class shopping at its excessive best. From Ferraris to Ferragamos, the Bazaar had it all. A placid stream wound its way through the expanse, lined with shrubs and flowering plants, populated with regal swans and a few ducks of different hues, and crossed at convenient intervals by arching footbridges. The waterway was the Babylon's rendition of the Euphrates, minus the silt.

Tonight, the grand sweeping entranceway of the front of the hotel drew the focus of a burgeoning crowd, who nudged and shifted like cows at feeding time. Everyone craned to catch a glimpse of the finalists basking in their fifteen minutes of fame.

I pulled my little trio to a halt before we got trampled. "I just don't get this whole reality tv thing—ringside seats to disaster from the anonymity of our living rooms."

"Oh, honey, it's everybody's chance at a dream." My mother squeezed my arm as she shivered with apparent delight.

"After you throw your teammates or housemates or mates in general and your dignity—oh, and your values—under the bus."

"It's the real world." Mona actually looked like she believed it. Logic never was her best thing—probably a coping mechanism. But, she did have a point: Civilization had abandoned civility in so many ways.

"This? The real world?" I unhooked my arm from hers as I caught sight of my assistant, Miss P, heading my way like a laser-guided missile. "I'm insulted. This is fantasy, smoke-and-mirrors." I waved my free arm over the crowd. "A carefully crafted illusion that, even if only for a weekend, we can all be who we want to be and have anything or anyone our hearts desire."

"What does your heart desire, Lucky, my love?" Teddie whispered in my ear. Before I could answer, he let go of my arm and was instantly swallowed by a swarm of fans. He whipped out a Sharpie and began decorating the various adoring females buzzing around him.

Momentarily distracted from thoughts of reality tv, I watched all the sweet young things pressing their soft flesh to his in a not-so-subtle display of availability. My reality. How he resisted, I couldn't fathom. How I would handle his temptations in the future was equally murky. A problem for another day.

Miss P trundled to a stop in front of me. "Lucky." A statement, not a question.

Right voice, wrong person. I squinted and refocused. I still hadn't gotten used to the hip, trendy, spiky-haired version of my old and frumpy right-hand man.

"I've been calling you," she continued, with more than a hint of exasperation. "Why don't you answer your phone?"

"For some silly reason, I thought I might take a moment to regroup without being hounded. I don't know what I was thinking." I grabbed my phone from my hip and thumbed off the silent switch. "Besides, I was momentarily distracted by an offer to join a threesome."

Miss P looked at me for a beat over the top of her cheaters. "Do I need to call the paramedics?"

"Not necessary—my rapier wit is only set to stun today." That didn't get even a hint of a grin. I was going to have to either change my act or take this one on the road.

With the middle finger of her right hand she nudged her

glasses farther up her nose as she raised her head to look at me full on, oblivious to the gesture she had just shot me. "The limos are five minutes away."

"Reroute them to the Kasbah."

"What?"

"The crowd is reaching the boiling point—security won't be able to hold them all back. Not good television and not the image of the Babylon I want to have splashed in prime time around the globe. I've already scrambled the tv crews to the vip entrance." My tone clipped the wings of any argument.

"And Trey Gold?"

My eyes went all slitty and Miss P took a step back. "Just the mention of that troglodyte's name triggers my gag reflex. Why they picked him to host a show about love is beyond me." I glanced around to make sure no one listened in—I didn't need that sound bite to be flashed around the world. "Jerry is riding herd. I've authorized the use of lethal force, but I suggest we be there to meet the limos. Bloodshed would be bad for business."

Mona leaned in as Miss P angled toward the Kasbah and its private vip entrance. "Ooooh, blood." She shivered in anticipation. "The reality fans will eat that with a spoon."

Shrouded in a carefully crafted myth of secrecy, the Kasbah served as the lap of luxury for the Babylon's most well heeled guests. Accessed through a long hallway that led to a set of large bronze doors, the Kasbah was zealously guarded by the most unctuous on our staff.

"Sergio, is everything ready?" I asked as I breezed into the hallway and swept our front desk manager up in my wake. Sergio was our resident expert in kowtowing without being obsequious.

"Of course, Ms. O'Toole. You have but to ask." Sucking up was also part of his repertoire. Given the fact that he had the body of a

Greek god, the face of an angel, and silky black hair hanging across his forehead that set off his doe-eyes, I didn't mind. Although he was a trifle fussy for my tastes.

Passing through a pair of double doors large enough to hold back an invading horde—and maybe even a rabid pack of paparazzi; we had yet to throw the crossbar, but you never knew —we entered a world of rarified air. Tall palms and shorter flowering trees flourished in the huge atrium, stretching their branches in salutation to the sun that streamed in through the bubbled glass ceiling high above. Following a path through a maze of individual bungalows, each one complete with a private pool and enough personal staff to keep even the most demanding sheik relatively content, we worked our way to the private drive-up entrance.

While the inner sanctum of the Kasbah had been quiet and serene, this entrance was anything but. Men shouldered cameras, and were trailed by minions managing the cables. Onlookers paused and craned their necks to catch a glimpse of whatever it was the group had gathered for. The small crowd had clearly reached the tipping point, adding to its mass like a positively charged atom gathering electrons, until the whole thing became unstable, an explosion waiting to flatten the surroundings.

Glancing over the mass of humanity, I saw Jerry's bald head sticking up above the milling throng and I made a beeline for him. As Head of Security, Jerry was always my friend in time of need—and a great equalizer.

Pushing my way through the thickening crowd, I managed to snag his sleeve. "Status?"

When Jerry looked at me I could see the whites of his eyes. "Combustible, but the limos should be here any minute. We've got two couples per car." He glanced down at a clipboard. "The first car, Couple Number One, will be Gail Fortunato and Rocco Traveneti. A couple of kids from Jersey now living on the Lower East Side."

DEBORAH COONTS

"At least they're not from the Jersey Shore and don't call themselves 'the Circumstance' or something."

"I think you mean 'the Situation.'" Jerry gave me a sheepish grin.

"Whatever. Don't tell me you watch this stuff."

"Keeps the wife happy," he said a bit quickly, his gaze shifting from mine.

I filed the topic for future ribbing.

"The second couple. Couple Number—"

"Two, I get it."

Used to my short fuse, Jerry didn't miss a beat. "Couple Number Two is Walker Worthington and Buffy Bingle." How he said that with a straight face, I don't know.

"Bingle. I would've changed that name for sure."

"Somehow that loses its punch coming from a gal named Lucky."

"Point taken. But Bingle? I'd bet my next month's salary she's a scrapper with mean playground skills."

"You're the expert." Jerry grinned at me. He knew I wore my rough-and-tumble upbringing as a badge of honor.

As advertised, a limo rounded the corner and then eased to a stop at the curb. Jerry and Miss P held back the crowd while Sergio and I stepped to the rear door of the car. Somewhere I had lost Mona, but I didn't have time to worry about that now.

"Everybody outta my way." The grating voice of Trey Gold, several decibels too high, echoed over the crowd. "You people, move!"

Reluctantly, they did as he ordered.

Red-faced, mopping his brow—which glistened despite his pancake makeup in an unnatural shade of orange—Mr. Gold pushed to my side. His jet-black hair, unmarred by even a hint of gray, and spiked with gel, clashed with the lines on his face. His cruel mouth curled in an imitation of a smile that didn't reach his eyes. Even in my low heels I had him by almost a foot. Although with his broad shoulders and well-camouflaged paunch, he most likely outweighed me—a fact which, swine that I am, gave me particular delight.

"O'Toole, glad to see you decided to put in an appearance. Just can't resist seeing your mug on tv, right?" He wheezed as if the short push through the crowd had been almost more than he could bear. He dropped the mike he'd been holding close to his face down to his side. His fake smile disappeared. "This is my show, O'Toole. Don't you forget it. Stay out of my way."

I opened my mouth to speak, but before I could get a word out, he reached an arm across my middle, pushing me out of his way. "Step back, girlfriend, and watch a master at work. You might want to take notes."

"Girlfriend?" My voice dropped an octave or two, my eyes got all slitty. "I'd slit my wrists if I was your girlfriend," I hissed.

Oblivious to everything but the seductive eye of the camera, Trey cranked up the wattage of his smile, turned to the cameras, and began babbling about the contest and the first couple as he reached for the door handle on the limo.

Seething, I was contemplating instruments of torture when Jerry grabbed my arm. "Later. Remember, we don't get back..."

"We get even," I said, finishing the familiar mantra. As I said the words, I felt myself relaxing. The Babylon was my world; I made the rules. Trey Gold was in my playpen now and he would get his comeuppance. I didn't know how, I didn't know where—I just knew for sure.

Glad that for once the spectacle wasn't my responsibility, I crossed my arms and watched it unfold. Couple Number One had the stage. Mr. Traveneti stuck his head out of the limo first, and his body followed. He reached back and grabbed the hand of his future mate, Ms. Fortunato. I liked that.

Trey stuck the mike in Rocco's face. "Welcome to Vegas. What do you think so far?"

As expected, Rocco was short and stout, with dark hair, dark eyes...Italian. And young. But his smile was warm and dimples creased his cheeks when he smiled. "It's cool."

Trey waited a second too long, expecting more, and then shifted the mike to Ms. Fortunato. "Gail, your impressions?"

Gail still squeezed Rocco's hand—I could see her knuckles turning white—but otherwise she appeared unruffled at all the attention. Her red hair was unexpected, as was her peaches-and-cream skin and blue eyes. Trim and toned, wearing casual clothes and low heels, she matched Rocco's height and his easy manner. "We're still sort of in shock, you know?"

She and Rocco stepped aside, making room for Couple Number Two.

Stepping out of the limo first, Walker Worthington reeked of stuffy boardrooms and the Upper East Side in his three-piece suit and Windsor-knotted silk tie. With his gray hair trimmed almost military short, plus his hard eyes and taut mouth, he was not the reality contestant I expected. Before he could help her out, Ms. Bingle clambered out of the limo and bounced to his side. Blond, twiggy, and gawky, with carefully contoured Tetons, a pouty smile, and a vacuous gaze, everything about her screamed *perky*.

God help me.

Trey was a bit more reserved when he approached Mr. Worthington. Guess the buttoned-up big shot had a bite. "Impressions of Vegas so far?" Apparently Mr. Gold was a one-question wonder.

Walker's eyebrows snapped into a frown. "All show, no substance."

I leaned into Jerry. "At least he's discerning." I grabbed Miss P, who had been standing silent guard at my side this whole time, by the elbow. "Enough of this sideshow. Let's make a last-minute readiness cruise through the bungalows."

Even though I knew of at least five trips she'd made to check the preparations for our contestants, Miss P followed me without a word as I plowed my way through the crowd. People quickly shoved their way into the vacuum we left, erasing any evidence that we'd ever even been there.

~

THE BUNGALOWS AT THE KASBAH WERE A PERMANENT FIXTURE ON every list of the best hotel rooms in the world—they were over-sized, opulent yet comfortable, with hot-and-cold running foot slaves. The price of admission included much more than wealth. Of course, our high rollers made it in—although the rooms were generally awarded based on a lottery of pecking orders. At a weekly meeting, our high-end casino hosts each listed which of their players would be in town, how much they regularly kept in play, and what their limit was, and then the head of the depart-ment made the room assignments. The players with the most potential profit to the hotel got the best room with the best perks. Fairly mercenary, I admit, but while the Babylon might be a play-ground, it was above all else a business. And as a business, it was profit or die—especially in the highly competitive world of sepa-rating the rich and famous from their money.

The key was to provide just enough pleasure and perception of freebies—or comps, as we referred to them—to keep the gamblers at the tables. All was negotiated, generally up front. A player would agree to gamble for so many hours, putting a specific minimum of action through the house. In return, we would offer discounts on losses, free use of the airplane and the Ferraris, fourth row center tickets to the best show in town—everything, constrained only by the limits of imagination and the legal system. Although I'd heard whispers of the latter being exceeded at some hotels, I'd never done it myself—and woe to any of my staff that put the hotel on the line by overstepping.

Adding insult to injury, this contest had thrown the pecking-order thing out the window. I had exerted my executive privilege and commandeered the very best of the Bungalows, which did little to endear me to the staff as well as some of our Kasbah regulars. Bruised egos would have to settle with opulent digs on our thirtieth floor—the über concierge floor. While the rooms didn't match the bungalows, the service was every bit as spectacular—the floor even had a private chef and a twenty-four-hour kitchen, all at no cost.

We stopped in front of Bungalow Five. "Who's in here?"

"Veronica Salter and Guy Handy." Miss P rattled the names off without consulting her clipboard—apparently these two were memorable. Guy Handy sounded like a stage name for a stripper in a gay club, but I was wise enough to keep that observation to myself.

"Any special requests?" I asked as I stepped into the room and wandered, looking for imperfections. I fingered a fold in the heavy damask drapes.

Miss P snorted, politely. I hid my smile.

"Vichy water, *sin gas*; Belgian truffles, 70 percent cocoa; Louis xiii." She paused as I whipped my head around. "No, not the Black Pearl," she said, in answer to my silent question. "Just the regular 1500-dollar-per-bottle swill plus Steuben brandy glasses—the tear drop pattern. A case of Château Lafite"—she glanced down again—"nothing younger than 1985; Irish linens; and Turkish towels, heated, of course."

"Of course." I ran my fingers across the top of the mahogany desk. Dust-free and spotless. "How did you find the tear-drop Steubens? The barware part of that pattern was discontinued before I was born."

"eBay."

"You deserve a raise."

"You just gave me one."

"You deserve another."

"You expect me to argue?"

"That would be overachieving." With one arm I circled her shoulders as we walked toward the door. A huge vase of unusual flowers caught my eye, and I abandoned Miss P. "Blue roses? Rare. I'm assuming another special request?"

Miss P nodded. If she was put out, she hid it well.

"Interesting." I turned the vase a quarter-turn, then stepped back. "Better?" At Miss P's nod, I once again circled her shoulders. "Did you know they signify unattainable love?"

"Really? I'm not even going to ask how you know that."

"My mind is a steel trap for worthless information."

"A walking, talking encyclopedia of little-known facts—next Trivial Pursuit game, you're on my team." A hint of a grin sneaked out as Miss P stopped to inhale the fragrance from the fresh-grown roses. "Unattainable love, you say? Probably a good thing, considering."

"Yes, I'd say someone is a wee bit high-maintenance, or just enjoying the power trip."

As I stepped back to allow Miss P to proceed me through the door into the common area, a well-heeled woman burst through. Tall, austere, her dark hair pulled back from her face and secured at the nape of her neck in a Tiffany hair clasp, the same one I had given several members of my staff last Christmas. Dark suit, gray cami, an oversized Breitling in no-nonsense stainless steel, black Loubous—the Glorias with the crystal heels that I lusted for—cheekbones so sharp they could cut meat, and dark eyes that never stopped moving. She peeled off one white glove finger by finger as she strode around the living room of the bungalow. I hoped she hadn't heard my assessment.

I was content to wait—while I didn't like overbearing people any more than the next guy, I appreciated a woman who walked into a room like she owned it, commanding attention.

After a quick tour, she stopped in front of me. "Are you with the hotel?"

I stuck out my hand, "Lucky O'Toole, Head of Customer Relations. I assume you are Ms. Salter?"

She took my hand in her long, thin cool one. I hoped my palms weren't sweaty. "A pleasure. This is lovely. Thank you."

I dipped my head and then motioned to Miss P. "This is my assistant, Miss Patterson. I can assure you, she is the oil in this machine. All of this is her doing. We both are at your service."

Veronica Salter shook Miss P's hand as well. So, she had manners to match the uniform. Done with the preliminaries, she turned to me as she worked off the other glove. "A manager who casts the glow on her employees. You and I will get along just fine, Ms. O'Toole."

"Lucky."

"Lucky, is it?" She arched one perfectly plucked eyebrow, and her lips curled into a grin. She was warmly pretty when she smiled. "Then you must call me Vera."

"I can't make any promises—generally such familiarity with our guests is frowned upon."

"Honey, I am no guest. I'm a paid contestant in this dog-and-pony show."

"Vera, where do you want all your shit?" The voice was masculine, but with a whiny quality that sent a shiver of distaste through me. "I mean, what?" he continued. "Am I one of those Roman slaves or something? What are they called?"

"Cretins?" Vera asked sweetly, a hint of honey dripping nicely from the two syllables.

I had to turn away and bite my lip. The man in question looked like Malibu Ken: blond hair, golden tan, buff bod, white shirt open one button too many, fitted slacks, and worn loafers with no socks. Well dressed, but lacking the polish of the well heeled. With his blue eyes, comfortable face, and broadness where he should be broad, he was male pulchritude at its finest—except for the pouty mouth.

"Cretins?" The man stretched out the word and scowled like a first grader struggling with phonics. "No, I don't think that's it."

"Don't think, honey, just put the stuff in the bedroom." Vera glanced at me, a question in her eyes.

"Back there, through the double doors." I pointed to the far end of the room. We both watched the man I assumed was Guy shoulder two trunks and head for the bedroom. I guess he'd beaten back the army of valets we had waiting in order to do his lady's bidding.

"Don't ask," Vera said, turning her attention back to me. "I have a habit of picking poorly." She glanced again at Guy as he maneuvered the luggage and his bulk through the double doors. The man-and-luggage mountain barely fit through the doublewide opening. "He is sweet, but not the right one."

"You and I have more in common than meets the eye."

"Really?" Her mask slipped a little, revealing the lonely lady underneath—she sounded wistful and a bit sad. "You are kind to say so."

Somehow, squeezing her in a hug seemed inappropriate, so, fresh out of ideas or words, I remained mute where I stood.

"Mr. Handy is an actor—the latest in a long line," Vera explained. She shrugged out of her suit jacket and handed it to the butler who had been lurking outside the door and who now rushed to her side. "He's not even a very good thespian, but he can remember his lines. We had no idea we'd get this far."

I wondered what she would do if she actually won.

Miss P and I left Vera and Guy to work out their arrangements—with the help of their personal butler and two bellmen. We hurried to check the last bungalow before the guests arrived. Bungalow Four was a mirror image of Vera's bungalow, but with vases of riotous orange tulips instead of the roses.

I took a quick turn around the space while Miss P waited just inside the doorway. "Tell me about this couple."

"Couple Number Four." Miss P consulted her clipboard. "John Farenthall and Melina Douglas. He's a plastic surgeon, and she is a newscast producer at the abc affiliate in Houston."

"Plastic surgeon? Interesting." I plucked a leaf that had turned brown from the stem of a day lily. "And Melina, what a beautiful name."

"Thank you." The voice, warm and smooth, startled me.

I turned to find myself staring at a tall woman—almost my height—dressed in a simple, bright-yellow shift, gold sandals, and a wide smile that lit her whole face. Her skin was the color of rich coffee with a dash of milk. She wore her hair cropped short, which accented her fine features and large, expressive eyes.

I extended my hand and once again made the introductions.

Pleasantries exchanged, Melina clasped her hands and held them to her chest as she wandered the room, her face holding a kid-at-Christmas delight. "This is lovely."

"There you are, darling." A voice boomed from the doorway.

Tall and lean, John Farenthall was the perfect matching bookend to Melina. His skin a rich mahogany and his eyes alight with a hint of mischief, his already warm smile deepened when he saw his future bride.

She extended a hand to him, which he stepped forward to take. "Isn't this perfect?"

"I'll say." His eyes hadn't drifted from Melina.

When she looked at him and caught his meaning, she ducked her head shyly. "Would you quit? Look." She gestured around the room. "Amazing, isn't it?"

He pursed his lips and nodded. "It'll do." Which elicited a giggle from his intended.

"We were conned into this, you know?" he said, turning to me. "Our families conspired against us, entering us in the competition. We never would've done it on our own."

Melina stepped closer to him, snaking an arm around his waist as she looked at me. "With John trying to get his practice up-and-running and my eighty-hour weeks, our family despaired of us getting married. They threatened us with bodily harm if we didn't play along."

"Woe be it to anyone who crosses my mother," John added, with a grin.

Melina looked a bit stricken at the mention of her future mother-in-law; when her happy-face slid back over her features, her eyes didn't mirror the smile. "And here we are."

"Well, welcome." I eased toward the door, herding Miss P in front of me. "If we can enhance your stay in any way, please let us know."

I took a deep breath and shook my head as I closed the door behind us, leaving John and Melina to themselves.

"Interesting cast," Miss P remarked.

I shrugged in agreement. "Let the games begin."

"Speaking of games, where do you want me to park Mr. Gold?"

"Put him in Room 30145."

Miss P looked at me for a moment. "Buttering him up, are we?"

CHAPTER TWO

*E*LLA BLUE usually spoke in exclamation points. Psychiatrist by day, mail-order clergyman by night, Ella presided over most of our formal couplings at the Babylon. Even with the noise of the shoppers in the Bazaar, the underlying happy music, and the cacophony of thoughts pinging around my empty skull, I could still hear her as I approached the Temple of Love. *"This is Lovely! Delphinia,* you are a *dear.* An absolute *dear!"*

Delphinia, the Babylon's resident wedding planner, and I had a noon appointment. Otherwise I would still be home asleep. Two hours of shut-eye. I groaned and rubbed my eyes as I paused outside the grand entrance to the Temple.

"I *love* these flowers." I could picture Ella, her hands clasped, dancing around like a Valley girl in a *Saturday Night Live* skit. I never could tell whether her mannerisms were affectations or reflections of an intellectual deficiency. "Everything is so...so...*perfect.*"

Perfect—not the adjective I would use. Ella wasn't exactly what the doctor ordered. There wasn't enough coffee in the universe to jump-start my day, so I was trying to ease into it. Stepping into the darkness within, I paused to let my eyes adjust.

From the outside, the Temple of Love resembled a ziggurat—huge stairsteps of large sandstone blocks, with a grand entrance flanked by double wooden doors replete with a beam to secure them against an invading hoard. We hadn't had to use it yet—although Rudy Gillespie and Jordan Marsh's commitment ceremony would have caused a stampede had it not been held in the Big Boss's apartment. But that beam might come in handy yet—I had a feeling the upcoming wedding that would finish off the tv show might spark a riot of shutterbugs eager to memorialize a fleeting pop culture moment.

The interior of the Temple was a vast space, uncluttered but for some reed mats covering the floor and subtle palms softening the corners—an empty room which the happy couple could furnish as they pleased. Flames under glass dotted the walls and provided a warm, welcoming glow.

Delphinia excused herself from Ella and rushed to meet me with a warm smile and a steaming mug of coffee clutched in both hands. To the casual observer, Delphinia was the personification of plain—until you looked into her eyes. Deep pools of violet, they were windows to an old, kind soul.

"Vanilla nut cut with milk, just the way you like it." At my raised eyebrow, she continued. "Miss P called. She said you weren't...up to speed today."

"That's one way of putting it." I smiled as I took the proffered mug. My body practically vibrated in anticipation. Caffeine, a drug of necessity—thank god it was still legal. "I left a warm bed and a hot guy so I'm not feeling all that magnanimous, I'll admit. So forewarned is forearmed."

She lowered her eyes and colored a bit.

One sip of coffee and my whole body sighed. "You will be rewarded by the gods, thank you. Now, come, show me what you're thinking for the wedding."

Apparently unwilling to be cast out of the spotlight any longer, Ella pounced. *"Lucky!"*

I winced. "Too many decibels, Ella. Can you please use your inside voice?" I took one of the three chairs that Delphinia had pulled together in front of the altar/dais/podium/whatever—the place where the minister would stand. Minister that would be Ella. With her over-the-top personality, she was just Vegas enough.

She collapsed in a heap into the chair across from me, her full skirt billowing like a parachute giving up the wind. As if beating glowing embers scattered on a breeze, she patted down the fabric. Finally, she came into view—all four feet, eleven inches and ninety pounds, including several pounds of strawberry blond hair that cascaded in a magnificent wave down her back and well past her butt. Batting her green eyes at me, she looked stricken.

"Isn't it a bit early for you, Ella? Aren't we cutting into your couch time?" I savored another sip of coffee and felt a few brain cells come on line.

"Oh," she waved a delicate hand. "I've cleared my calendar for the next few *days*. Can you *believe it?* They hired me as an *expert* on the *Forever Game*. I'm to give some insight into what makes a couple, you know, *compatible*. We're looking for the couple most in love!" She clasped her hands together and wiggled like a puppy. "Isn't this *fun?*"

All of this came out in a mellifluous accent carefully steeped in the cauldron of the Deep South—if I remembered correctly, some tiny burg outside of Birmingham, the name of which always eluded me. Why did a Southern accent sound stupid on men—but sound like mint juleps, cool linen, and gentrified manners when dripping off a female tongue? I had a feeling I wouldn't like the answer. It probably had something to do with stereotypes and expectations that would flip me to the pissed-off position, so I didn't waste the tiny dollop of energy I had thinking about it.

"And of course I'm going to preside at the wedding!" Ella emoted, punctuating her words with grand gestures. "That's why I'm here, actually. What will you be providing for the *production?*"

"Local color," I said, with a straight face.

Delphinia, who had taken the chair next to mine, also kept a bland expression, but her eyes sparkled as she refilled my mug from a coffee pot I hadn't noticed on a side table.

Ella's forehead creased into a frown. "oh. Well, that's just *great*, isn't it?"

"Yeah, I'm lucky that way."

"You do know that your sarcasm is a defense?" Ella announced in an unexpectedly quiet voice. "We should have a session on that."

So, she did have an inside voice. Who knew? I looked at her over the top of my mug as I drained the steaming brew. "In my line of work, an offense is rarely available, so a defense is vital."

"You always have a quip."

"A substitute for an answer when I don't have one. But, I really don't want to go there."

Ella pouted as she looked down, picking at a thread sticking out from the bottom buttonhole in her perfect little cashmere cardigan—in a dusty rose that just missed clashing with her hair color. Her shoes matched her cardigan.

How did one do that? Better question—why? I preferred being a fashion casualty—that way no one had any expectations. "Thank you, though."

That perked her up. Southern women and their manners: comfort in insincerity.

Delphinia cleared her throat. "I thought perhaps I would start, then Ella can have her say."

THE MEETING TOOK A BIT LONGER THAN I'D BUDGETED, AND I WAS hurrying with my goodbyes when Teddie's voice boomed from the doorway. "Lucky, woman, are you in here?"

Delphinia glanced at me, a question on her face.

"The hot guy."

"Oh." Interest sparked in her eyes, turning them an interesting shade of purple.

"Come, we can all say hi."

Teddie remained outside, lurking as if afraid to enter into the House of Matrimony. I chose not to be worried about that—to be honest, I wasn't all that comfortable there either.

Ella bolted in front of Delphinia and me. She waggled her fingers at Teddie, "hi, handsome."

Teddie bussed her cheek as expected. "Ella, you look competitive, as always."

"Oh, you say the nicest things." Ella swatted his arm.

"And you," Teddie said, turning his attention to me. "You look good enough to eat—a feast for the eyes and food for the soul."

Now it was my turn to color as he grabbed me, dipped me over bended knee with a flourish, and then righted me. Pulling me close, he wrapped me tight and kissed me—slow and purposeful, like he really meant it.

My knees went weak. My breath caught. Nothing like a distraction to keep me focused.

When Teddie had made his point and air once again filled my lungs and blood reached my brain, I let Delphinia engage Teddie in a bit of small talk while I tried to marshal my elusive composure—something near impossible when Teddie was close by.

With pleasantries exchanged and quick goodbyes said to Ella and Delphinia, Teddie grabbed my hand, pulling me toward the hotel lobby. "Come on. Hurry."

"What?" I laughed as I let him pull me along. "Is Hugh Jackman stripping in the lobby?"

"If he was I sure wouldn't tell you." Teddie slowed his pace a bit. "They're taping the first segment of the game show—the initial interviews. They asked me to be the Vegas celebrity judge."

"Since you're such an authority on long-term relationships," I teased, with just the teensiest hint of sarcasm.

"Hey, I'm staying a chapter ahead of the class."

"I guess that makes you an expert."

BY THE TIME WE HIT THE LOBBY I'D TAKEN TWO PHONE CALLS, AND messages were cueing up faster than fans waiting for Lady Gaga tickets. Clearly, I was out of fun time. Teddie didn't seem too broken up about me not being able to play. He was harder to read than ancient hieroglyphics, even with the friggin' Rosetta stone. Lately, though, he'd been stuck in "me" mode—one of the curses of the chromosomally challenged. To be honest, I found it really tiresome, and a bit insulting. As if my responsibilities didn't matter. Perhaps I was being petty. Perhaps not. Frankly, I didn't have the time to tackle that Gordian knot.

Nor the patience. Today, crossing the lobby was like trying to fight my way downriver during spawning season. Two-by-two, hand-in-hand, couples streamed in through the front entrance, making a dash for the casino and Teddie's theater beyond, where preparations were underway for the game show taping. No one stopped to gaze in awe at the thousands of blown-glass humming-birds and butterflies that swooped across the high ceiling, nor at any of the other awe-worthy features. A river of humanity flowed past, effectively cutting me off from the stairs to the mezzanine and the relative serenity of my office.

My phone rang just as I was timing my leap into the throng, risking bodily harm in the name of five-star service. I glanced at the caller—my office—then pushed to talk. "Make a note. When the time comes to renegotiate my compensation package, I want to add hazardous duty pay as a benefit."

"It's too early for whining," Miss P stated, as if it was a rule written somewhere.

"It's never too early for whining, but there are times when it may be way too late." I switched my phone to my right ear as I ducked into a small alcove, and stuck my finger in my left. Why had no one thought of inventing a noise-cancelling cell phone? "What can I do for you?"

"Have you seen Rocco Traveneti and Gail Fortunato?"

"Couple Number One? No. Why?"

"They're a no-show for the taping. Trey Gold is starting to panic."

"Can security shed any light?"

"Jerry said he lost them in the Bazaar." If Jerry lost them, they had skills.

"I was just there at the Temple and I didn't see them—not that I was looking—but I'll head back that way, see if I can pick up their trail." I turned to scan the lobby. "Keep security on the lookout. The eye-in-the-sky is our best bet. This place is a zoo." The eye-in-the-sky was our system of highly sophisticated cameras monitored by security. Of course, the casino was the most closely watched, but we had feeds from all corners of the property.

I reholstered my phone and considered my options. The entrance to the Bazaar was just to my right, between the entrance to the casino and Reception. For once I was glad my progress had been impeded. After negotiating along one wall, I retraced my steps and once again ducked into the Bazaar. The crowd was thin. I popped my head into a few shops, but no luck. A bit too glitzy for New Jersey tastes, I thought.

Now where would two kids from the Garden State choose to land?

Trey Gold caught me in front of Samson's, the Babylon's beauty salon where females of all shapes and sizes could be primped, polished, and attended by in-the-flesh facsimiles of the Biblical hero. "You!" He stepped into my space—we would've been nose-to-nose but for a rather serious height discrepancy in my favor. He smelled like cheap gin, or bad cologne. "This is your fault."

"Most likely—along with the balance of trade deficit, inner-city blight, poverty in Africa, and all the rather unsavory uses for a Saturday Night Special, which, by the way, conjures something altogether different here in Sin City. No doubt about it, I am a one-woman wrecking crew. You'd be well advised to steer clear of me."

A few strands of his helmeted hair had broken free and ran across his forehead. His countenance, still an unsettling orange, held not a hint of the fury I could see in his eyes. His breathing was shallow and rapid, and he didn't look well—the same as before, but not well. He stared at me a moment through red-rimmed eyes. Then, like a puppet whose strings had been loosened, his posture, rigid with righteous indignation, sagged. His shoulders started to shake.

"Are you okay?" I asked, as I grabbed his arm.

He nodded as a grin lifted the corner of his mouth. Tears sprung to his eyes. The guy wasn't stroking out, he was laughing —clearly an unusual state. Reaching for his back pocket, he extracted a purple handkerchief and dabbed at his eyes, careful not to dislodge his war paint.

Weakly, he patted my shoulder. "I can't decide whether I like you or I want to kill you."

"I have that effect on people."

"Those two kids like to cook. The restaurants would be a good place to start." He turned to go. "Find them. Now."

As he walked away I thought I heard a very faint, "Please."

That was...unsettling. Okay, restaurants. There was only one in the bazaar, the Burger Palais.

My father, the owner of the Babylon, had recently acquired a run-down local property. Before the remodeling plans had even been finalized, he hired a very well known French chef, Jean-Charles Bouclet, to conceptualize, develop, and manage an eponymous restaurant at this new property. A wee bit precipitous, in my opinion, but my father dangled the chance of opening a gourmet burger restaurant in the Bazaar at the Babylon to lure his gastronomic *coups de grâce*. Hence, the Burger Palais. To be honest, it was a great use of a space vacated by a forcibly evicted Italian joint that hadn't been up to snuff.

It was early yet for dinner, and there wasn't much of a crowd when I charged through the doors. Blinking my eyes in an attempt to force them to adjust to the relative darkness, I paused just inside the restaurant. I didn't see Paxton Dane until he spoke.

"You're not at the taping?" His smooth voice held the honeyed tones of Texas and made me smile. Dane and I, well, I didn't know what we were. There was an attraction...or something, but I wasn't going there. Despite my awe-inspiring skills, I could handle only one man at a time.

"Watching those shows is like sitting at a dangerous intersection waiting for a crash."

"I've been told that's their charm."

Finally my eyes adjusted, and I could see the smile in his emerald eyes. He had me by a few inches, and it was nice to be able to look someone in the eye without looking down. I never figured out how to look down *at* someone without seeming to look down *on* them.

Dane worked in security, so I assumed he might be wise to my mission. "You looking for our two runaways, too?"

"Yeah." Dane moved me further inside with a slight touch to the middle of my back.

I could feel the warmth of his skin through my shirt. A shiver chased down my spine.

"They don't seem to be in here," he said as he scanned the eating area, "but let's look in the kitchen just to be sure."

Jean-Charles had a habit of inviting folks into his inner sanctum. Once I had been so blessed, and I'd never been the same. There was something about that Frenchman...sizzle and burn and an odd connection. He made me nervous in a way I'd never felt before.

As I peered into the kitchen through the wall of glass separating it from the dining area, I saw him bending over the stove. Trim, handsome, his brown hair curling over his collar, he glanced up and caught me staring. I reddened. Even though I couldn't see his eyes, I knew they were a robin's egg blue that went all dark and stormy when he became serious. Flashing a smile that had probably melted more hearts than I cared to think about, he motioned us inside.

Dane threw me a look as he stepped around me. "Our runaways are right where we thought they'd be." He motioned with his head toward the prep table on the other side of the stove.

Rocco, his head bent and face scrunched in concentration, worked on some vegetables with a knife large enough to cut out someone's heart. His strokes quick, his movements precise, he created a mound of chopped greenery in a few seconds—apparently without shedding blood or sacrificing body parts. I was in awe.

Gail stood between Jean-Charles and Rocco, so slight and still I'd missed her on my first visual reconnoiter. Engrossed, she listened as Jean-Charles continued a running commentary punctuated by his pointing from pan to pot to oven.

Focusing on the youngsters, I strode into the kitchen, trying my best to override that silly schoolgirl nervousness by ignoring the chef. "You guys do know Trey Gold has threatened to shoot the entire staff of the hotel if we don't get you to the theater posthaste?"

Rocco glanced up, his dark curls hanging in his face. His dreamy look reminded me of the face of a child lost in his imaginings. "What time is it?"

"Way past pumpkin time."

Gail seemed oblivious to all of us, her fresh face creased into a frown. "So, you would make a plate of *osso bucco* with the cranberry wild rice?"

"*Oui.*" Jean-Charles pursed his lips as he thought. "A simple poached pear salad with goat cheese to start, perhaps? Something savory, something tart…"

"Something sweet," Gail chimed in. "Perfect. Paired with a smooth pinot noir?"

"Nothing too heavy, though," Jean-Charles agreed, a smile playing with his lips. "You have good instincts. The plate will be pleasing; the meal, satisfying."

"Excuse me," I said, pretending to be perturbed. "Playtime is over. Time to earn your keep." I motioned to the Jerseyites. "You two better skedaddle—you're holding up the show. Dane, could you deliver them to Mr. Gold, personally? He's out for blood."

The Texan glanced between Jean-Charles—who stood wiping his hand on a white towel that hung from his waist—and me, then nodded. "Come on, guys. You've got a lot of folks chasing their tails."

"I am sorry," Jean-Charles said after the trio had left. "When I create, time loses meaning."

"Especially when you have a rapt audience and a skilled accomplice."

He tossed me a hand-caught-in-the-cookie-jar look and rewarded me with a Gallic shrug and brilliant grin. "He is very talented, Rocco. And Gail has a gift for menu design, pushing the boundaries slightly while keeping things comfortable for modestly educated palates." He pulled a stool next to the stove where he continued to work while he talked. "Sit. Stay with me."

I didn't need a second invitation—the aromas were enough, but the Frenchman was an added delectable. Straddling the stool, I reached for a bottle chilling in a cooler on the counter and poured us both a glass of wine. I held the glass up and swirled its contents. "Not a Bordeaux, something lighter." I held it to my nose, inhaling its fresh, fruity bouquet. "A Syrah?"

"Hmmm, from the Oregon AVAs." He peeked under the lid of a pot, dipped a spoon in, and then blew on the steaming liquid before tasting. He shrugged but said nothing as he took the wine glass. After sniffing and swirling, he took a sip, held the liquid in his mouth a moment, and then swallowed. "Nice, but not nice enough for the price point."

"Your call." I wasn't about to question his heretofore-impeccable taste. We could quarrel over costing-out his restaurant, but the food and wine were his sole province. "How did you happen to corral the runaways?"

"They corralled me. I was working on some menu ideas for the new restaurant, and they wanted to help. They are a good pair, those two. But they do not yet know they are in love."

"They entered a game show to win a wedding."

Jean-Charles stirred something in a saucepan that started my mouth watering. "*Non.*"

"What is that?" I leaned forward, breathing deeply of the delicious aroma. "And what do you mean, *non?*"

"A red wine reduction with a special addition I am trying." He took a sip of wine as he leveled those baby blues on me. They held a smile that made my heart do a somersault. My heart was apparently playing hooky from the School of Teddie. "And *non*, they entered the contest to get to Las Vegas and our restaurants."

"I see."

"And Rocco is going to teach me how to make his grandmother's secret marinara sauce." Jean-Charles actually looked thrilled.

"I thought you stuffy French-types were above something so mundane as tomato sauce."

Seeing that the level of wine in my glass had dropped an inch or so, he grabbed the bottle and reached to add more. His hand brushed mine with an electric shock. The muscles in his jaw clenched—he felt it too. Man, I so did not need this. Teddie had my heart, but my body had clearly missed the memo.

He poured the wine with a studiousness the act didn't deserve, and replaced the bottle before answering. "Not only is food nourishment, it is also pleasure—a feast for the senses. Like love, it does not need to be complex or exotic to be satisfying. Simple, direct, rich, and spiced with the flavors of passion, it feeds the body as well as the soul."

Enraptured, I was holding my breath as the chef captured me like a snake charmer weaves a spell over a cobra. I let my breath out in a whoosh and shook my head slightly, trying to break the spell. "And the complex and exotic?"

"Feed the ego."

I STILL FELT AS IF I HAD FILLED MY LUNGS WITH HELIUM OR something as I pushed through my office doors—a couple of hours with the chef, sharing dinner in his lair, was enough to do that to any female. "Crisis averted. Harmony in the universe has been restored." I didn't sound like Pee Wee Herman so the whole helium thing had been a figment of my imagination. One small thing to be thankful for. That fact that I appeared to be in lust with our new chef was *not* on that list. Usually, meaningful sex was an antidote to libido overdrive. I wondered why it wasn't working this time. With no answer, I abandoned that line of self-interrogation as being a threat to the status quo.

Miss P, holding the handset to her phone in one hand, looked at me over the top of her cheaters. "Alert the media. How are you coming on the world peace problem?"

"I've added it to my Christmas list along with a plea for super-powers. That's the best I can do." I picked up a pile of messages in her outbox—my inbox—and waved them at her. "Any of these important?"

"I guess that depends on your point of view."

I gave her a glare, but I think my grin sort of killed the effect. I plopped down in a chair across from her, my legs stuck out in front of me. "Your job is to prioritize. Give me the top five, then we delegate."

Being at the top of the food chain had its disadvantages—I

drew the short straw every time. "A wife mix-up?" I read from the message on top. "What is this about?"

"Bungalow Five." Miss P couldn't hide her grin. "Mr. Handy?"

"The brawny half of Couple Number Three?"

"His *wife* is looking for him and she's *not* happy."

THE DOOR TO BUNGALOW FIVE WAS STANDING OPEN WHEN I skidded to a halt in front of it, short of breath and ideas. "Hello?" I knocked on the doorjamb as I peeked inside. The living room was empty. "Anybody here?"

Angry voices emanated from the direction of the master bedroom. "I told you not to come. You'll ruin everything." A male voice. Guy Handy. I still couldn't get my mind around the fact that with that name and that body, he wasn't in a male revue or stripping somewhere.

Throwing protocol to the wind, I charged inside and headed for the escalating argument.

"But, honey, I know we agreed to let this play out." Female voice. Mrs. Handy, perhaps? Without even a hint of ice, the voice clearly didn't belong to Vera.

"You have to leave. Now. Before the bitch shows up. She'll have a capillary."

I stuck my head in the room in time to see a petite brunette put a hand in Mr. Handy's chest and say, "Coronary."

Guy wrinkled his brow, but the word obviously took his mind of the issue at hand. "What?"

"She'll have a coronary. A heart attack," the brunette explained, with staggering composure. "A capillary is…"

Since no one seemed to be brandishing a weapon, I felt brave enough to step into the room and make my presence known. "Excuse me?"

They both whirled, and then seeing it was me, sagged in relief.

Mr. Handy was the first to find his voice. "God, I thought you were the..."

"Vera?" I interrupted.

As if on cue, a tornado of seething anger whirled into the room—Vera. Pointing a finger at the brunette, who scurried to hide behind the formidable form of Mr. Handy, the female half of Couple Number Three adopted an imperious stance. "Who the hell is this? And why is she here?"

CHAPTER THREE

I PUT my body between Vera and the Handys. Today seemed to be my hazardous duty day. "Let's all calm down. I'm sure there's a good explanation." I glanced at Guy for affirmation.

His eyes stricken, he shook his head.

"Okay," I said, as I took a deep breath. "No good explanation."

"This is my wife." Guy clutched the small woman to him. She leaned into him, disappearing into the crook of his arm, which circled her protectively.

Directly in the line of fire, I didn't have enough time to formulate even one mediocre idea. Vera launched herself at the couple with talons drawn, fangs exposed. Instinctively, I pushed Handy and his wife behind me, and then turned to shield us with my shoulder as I closed my eyes and braced for impact. Hell hath no fury and all of that... This wasn't going to be pretty.

"Vera!" a voice boomed. A male voice.

When Vera, the human missile, failed to make contact, I inched one eye open.

Walker Worthington, the buttoned-up half of Couple Number Two—still spit-and-polished and looking like he'd stepped out of a Brooks Brothers ad—had Vera by the waist in a bear hug. She kicked and fought, but he held tight. "Calm down, honey. Double-digit boy-toys are a dime a dozen."

With superhuman self-control, Vera pulled herself together. Throwing her shoulders back, she stretched to her fullest height and pushed at Walker's arms. "I'm fine now. Thank you." Her voice was sharp and cutting, but cool. "Dignity is too high a price to pay for that..."

"Man," I interjected.

She shot me a venomous look. "Fine. Although, Walker, I'll have you know I paid considerably more than a dime."

Walker Worthington gave Guy Handy the once-over. "You overpaid."

With that, Vera wilted like a starched shirt on a humid day. She put one hand on her hip as she worked her strand of pearls with the other, and eyed the couple. "Guy, perhaps you would be so kind as to shed some light?" Her voice dripped with honeyed sarcasm. I was proud.

Keeping a watchful eye on Vera, Guy hissed at his wife, "Honey, you said I could see this through. We both agreed we could use the money."

If he and Vera actually won the contest, I wondered how he planned to leap the polygamy hurdle, but I didn't think this was the time to ask. Instead I said, rather stupidly, "This was about money?"

I'm sooo naïve. Pity me.

Vera cocked one eyebrow at me. I knew the look. She said, "Did you really think I could put up with this...this..."

"Man?" I once again offered.

"Fine." Vera tossed her head and rolled her eyes. "Of course it was about the money. What else would it be about?"

"Gosh, next you're going to tell me there's no Santa Claus." I know, I know, not particularly helpful, but it was better than saying what I was thinking: that it could be about the sex. Even I was smart enough to know not to poke the bear if I was in the cage with her.

The four of them stared at me wide-eyed, as if expecting me to fix this mess.

I blew at a strand of hair that tickled my left eye, stalling for time. Reality tv shows were as baffling to me as the game of love. If you stacked the deck, did you really win?

Trey Gold found us stuck in that awkward silence—like a herd of lemmings looking for a cliff to plunge over—and rushed in to fill the momentary silence. "What the hell is going on here?" Without his makeup he looked almost normal...almost. His hair still didn't move, which bothered me. "We can hear your voices halfway to Pahrump. The reporters are circling like wolves around a herd of pigs."

Okay, not a metaphor I would have reached for, but it seemed to fit.

Trey pointed an accusatory finger at the brunette. "Handy, who is this?"

"My wife."

The bombshell exploded, rendering Trey Gold speechless. A rarity, if I could hazard a guess. Wild-eyed, he turned to me. "Is this true," he sputtered, when he found his voice.

I shrugged. "He should know."

Trey whirled on Handy's supposed other half. "Vera?"

She couldn't look him in the eye. "All right, I paid him."

Trey blinked rapidly, as if that would help get his pea-brain around the problem. "I should throw you off the show. That's a clear violation of the rules."

"What about my money?" Guy Handy whined.

Vera shot him a lethal look. "Read your contract. You haven't fulfilled your duties."

"You have a contract?" I couldn't keep the incredulity out of my voice. "You put this in writing? You have a section spelling out 'duties of the parties'?"

Vera gave me a terrified look as reality hit her right between the eyes. "Very specifically."

"They say the devil is in the details." I'd never write anything I didn't want to see on the front page of the paper. "Serious damage control is in order." I reached for my phone to alert my team.

"I wouldn't get involved, if I were you," Trey said, through clenched teeth. "This is my show. And I'm sure you wouldn't want the Babylon to be presented in an unsavory light, now, would you?"

My hand dropped to my side, my fingers itching to circle his neck. "Is that a threat?"

"Of course."

At least he was honest...a snake, comfortable in his skin.

Dismissing me, the little reptile turned to Vera. "How'd you get around my investigators? They should've discovered your ruse." I could almost hear the rusty cogs grinding in his tiny, self-serving, narcissistic mind.

Vera gave him a look normally reserved for mongrel dogs. "Please, I run a Fortune 1000 corporation. Shuck and jive is part of the skill set."

If recent Wall Street shenanigans were any testament, I'd say she was stating the obvious, but I'm not sure I'd admit it.

Since no one else seemed to be willing to pose the obvious question, I did. "Mrs. Handy, if you agreed to all of this, why are you here? Why now, so close to the end?"

Blinking her huge doe-eyes, she seemed to shrink within herself as she ducked behind her husband again, hiding most of her body. "I'm pregnant."

For a moment Guy stood there, dumbstruck.

I fought my smile at the tortured pun. And I fought the urge to make sure he understood the meaning of the word "pregnant."

Grabbing his wife at the waist, he picked her up and spun her around. She giggled, her hands on his shoulders. When he stopped twirling, he slid her down his body and wrapped her in a hug.

Teddie used to do that to me, but I couldn't remember the last time. There was a red flag in there somewhere, but I chose to ignore it.

"People." Trey clapped his hands like a kindergarten teacher trying to get a room of five-year-olds to focus. "Attention!"

All heads swiveled his direction.

"This is perfect," he announced with glee. "Think about it." Driven by an inner need to move, he began to pace. We all watched him going back and forth, like fans at a tennis tournament. "Folks, this is reality television at its finest."

"A train wreck," I gasped, as reality hit. "You wouldn't?"

His face split by a huge grin, he nodded at me. "Oh, I would."

"I'll sue," Vera threatened, in a voice that left little doubt that *sue* was just a nice way of saying *disembowel*. She'd obviously found the page in the book we were all reading from.

Trey waved her off. "Honey, read your contract." Turning to the Handys, he said, "You two come with me. We need to strategize. You guys are going to be bigger than Snooki and the Situation."

Dollar signs in their eyes, they followed him like lambs to slaughter.

Vera leaned into Walker as his arm circled her shoulder. She looked stricken. I didn't blame her—nothing to take the starch out of your shirt like the prospect of the world knowing that you were so desperate you had to pay an actor to pretend to love you. Well, you live by the contract, you die by the contract. No wonder everyone hated lawyers.

"Walker, what am I going to do?" The ice had melted.

"You two know each other?"

"We've done several deals together," Walker explained, before turning to Vera. "As ceos, you and I know how to spin anything to our advantage. Why don't you let me buy you a drink? We can put out heads together."

~

My father found me in Delilah's Bar, contemplating various healing waters. "Pick your poison, I'm buying." He snaked an arm around my waist and gave me a squeeze, then let go as he straddled the stool next to mine. He was a handsome man, shorter than me by several inches but fit and trim, with chiseled features and salt-and-pepper hair. He looked twenty years younger than his mid-sixties age. Tonight, he had abandoned his normal suit and tie in favor of an open-collared pink button-down and charcoal grey slacks.

"You sure? Tonight calls for a double dose." I'd left the contestants to solve their own problems. Usually, not being able to bring about a good solution made me twitchy. Not tonight. Besides, I didn't see a ready happy ending, which took a bit of rose tint off my glasses.

"That bad?" My father nodded at Sean, our head bartender, who set to work. Apparently the mixologist had heard enough of the conversation. With a flourish and a smile he slid a tumbler filled with Wild Turkey to me, then put the same in front of my father.

Holding the glass to the light, I eyeballed the contents. More than a double. To hell with the Self-Betterment Program. "I'm seriously considering serial monogamy."

My timing was impeccable—my father had just taken his first sip. He spluttered and choked until I thought I might need to hammer him on the back.

"I don't know," I continued. "It seems there comes a point in every relationship where something changes. One or both quit trying. The honeymoon ends. Whatever. It just doesn't seem to work so seamlessly anymore." I cast a forlorn look at my father.

His face red, he dabbed at his eyes with a cocktail napkin and still could not draw a full breath.

"This is where the serial monogamy comes in. After a couple

of years, when things start to settle into that whole taking-each-other-for-granted phase, my friends and I could get together and trade."

"Trade?" My father managed to choke the word out. I ignored the fact that he looked ready to do something rash.

"Yeah. We could pass the guys around, sort like musical chairs, and we each could move one spot to the right. Then it would still stay fresh. Know what I mean?"

My father looked defeated. "I'm sure there's a law against that, or something."

"Please, it's Vegas. Long-term relationships here are measured in hours, not to mention paid for in similar increments." I took a dainty sip of my Wild Turkey and relished the ball of fire that chased down my throat and exploded in my stomach. Bliss. "Speaking of which, where's Mother? Aren't you two attached at the hip or something?"

"I know you love her, as I do, so I'm not going to give you the fight you're angling for."

Fathers. They could see right through you. I hated that part.

"I'm not really picking a fight, but something's bugging me, I'll admit that. I just don't know what exactly."

My father seemed to think that over for a minute as we both worked on our firewater.

"Seriously, where's Mother?"

"She knows me well," my father said. He spun around on his stool. Back to the bar, he leaned back resting his elbows on the polished mahogany as he surveyed the casino. "Sometimes I just need to wander, check the pulse of the hotel."

I followed his lead, turning my back to the bar and my face to my world.

Understanding, I nodded as we both gazed on the crowd in silence. "Seriously, how do you keep that whole wild-sex-on-every-piece-of-furniture phase going?"

"Should I be having this conversation with you?" My father,

looking decidedly ill at ease, reached for his wallet. He extracted what I knew to be a hundred dollar bill and then replaced his wallet. Studiously avoiding my eyes, he began to crease and fold the paper. When under stress he turned to origami to calm his nerves. Funny he should need it now—sorta sweet.

"Who else would I trust to not only understand me, but to care enough to soft-sell any bad news? Mother?"

Out of the corner of his eye, he glanced at me. "Good point." He made a number of meticulous folds before continuing. "Can you give me a hint as to who might have put this particular burr under your saddle?"

"I think I'm becoming cynical about love."

That got a huge grin out of him, which, to his credit, he tried to hide. "Honey, you still believe life is a Rodgers and Hammerstein movie. 'Some Enchanted Evening' is your theme song. I love the fact that you think true love is just going to swoop in someday."

"Like a buzzard, to pluck my heart out." I watched a little figure take shape in his hands—a bird. Cute. "Stupid, huh?"

"Charming. And encouraging." He stopped a young couple as they walked in front of us. "Here." He dropped the bird in the young woman's hand and smiled at her delighted gasp of surprise.

"One in the hand, right?" I commented as we watched the couple walk away, both of them talking excitedly, their heads bent together.

"You and Miss P. What is it with you two and your clichés and platitudes?" My father angled his stool so his knees meshed with mine, and I could no longer avoid his eyes.

"Ella says it's a defense mechanism, along with the sarcasm," I said, not even trying to sugarcoat it.

My father's eyebrows shot toward his hairline. "Ella has that kind of insight? Who knew?"

"Our resident answer to Dr. Phil." I took another sip of my Wild Turkey, this time a not-so-dainty one.

My father took both of my hands in his. "Promise me one thing, Lucky."

"Sure."

"Don't ever change."

AFTER FINISHING OUR DRINK OVER MORE BENIGN TALK, MY FATHER went in search of his true love, and I went looking for love in all the wrong places. The game show had finished taping all the interviews and the crowd now spilled into the casino. Throngs of people three-deep ringed every table, which put a spring in my step. Bringing folks into the hotel to spend money was the sole motivation behind subjecting myself to Trey Gold and his little band of cutthroat attention-seekers.

Pausing by a row of slot machines, I absorbed the energy that shimmered off the crowd as I watched the scantily clad cocktails waitresses work the room. They moved quickly, with precision— as much to keep warm in their lack of clothing as to earn more tips. Shouts rang out from the tables, competing with the subtle come-on songs from the slot machines. Music with a pulsing beat served as an undercurrent to the enthusiasm. Basking in the glow of unfounded optimism, I spied a possible love match at one of the craps tables. I sidled up behind him and leaned close. "Hey, handsome, want to buy a little fantasy for the weekend?"

Clearly Teddie had seen my stealth approach from behind and had decided to play along. At my whispered invitation, he spun around and grabbed me, burying his face in my neck. "Could you make room on your schedule for something longer than a weekend?" His words were muffled as he nibbled on my ear lobe, making me giggle.

Giggling used to appall me—a personal affront to my dignity— but somehow I no longer felt that way. Giggling made me feel good. "Tough to do. I might need convincing."

Holding me close, he looked me in the eye as his playful mood morphed into smoldering passion. After slowly tracing my lips with his thumb, he cupped a hand behind my head and pulled me into probably the most delicious kiss ever. Every nerve tingled as he assaulted my mouth with his tongue.

When he pulled back, he gave me a quizzical look. "You smell like sautéed onions and charcoal. Where have you been?"

I stepped away so I didn't have to look him in the eye. Afraid of what I might glimpse lurking in the depths, I didn't want to look too deeply. Taking his hand, I pulled him away from the table and into the flow of the crowd. "Trey Gold needed help finding your Couple Number One. I managed to corral them in the Burger Palais."

"Yes, they both have a passion for food." Out of the corner of my eye I could see him looking at me. "Your new chef, was he there?"

"He's not *my* chef—the Big Boss threw him into my lap. And yes, he was there taking lessons in Italian sauces from Rocco."

"Someday I'm going to have to meet this chef of yours." Teddie looked at me as if he could see into my soul. "He sounds interesting."

"He's here to make money for the hotel." I forced my eyes to meet Teddie's. "That's as far as my interest extends. So, tell me, how did the initial taping of the show go?" A deft change of subject that puffed my chest with pride. What had Vera said: shuck and jive were part of the skill set. *That* didn't make me proud.

"Interesting cast of characters for sure," Teddie started in, clearly relishing his role as arbiter of love. "The young couple, Rocco and Gail, should be the early favorites. They really seemed to be on the same wavelength, as did that weird couple—the young guy and the boardroom gal. They were in tune. Go figure."

I took a quick survey as we climbed the steps to the elevated platform of Delilah's. "Yeah, go figure."

Teddie's perceptive abilities clearly needed some fine-tuning. Of course, the whole show was a staged farce, which disappointed me. I don't know why—I was certainly way more than a bit player in the Vegas fantasy show. Perhaps it was something about Teddie, recently—a more tenuous connection? And my fear that our relationship was some sort of superficial game. A figment of my imagination, or was it real? Who the heck knew anymore?

With bougainvillea trellises, a stone water feature forming the wall behind the bar, and a white baby grand in the corner, Delilah's was a nice oasis from the raucous, desperate energy of the casino floor. Of course video poker games were embedded in the bar top, and a camouflaged ATM lurked discretely in a corner —subtle signs that this place was still all about wagering. At least here, one knew the odds.

Sean, drying clean glasses with a rag, still manned the bar. "You back for more?"

I sidled onto a stool as Teddie broke away and slid onto the empty piano bench. With no apparent thought, he began to play and sing. His rich tenor always turned heads—the bar quieted as people stopped to listen. He played my song, the one he'd written for me, "Lucky for Me." When he caught my eyes, he held them. The room fell away. The past and the future faded, distilling life to the now.

After exactly two bars and a chorus, a call from my office broke the spell.

"Lucky?" Miss P's voice emanated from the phone at my hip. "We have an emergency at 3M. And you'd better hurry." Her voice held a note of panic. History had taught me that when something rocked Miss P off center, I'd better pay attention.

With an irritated swipe, I grabbed the offending device and held it to my lips. "On my way. Have Paolo waiting out front in two minutes."

Teddie didn't even miss a beat, or a note, when I waggled my fingers at him and bolted.

3M was our code for Miss Minnie's Magical Massage Parlor. I know, that's four M's, but after dealing with the proprietress and her establishment more times than we could count, we no longer found it magical. And, to be honest, three out of four was still formidable.

One of the hotel's limos slid to the curb as I burst through the front entrance. Without waiting for Paolo to come around to assist me, I yanked on the handle, threw the door open, and dove inside. "Miss Minnie's and make it quick."

The acceleration threw me back against the seat as I pulled the door closed. Paolo glanced at me in the rearview, but said nothing. He was a small man, and behind the wheel he looked like a kid taking a joyride. Granted, his chauffeur's cap made him look a bit more professional, but not by much.

"You okay, Miss O'Toole?"

Taking a deep breath, I tried to marshal my thoughts. "Fine, thank you." I leaned back, savoring the silence, quieting the cacophony in my head. "Say, Paolo, you wouldn't have taken anyone to Miss Minnie's this evening, would you?"

Although I'd never been a driver in Vegas I knew how the system worked. Many of the local establishments, from fine dining to spouse-swapping party houses, offered drivers a kickback if they delivered a paying customer. As wily as a snake after a rabbit, Miss Minnie worked the system like a pro.

I opened my eyes in time to catch Paolo's gaze flicking to me in the mirror, then away again. Guilty. I knew it. "Paolo, we had a talk about this. Miss Minnie is trouble."

He ducked his head. From where I was sitting, he disappeared from view, which was a bit unsettling. I hoped he still could see where we were going. "The money, Miss O'Toole. It is hard to resist."

"You make a tip. I get a problem dropped on my head." I moved to the bench seat behind him and stuck my head through

48

the open window separating the driver from the passengers. "It's really unwise to piss off your boss."

"Yes, ma'am."

"So, tell me again, who is your boss?"

"You are." His voice lost some its normal exuberance.

"Look at me, do I look happy?"

His eyes glanced up the rearview and I gave him my best frown.

"No, ma'am."

"Remember that the next time Miss Minnie dangles a twenty in front of your nose, okay?" I returned to the deep, forward-facing seat and leaned my head back. "Tell me whose ass I'm going to have to drag out of the fire."

"That game show guy...Mr. Gold."

This time, when I shut my eyes a grin tickled my lips. In a particularly spectacular twist of fate, life had dropped a golden goose in my lap.

As Jerry said, we don't get mad, we get even.

SUBTLETY WAS NOT MISS MINNIE'S FORTE. HER ESTABLISHMENT lurked in a nondescript strip mall in the bowels of Koreatown. Small and dark, with blackened storefront windows, it would have been easy to miss...except for the neon sign. Huge, pink flashing neon screamed, "Miss Minnie's: Let Us Rub You the Right Way."

The parking lot was packed, so Paolo eased the big car to a stop in front of the door. I jumped out and burst through the doors, taking in the sign on the door that read, "Tonight's Special —A Happy Ending for Everybody."

Great. Giving Trey Gold a rub and a tug sent a shiver of revulsion down my spine. I'm very visual, which at times can be traumatic. This was one of those times.

Someone must've alerted Miss Minnie to my presence. Dressed in full geisha regalia, she rushed to greet me with hurried, mincing steps, her hands clasped at her stomach, her head bowed in a false show of respect. "Miss O'Toole." Keeping her head lowered, she stopped in front of me. "You please us with your presence. It's not often a woman such as yourself—"

"Cut the crap, Minnie," I growled, using my full height to intimidate as much as possible. "Where's Trey Gold?"

A door opened behind Miss Minnie, about halfway to the end of the long hall. Trey Gold stuck his head out. "Help me, Lucky!" His head disappeared. "Hey!" he shouted, and then the door slammed.

Pushing Miss Minnie aside, I charged down the hall. She grabbed my arm, but I pulled her along as easily as a hooked shark would tow a dingy.

"He no pay," Miss Minnie whined as she clung to me. "He not nice man."

Although I agreed with her, I wasn't about to say so. He was a guest in my hotel, and as such, he had my fealty. I stopped in front of what I thought was the right door and tested the knob. As expected, it was locked. I gave Miss Minnie a grin, then put some muscle to it. The cheap pot metal gave easily.

Taking a deep breath, I charged inside—I'd only have a moment to assess the situation. Trey cowered in the corner with a towel around his waist as a dark-haired woman clad only in lace panties shook a finger in his face, letting him know exactly how she felt...in Korean. Nearby, a short, stocky guy, dressed in wrinkled black slacks and a white dinner jacket that strained across his shoulders, narrowed his eyes at me—Miss Minnie's muscle. Unsure of whether I was a threat—me being female and all—he moved toward me, a hand reaching inside his jacket. I grabbed his lapel with one hand, surprising him. As I knew he would, he stepped back, expecting me to pull him toward me. Instead, I moved into him, throwing him off balance. Stepping in between his legs, I braced myself. I threw an elbow at his temple with all I had. Bone connected with bone, a hollow thunk that reverberated through my shoulder. He dropped like a rock.

Miss Minnie lurked in the doorway. Before she could bolt, I grabbed her, pulled her into the room, then kicked the door shut.

Stepping over the inert body on the floor, I advanced on the young woman and Trey Gold. Both of them stared at me, their mouths hanging open.

"One of the advantages to having been raised in a whore-house," I explained, as I took stock of the surroundings. Miss Minnie usually had only one strong-arm guy, but I kept her at my side as added insurance in case tonight she had doubled up.

"I'm going to call the police," Miss Minnie said. "You can't come in here like big, tough broad."

"You're going to call the police?" I pulled my phone from my hip and extended it to her. "Go ahead."

Trey started to snivel. I silenced him with a look.

Miss Minnie gave me a hard-eyed stare, then shrank back.

"Thought so." I re-holstered the phone as I herded everyone into the far corner of the room, where I could keep them corralled and still have an eye on the door. "Okay, somebody tell me what's going on."

"He want happy ending." The young girl looked ready to spit nails.

I wanted to give her a hug, take her home, and feed her a hot meal. "And?"

"I paid the price," Trey interjected, managing to actually sound irate rather than mortified. His psychological profile would prob-ably turn my blood to ice. "She said it would be ten dollars more."

Ten dollars for a hand job. Men. Why the hell would he pay for something he could do himself? As much as I'd like to know the answer, a philosophic discussion with Trey Gold would probably destroy any illusion I might still harbor regarding the future of the human race.

I turned to the young woman and raised an eyebrow.

"Ten dollar!" She rolled her eyes. "For normal man maybe, but he old. He take too long."

Ah, the glorious indignity of it. I was enjoying this far more than I should.

Trey didn't even look bothered by her assessment. "Hey, I took a purple pill. I was rarin' to go. If she'd just done it right. She needed to grab it hard. You know, with her thumb and forefinger, like this…"

I held up my hand. "Spare me the specifics." My stomach turned queasy as a visual took shape. I shook it away as I glanced at the other three, all of whom seemed to think this was an acceptable topic for casual conversation. "And aren't the pills you want blue?"

Trey's face fell as his brows snapped into a frown. Then he brightened.

His line of thinking wasn't hard to follow, and I did not want to go any further down that path. I turned to the girl. "How much do you need, then?" Before she answered, I pulled a roll of bills out of my pocket and peeled off two hundreds. "Will this do?"

Interest flared in her dark eyes as she reached for the money.

So two hundred would crack her hardened shell—she hadn't fallen so far down the rat hole she couldn't climb out. I pulled the money back. "There's just one thing I want you to do."

The woman's face closed down. "I no whore."

I smiled as my heart broke. "Keep it that way." I peeled off two more hundreds and handed them to her. "Are you in this country legally, with a work permit?"

"Don't be moron."

I took that as a yes, though that wasn't exactly clear. Through narrowed eyes, I scanned for any sign that she was lying or nervous. I didn't see any.

Miss Minnie sniffed. "What? You think I stupid? I no need no ins problems. That's really bad voodoo."

"Good." I ignored Miss Minnie and kept my eyes trained on the girl. "Go home. Get a good dinner. And come to the employment center at the Babylon tomorrow. Tell them I sent you. The money isn't as good, I'm sure. But it's an honest living with opportunity."

"Really?" The mask disappeared, revealing the girl inside.

"Tell them Lucky sent you. Have them call me."

"For real?"

"For real." As she eased by me, I stopped her with a hand on her arm. "You let me down, I'll kick your ass."

"Yes, ma'am."

Without the woman as his shield, Trey Gold shrank under my gaze.

"You owe me four hundred dollars." As I looked down at the miserable excuse of a man, I thought about adding, "Asshole," but I wasn't as ready to shed my dignity as everyone else appeared to be.

"Done." Holding his towel, he started to step around me.

"Not so fast." I crossed my arms and stepped into his path. Pausing, I took a deep breath and savored the sweet taste of revenge. "The money's only part of the deal."

He feigned indignation—hard to do in his position, and with his lack of clothing, but he came close to pulling it off.

Life was hard enough without having to share it with people who had no shame and no decency. It's amazing the opportunities that present themselves when you don't have a gun.

"We're done here, O'Toole."

I still couldn't process the fact that his body was lily white while his face still held that weird orange color, so I tried to keep my eyes on his. "It's O'Toole now, is it?" I stepped into his space, using that whole height thing. "Let me tell you something, little man. We are *so* not done. Here's how this deal is going down. In return for my bailing your ass out and for keeping your name out of the papers, as well as for keeping the video off of YouTube, you are going to do something for me."

"Video?" Trey's voice held a tremor.

I pointed to a small vent in the ceiling where a tiny, blinking red light was barely visible. "Video."

Trey's shoulders sagged and I moved in for the kill. "In return, you will not throw Vera to the wolves."

"Oh." Trey's tone hit a plaintive note. Tonight he was running through the full arpeggio of emotion. "You can't do that. It's perfect reality tv. I'll be famous." Ah, a hint of glee, which made me just the teeniest bit angry.

My eyes got all slitty—they were doing that a lot lately. Where had I lost my smile? I leaned down, putting my mouth next to Trey's right ear. "If famous is all you want, I can spread that video-tape around—that ought to get you your fifteen minutes."

"Is that a threat, O'Toole?" He tried to make himself taller. It didn't work.

"Of course." I threw his answer back at him. "I don't care how you spin it, but I will not let you sacrifice a brilliant CEO's dignity on the altar of Nielsen ratings." I poked him in the chest for emphasis. "Whatever you do, Vera gets veto power. If you serve her up for public ridicule, you're gonna see that lily white ass of yours on the widescreen. You got it?"

He swallowed hard. "I got it."

"Deal?" I extended my hand.

He reluctantly took it in his limp, clammy one and gave my hand a weak pump. "Deal."

AFTER HE HAD DRESSED, I SENT HIM BACK TO THE BABYLON ALONE in the limo. Maybe I thought if I shared the same air with him, some of his despair, some of his disillusionment, some of his lack of faith in the grandeur of the human spirit might rub off on me.

The guy had a black hole for a soul. And right now, I felt the pull of the darkness. It hid in the shadows, waiting like a hellhound to snatch the nugget of optimism glowing inside of me and lighting my way.

Besides, Miss Minnie and I still had a bit of business to transact.

She was sitting behind the reception desk when I returned—an imperious little Korean geisha, to the extent those terms fit together. Her hands were clasped in front of her, and her little bow-tie, painted-on mouth puckered with disapproval.

I held out my hand and snapped my fingers, then extended my open palm. "Give it to me."

"You took my best girl. You no get nothing."

My eyes never leaving hers, I reached for my phone. With my thumb, I felt the raised buttons, found the one I wanted, and pressed. When it started ringing, I held it to my ear.

"Who you calling?" Miss Minnie tried to hide fear with indignation as she pulled herself straight and threw her shoulders back. "You no scare me."

I thought we'd established that that wasn't true, but since mentioning it probably wouldn't be helpful, I didn't. "I work closely with the Pandering Investigation Team. I'm sure you're familiar with the vice team at Metro. Sheriff Gillespie is a personal friend."

"I a businesswoman. " Shooting me daggers, Miss Minnie pulled the videotape from under the desk and slapped it on the counter. "You win."

I pocketed the tape. "Yes. I win." I didn't even try to hide my gloat.

When I walked outside, victory had beaten back the pull of darkness—not a bad evening, all things considered. As I paused at the curb, a taxi flashed its lights and then eased to a stop in front of me. I opened the back door and peered inside at the driver. "Hey, Watalsky. Fancy meeting you here."

"I could say the same," he replied, grinning at me through a full beard. River Watalsky was an inveterate poker player. He'd won and lost more fortunes than he could keep track of. Recently on a downward trend, he'd come to me for a job. I'd found him one with the cab company. "Your office called the company. When the dispatcher said the pickup was you, I took the call."

Miss P and Paolo—they took better care of me than I could. I shut the back door and climbed in the front. "Follow the yellow brick road back to Oz, please."

He turned and put the car into gear. "The Babylon?"

"No, home. I think I'll knock off for the day."

"Had enough crossing swords with the Wicked Witch?"

I settled into the seat and tried not to think about why commercial-grade rubber covered the entire inside of the car. "Why don't the cops put her out of business?"

"Honey, without the bad, how do we know the good?"

CHAPTER FOUR

*T*HE PRESIDIO, a tall cylinder of steel and glass, served as home and home-away-from-home to financiers, entertainers, athletes, celebrities, and me. One of the toniest addresses in Vegas, the Presidio had impeccable service and unrivaled views, but I wouldn't know—all my home time was spent sleeping or changing clothes. More than once I'd thought about just moving into a small apartment at the hotel, but Teddie also lived at the Presidio. Giving up proximity and privacy seemed too high a price for expediency.

After rewarding Watalsky for his business acumen, I pushed through the double doors into rarified air. Filled with wood, brass, knotted silk rugs, and important artwork, the lobby reeked of class and exclusivity. To be honest, had I not bought my place at pre-construction prices, I would no longer have enough green to even worm my way onto the waiting list. Not that that would bother me—I got enough attitude at work, I didn't also have to live with it. Frankly, the whole thing had been Teddie's idea—he bought the penthouse and I bought the floor below. A good investment, he had said, and he'd been right.

Forrest, our resident concierge/bouncer/doorman/friend,

rushed from behind his desk. A former NFL player, Forrest now hobbled on creaky knees, but he still managed to make it to the elevator before me. The mountain of a man pressed the up button. "Miss Lucky, you get fired or something? I never see you before the wee hours."

"I wish. But, I have learned that if I'm really disagreeable they'll send me home early." I stepped into the elevator, which he held open for me.

"Not you, Miss Lucky." Forrest reached in and punched the button for my floor after I had swiped my magic card. "Mr. Teddie is home. Thought you might want to know."

The doors closed on his mile-wide smile. Why I felt like an inside joke, I didn't know, but I wasn't sure I liked it.

The elevator deposited me in the middle of my great room. A vast open space with polished wood floors, whitewashed walls, splashes of furniture, and rugs in bright colors, my apartment was my sanctuary. Quiet, open, serene—the antithesis of the Babylon. A place where I could breathe. As I tossed my phone on the couch —I'd left my purse in my office—I felt my tension ease. Wandering into the kitchen, I reached into the fridge, grabbed a Diet Coke, and popped the top. As I guzzled the cool bubbles, I grabbed the cover on a cage in the corner and whisked it off.

My multicolored macaw, Newton, eyed me through sleepy eyes, one leg tucked under him as he perched on his high bar. "Whassup, bitch?" The product of a hazy upbringing, his potty-mouth always made me smile.

From a bowl on the sideboard, I chose a piece of browned apple and carefully stuck it through the bars of the bird's cage. He'd been known to take a chunk out of my finger when I got sloppy. "Here you go, birdbrain."

The look he gave me made me wonder if birds understood the concept of disdain. They couldn't, could they?

With a quick strike, he grabbed the apple. "Asshole!" he sang out, then retreated to the other side of the perch to savor his prize.

As I watched him gnaw, it dawned on me that ours was the only relationship I had that I understood. I fed him; he pretended to hate me—it worked for both of us. Why couldn't all relationships be as simple? I drained the last of my Diet Coke, crushed the can, and tossed it into the garbage can in the corner. And, while I was dreaming, why couldn't every day be Christmas?

Time to get comfortable and then go find a hug.

TEDDIE, IN HIS INFINITE WISDOM, HAD CONTRACTED FOR A BACK staircase connecting our two apartments. Actually, he had done it before I could think it through, but since we'd started as best friends, I don't think "thought" would've changed the outcome. Music wafted from his apartment as I hit the stairs, trudged up the thirteen steps—which I tried not to count—and stepped into his kitchen.

A similar space and layout to mine, but with higher ceilings, Teddie's apartment reflected his own eclectic style. Comfortable furniture clustered on small rugs. Sketches of various musicians—some famous, some not so much—dotted the walls, all of them done in Teddie's hand: one of his many talents. Various instruments on stands sprouted from the floor like small brass bushes, surrounding the centerpiece—a gleaming white baby grand under a spotlight.

Teddie, sitting at the keys, looked up when I leaned on the piano. "I didn't hear you."

"You were lost." I handed him a glass of Bordeaux I had poured on my way through his kitchen. The second glass I kept for myself. "What's that you're working on?"

"This." He played me a riff. "What do you think?"

"Sounds like the start of something good." We clinked glasses in a silent toast.

Teddie looked delicious. Short, spiky blond hair, huge blue eyes fringed by lashes Cover Girl would kill for, high cheekbones, and full lips. He could look sexy as hell dressed in Chanel. Tonight, in his Harvard sweatshirt with the collar cut out—a remnant from his MBA days—and his threadbare jeans, he inspired thoughts that, well, didn't require clothing...which was a real testament to his appeal, given my near-dead state.

Pushing back from the piano, he rose and came around to greet me properly. The kiss flowed through me like a sweet rush of warm, molten chocolate, gooey and good. I let my hands explore the broad expanse of his chest, then drift lower, savoring.

He moaned against my lips, then pulled away. Grabbing my hand, he tugged me over to the couch, where I curled into him, my head on his shoulder.

"How is the music coming?" I was afraid to look at him. I knew I'd see his excitement. Right now I didn't want to think about his music—his mistress, the one huge hurdle for us to overcome. Personally, I'd liked it better when he'd been Vegas's foremost female impersonator, and I'd come home to see him prancing around channeling Cher in silver lamé and stilettos. Of course, he'd been brilliant at that as well. He could wear Oscar de la Renta like nobody else—something that used to worry Mona and turn me green with envy.

"Dig Me O'Dell has been on my ass. As has your Miss One Note Wiley." He took a sip of wine as he tangled the fingers of his other hand in my hair, which made it hard to concentrate. "They want ten original tracks by yesterday."

Dig Me O'Dell was a record producer of some serious fame. He'd contracted with Teddie, launching my love's dream. One Note Wiley was Teddie's agent. I'd made the original introductions—something I now felt pretty conflicted about. Launch a dream; torpedo a future. Teddie didn't seem concerned. Which was fine—I had enough paranoia for both of us.

"How many tracks do you have so far?" My hand shook a bit as I lifted my glass to my lips.

"Seven. Three good ones, two mediocre, and two totally blow."

"How can blow be the opposite of suck but mean the same thing?" I asked, clearly avoiding something: Teddie, myself, the topic at hand, the one we never spoke about, all of the above.

"You think about the weirdest stuff," Teddie said, with a laugh. "The music will come, it always does."

"Hmmm."

"When you bolted from the bar, where did you go? Was it something serious?"

"Serious enough, but I smoothed it over."

"You're good at that."

"One of my many talents." I uncurled myself, then stood. "Would you like me to show you some of my other skills?"

He grinned up at me. "I thought you'd never ask."

CAFFEINE WAS THE ONLY ANTIDOTE TO MORNING—OKAY, EARLY afternoon—the cruelest part of the day. What could be camouflaged under the cover of darkness now lay bare, exposed in the bright birth of a new day. As a creature of the night, I was not at my best before nightfall, and especially if not fully caffeinated.

Pulling the pillow off my head, Teddie waved a steaming mug at me. "Vanilla nut, your favorite. With enough milk to take the bitter out."

I rolled over and groaned. My place or his? I couldn't remember. Not a good sign. I pushed myself up then plumped the pillows behind me. My place. I didn't even remember how I had gotten here, but I'd never admit it. Talk about sleepwalking. I smiled at him and cupped my hands around the mug, absorbing the warmth and inhaling the aroma. After a test sip, I took a long pull and sighed. "You are a prince among men."

"I have you fooled." I don't think he meant it like I heard it. One thing for sure, if he kept standing there looking all tousled and sleepy-eyed I was going to be seriously late for work.

I reached up and tugged on the elastic band of his pants—a pair of tattered warm-ups that were the only things standing between him and indecency.

"Ah, what a difference a good night's sleep makes." He took my coffee mug and set it on the nightstand. Then he slid out of his pants—clearly my suggestion had raised...expectations. Lifting the edge of the duvet, he slid in beside me.

"Hot coffee. Hot guy. Am I lucky, or what?"

He nuzzled my neck as I circled him and spread my body the length of his. For a moment he arrested a hand against my stomach, spreading a warmth that exploded when he moved higher, cupping my breast and teasing my nipple with his thumb. When he covered my lips with his and plundered my mouth with his tongue, the world disappeared. Sensation alone remained.

My hands roamed, retracing, memorizing anew every peak and valley. Closing my mind to my worry about our future, my confusion at how to still believe in forever love when surrounded by the carnage of so many relationships, I reveled in the here and the now.

The future would take care of itself. Or not. And somehow, I'd survive.

SHOWERED, DRESSED IN BLUE LINEN DANA BUCHMAN PANTS, a silver silk cami, a blue cashmere cardigan with silver threads running thorough it, and my very first pair of sensible blue Ferragamos, which had been rebuilt at least five times, I was not only sated and caffeinated, but feeling pretty self-satisfied. A lingering kiss from Teddie had launched me out the door and into a delicious early fall day. Walking had seemed like a good idea—the stroll from the Presidio to the Babylon took twenty minutes, if I dawdled, and today was a dawdling kind of day.

With so much to do, there was rarely any time to think, to reach for elusive perspective. So I enjoyed the quiet time alone with myself. Life. Love. No easy answers. But, if it were easy, then everyone would do it, right? Of course, everyone *did* do it. So was it just me who made it harder than it should be?

Lost in thought, I hiked up the long curving driveway to the Babylon. Bordered by palm trees tall enough to turn Donald Trump green with envy, it reminded me of a tropical Appian Way —but without the burial monuments alongside or the catacombs underneath, which I thought was a good thing.

Paolo was just pressing his hat on his head as he burst through the doors and made a turn toward the limo park. Spying me, his face creased into a lower-wattage smile—apparently he remembered our last conversation—as he altered course and headed toward me. "Good afternoon, Miss O'Toole. I see, we are both starting the day late."

"I prefer to think of it as getting a jump start on our evening." I thought about adding that I also believed that love came to those who waited, but I was losing a bit of strength in that conviction. Besides, clichés were more my thing—I'd leave non-sequiturs to someone else.

Paolo stopped in front of me, bowing slightly from the waist. "I was just coming to get you." He turned toward his car, then stopped mid-stride. Turning to me again, he asked, "Did your office reach you?"

"No. I accidentally left my phone at home. Why?"

"We have a bit of a problem that will take your special skills." He moved to the rear of the limo, opened the door, and motioned me inside. "Let me fill you in on the way."

"Anything to keep me out of the office." I dove through the

opening and settled into the deep seat. I waited until we were out of the traffic on the Strip. When we were traveling sedately west on Tropicana, I moved over to the bench seat and leaned through the opening—déjà vu all over again, as Yogi Berra once said. "Want to tell me what's so important?"

"The bottom-feeders have staked out one of the contest couples. They got 'em pinned down."

"A rescue mission from the paparazzi. You've could've done that with a security guy or two."

"No, ma'am. They got them trapped at Spanish Trail." Paolo gave me a knowing look in the rearview, bursting my little bubble of *joie de vivre*.

"Let me guess. Phil Stewart's house?"

He didn't answer. He didn't have to. The look on his face told me all I needed to know.

Phil Stewart. Just the thought of him made my skin crawl. Phil was a swinger. And he loved to host spouse-swapping parties at his estate in Spanish Trail. I attended one once...as a spectator. Before you take that the wrong way, Teddie and Dane had conspired with Detective Romeo to catch a killer at one of Phil's little soirées. One had been more than enough.

Spanish Trail was the first gated community in Las Vegas. Built almost thirty years ago, it was so far west of the Strip, on a two-lane dirt portion of Tropicana Avenue, that most thought it should have been called East Los Angeles. The power-trust running Las Vegas had deemed the developers fools. Now that section of Trop was a six-lane speed trap, and Spanish Trail was in the middle of suburbia and one of the most sought-after developments of its kind in the Valley. The developers had laughed all the way to the bank, and were probably living on their own islands in the South Pacific or the Med. None of that mattered right now, of course. But the fact that Spanish Trail was not only gated, but also had gated communities inside the gated community, mattered a lot. Phil Stewart's house sat on a primo lot behind two gates.

Paolo rolled down his window as we turned into the east gate and eased up to the guard shack. A bored adolescent in a yellow shirt black pants with a gun holstered on his hip gave us the once-over. "Help you?"

Why, with each passing day, did everyone look younger and younger? I stuck my head out the back window and introduced myself. "I hear you got a bit of a problem in the Estates?"

"Shutterbugs all anglin' for a *People* magazine paycheck."

"I'm here to take the persons of interest off your hands."

His eyes widened. "Hope your life insurance is up to date." He punched a button and the gates slowly inched open. "You got the code to the second set?"

Paolo flashed a piece of paper and nodded as the guard waved us through.

"We need a plan," I said, trotting out my flair for the obvious. I watched Paolo maneuver the big car past the golf course on our right and the clubhouse on our left. I thought for a moment, but inspiration refused to strike. "We couldn't do something so simple and bold as to pull up to the front of the house and grab them, could we? Who are we grabbing anyway?"

"I don't have the names. But no one can see in the windows on this car—the tint is several shades past legal." Paolo grinned, but lines of tension bracketed his eyes. .

"Well then, pull right up to the front door. After that, I'll make it up as I go."

After opening the second gate with the magic numbers, Paolo eased the car through. Two white pickups with yellow lights and emblazoned with the Spanish Trail logo sat like sentries forming a gauntlet through which only the worthy would pass. From behind their mirrored Ray-Bans, the guards watched us.

"Are rent-a-cops supposed to make us feel better or worse?" I mused out loud, not really expecting an answer.

"Mostly they are here to make the residents behave. And to write tickets for exceeding the twenty-five-mile-per-hour limit."

DEBORAH COONTS

"I feel safer already." I leaned forward through the opening. "The house we want is that big one at the end—the one with the party house out back, and the naked dancing girls in bronze relief on the front door."

As it turned out, we couldn't have missed it. A crowd ringed the front of the house—men and women with cameras and huge telephoto lenses looped around their necks, jockeying for position. All that was missing from this sideshow was a snake oil salesman and a guy selling funnel cakes out of his van.

Paparazzi were like ants—once they got the scent, they closed in on the target, angling for a kill. You could push them, squash them, or run them off, but they always found a hole in the fence to get back in. I guess the members of the Spanish Trail security force either understood their limitations or had been contractually excluded from hazardous duty. Either way, they couldn't be counted on for reinforcement in case we got in over our heads.

As Paolo eased the big car into the driveway, he honked to clear a path through the throng. Experience had taught him to never allow the car to come to a standstill, so he kept it rolling, pushing people out of the way with the front bumper if he had to. Disembodied faces with hands cupping their eyes pressed to the glass, trying to see through the dark film. I could see them, but hopefully, my identity remained obscured. My name and photo included in an unsavory article about alternative sexual practices would probably do little for my upward career mobility. Although, worse things had been said about me.

Clearly someone had told the photogs they had to remain off private property, so they lingered at the fringes. Of course, we were in a gated community so it was technically all private property—but, in an Orwellian sense, apparently some was more private than others. Once we made it through the throng, we traveled the rest of the way up the curved driveway unmolested.

When Paolo brought the car to a stop under the porte cochere, I slipped over to the driver's-side door and let myself out. I didn't try to shield my face in case someone had found a good vantage position for a photograph—no need to look guilty when I wasn't.

Tape covered the doorbell so I was forced to use the knocker, which, as expected, was a set of brass...knockers. D cups, if I could hazard a guess. I wasn't amused.

The door opened after the first...bang, and Phil Stewart, in all his sleaziness, ushered me inside. "You have to get those camera people out of here. My guests are peeved. While they don't try to hide their identities, they don't seek publicity either. And some of them would be less than thrilled to have their faces on the national news." Phil had unnaturally black hair, a perpetual dark tan, evasive eyes, and a manner in keeping with his overall repugnance.

He turned and I followed him through the marble foyer to the back of the house. The house was unexpectedly quiet. The last time I'd been to one of his parties, all manner of activities I'd rather forget had been going on in the pool and the hot tub—although I did rather like the naked mariachi band. "Didn't your mother ever tell you not to do anything you wouldn't want to see on the front page of the *Review-Journal?*"

"Mothers say a lot of stuff they don't mean."

Even with Mona being what she was, that hadn't been my experience, but I wasn't about to share a personal tidbit with the likes of Phil Stewart. "If you didn't want the publicity, why'd you let the celebrity couple in?"

He waved a hand at me. "I don't watch reality tv. How the hell was I supposed to know they were pop-culture curiosities? I just thought they were a tv producer and a plastic surgeon from Texas."

"Wait." I grabbed his elbow, pulling him to a stop. "Are we talking about a nice, clean-cut African American couple? Tall. Thin. Warm smiles."

A sardonic grin lifted on side of his mouth. "What? You think *normal* people don't swing? Normal is so boooring. Needs some spice. Know what I mean?"

When fringe folks use logic, it weirds me out—especially if I find myself semi-agreeing. I mean, who aspires to "average"? I got it. Phil's lifestyle might be unpalatable, but his logic was unassailable, which scared me. "Who's that?" I pointed to figure skulking behind the bushes at the edge of the pool. As I watched, a hand parted the branches and a face peered through...a face I knew. With two angry strides, I reached the sliding glass door, threw it open, and charged through. "Flash, what the hell are you doing?"

She popped out of the bush as if she'd been Tasered. "It's my job. What's your excuse?"

"Same."

"There has to be a better way to make a living." Flash brushed the leaves from her sweatshirt and jeans as she stepped into the open.

"Selling my organs one at a time springs to mind." I motioned her inside, which was akin to inviting the fox into the henhouse. Flash might be my best friend, but she was also the primo investigative reporter in Las Vegas. But, as all good friends do, I had major blackmail material on her, so I wasn't too worried about her spilling the beans on my wayward Couple Number Four.

"Nice to have a plan B." With her red hair piled on her head in riotous curls, she looked like a cute troll, to the extent that wasn't an oxymoron. Overdeveloped and overdone, she screamed *Vegas*. She also screamed *bimbo*, but that would've been way off base. She was as sharp as a card-counter with a new shoe.

"What's she doing here?" Phil Stewart asked, coming late to the party.

"Good question." Hands on my hips, I used my full twelve inches of height advantage to look down on Flash. "What's your angle?"

"An inside piece on why folks pick the swinging lifestyle."

Phil looked interested. "Names and faces?"

"If anybody wants the publicity, sure. Otherwise, not necessary. I'm just curious, that's all. And if I'm curious, I figure other folks are, too."

"Any money in it?" Phil narrowed his eyes like a cat eyeing a canary. He didn't know it yet, but he was in way over his head with Flash.

"Look," I interrupted. "I'm in a bit of a hurry here. Can you hammer out the details later?"

Flash looked at me, her investigative radar on high alert. "Where's the fire?"

I'd trust Flash with my life, so I told her.

"Wow," she said with wide-eyed wonder, when I'd finished. "That would hit the highlight reel for sure." She gave an appreciative whistle.

"Yeah, best plays of the week." I grabbed her elbow. "But not this week. You owe me for giving you the inside track on the gal who took a header off the hotel."

"You're writing the rules today." She gave me her trademark grin.

"Thanks." I turned to Phil, who was still clearly contemplating all the media opportunities. "Where is everybody?"

"We had to move the party to the gym." He motioned me down a hallway to the right. "This way."

I wasn't about to admit I knew the way. The last time I'd been aware of a party in Phil's gym, Dane had gotten sucked into some sort of grope-fest in the dark—he'd been a little hazy on the details.

"If you take your happy little couple from Houston back to the Babylon, then maybe, without the photo op, the Spanish Trail swat team can round up the voyeurs and the party can go on as planned." Phil pulled open one of the double doors to the gym and walked through. He let the door swing back.

Bad man, bad manners. Hot on his heels, I blocked the door with a stiff arm and kept on motoring. Of course, the last time I'd been his guest I'd spilt blood and threatened him with all manner of unmentionables, so no love lost.

One of the Bee Gee's classics played over the speaker system, which struck me as funny. Something about bartering sexual favors to a melody sung by a guy who sounded like he hadn't reached puberty...I don't know. Maybe I needed a very long vacation.

People clustered in small groups, talking animatedly, sipping the beverage of their choice—while they evaluated the other...opportunities. Casual sex made me queasy. I needed to find my quarry and boogie.

"Hey, O'Toole!" A booming voice. Male. "You come back to give us a try?"

I turned and found myself face to face with the Most Reverend Peterson J. Peabody, otherwise known as Jeep, primarily because they had the same body style. At four hundred pounds, give or take, Jeep had the whole wide-body thing going on, yet he was a swinger. As was the missus, a petite little woman who never said much but smiled all the time. Maybe I should have some of what she was getting. A shiver of revulsion chased through me. Jeep and I had met under perhaps not the best of circumstances—someone had slipped him a mickey and my staff had found him out cold, naked as the Lord had made him, sleeping it off under the stairs.

"Jeep! How the heck are you?" I wrapped him in a bear hug.

He did the same to me—nice man, nice manners.

"I didn't expect to see you back so soon," I said, as I stepped out of his embrace.

"Well, our last trip sorta got interrupted by the whole...mess. You know." He looked a bit sheepish. "So, we thought we'd come back for what we came for."

I knew there was a really interesting pun in there, but I rose above it. Instead I blushed—being visual can be traumatizing, trust me.

Phil, who had rushed off when Jeep had waylaid me, returned with my targets in tow. Melina, carrying her shoes in one hand while trying to shrug into her dress, looked...as calm as if she was rushing to a hair appointment. John glanced furtively over my shoulder, eyeing the prey as he buckled his belt. He shot someone a wink, but I didn't turn to see who.

"I hear you guys need a ride back to the real world." I crossed my arms, trying to look stern.

"We just thought we'd have some fun," Melina said, sounding as if they'd just gone dancing or something. "Burn off some steam. Know what I mean?"

I wished everyone would stop asking me that. I didn't know what they meant, not exactly anyway. And I didn't want to.

"I think you're spoiling everyone else's fun." That took the smile out of her eyes. I poked John in the chest, trying to get and hold his attention. "You two have got to come with me." I turned to Phil, who was licking his lips over a sweet young thing talking to some cowboy dude in the corner. "Phil, focus. Is there room in your garage to move the limo in there?"

"Of course. It's a ten-car garage and I keep most of my toys in Jackson."

"Can I borrow your phone?"

He handed it to me and I called Paolo. He answered on the first ring, and I gave him the details of my plan, short and sweet. After disconnecting, I bade farewell to Jeep and turned to Melina and John. "Come on, you two." I turned on my heel and marched out of the gym with happy Couple Number Four following behind. Phil Stewart trailed us like a coyote hoping snatch a lamb. I pretended he was a disgusting relative at Christmas dinner and tried to ignore him. In fact, I tried to ignore all of this. The concept of marriage as an overlay to the swinging lifestyle made my head hurt. It didn't do too much for my heart either, so I shut it out as best I could.

Love...in all its bastardizations. Enough to makes us all hard-hearted cynics. I hated it when people messed with the magic.

Paolo had just squeezed the limo into the garage and was closing the door when I peeked my head in. I shielded my guests in case a wandering cameraman had sniffed out the plan.

"All, clear, Miss O'Toole." With his hat tucked under one arm, Paolo opened the back door with a formal flourish.

"Quickly." I stepped aside and directed Melina and John to the limo.

Without a word, they scurried to the car and dove inside. After securing them in the back, I rode shotgun. As Paolo took his place and put the car in gear, Phil Stewart punched the garage door button, releasing us to the outside world.

"You two keep your heads down," I hissed through the window to the back. "I think you're safe behind the tinting, but right now is not the time to test my theory."

We made it through the gauntlet of popping flashbulbs and crushing crowds, going back through the east gate and out onto Tropicana, where Paolo picked up speed. As we moved with the traffic, I began to relax. No one seemed to be following us, so that was good.

Propping my elbow on the ledge between the driver's compartment and the back, I rested my chin on my arm as I eyed my charges. Both of them seemed unflustered, their smiles in place as they held hands. "I must admit, very little surprises me these days, but you two managed just that."

"Why? Because we're the perfect couple?" Melina asked with a sigh. "Everyone says so, you know."

"That you're the perfect couple?"

"Yes," John weighed in. "We're tired of hearing it actually."

"You don't agree with them?"

Melinda shrugged as she glanced out the side window, then back to me. "I don't really know. We certainly seem to agree on a lot of things."

"Yes." John nodded. "Like the Hockney painting we acquired recently for our living room. What a coup!"

"We practically stole it out from under a French investor. He was livid." Melina settled back with a self-satisfied look.

"Hockney." I pursed my lips as I mentally reviewed some of his works I was familiar with. "What was it about the painting that called to you?"

Melina and John looked at me as if I'd switched from English to Swahili.

"How do you feel when you look at it?"

"Feel?" They said in unison.

Clearly communication was not in my skill set today. "Why'd you buy it?"

"It made sense," John answered.

"A brilliant investment," Melina added.

"Do you like the painting?"

Both of them shook their heads. "Not particularly," John said, with a quizzical frown. "Why?"

"Art is like love," I explained, as if I really knew what I was talking about. "It should hit you on a visceral level. Of course, the purchase can be intellectualized, but the connection to the piece should be emotional." I ignored all the puns in that statement. I had no intention of undermining my own beliefs—my hold on them was tenuous enough as it was.

"Really?" Melina asked in a small voice. "Is that what love does?"

"I'm no expert, but that's been my experience." I sort of rolled my eyes—me counseling anyone on the meaning of love was like a jackleg preacher proselytizing from a bible he'd never read. "What were you looking for at that party back there?"

John chewed on his lip as he looked past me, over my shoulder. "I don't know. Something that's missing, I guess."

The three of us fell into silence, lost in our own thoughts.

Love. What folly to try to intellectualize an emotion. "Do you mind if I ask you guys a question?"

"Fire away," John said as he leaned back, his face open, his posture inviting. Melina nodded her agreement.

"Why are you getting married?"

"One, we're compatible." John started ticking the reasons off on his fingers. "Two, we both are well educated, intellectually curious, and seem to see the world through a similar prism. Three, our families will stop bugging us. And four, we'll make beautiful children—if we ever find the time."

"Looks good on paper," I agreed. "A sound intellectual decision. But something's missing. Can you live with that?"

"You never get everything you want." John announced. Hurt flashed across Melina's face.

"But what you have, is it enough?"

"Of course," John announced, crossing his arms across his chest and narrowing his eyes.

Melina still looked hurt. "I don't know," she added in a small voice.

MISS P WAS JUST DISCONNECTING FROM A PHONE CALL WHEN I pushed through the office door. "Do you believe in happy endings?" I asked, hoping she would restore my faith.

As she re-cradled the phone she gave me a quick perusal. Today she sported vintage Versace—scalloped skirt, lace cami, and fitted jacket—a pair of sensible Ferragamos, hints of gold and diamonds at the appropriate spots, and a knowing look. "I will assume you are not referring to the kind of happy ending men buy from Miss Minnie."

Her short blond hair was gelled into pointed tips, which I thought sort of matched her personality. Tired of sitting and still a bit antsy, I parked one cheek on the corner of her desk as I glanced through the pile of messages. "Let me rephrase. Do you believe in happily ever after?"

"Are you finding it hard to keep your head when all around you are losing theirs?" Miss P could cut to the heart of the matter even better than Mona, who was an expert at wading through my obfuscation. A peaceful look settled over her face, softening her features. "Love shows up when you stop looking."

Miss P had been resigned to a life of comfortable solitude when the Beautiful Jeremy Whitlock showed up. Fifteen years her junior, a walking, talking Australian god straight off Bondi beach, and one of Las Vegas's best private investigators, Jeremy had taken one look at Miss P and lost his heart. Despite all of his obvious assets, kindness was his best feature—proving once again that good things can come in pretty packages.

As if he'd been waiting outside the door for his cue, Jeremy burst into the office. "Hey, Beautiful." Offering Miss P a perfect yellow tulip, he leaned across the desk and bent to kiss her.

With a soft smile, Miss P put a hand to the side of his face and met him halfway.

"What am I? Chopped liver?" Apparently my words fell on deaf ears. When the phone rang, I reached for it. "Customer Relations, Lucky O'Toole speaking."

"Lucky, oh I'm so glad I found you." Mona sounded out of breath.

My heart tripped. "Are you okay?"

"Me? Of course, don't be silly. I'm here with one of the game show couples and, well, we have a situation."

"Of course we do." Mona mixing with the reality folks...God help us all.

"You don't understand. They're going to call the police."

That got my attention. "Where are you?"

"Smokin' Joe's Sex Emporium."

CHAPTER FIVE

*S*OMETHING ABOUT a trip to Smokin' Joe's just screamed for a Ferrari.

Maybe I was feeling sorry for myself. Maybe I needed a pick-me-up. Maybe I just needed a dose of the real world. Who knew? Who cared? A simple phone call was all it took to strong-arm the dealership into letting me put my ass in some of their class.

A new F430 Spider, top down, awaited me at the valet stand when I hurried through the front doors, dodging the crowd surging in. Red, of course, with a tan interior and enough wow-factor to make grown men weak with envy. I traded a twenty for the keys from a wide-eyed kid in an ill-fitting uniform, who drooled as he eyed the gleaming machine. "I agree," I said, as I slipped into the car through the door he held open for me.

He closed it with reverence. "Is it as great as I think it is?"

"Superb in every way." Well, except for the fifteen-hundred-dollar oil change and the fifteen-thousand-dollar service at eight thousand miles. I didn't bother to bring those up—they would be mere trifles for those plunking down close to three hundred grand to buy the thing anyway.

I pushed the start button and the engine growled to life, lifting my spirits. Easing it into gear and away from the curb, I pushed my worries to the side. There was something so freeing about strapping on almost five hundred horses and kicking them into a flat-out gallop. Crossing the Strip, I took my time—I didn't need to turn a couple from Peoria or somewhere into a hood ornament. Hanging a left, I hit the on-ramp for the I-15. Powering through the paddle shifters, I reveled in the visceral joy of speed. The wind whipped my hair, stinging my cheeks with its bite.

Smokin' Joe's was barely far enough to lift my spirits. A right off the 15 onto Trop, straight a few blocks, and then I wheeled into the parking lot. Flashing lights and squad cars were conspicuous in their absence—either Mona had forestalled the call to Metro or I'd beaten them there. Either way, the absence of cops simplified my problems dramatically.

I probably knew more about Smokin' Joe's xxx Video Parlor and Sex Emporium than any well-adjusted person should—a fact that worried me when I allowed myself to think about it, which wasn't often. A full city-block long, Joe had cobbled together an incredible assortment of toys, costumes, magazines, and videos with one purpose—to launch libidos. To hear tell, he was enormously successful. Heck, even I had an account there. Before you leap to the obvious conclusion, I used to buy videos for Mona's bordello in Pahrump...before she'd found legitimacy.

After making one circuit of the parking lot, I angled the car across two spaces far from neighboring cars then levered myself out of the low-slung vehicle. It was still early, and the hookers had yet to man their posts on the street corners. But with cocktail hour easing into dinner hour, they'd be along soon. Not that I was overly concerned.

Mona lurked inside the front door. She pounced when she saw me. "Lucky, don't be mad. I did what I thought you would do." She ran a shaky hand through her hair as she took a shallow breath, and looked at me with eyes that seemed a bit haunted. "But the woman came at him like a banshee! Blood went everywhere. You know how a head cut can bleed. Joe freaked. He wanted to call the cops, but I convinced him you would be a better choice."

I took her arm and led her over to a swing that hung from the ceiling. "Mother, sit a minute. Can I get you water or something?"

She shook her head as she eyed the swing. "I'm all right. And, honey, I am not going to sit in that. It would be so...undignified."

Pointing out the obvious indignity of the whole scenario unfolding would be lost on Mona, so I didn't waste my breath. "You said there was blood?" I could handle most anything— through the years I'd been spit on, vomited on, had countless beverages thrown at me, but I really wasn't all that keen on blood. Although I'd been know to spill some of it myself, when circumstances warranted.

"The woman, she was fast. She laid open a three-inch gash on his temple."

"With what?"

"One of Joe's high-end toys. I had no idea dildos could be inlaid with real gold and diamonds and stuff, did you?"

"I'll cop to the Fifth on that one." I couldn't decide whether to laugh or to run. "Why don't you give me a few details?" I glanced around and the furor seemed to have died down, so I assumed the guilty parties were sequestered under Joe's watchful eye. Better to go in prepared, so I took a minute to grill Mona.

She took a deep breath, smoothing the pleats in her broom skirt, arranging the turquoise belt that rested on her hips, nipping in the peach silk tunic. The gold sandals were a nice touch. She glanced toward the rear of the building before she started in. "I was having breakfast by myself in Neb's when I overheard the couple at the next table discussing, well...things." She glanced at me through lowered lashes then looked away. "I really didn't mean to interfere."

"I understand." She looked genuinely concerned, so I took pity on her—usually not wise, but I had nothing to lose. How much worse could the day get? Besides, I just had to keep the lid on until tonight's taping of the final installment of *The Forever Game*. The audience and the judges would vote, we'd have a winner, and I'd have my life back, such as it was.

"Anyway, the long and the short of it was, they apparently had broken one of their own toys and were looking to replace it. I offered to introduce them to Joe."

"It was the least you could do." I bit down on a grin.

"Right." Mona stood a bit taller—I think she even preened a little bit. "Anyway, how was I to know the woman with him was not his fiancée?"

Somehow this little tidbit didn't rock my world. Dealing with interesting choices was part of my job description. "And the fiancée?"

"The dildo-wielding banshee." Mona looked at me matter-of-factly, with her hands on her hips, like a teacher ratting on a student to the principal.

"With all this bed-hopping, Viagra missed an incredible promotional opportunity." I grabbed Mona by the elbow and spun her around. "You'd better take me to them. We just have to prevent homicide until eight p.m. After that, they can kill each other during prime time for all I care."

"The ratings would go through the roof." Awe infused each of Mona's words.

"And add a dose of reality to reality tv."

We'd made it past the toy display and the private viewing booths when a thought hit me. "I'm not that great at math, but it seems to me there were three of them and two of you. Did you and Joe stop the bloodshed all by yourselves?"

"With a little help from Detective Romeo." Mother glanced at me through narrowed eyes, reading my pulse. Apparently she deemed it safe to continue. "When I couldn't get hold of you...that brings up a point, why does Teddie keep answering your phone?"

"I left it at home, and he's untrainable."

"They all are, honey. Remember that." My mother shot me a

look that saw right through me. Thankfully, she didn't belabor the point—a first for her. "As I was saying, when I couldn't get you, I called Romeo. Told him to keep it on the qt. He calmed everyone down."

"Yes, a man with a gun can have a chilling effect. You did the right thing."

This time I know she preened.

Detective Romeo, my ally in the Metropolitan Police Department, had a knack for making the right decisions despite his lack of experience. The fact that he was a bit older than he appeared— he looked all of twelve—also weighed in his favor. Today he sported his ever-present rumpled overcoat, a creased suit that looked like he'd slept in it, probably for good reason, a tie loosely knotted around his thin neck, and a wilted shirt. He wore his sandy brown hair shorter than the last time I'd seen him—he'd probably grown tired of trying to tame his cowlick. The short hair looked good on him, framing his open face, blue eyes, and mischievous smile—which grew wider when he saw me. "About time you showed up."

"I learned long ago it's best to let someone else do the heavy lifting." I squeezed his shoulder, feeling bones. Not good. "If I time it right, when I show up there's nothing left to do but take the credit."

"You'll have to teach me how to do that." Romeo reached into his inside coat pocket and pulled out his notebook, which he flipped open. "We got one Walker Worthington in Booth Three over there." He pointed behind me. "He's going to have a pretty good shiner. And he could probably use a few stitches, but he refuses. The lady"—he pointed to another booth on the far side of the room—"popped him pretty good."

"Really? With what?" Call me ugly, but I just had to jerk his chain a bit. Hey, I got my jollies where I could, not that it made me proud.

"This." Romeo's face turned bright pink when he held up the

80

weapon: a gold-inlaid, diamond-encrusted penis, which gave a whole new meaning to rough. He must've punched a button or something because the thing started vibrating and flashing lights through the jewels. "Someday, you're going to have to explain why this is so..."

I held up my hands, stopping him. "Barking up the wrong tree, my friend." I shook my head as I eyed the battery-operated boyfriend. "Even I have no explanation for...that."

Mona heard her cue. "Oh, well, I think I can explain it. You see, women, because of their anatomy—"

"Not necessary, Mother," I snapped.

"Perhaps another time," Romeo added, a red flush coloring his cheeks.

"Well." Mona pouted. "You don't have to get so huffy."

Romeo started to comfort her, but I waved him off. Playing into her little games only made things worse.

"Which lady popped our banker with the penis?" Briefly, I wondered if my counterpart at a Four Seasons property in some wildly exotic location, like Cairo or something, had my particular set of problems. How many times in the average day did they have the opportunity to say *penis* in public? Not many, if I ventured to guess. It would almost be worth putting myself in the crossfire of political strife to avoid ever having to trot out that word.

A door crashed open behind us. "I hit the lout."

At the sound of the high-pitched voice, our heads swiveled as if pulled by the same string.

Buffy Bingle. I'd read in her profile that she liked to watch cartoons. Today, in a skimpy little red dress with her assets on display, and carrying a purse shaped like a little white dog, which could double as a stuffed animal in times of crisis, she was reading from the Betty Boop book of fashion. Her blonde hair had been gathered in two knots, one protruding from each side of her head. I think Mona had done my hair like that...once...when I was six.

"Why the penis?" I don't know why I asked that. I guess I needed a moment of self-flagellation.

"Because it was the only thing within reach." Ms. Bingle looked at me like I was severely IQ-challenged. She wasn't far from the truth.

When I glanced at Romeo, he looked at me with wide eyes and a blank expression, clearly trying not to laugh.

"Why did you hit him with it?"

"Because he already had a stick up his butt."

Romeo snorted, and she whirled on him. "You think this is funny?"

"No, no. Of course not." He straightened and tried to wipe the grin off his face, with little success.

"All of you think this is funny." Buffy/Betty wilted. "Men. Why're they always doing their thinking with the wrong head?"

"Mother?" I turned to Mona. "I believe it's your turn."

As I knew she would, Mother stepped up and put an arm around Buffy, leading her to the side. This was in her wheelhouse—I'd lost count of all the young women my mother, the Madam, had saved from a life in the sex trade. I know, she's a walking contradiction. It's one of her charms.

"Okay, let's go tackle the others." I stepped aside for the young detective to move by me. "Lead on, McDuff."

Smokin' Joe himself stood guard in front of Booth Three. A tall, thin Native American man, with dark hair, sad, soulful brown eyes, and tats covering every square inch of skin visible below his rolled-up sleeves—he even had m-o-m tattooed on the three middle fingers of his left hand, one letter on each finger—Smokin' Joe reminded me of an addict either just out or on his way back in. He had trust issues and didn't play well with others, but he'd taken a shine to me, which worried me a little. "Man, Lucky, what're you bringing your low-rent clients here for?" He grinned a half-toothless grin, which shocked me. Normally a dour personality, he'd never smiled in my presence before.

"Thought I'd give them a taste of hangin' with the highbrows."

"They could do worse." He stepped aside and opened the booth door for me.

Walker sat in a low, cushioned chair with Vera on his lap, holding an ice pack to his right eye. A movie played on the screen, but I made a point of not looking at it, although the two of them seemed engrossed.

"Well, you two are certainly taking this whole 'what happens in Vegas, stays in Vegas' thing to heart, aren't you?"

At the sound of my voice, Vera pushed herself off of Walker's lap, then reached a hand to help him out of the deep chair. Neither looked embarrassed, nor did they offer any explanation. Walker kept the ice pressed to his face. Blood, dried to a brownish hue, crusted the left side of his face. A stain—looking like a darkening red tie—marred the front of his beautifully tailored white shirt with his initials in blue on his right cuff.

"Looks like you two put more than your heads together."

That cracked Walker's reserve. "What?" He lowered the ice pack, revealing the start of a nice shiner plus a long red gash across his temple that disappeared into his hairline.

"That's what you told me you were going to do, the last time I saw you." I moved in to get a closer look at him, squinting my eyes in the darkness. "Shouldn't you get that sewn up or something?"

"It'll be fine," he growled.

"I wouldn't want to explain it either." I stood and looked him straight in the eye.

"A bit messy, I admit." To his credit, a little bit of color rose in his cheeks.

"A wee bit," I agreed.

Vera stepped into the abyss. "We've always enjoyed each other's company—we do have so much in common, a shared value system. We'd just been denying the obvious."

"Interesting attestation in a sex toy store, but hey, common ground is a wonderful thing."

Vera eased closer to Walker and clutched his arm.

"Your timing sucks, but I'm happy for you, truly I am." I fought with myself—I really wanted to shoot them and put them out of my misery. But idiots were probably out of season, and justifiable homicide was so tricky to prove. "I hate to throw a blanket on the fire, but we have the little issue of a televised contest tonight...with your respective betrotheds. Remember?"

Reality dumped on their heads like a bucket of ice water.

"What exactly do you propose we do about that?" Walker asked.

"Well." I looked at Vera. "I've saved your stones once today already." I expanded my gaze to encompass both of them. "I'd say I've done my job. How you two play it from here is up to you."

As DARKNESS SETTLED OVER THE VALLEY AND THE LIGHTS OF VEGAS worked their magic, I actually felt fairly happy with how the day had turned out—I hadn't killed anybody, and all the couples had been delivered to Trey Gold for pre–prime time primping. We'd patched up Walker as best we could; the make-up artist would have to do the rest.

As luck would have it, the final show was to be broadcast live from Siegfried & Roy's Secret Garden, behind the Mirage. Yes, the moveable feast had decamped; the Babylon's responsibilities were officially over.

Ella found me standing in the lobby. I must've looked a bit the worse-for-wear as she said, without preamble, "Those *contests* folks are *nutcases*."

"Is that a technical term?"

"A professional diagnosis, dumbed-down for you lay people." Once again, she used her inside voice—the second time in as many days. She must be coming down with something. "The whole thing has left a bad taste in my mouth."

"Dysfunction on display."

Ella gave me a slight smile. "Welcome to my world."

"You and I occupy different sides of the same street. On my side, we just pretend everything is fine."

"You can't hide there forever, Lucky."

"Watch me." I spied Teddie as he rounded the corner and waved.

"Hope it doesn't bite you on the butt."

Teddie grabbed me, pulling me close. "If anyone's biting you on the butt, it's going to be me," he murmured, before he covered my lips with his.

The man took my breath away. When he righted me, my thoughts had tumbled. I knew there was a witty response in there somewhere, but I'd be damned if I could find it.

"How're you getting to the Mirage?" he asked. "As one of the judges, I have to get going. Want to head over with me, ladies?"

Ella grabbed one arm; I grabbed the other. "Safety in numbers," I said. "It's a beautiful evening. Feel like a stroll?"

The Mirage wasn't far, but we enjoyed the intervening stretch of the Strip—perhaps me more than the other two. Wandering with the revelers recharged my personal stores of magic. Ten minutes of walking with them, and I'd learned to say "give me a kiss" in several languages, where to buy the strongest drink for the best price, and how to get to the second floor of Margaritaville before it opened in order to watch the fountains at the Bellagio. Several young men decided I ought to join them later, which I found charming. Teddie disagreed, and I enjoyed that, too.

Lured outside by the air that held a hint of fall—as refreshing as a cold beer on a hot day—other couples...or trios...hiked up the driveway with us to the entrance of the Mirage. We ambled, matching our pace to the flow of humanity. As we rounded the volcano in front, we slowed further, waiting for it to belch fire. At the first rumble, we stopped at the railing to watch. Fire and steam belched and flowed. The crowd *ohhhed* and *ahhhed*—me included. I loved the magic, all that was Vegas. The faces of the people reflected all that I felt. Even if only for a weekend, Las Vegas could lighten the burden of reality. It was a special kind of magic.

Steve Wynn and his building of the Mirage had started the mega-resort boom on the Las Vegas Strip. Still the visionary, Mr. Wynn remained the single most influential man in the city. He shaped the town, built its skyline, and gave us all Siegfried & Roy by luring them into the spotlight. They rose to the occasion and became icons revered the world over. Although they no longer performed, Siegfried & Roy still drew the crowds to see their Secret Garden and its population of wonderful white cats.

Like the city itself, the Secret Garden was best at night. The canopy of trees hung ripe with twinkling lights, obscuring the high netting designed to provide separation between felines and their prey. The cats lazed and played, in expansive holds lush with grass and waterfalls cascading into refreshing pools. A huge white Siberian tiger padded to the edge of one pool, then lay half-submerged. If he could've smiled, I'm sure he would've—or at least groaned with pleasure. In another enclosure, two huge, magnificently maned white lions sat like statues, watching us but pretending not to care. While men trolling the Strip could make a woman feel like a piece of meat, the lions made me feel like dinner. I wasn't sure which was more unnerving.

A magical place. The Secret Garden hid a secret of its own.

We pushed through the crowd already gathering for the taping, looking for a set of guarded gates. Taking the lead, I pulled Teddie by the hand. Ella clung to his trailing arm. As we arrived at the gates, the guard nodded and opened them wide enough for us to squeeze through into another world.

Animal lovers from childhood, Siegfried and Roy—especially Roy—were forced through circumstance to give up their show, but they never abandoned their animals. In a huge aluminum building behind the Secret Garden, the famous magicians nurtured a menagerie of snowy felines and other beloved creatures—a conservation effort designed to perpetuate the breeds and eventually to reintroduce them to the wild. Tonight, the animals stalked the length of their cages, nervous at the increase in human activity.

At the call from a group of friends huddled by a white lion's cage, Ella veered off, leaving Teddie and me alone in the crowd. I pulled him along the wide path through the center of the building. Cages lined each side. The cages were clean, the animals luminescent. And the place smelled like...hamburgers.

"I've got to go meet the other judges," Teddie whispered in my ear. "Some sort of logistics thing. I'll meet you back here when they start choosing the animals. Okay?"

"Choosing the animals?"

"The final test." Over my shoulder, he eyed the crowd behind me. "Each couple has to choose the animal they think most represents the traits of their partner."

"Good thing there's no reptiles in here," I muttered.

That brought his focus back. "What?" His baby blues focused on mine.

"Never mind." Secrets were meant to be kept. "You were saying?"

"They each choose the animal—it's done in secret, like a blind ballot. Then they reveal their choices on live tv."

"Interesting."

"Fairly benign, I should think."

He hadn't a clue.

Bending to give me a distracted kiss, he segued into his in-front-of-the-crowd mode. "I gotta go. But I'll be back. Don't wander off with any strange men."

"All men are strange."

I watched him as he walked away. He had a nice ass. It was perhaps his best feature. Although, all his features were pretty yummy—from his dancing eyes and full lips, to his broad shoulders that squeezed into taut abs and a teenage waist. I flushed at the assault of a memory—that whole visual thing could so get me into trouble. The crowd finally swallowed him, saving me from doing something spontaneous and potentially embarrassing.

"There you are." Mona's voice carried over the crowd and jerked me back from my musings. She and my father wormed their way toward me. I loved seeing them together. Whatever strident notes they hit separately, as a couple they melded into a pitch-perfect melody, a symphony of synchronicity.

Mother wore slacks in a browned butter shade with a matching cashmere sweater set, rich with a hint of gold. The gold flats still sparkled on her feet. She wore her hair in soft curls that brushed her shoulders. Her face, barely highlighted with makeup, shone with love as she clutched her man's arm. Tall and thin, she ducked her head toward her man to minimize the difference in their heights. Clearly, he had no issues with being the shortest in the family. Besides, he was larger than life; everyone said so.

Spit-and-polished as usual, my father sported a gunmetal grey suit, a starched white shirt with a diamond-encrusted collar bar, a bright pink tie—which made me grin, no doubt it was my mother's influence—and a huge smile. "My two women. I am a lucky man."

"So have you picked your animals?" I asked when they stopped in front of me. "I think we all should play, don't you?" At their puzzled expressions, I quickly explained the game.

Mother's face immediately lit. "Oh, that would be so fun. Come, Albert, let's pick."

He shot me an amused look, then let her pull him toward the row of cages. With my responsibilities completed, I found myself in the unusual position of having nothing to do and no one to do it with, so I followed along. It felt good just to be part of the crowd and not in charge of anything.

Mother stopped in front of a small sign. "Look, Albert. It says a bull symbolizes masculine strength and vitality." She clutched his arm and giggled as she whispered in his ear. He ducked his head and grinned.

"Look, Mother." I pointed to the sign, drawing her attention. "This one says a badger denotes a person with a nagging personality—usually someone who interferes in someone else's life. I'm thinking..."

"I know what you're thinking," Mona snapped as she stuck her nose in the air. "And you're lucky to have me."

"True." I gave her a quick squeeze. "But admitting that is not part of the game."

With one hand, Mona flipped her hair and gave me a wicked grin as she pulled her reading glasses from the top of her head and put them on. "Now it's my turn."

Silence fell between the three of us as we meandered, reading the signs describing the symbolism of various animals. The big cats padded silently as they watched us—whether they were looking *for* morsels or looking *at* morsels was anybody's guess.

"Here it is," Mona announced, triumph in her voice. "If there is an animal reflective of all that is my daughter, this one is it."

I bent down and looked. "An owl." Hands on hips, I turned to my mother. "You think I'm an owl?"

"Read it," she urged, as she pulled off her glasses and chewed on the end of one of the earpieces, a superior look on her face.

I read aloud: "A symbol of knowledge and heightened observational skills. It can also mean to use more judgment in a life situation." When I finished, I looked at my mother with a raised eyebrow.

She shot me a look of pure innocence, which for her was an Oscar-worthy effort. "Romance is a 'life situation.'"

"I get it. I know you're proud of yourself, but an owl is also an evil omen, a harbinger of misfortune," I added.

Mona slapped her glasses back on and bent to read. "Where does it say that?"

"It doesn't," I admitted. "It's part of Chinese animal symbolism. When you deal with Asian clients you become sensitized to that sort of thing."

"Well, I'll handle that the same way I handle organized religion."

My father glanced at me and gave me a shrug. Mother's logic always traveled a circuitous path.

"From animal symbolism to organized religion—not too far a leap. I know I shouldn't ask," I said, completely unable to prevent myself from charging in where most angels would fear to tread. "But how exactly do you handle religion?"

"I pick the parts I like and ignore the rest."

"Interesting approach."

"Spirituality connects us as humans." Mona's smile morphed into a serious expression. Her voice was hushed, yet vibrating with conviction. "Religion, on the other hand, is a power struggle. In the wrong hands it tears us apart. I don't think the powers that be would like that."

The little pearls of wisdom Mother was trotting out surprised the heck out of me. I don't know why. She'd preached from the her Gospel of Simplicity so often throughout my life I could probably quote it from memory. "As you know, Mother, I'm a Golden Rule gal, myself. Everybody else can fill in as they see fit."

"A good place to start, honey," Mona said, taking my hand and threading it through the crook of her arm. "As you get older, you begin to see more of the connections."

"I can wait. I'm having enough trouble with the connections I already have."

She gave me a knowing smile.

Never enjoying third-wheel status, I gave my parents a group hug then ambled off by myself. I spied three of the couples— acting couple-like—as they strolled the hall. The kids from New Jersey were awol as far as I could tell. Each of the other contestants scribbled notes on individual pads of paper as they read the animal symbol signs, careful to keep their choices hidden.

After walking the full length of the building then retracing my steps, I knew one thing: Couple Number One was definitely late to the party. Not really my problem, but I never met a problem I could resist trying to solve, mine or not.

Following my nose back outside and through the gates into the Secret Garden, I chased the scent of hamburgers through the gathering throng to a small, open-sided building near the exit—I'd missed it on the way in. Stepping inside, I had to grin. Jean-Charles in his chef's whites and toque flipped burgers on a huge grill, mirrored by two similarly attired, equally focused chefs-in-waiting, spatulas at the ready: Couple Number One. They didn't play by the rules, but at least they were consistent.

"I'd like a Whopper Junior, hold the mayo."

All three glanced up and smiled. Jean-Charles whispered something to his charges and stepped back, relinquishing his spatula. "Lucky!" He reached out a hand as he rounded the counter between us. "Come. I have something for you."

I let him take my hand, I don't know why, and I felt that tingle again, a lightness in his presence. Why did I need enemies when I had me as a friend? But flirting, it's a good thing, right? The French certainly have elevated it to an art. And what's wrong with it—as long as everyone knows the rules. Jean-Charles knew the rules, didn't he?

We stopped under the twinkling lights. He lifted my hand, turning it palm up. With a smile, he reached into his pocket, pulled out a coin, and set it in my open hand.

"What's this for?" The coin had an animal on one side. A horse, I thought, as I looked at it more closely.

"It is an old French coin," Jean-Charles said, suddenly looking a bit ill at ease. "I know we are not playing the game, but when I thought of you, this is what I thought."

"A horse?"

"Ahhh, a very special horse."

"French, of course."

"*Oui*. This breed, my parents raised on their farm." He looked at me, his eyes dark and deep. "It is a spirited animal, but sensitive and beautiful...like you. The perfect blend of..." He suddenly blushed.

Words and thoughts tangled with emotions. "I don't know what to say."

He closed my hand over the coin, holding my hand with both of his. "Keep it. Perhaps it will remind you of me."

"I can't."

When he smiled, I knew he understood. "It is my gift. It is bad manners to reject a gift."

I was about to disagree when the lights dimmed three times— the signal to gather at the Dolphin Pool. The taping was about to begin.

"It's a beautiful gift. Thank you."

He nodded. "Now, you must go. The show is to begin. And we must cook—there will be many mouths to feed when the show is over."

"You will send Rocco and Gail?"

"They were voted off the show last night. Did you not know?"

"I've been chasing my tail all day." At the look of confusion on his face, I explained. "Busy doesn't begin to describe my day. I haven't kept up."

Understanding dawned, turning his eyes a lighter blue. "They are in love. They will be happy. They will cook together. It's as it should be. Life has a rhythm."

"Life, nothing but a timing issue," I concurred. And mine seemed to be a bit out of synch.

"Timing issue? What is this?"

"Don't mind me." I finally found the energy to pull my hand from his. "Gifts make me uncomfortable. Not the giving, but the receiving." I opened my hand and looked at the coin. "And thank you. You've brightened my day."

"Then mine is complete as well." He gave me a smile and a slight bow, then hastened back to his grill, barking orders at his two acolytes.

CHAPTER SIX

*T*HE FINAL test in the *Forever Game* was an invitation-only kind of thing. The hand-selected audience circled the largest of the dolphin pools—not technically a part of the Secret Garden, but adjoining. Gray torpedoes circled under water, breaking the surface occasionally, or leaping onto an angled concrete slab and sliding in circles before slipping into the water again. So playful. Dolphins were always good for a smile. Tonight, two of the aquatic mammals were shadowed by little ones—the results of the breeding program. Handlers in wet suits stalked the side of the pool. The dolphins circled, awaiting a signal. When they got it from their human, they performed the requested tricks —jumping through hoops, tossing balls, leaping then falling broadsided into the water, splashing the crowd.

From his chair in the front row, Teddie waved to me, motioning me to join him. Fighting through the crowd, I finally eased into the seat next to him just as Trey Gold took the stage. He blew into the mike in his hand. "Testing. Testing, one, two, three." He looked toward the mixing console behind the crowd. "Good?" he asked.

A guy gave him a thumbs-up. Trey turned to the crowd. "Okay. Are you guys ready to crown a winner?"

The crowd hooted and hollered.

His orange color had grown on me, as had the dark, immovable hair—overdone for an overblown personality. Hollywood expectations. While Trey stalked the stage—working the crowd, distracting them—the contestants filed on, each taking a stool next to their supposed future mate.

Teddie leaned in next to me. "If you were an animal, you'd be an ox."

I leaned back and turned to look at him. "A *farm animal?*"

"Would you stop? It's a good thing, I swear." He adopted that listen-to-me-I-went-to-Harvard look. "An ox symbolizes a hard worker, someone who pulls more than her own weight."

"I'm underwhelmed," I murmured, but he'd stopped listening. Part of the Curse of the Y Chromosome was an unerring ability to retreat from the conflict they'd created.

An ox. No matter how I spun it, I didn't like it. I tried to muster a smile as I fingered the French coin, the one with the majestic horse, tossing its head in defiance, its mane flowing, its nostrils flaring. Passion. Adventure. I could live with that. But work? Please, I'd rather not.

Once comfortable in a relationship, why did a man go from the "we" mode back to the "me" mode? Romance—yet another casualty to time and complacency.

"Okay, contestants," Trey Gold emoted into the mike. "We're going to start taping. You know how it goes. We'll start, and then at set times, I'll cut for a commercial. After that, we'll pick up again. You guys just be yourselves and have some fun." In front of the cameras, he preened like a peacock, his plumage on display. If the situation at Miss Minnie's had ruffled any of his feathers, he hid it well.

People cheered and clapped—a few whistles pierced the night air, which was cooling rather rapidly, making me glad for my

sweater. Then the audience quieted as Trey went into his intro-
ductory spiel. Scanning, I only half listened. To be honest, I would
have rather been eating a juicy hamburger than sitting here
watching this circus.

Trey had buried Vera and Guy's "arrangement," but exactly
how the whole thing was going to pan out was anybody's guess.
John and Melina had a warm congeniality, the shared spark of
common interests and goals—a sort of love-the-mind-can't-
love-the-person kind of thing. No vibrancy. And Walker and
Buffy? No comment needed. Sexual and superficial—buying the
perfect accessory. None of them had that spark of true love I
was looking for. The spark I saw between my parents. The one
that lit the Beautiful Jeremy Whitlock's eyes when he looked at
Miss P. And, as Nora Ephron said, marriage is hard enough
without such low expectations. The whole show was demor-
alizing.

Ella materialized at my side and squeezed in next to me. "This
whole thing is a farce."

"Perfectly staged for the consumption of the masses."

"You know, *lucky*, you're becoming a bit of a *cynic*."

"Weren't you the one who called this a farce?" I watched the
contestants as they fidgeted on their stools. They looked...falsely
animated, except for Walker, who simply glowered.

"I was hoping you would disagree." Ella once again trotted out
a serious observation in her inside voice—I was beginning to see a
pattern. "If you ask me, they are all..."

"Looking for love in all the wrong places?"

"Ah, there you are. I knew I could count on you." She squeezed
my hand with her tiny one. "You're a hummingbird."

"What?" I stifled a laugh. "A hummingbird is the smallest bird
on the planet. I'm an amazon."

"Perhaps, but if you have hummingbird magic, then you have a
talent for finding the good in people. And you never look back
wishing for what was. Instead, you make the most of what is,

spreading joy." She gave me a kind smile, one I'd never seen on her before. "If that describes anyone, it's you."

"I don't know what to say." I truly was blindsided. I never knew Ella to be particularly insightful, although she was a trained therapist.

"It comes with a warning, though." Her expression turned serious. "You have an abundance of energy and a spirit that cannot be confined—you must fly free."

"Is that figurative or literal?"

"Perhaps both."

With nothing more to say, we turned our attention back to the stage. This was the weirdest day—nothing was as I thought it was, or as it appeared to be. Unexpected people lifted my spirits. And the ones I normally counted on...not so much.

Trey again addressed the audience. "Remember, we are down to three couples. Melina and John are in the lead, Walker and Buffy and Vera and Guy are trailing, separated by only a point. Guy and Vera, as the couple in third place, will lead off tonight."

"Guy, you go first. If Vera were an animal, which would she be?" Trey Gold stuck the mike to Guy's face.

"A peahen. You know, the girl peacock." He looked smug—still like Malibu Ken in his Hawaiian shirt and khakis, with his tan and his hair gelled to spikes—but smug nonetheless. "She's not much to look at. Know what I mean?" He gave an exaggerated wink to the crowd. "She can't hold a candle to the guy."

The crowd went nuts as Vera leaned back, eyeing Guy with cool disdain. Tonight Vera had ditched the Brooks Brothers attire in favor of a soft, feminine skirt and a light pink silk top. With her hair falling loose and free she looked almost pretty—except for the pinched look on her face and the venom in her eyes. "Perhaps her plumage isn't as fine, but a peahen sticks by her mate. Pretty on the inside instead of the outside. That's more than I can say for you," Vera said.

The crowd hooted and jeered, egging them on.

"Those two have lost their magic," Teddie whispered.

"You have no idea." Despite his questioning look, I refused to give him more.

"Okay, Vera, your turn." Before Vera launched in, Trey turned to the crowd. "This is going to be good. Nothing like a woman scorned." Then he turned back to Vera. "Okay, if Guy was an animal..."

"What makes you think he's not?" Vera's coy manner seemed out of character, but the crowd bought it, cheering at her innuendo.

Trey laughed along. "Good one. So, what'll it be?"

"Well." Vera milked it, working the crowd. "At first I thought maybe a unicorn."

"What?" Guy hissed, his face flushing red. "You're telling them I haven't got a..."

Vera turned to him and asked sweetly, "A what?"

"You know." Guy lowered his voice further. "A...thing."

"I said unicorn, Guy," Vera said, patting him on the knee, "not eunuch."

The crowd erupted. Gales of laughter washed over the stage. Guy looked like a man ready to hit someone, but he didn't know what for. Trey let them laugh. Conflict was good for the show—or so I'd been told.

"I don't know what she sees in him," Teddie whispered. "Do you?"

"A pretty package?"

"Yeah, but you still gotta talk in the morning."

"Perhaps talking is overrated?" I teased, just to see what he'd say.

Before Teddie could respond, Trey once again established order. "Vera, be serious. A Las Vegas wedding extravaganza is on the line here."

Vera heaved an exaggerated sigh. "If you insist. I would say that Guy is a lion."

That made Guy sit up a bit straighter, pulling his shoulders back. He even sucked in his stomach and flexed his biceps a bit, but maybe I imagined that part.

"Yes, a lion," Vera continued. "The male of the pride who sits around admiring himself while the females do all the work."

Again, gales of laughter. Guy sulked as the truth finally hit home. He was going to be the butt of the joke on national tv and there was nothing he could do about it. Of course, the tv audience voted and they might think Vera was being a bitch, but I don't think she gave a rat's ass.

I crossed my arms and settled in for the show. Not that I liked bitchiness—I always thought there was a nicer way to get your point across—but I did appreciate a woman who stood up for herself.

Trey turned to the camera. "Audience, it's time to vote." He rattled off the number to call. Apparently the couples were supposed to be rated on a compatibility index of one to ten, with one being the least compatible. And, curiously enough, there was some flexibility built in to the show. If someone didn't like any of the couples, they could vote accordingly, and explain why in a comment box. "Remember, you have the rest of the show to call in. All votes will be tabulated at the end."

Walker and Buffy were next.

"Buffy, your turn."

"A jaguar," she said, in her high, squeaky voice. She still channeled Betty Boop, but tonight the dress was black. Although the purse was the same—a fashion faux pas of epic proportion. I'd shoot myself before I appeared on national television carrying a stuffed animal.

Walker didn't react—he sat stoic in his buttoned-up silence. The makeup artist was truly that, an artist. She must've used Spackle or applied foundation with a trowel—Walker's wounds were invisible.

"Jaguars are known for their sneak attacks," Buffy recited, as if she'd memorized her part in a play...or a farce, as Ella had observed. "A jaguar's prey never sees it coming."

The crowd *awwwwed*. Apparently they interpreted this as something cute—like love bites you when you least expect it. I knew better, but I wasn't giving it up.

"Walker?" Trey asked.

"Buffy would be a white rabbit."

Buffy bounced up and down on her stool as she clapped her hands. "How sweet. A cuddly rabbit."

"Who can't hide in the wild due to its color, so it needs protection." Walker delivered his lines stiffly and without emotion. He came across harsh, but Buffy pretended not to mind as she threw her arms around his neck and gave him an exaggerated kiss.

"That was weird," Teddie said. The crowd clearly agreed, as their response was ambivalent and muted. "There's something going on there, but it's hard to read."

"If you can't have his heart, take his wallet."

"Harsh."

"Money, a substitute for love."

"You believe that?" Teddie sounded surprised.

"We're not talking about me...or you." I shot him a look. "But, the term *gold digger* must've come from somewhere."

"True." Teddie shook his head and grimaced. "The two of them together makes me feel like nothing is right in the world."

"Happiness can't be bought."

"Right."

At least we agreed on something.

Trey waved his arms with a flourish. "Now, last but not least, our leaders, Melina and John."

The crowd applauded politely—no wolf whistles, no shouts, no emotion. Somehow that seemed to fit.

"John, what animal would Melina be?" Trey asked, still energetic, but almost falsely so, as if he was trying to inject his own energy into the game. Not a bad idea—John and Melina's cool reserve acted like a wet blanket on the fire of the crowd's enthusiasm.

"A snow leopard."

"Ah, now we're getting somewhere." Trey brightened. "Tell us why."

"The snow leopard is regal, reclusive, almost mythic in its desirability, but very difficult to find." John had no inflection in his voice. No real emotion in his eyes when he reached for her hand. A pragmatic choice. A life box checked.

I looked at the crowd around me. Underwhelmed, and so not fooled.

"Almost mythic in its desirability?" Trey repeated, looking for a foothold. "A beautiful sentiment."

"Melina?"

"That's very sweet." She smiled. She seemed pleased...reserved, but happy enough. In her red dress and kick-ass stilettos, with her hair perfectly coiffed and her makeup subtly applied, she personified perfection in a Grace Kelly kind of way. Removed, and somehow above it all. "John, I picked a cheetah for you. Regal, graceful, fast, almost unattainable." A frown skittered across her face then was gone, leaving her brows slightly furrowed.

"This is like voting for president," I whispered in Teddie's ear. "May the least awful win."

Trey Gold cut to his going-to-commercial patter, thanking everybody and telling everyone to vote. During the break he talked to the couples, joking, trying to loosen them up. As a pro, he knew the energy was lacking, and the show would lay an egg if something didn't happen.

"Who're you voting for?" I asked Teddie, my celebrity judge.

"I don't want to vote for any of them."

"The rules state you should pick the best couple. So, pick the best couple." He looked at me like I'd started drinking early. Which, all things considered, wouldn't have been a bad idea.

"I don't understand you."

I just smiled—that statement opened a whole can of worms. Ox, my ass.

~

THE CROWD MILLED AROUND WHILE THE VOTES WERE TABULATED. Open bars dotted the circumference of the dolphin enclosure, and most people took advantage, grabbing the libation of their choice. In short order, the mood elevated, fueled by a steady supply of eighty proof. People chatted animatedly as they made their way back to their seats.

Teddie and I once again settled in. Ella had disappeared, which didn't bother me. I scanned the crowd for my parents, spying them in the back, next to one of the bars. Behind the hedges near the exit, smoke rose in a plume—hamburgers sizzling on the grill, nearing perfection. I could picture Jean-Charles, spatula in hand as he worked in concert with Rocco and Gail, smiles of contentment competing with frowns of concentration. Off to the side, Miss P nuzzled Jeremy, who held her close with an arm around her shoulders.

Trey Gold bounded back on stage and the crowd quieted. The stools had been removed and the three couples stood in a semicircle behind Trey. With various expressions on each of their faces, the one universal emotion evident seemed to be relief.

Drums rolled, commanding everyone's attention.

My heart beat faster, I had no idea why. Perhaps it was the terror of knowing there would be losers once a winner was chosen. Nobody should be branded a loser, unless they deserved it, of course. And none of these people did. Oh, they'd made interesting choices, for curious reasons. But hadn't we all?

Trey waited for the crowd's absolute attention, then milked it a few beats more, ratcheting up the suspense. Finally, he presented the envelope and worked a finger under the flap. He pulled out the card and scanned it. A stunned look. I know I saw it, but it was quickly concealed as his professional mask fell back into place.

"Now this is interesting, folks. Very interesting. Not quite what any of us was expecting." He looked at the crowd, then focused on the camera. "And the winners are…"

The crowd didn't move. I didn't think anyone even breathed. The soft calls of the animals in the Secret Garden and the muted rumble of traffic from the 15 were the only sounds—besides the pounding of my heart in my ears, but I didn't think anyone else could hear that.

Trey licked his lips and smiled as he gave a slight shrug. "The winners are Vera and…"

Guy Handy clutched his chest. I'm sure visions of a polygamy reality show danced in his head. Some in the crowd cheered. Some laughed. Some tossed out a *boo* or two.

Trey held up his hand. "Wait."

The crowd quieted.

"The winners are Vera and…Walker."

A moment of stunned silence, then the crowd erupted. I couldn't help myself as I laughed along with them. Surprise hit Vera and Walker as they looked at each other with disbelieving smiles. Then Vera leapt into Walker's arms, her legs wrapping around his waist, her arms circling his neck. Their kiss lasted a very long time…much to the delight of the crowd.

Teddie whirled to me. "Vera and Walker? How'd that happen?"

I studied the man I called the love of my life, then let my gaze drift to the gentle wafts of smoke curling upward into the dazzling lights of Vegas. Life could take the most surprising twists. Who knew where mine would lead?

"Teddie, my love. Don't you know by now that love always finds a way?"

THE END

Thank you so much for going on a Lucky adventure with me. I hope you enjoyed the ride.

As you may know, reviews are SUPER helpful. They not only help potential readers make a choice, but they also help me win coveted spots on various advertising platforms.

So, if you would please, do me the favor of leaving a review at the outlet of your choice.

LUCKY BANG

A LUCKY VEGAS NOVELLA

NATIONAL BESTSELLING AUTHOR

DEBORAH COONTS

CHAPTER ONE

$\mathcal{T}$HE BOMB was small, crude...homemade but lethal. And familiar. The last time I had seen a device like this one had been a lifetime ago. Frankly, I thought I'd never see one again. And I certainly hadn't expected to find another ticking time bomb in the ladies' bathroom at Jimmy G's new family restaurant. Had I not spilled the entire contents of my purse while doing my business in the far stall, I never would've found it. But there I was, on all fours, chasing a runaway lipstick when I came nose-to-nose with a couple of sticks of old dynamite taped together and wired to a battery. An old wind-up clock ticked off the seconds.

Three minutes.

And, with the Fourth of July celebrations this weekend, the city was bursting at the seams—Jimmy G had a full house.

I glanced at my watch, marking the time.

Forgetting the rest of my wayward personal items, I backed out of the tight space, grabbed my purse—no one leaves a Hermes Birkin anywhere, bomb or no bomb—and hurried out of the bathroom.

Jimmy G was at his normal table in the bar by the piano,

nursing his ubiquitous glass of Pinot Noir, and bending the ear of some enraptured, sweet young thing. He paused to wet his whistle when I stepped in next to him and bent down to whisper in his ear.

"Jimmy, there's a bomb in the ladies' bathroom." His eyes widened, but that was the only reaction I could see.

"Can you take care of it?" He spoke out of the corner of his mouth.

"What do I look like? I don't know jack about bombs. For all I know, it could be rigged to blow when touched—like the last one." I checked the time. "We got two and a half minutes."

Lacking his normal grin, Jimmy stood to his full height of a wiry five feet five inches, his face grim, his manner all-business as he motioned to the waiters. They understood the silent order and began going from table to table encouraging the patrons to leave quickly.

Jimmy tinged on his glass with a spoon. "Everyone, listen up. I apologize, and there is no time to explain, but please, we need you to exit the building and move away, across the parking lot out front. As far away as you can get. Quickly, we don't have much time."

A silence fell over the crowd for a moment, patrons casting shocked glances around the room. The soothing voice of Dean Martin singing an oldie but goodie and the dinging bells of the games in the kids' room filled the empty air. A moment suspended in time, captured by confusion, disbelief. Then the sound of chairs scraping back. Voices elevated now, hints of panic, but the crowd remained calm as they gathered the kids and moved to the exits.

Two minutes.

I posted myself at the back of the main dining room and began ushering everyone toward safety. As a customer relations expert at the Babylon—Vegas Strip's most over-the-top casino/resort—I have some experience with clearing rooms and herding crowds.

One lady stopped to gather her purse and a backpack, presumably a child's—the purple dinosaur was a dead giveaway.

I put a hand on her back. "Leave it." I kept my voice low, calm but firm. For a moment I thought she would argue. Instead she turned and hurried toward the door, rounding up children as she went.

I heard faint sirens growing louder.

A minute forty-five. They wouldn't be in time.

Sweat trickled down my sides as I forced myself to stay calm, to think clearly. A glance around the room confirmed that folks were doing as asked. Except for one man at a table on the far side. Resolutely forking in spaghetti, he remained seated.

Dodging the detritus of haste, overturned chairs, abandoned coats and bags, I hurried to his side. "Sir, you need to leave. Now."

His fork poised between plate and mouth, he glanced up at me with a smile. "This sauce Bolognese." He put two fingers to his lips and made that Italian kissing thing that is supposed to convey supreme satisfaction, but just comes off looking silly to us non-Italians. *"Perfecto."*

One minute.

"Sir," I grabbed the back of his chair. "You need to leave."

He waved a hand as if shooing away a pesky gnat, then dove in for another bite. "These fire drills, they never mean anything—all smoke and no fire," he announced even though his mouth was full.

"This one is the real shebang." I tugged on his chair. Even with my considerable weight behind it, the thing wouldn't budge, so I grabbed his arm with both hands and pulled. "Come with me." My voice carried the sharp prod of an order.

"But my Bolognese," he whined as he reached for his napkin and started to stand.

Now I had some leverage. Feeling time breathing down my neck, I pulled him up. With a shove, I pushed him toward the door. "I'll buy you a new plateful when this is over." *If there's a restaurant left.*

A glance over my shoulder and confirmed that we were the last two out.

With forty seconds to spare.

We rushed across the parking lot to join the crowd on the opposite side as the sirens grew louder. Through the rows of spindly trees in the parking lot, I saw the flashing lights of the first fire truck.

Thirty seconds.

Too late.

"Oh my God!" A voice filled with panic. "Where's my daughter!"

I whirled to face the throng. "Who said that?"

"My daughter!" a woman wailed as she separated herself from the crowd and pointed toward the restaurant. "She's still inside. I have four children. Two of them brought friends. I had them all. And now she's not here." She clutched three children around her while two others huddled close.

I dropped to one knee so I was eye-to-eye with a tow-headed little boy, his eyes wide with fear, his lips trembling. "Do you know where she is?"

"It's my fault." His chin trembled as he fought tears. "We were playing Whack-a-mole. She lost her bear. I was supposed to watch her. She wouldn't leave without the bear."

"Her name?" Pushing myself to my feet, I turned and ran, shrugging out of Jimmy G's grasp as he reached to stop me.

"Elise," her mother called after me. "Her name is Elise."

I ducked back inside the now empty restaurant. In three strides I was at the entrance to the game room. My eyes searched the room, probing every corner. I missed her the first time. The small girl, a riot of long sandy curls, a pressed pinafore, her eyes big and round, hunkered under a Skee-ball machine, a small brown teddy bear with one eye clutched to her chest with both arms.

"Elise, come on, honey." I reached down, grabbing both her

arms and lifting her to my hip. "I'll take you to your mother, but we have to hurry."

Turning, I ran.

Ten seconds, I guessed. Nine. Less. I didn't take the time to look.

Two strides from the door.

One.

A huge sound behind me. Instinctively I ducked. The compression wave hit me. Staggering, I dropped to my knees, then to my side. Sheltering the girl's small body with mine, I curled around her, then covered my head.

Sound and fury. A maelstrom of debris. Shrapnel whizzing through the air. Heat. Stinging pain.

Then darkness.

A HAND ON MY SHOULDER. MOVEMENT. MY EYES FLUTTERED OPEN.

For a moment, I couldn't remember. Where was I? Flashes of memory zinged across my synapses. Jimmy G's. A bomb. A little girl. A jolt of adrenaline. Yes, a little girl. My eyes flew open, as I took a deep gulp of air.

Detective Romeo knelt in front of me, worry etching years into his boyish features. His mouth formed words, but I couldn't hear him. In fact, I heard only an intense, piercing screech. Shaking my head, I pushed at him, forcing myself to a seated position. Stars spun in my vision. I didn't care. I cast around frantically, searching. Finally I saw her, my small young friend. Wrapped in a blanket, still holding her bear, she curled into the crook of a fireman's arms.

Safe. Her mother followed close behind, herding the other children.

Breathing easier, I swiped at my forehead. My hand came away wet. I felt my face scrunch into a frown as I stared at the red smear on my palm. Sounds, disjointed and far away, filtered past the shrill buzz in my head. The rush of pressurized spray from the fire hoses. Dripping water. Boots clomping. Hot embers sizzling. Snippets of reality, random pings on my real-world radar.

Someone shaking me. Gentle pressure. "Lucky?" The word, muffled yet distinct, focused a few brain cells.

For the first time, I looked around and took stock of my surroundings. Still on the floor, I was just inside the doorway to the restaurant. The picture windows across the front were gone. A few jagged shards, still clutched in the frame, hung like lethal icicles, but the rest of the plate glass was missing. Smoke hung in the air, a dark roiling cloud clinging to the ceiling, then drifting through the windows to be carried away on the breeze. Acrid and heavy, the air stung my eyes and seared my lungs. In full fire-fighting garb, firemen snaked their hoses through the gaping holes, then disappeared behind me.

"Lucky?" Romeo's voice came in clearer now, the scream in my ears retreating. "Can you hear me?"

Looking into his blue eyes clouded with emotion, I nodded. My hearing might be normalizing, but my thoughts still bounced around the inside of my skull compounding a blistering headache. "Everybody okay?" I pressed my palms to my temples, holding my head in a vise—pressure against the pain.

"Yes, thanks to you." The young detective grabbed both my shoulders, forcing my attention. "Who are you?"

Letting my hands drop—the vise thing wasn't working—I tried to give him one of my patented snorts, but it came out as an anemic wheeze. "You know who I am."

"Yes, but do you?" He looked serious.

Oh. I chewed on my lip as I exerted all the energy I could muster on marshaling my thoughts. "Lucky O'Toole."

A grin bloomed, cracking his stone-face. "Where do you work?"

"The Babylon."

"And what do you do there?"

"Solve problems." I took a deep breath. My head pounded, an ice pick of pain stabbing behind my right eye. I dabbed at my forehead again, then looked at my fingers. Fresh blood. "And I put up with irritating detectives with the Metropolitan Police Department."

Romeo sat back on his heels, his grin widening, which I didn't think possible. He motioned to one of the EMTs who came over and knelt in front of me. Cute, buff, with wavy dark hair, hazel eyes that bordered on gray, and dimples, he was the paramedic from Central Casting. With gloved hands, he gripped my head and probed my forehead with his thumbs.

"Do you know me well enough to take such liberties?" I asked.

"Does this hurt?" He pressed with a thumb.

I yelped.

"I'll take that as a yes." He popped the latch on a black box that looked suspiciously like a tackle box.

"If you plan on sewing me up with a fish hook and eight-pound test, we need to talk."

Once again he flashed those darn dimples as he pulled out and opened a package of gauze. He used it to dab at my forehead. "You've taken a pretty good lick. Good thing you're tough." The gauze turned red. He discarded it for a fresh wad. This time he added a dose of peroxide. "You'll need to get this checked out—there can be things going on inside your skull that we can't see. They can be fatal if not taken care of. And, as pretty as you are, you'll want a plastics guy to stitch you up."

"Are you flirting with me?"

Romeo punched the paramedic on the shoulder. "I told you she was one ballsy broad."

I puckered my lips as I glared at Romeo, then turned and ran headlong into the medic's bemused expression. Afraid my brain might leak out my ear, I cautiously cocked my head at the young detective. "The kid has a death wish."

That got a laugh out of both of them. Defusing tension, I can do.

With a couple of Steri-Strips in place, I felt good enough to try standing. Romeo extended a hand, which I gladly accepted.

The EMT steadied me with one hand holding my elbow, the other firmly pressed into my lower back.

"How're you doing?" he asked as I tentatively stretched to my full six feet.

For some reason, the fact that he still had me by a couple of inches made me feel infinitely better. "I'll rally."

"You don't know how lucky you really were." Still holding my elbow, he eased me to the door. "When those windows blew..." Leveling those eyes, now dark and serious, like the sky before a storm, he captured my eyes. "Have you ever seen a human flayed alive by flying glass?"

SITTING SIDEWAYS ON A GURNEY PARKED IN SOME OBSCURE HALLWAY at University Medical Center—UMC to us locals—I half-listened to the conversation in the curtained-off cubicle across the hall, straining to hear through the residual ringing in my ears.

A bored voice with forced energy—presumably the doctor's— said, "So," a pause as papers rustled, "Mr. Jones. What do we have?"

A male voice, mellifluous, melodic, sexy...vaguely familiar. "Well, a few years ago my girlfriend and I were into some pretty rough stuff."

"S and M kind of stuff? What are we talking about?"

"Cock stuffing."

I blinked. The doctor didn't say anything—I would've paid good money to see his expression. Or mine for that matter.

"You know, that's where you take—"

"I understand, Mr. Jones."

Wait. Don't cut him off! I didn't understand. What were they doing? My mind freewheeled until I stomped on the brakes—imagination is a terrifying thing. And I was dizzy enough as it was. I didn't need to add hurling to today's indignities.

The patient continued. "Anyway, the thermometer broke… inside. I bled…a lot. But the doctor got everything under control, said there was no permanent damage."

"I hope they also told you to never use thermometers. They have surgical instruments; you can purchase them at any S and M store. They're called sounds. Same sensations, none of the downside."

"Good to know, but that sort of play was a short term thing. I'm married now and my wife has her limitations."

I narrowed my eyes. He made it sound like not getting her jollies from bondage and stuff was a shortcoming to be over-looked. To be honest, I sorta agreed.

"And you are here because…?" The doctor sounded nonplussed by all of it—just another night in the asylum.

Mr. Jones continued, "My toddler, he's only three. Would you like to see a picture?"

"Perhaps later."

"He's the greatest kid." Mr. Jones chuckled in that doting-parent way. "Anyway, he was running and, well, he head-butted me in the groin. And, I've got a bit of a problem."

I heard the doctor set down his chart, then snap on a pair of latex gloves. "Let's see what's going on. You can take the towel off."

"Oh."

Then silence. Leaning so far toward the curtain closing them off from view, straining to hear every word, I almost fell off the gurney. I caught myself, barely. Thank God somebody had locked the wheels.

"Oh my!" Pained or alarmed—or a bit of both, it was hard to tell—the doctor no longer sounded bored. "Put that towel back on. I'll be right back." He rushed out of the cubicle, glanced at me, then charged down the hallway in a flurry of white coat-tails. He disappeared through the door, which closed behind him.

Well that was fun. Show over. Tucking my hands under my thighs, I swung my feet and tried to picture what in the world that guy had been doing with that thermometer. Then I decided, being visual and all, I'd had enough trauma for the day. I thought about asking him myself but abandoned that idea as being a bit tacky. Although, I *was* really bored.

An orderly had brought me down here months ago, parking me outside radiology while he went to check on the timing for my CAT scan. My stomach empty, my patience long since exhausted, I glanced through the curtain and up and down the abandoned hallway, plotting my next move. Aspirin had dulled the pain behind my right eye. The ringing in my ears had muted to the point where I no longer had to strain to make sense through the noise.

The door at the end of the hall banged open admitting two orderlies who ran in my direction. They dove into the cubicle next to me. "Sir, you need to come with us."

"Where are we going?" Mr. Jones's voice held a hint of panic.

"The doctor needs to get the swelling down, relieve some of the pressure, before permanent damage is done."

As they wheeled Mr. Jones out, I strained to catch a glimpse.

Oh my God. I was right! I knew him.

Mr. Jones, my ass. That was Creighton Crider. He'd been a big shot at Metro when I was a kid. We used to call him Crayfish Crider—a Bayou Boy with a limp, clammy handshake. I guess his handshake wasn't the only limp member he had. Somebody I knew had dated him—sort of a walk on the wild side with an older guy as I recall. One of those stupid things young women do. Which friend was it who had done Crayfish? I couldn't remember —my brains were all scrambled.

I shuddered at the thought as I watched the trio trundle down the hallway.

The doorway at the end swallowed them whole leaving me, once again, alone with my thoughts. Normally, I could tolerate my own company, enjoy it even, but I'd been alone with me so long I was boring myself.

With the entertainment over, I seriously considered making a run for it. Somehow I couldn't work myself down to the indignity of an ignominious escape, mooning the world as I dashed away in my hospital gown. Pride can be such a hindrance.

On the verge of throwing dignity out the window, I sipped off the gurney, clutching my gown closed behind me. I whirled at the sound of the pneumatic doors at the far end of the hallway swinging inward.

My mother, Mona, charged through the opening. In leggings and a loose white tunic to hide her baby bump, with her brown hair swinging loosely to her shoulders, her make-up impeccable, her skin glowing, and her eyes dark with emotion, she looked like my kid sister. *That* certainly made me feel better. Add her unparalleled ability to punch every button I had, and her presence had me clinging by my fingernails to the ledge of civility.

Returning to my previous position on the gurney, I pasted on a weak smile and promised myself I would shelve the sarcasm. Okay, I would *try* to shelve it—making promises in my condition was iffy at best.

Mona hurried to my side, then clutched one of my hands in both of hers. Her skin was cold. I guess she really wasn't faking her worry, although, with Mother, one never could be certain. "Lucky! My God, honey!" She leaned in and whispered, her voice shaking. "It's like before."

Another time. Another place. Another bomb. I shut my mind to the assault of the memories. "Don't go there, Mother. I'm okay." I looked around her but didn't see anyone.

Amazingly, Mona understood. "I left your father out front

talking to the doctors. He'll be here in a minute." She grabbed my hand her face turning serious. "There's something going on, Lucky."

"I'll say. *That* message was delivered with quite a punch this afternoon."

She waved her hand as she glanced over her shoulder at the hallway doors. "Not with Jimmy G. It's your father. He got some kind of note yesterday. It made him nervous...and angry. I haven't seen him like that in a long time."

"What did the note say?"

"He wouldn't tell me. But I thought, with you two being thick as thieves, maybe he might tell you."

If she was jealous of my relationship with my father, she kept it hidden. Our bond was understandable really—my father and I had the hotel business in our blood. A businessperson as well, my mother had experience of a different kind, although it was remarkably similar in some respects. Until a couple of months ago, she'd been the proprietress of Mona's Place, the self-styled best whorehouse in Nevada. She and Father had married recently, terminating my illegitimacy. I still wasn't sure how I felt about that. Glad for them, of course, but missing a ready excuse for the boulder I carried on my shoulder.

"Father can be awfully private, but I'll try...when the time is right."

Mona's worried look fell away—transferring responsibility always lightens the load. She graced me with a soft smile. "I heard you're a hero," she said, her voice breathless with a grudging awe.

"Overstating." I tried to extricate my hand, but she wouldn't let go.

The doors swung open again, this time admitting my father, Albert Rothstein, lovingly referred to as the Big Boss. One of the top-tier players in town, he was integral in making Vegas what it was today. Currently he owned several properties, the Babylon by far his most grand. Yes, not only was he my father, he was also my boss. Not really advisable, but we seemed to be making it work.

Hands in his pockets, he strolled toward me, his weak flash of a grin unable to fully camouflage his concern. A short man with salt-and-pepper hair, a square face, and chiseled physique, he oozed masculinity and something else—power, perhaps? In his perfectly tailored, dark gray Italian suit in summer-weight wool with a very faint pinstripe, starched white shirt, deep purple tie, diamond-encrusted collar bar, and Gucci wingtips, he was every inch the power broker. With worry tingeing his eyes and pulling his lips into a taut line, he was also every inch a concerned parent. He moved close but didn't reach out to me. "The doctors say you're going to be fine. The CAT scan is just prophylactic."

I gave him a lopsided grin. "You know how I feel about prophylactics."

"Lucky!" Mona feigned shock.

I rolled my eyes. Apparently playing the owner's wife included heightened sensibilities not normally found in a former hooker.

Father patted her hand. "Humor, honey. It's how Lucky deflects, you know that."

Most people yearned for that kind of insight from their loved ones. Not me. It just made me uncomfortable. Picking at the hem of my gown, I stared at the floor commanding my thoughts into a logical formation, which sounds way easier than it was. "Father, you remember Boogie Fleischman?"

"Boogie the Bomber." His eyes widened slightly as they held mine. A few beats passed before he answered. "That's going way back." My father reached into his back pocket and tugged at his wallet—a slim, well-worn piece of leather. He opened it and extracted a hundred dollar bill. Flipping the wallet closed, he tucked it back where he'd found it and began working the paper bill. His hands shook a bit, which surprised me. Creasing and folding, he glanced at me. "What'll it be?"

"Your choice."

My mother and I watched him, his brows scrunched in concentration, as he created. A few moments, and he was finished. Taking my hand, he turned it over and pressed the finished product into my palm. After leaning in for a quick peck on my cheek, he let go of my hand and stepped back.

Glancing down, I smiled. A heart. "Origami," I said. "Your way of deflecting." I hoped he'd heard my smile. "Now, Boogie and Jimmy G? Weren't they partners or something? I can't remember; I was young."

"Very." My father's eyes had turned dark, his expression serious as he crossed his arms. "This reminds me of that time…"

"Yeah, startling similarities." My tone shut him down. A close call, so long ago. "A bomb. Jimmy's Place."

"You don't need to remind me." My father's voice was flat, hard.

"Tell me about Boogie and Jimmy G," I prompted. "You've never really talked about it before—I've never heard your take."

"Never had to give it to you."

"Perhaps now might be a good time to fill me in."

Amazingly, he didn't argue. "Not only partners, but the best of friends, they'd moved out here together. I can't remember exactly, but neither one of them was much more than legal at the time."

I finally extricated my hand from Mona's. When I patted the gurney next to me, she boosted herself up. Reflexively, my father helped her, right-side-of-the-tracks manners from a wrong-side guy. "This was when? The sixties?"

My father nodded. "They'd both grown up in the restaurant business back in Jersey. So they came out here and set up shop together—a popular little Italian joint over on Eastern. The neighborhood was much more upscale then—all the casino folks and their families lived there."

"What happened between them?"

My father ran a hand over his eyes. "Why're you asking me this? You can't possibly think…"

For a moment I chewed on my lip, remembering.

Mona looked at me owl-eyed. "Lucky?"

I shut them both down with a look. "I don't know what to think. Tell me what happened."

He shot me a questioning look but did as I asked. "Boogie fell in with the wrong crowd. You know Jimmy, he kept his nose clean, ran a nice place. Jimmy forced Boogie out—he didn't need that kind of trouble. Jimmy paid him fair, but Boogie held a grudge." My father glanced around. I knew what he was looking for—a window. He loved to stare out through a window when he trotted down memory lane.

"No pretty vistas here, Boss. This is a hospital, one of the most depressing places on the planet. I'm sure the lack of ambiance, although a bit sadistic, is purposeful. Makes us all want to go home."

My father shrugged. "You know the rest of the story."

"Tell me again. I want to be sure."

"I'd like to hear it again, too," Mona said, adding an encouraging nod.

"In the seventies, the corporations moved in. There was a huge push to move the Family out. We all knew that's how it'd have to go if we really hoped to put Vegas on the map." Clearly on edge, my father again reached for his wallet, extracted another bill, then stuffed his wallet back in his pocket. Drawing on a lifetime of memory, he began working the bill as he talked. "Jimmy's place was doing real good. A high-class joint, you know?"

At his glance, I nodded.

"A lot of money was at stake in polishing Vegas' image. The dirty history was swept under the rug, until the Union moved in." Absentmindedly, he folded and refolded, his fingers dancing to a memory.

"The Culinary Union?"

"Yeah, they tried to fill the power vacuum left when the Family got escorted out of town. As you can imagine, the business owners wanted no part of the Union. To them, it was just more of the same."

"A poor substitute for the Mob."

"Yeah." My father gave me a rueful smile, then took a quick glance at the figure forming as he worked. "At least with the Mob, they took care of their own. You knew what the rules were, and the price for breaking them. With the corporations and the Union, it was warfare—a game with no rules."

"But the Union won," I said, mainly for Mona's benefit.

"A lot of blood was spilt," my father continued, a lost, angry look in his eyes. "The Union had these thugs that would bomb restaurants that refused to become unionized. It was an ugly time in this town."

"And Boogie Fleischman? What role did he play?"

"He found his calling: he loved blowing things up. Got pretty cocky about it, as I recall."

"And that night at Jimmy's, was the bomb his?"

"They didn't pin that one on him, but we were pretty sure it was." My father glanced at me, then his eyes skittered away. If I didn't know better, I'd say he was nervous. He pretended to be absorbed in the tiny figure in his hands, putting the finishing touches on a swan with a graceful, arched neck. Taking one of Mona's hands, he pressed it into her palm, then closed her fingers over it.

"Why didn't they pin it on him?"

"He had an airtight alibi."

"What?"

My father didn't meet my eyes. "I don't know, but it stuck."

"But he was sent up, right?"

"Lesser charges, another incident."

My feet stopped swinging as I stilled. "Then why were you sure the bomb had been his?"

"A few bits of the bomb were found in the wreckage. Parts of a wind-up clock, pieces of a secondary trigger." He rubbed his eyes, then took a deep breath. "Making a bomb is an art. The folks that do it usually have some particular background or knowledge that shapes how they fashion the device. With Boogie, he only knew one way."

"Unique, like a signature?"

"Exactly."

"Ah, the punch line." I leaned back against the wall, once again glad the wheels on the gurney had been locked.

They both looked at me owl-eyed. Silence stretched between us.

"Today's bomb and the other one, all those years ago; they were exactly the same," I said with a little more bravado than I felt.

My father stared me down. "Are you sure?"

"An old wind-up clock that probably hasn't been for sale for decades. Seriously old dynamite."

"Boogie paid his debt and went back east, last I heard." My father sounded like he was working real hard to sell the story. But to me or to himself? I didn't know. "He didn't have anything to do with this, Lucky."

"Why are you so sure?" I pressed. Mona was right; something was definitely going on with the Big Boss. Behind the paternal façade, he looked tired. And angry.

My father started to answer, then clamped his mouth shut at the sound of the doors opening one more time. This time, they admitted Romeo with my EMT Galahad on his heels.

As they approached, my father leaned in close. "We need to talk. Soon." He touched my face, a lost look in his eyes, then he stepped back, turning a smile toward the two men hurrying in our direction.

Romeo, his clothes rumpled but his face bright, looked a whole lot better than I thought he should. Apparently he could take bombs and late nights in stride far better than I. His sandy hair was cut short and gelled with not a hair out of place...well, except for the cowlick at the crown of his head, which so far had defied every styling substance short of Super Glue. His blue eyes clear. A bounce in his step. A ready smile creasing skin otherwise unmarred by the passage of time. Looking at him, I had a glimmer of why people would mortgage their souls for a brief taste of lost youth.

After nodding a greeting to my parents, the young and way too perky detective hooked a thumb over his shoulder as he stopped in front of me. "The ATF guys are chomping at the bit to talk to you."

"I can't tell you how good that makes me feel."

"Bombings attract a lot of attention, and you're the only one who got a look at the device."

"Besides the one who put it there." I gave him the best stern look I could muster. "Speaking of which, shouldn't you be out chasing leads or something?"

"I'm working on it." Romeo didn't seem to buy my act. "There's precious little to go on. Jimmy didn't have any video, so we're trying to get a bead on what folks saw."

"Or thought they saw."

"Eyewitnesses aren't the most reliable," the young detective agreed. "So you can understand why ATF wants to get your take."

"I have a head injury, haven't you heard?" I pointed toward radiology. "I'm waiting for them to diagnose the extent."

Romeo smiled. "Nice try."

"I could use some help here," I said to the EMT. "I still don't know your name."

"Nick." He flashed those dimples.

I was so glad I wasn't hooked up to one of those heart rate machines or the thing would be having a coronary about now.

"And I'll be glad to testify to your instability if you'll go out to dinner with me. The detective here told me you were flying solo." He colored a bit at my scowl.

Romeo, on the other hand, seemed unfazed.

"Sweetheart," I cooed to the young detective. "I don't need you pimping me out." He just gave me an open, innocent look, making me smile.

My mother, who had grabbed my hand again, cutting off the blood flow, leaned in and whispered so everyone could hear, "Honey, he's yummy."

None of this seemed to knock Nick off base. Not even his introduction to my parents. Either he was clueless or supremely secure. Perhaps he merited some study. As I opened my mouth to respond to his invitation, the doors behind me slammed open, making me swallow my words.

The orderly, who had abandoned me a lifetime ago, stepped into the group and announced, "They're ready for you."

As he reached to wheel me away, I gathered my dignity—hard to do in my current attire—and announced, "Well, today's the day we finally find out if I really do have mush for brains."

BY THE TIME I'D BEEN STITCHED UP, DECLARED OF SOUND MIND AND body, and given my discharge papers, the energy in the hospital was at an ebb—daytime bombings under control, nighttime stabbings and overdoses still to come. Thankfully, my father had taken Mona home, relieving me of the energy drain. Romeo had left, presumably to tilt at windmills and right wrongs, keeping the world as we know it status quo for yet another day.

My clothes had been stuffed into a sack and unceremoniously thrown into a corner of my emergency room cubicle. Weariness crept through me—the aftermath of an overdose of adrenaline—as I pulled my Dana Buchman slacks and matching sweater in a deep midnight blue from the bag. Crumpled, peppered with holes, and reeking of smoke, they were all I had. It took me three tries to get my foot fully through the left pant leg without it coming out the large tear in the knee. Then I pulled my sweater on over my head—a bra seemed beyond my capabilities at the moment so I left it in the bag. Reaching into the bottom, I came up empty—no shoes. And as I recall, they'd been my favorite Ferragamos, also in blue. I'd had them resoled seven times. Or was it eight? Not that it really mattered. Finally covered, but still far from presentable, I scrawled my name on a stack of release forms left by the attending physician and padded toward the exit.

Paxton Dane pushed himself upright and into my consciousness. How had I missed him holding up the wall next to the nurse's station? He ambled in my direction. "Man, you look like forty miles of bad road."

Too bad I couldn't say the same about him. Several inches over six feet, with wide shoulders tapering to a boyish waist, dark wavy hair, emerald green eyes, cheekbones so sharp they looked carved out of stone, and a ready grin, he was spit-and-polished in his creased 501s and starched button down. Normally, his presence made me wary. Not only did he ooze some sort of male pheromone or something—which ought to be illegal around women in my weakened state—he also had a penchant for bending the truth. However, tonight I'd never been so happy to see a friendly face. A former co-worker and rebuffed suitor, I thought we now had weathered the rocky road to friendship. His smile gave me a hint he agreed.

"What are you doing here?"

"Trying to get a jump-start on my damsel-in-distress quota."

"I'm honored to be the beneficiary of such self-aggrandizement." I took his proffered arm, looping mine through it. "It's been a less-than-stellar day."

"Oh, I wouldn't say that," he said as he steered me away from the front entrance. "You don't want to go out that way."

"What about the ATF guys? I heard they were looking for me."

"They agreed to meet you in your office. The packs of bloodhounds feasting on small children and old people around here scared them off. My truck's in the garage on the other side of the hospital."

I happily leaned on Dane as I let him lead me through the labyrinth of UMC. We both knew the drill—the reporters would be corralled out front, while we sneaked out the back. "The newshounds are waiting to tear out my throat, are they?"

"Or anoint you queen for a day. Nice touch saving the kid."

"You know me, anything for good copy."

"Seriously." His grip tightened on my arm. "Good job."

I felt heat rise in my cheeks. Praise made me uncomfortable. Praise for doing something I should have done made me mad.

Thankfully, we were saved from embarrassment by Jimmy G barreling around the corner. He almost took us both out before he skidded to a stop.

"Lucky, man, where they been hidin' you?" He looked like he was loaded for bear. "I've been lookin' for you all over. This guy out there," Jimmy, his face a mask of indignation, hooked his thumb over his shoulder, "he was talkin' to me like, you know, all highfalutin, like he had more degrees than a thermometer, you know? But he was tellin' me something ain't right with your head."

Dane managed to keep a straight face. I, on the other hand, lost that battle. "Jimmy, you know I come from a long line of nutcases. If somebody knocked some sense into me, it'd be a good thing."

Jimmy pulled a handkerchief out of his back pocket and dabbed at his forehead. "True."

I tried to scare him with a frown—I don't think I pulled it off. "You could argue a bit, just to make me feel good, you know."

Jimmy seemed to ponder that concept as Dane and I gathered him in our wake and we hurried through the hospital to the garage. Dane's F-150 languished across two parking spaces. A crew cab with four doors and a full eight-foot bed, it also stuck out so far that cars could barely squeeze around it. But in desperate need of a ride and a knight in shining armor, I decided now wasn't the time to point out his lack of consideration for the other drivers.

The three of us piled in, Jimmy riding shotgun while I hunkered down in the back, making sure to keep out of sight even though this game of cat and mouse with the reporters was more for show than substance. After all, being the mouthpiece of the Babylon, I was pretty easy to find. But if I could lure them to my turf, then I held the upper hand... in theory.

Ducking as Dane pulled out of the garage, I asked Jimmy, "What's left of your place?"

He swiveled around to look at me.

"Look out front, Jimmy," Dane barked. "We don't want them to see Lucky in the back."

The little man whirled around like he'd been bitten on the ass by a rattler. As he stared straight ahead, he pulled down the visor in front of him. His eyes flicked to the mirror as he talked. "It's like almost stranger than those books, you know?"

"Books?" Sometimes Jimmy's circuitous train of thought had me making nothing but left turns. I racked my brain. "You mean fiction?"

"Yeah, yeah. Stranger than fiction." He shook his head, "Those folks who make that stuff up. They gotta be touched, you know?"

"Borderline personality disorder... all of them."

Jimmy turned around to look at me. "Really?"

"Jimmy!" Dane barked again. "Out the front. Lucky's not here."

"Well, technically, I'm here, but I'm not *all* here."

I could see the smile in Dane's eyes when he looked at me in the rearview mirror. "Jimmy, now that we've established that writers are nuts and truth is really stranger than fiction, why don't you give it to me straight?"

"That bomb." He said the word 'bomb' with such reverence it gave me the chills. "That bomb didn't pack the punch it was meant to."

"So I have to turn in my hero badge?" I asked, not sure how I felt about that. It was sorta fun being held up as a paragon of virtue—of course it couldn't last, but I'd ride that horse as long as I could.

"They gave you a medal? Really?" Jimmy sounded awestruck.

"Kidding."

"Oh, right." He didn't sound too pleased that my sarcasm had done a flyby.

Couldn't say I blamed him. I even irritated myself on occasion so I sympathized.

"I was saying," Jimmy groused, "according to the ATF guys, it looked like the bomb was made with some old stuff."

"So not as much bang for the buck?"

Jimmy didn't laugh. "Even still, it coulda killed somebody—a lot of somebodies if it hadn't been for you."

"So the bomb," I said. Decidedly uncomfortable when hip-deep in emotional quagmire, I redirected the conversation back to solid ground. "Was it like somebody maybe used an old blueprint?"

"Yeah, they found pieces of an old clock that hadn't been for sale for decades. They said the bomber had to buy that thing at a flea market or somethin'."

"Or they got it from somebody's stash…from a long time ago."

This time, when Jimmy swiveled around and stared at me, his eyes huge and angry, Dane didn't bark.

I nodded at Jimmy's silent question. "You wouldn't know where Boogie Fleischman is, would you?"

"Boogie." Jimmy's voice was low with a hint of menace that gave me goose bumps. Turning inward, he was quiet for awhile. When he spoke, his voice was hoarse and soft. I had to strain to hear him. "I went up and saw him the day he got sprung."

"I didn't know that." I pushed myself up onto the seat and leaned back. If the reporters were around, they had to be behind us. Good thing Dane had several shotguns hanging in the back window—not only was the view inside the truck obscured, but we could defend ourselves if necessary. "How many years did he do?"

"Thirty's what he got. I don't recall exactly how many he did.

But he got out—" He paused then whistled. "It's been maybe twenty years ago, I bet."

"Hell of a long time to keep a grudge," Dane muttered. I couldn't read the emotion in his voice, but there was something there.

I leaned forward, closer, but still scrunched down a bit. "When you went to see him, what'd you guys talk about?"

At the Strip, Dane took a left toward the Babylon. "Old times?" he offered. For once, someone else said what I was thinking.

A sad expression tugged at Jimmy's features. "I know you're makin' fun, but that's all we had to talk about. There was nuthin' else. I tried to make it right between us, but he wouldn't have nuthin' to do with it."

"Some people just have to hang onto bad feelings, Jimmy." I reached over the back of the seat and squeezed his shoulder. "Not much you can do about it."

"Last thing Boogie said to me, he was going back to Jersey to pick up the pieces. Then he'd be back. And he'd be gunnin' for me." Jimmy's face hardened, his eyes narrowing to dark slits. "But not just for me."

"Who else was in the creep's crosshairs?" I asked. Could Boogie really be back? Or did we have a copycat? And who was the target? And why now? Hell, most of the bit players were probably dead by now.

"Your father."

Okay, that grabbed me by the short hairs—me and my misplaced smugness. "The Big Boss?" My stomach clenched as my blood ran cold. I touched the bandage on my forehead. A throbbing pain had pierced the heavy dose of local anesthetic. Waving away the offer of pain medication probably wasn't the smartest stunt I'd pulled lately. I was never quite as tough as I thought which, all things considered, probably wasn't a bad thing.

"Yeah, back in those days, your father was willing to help clean up Vegas. He made a lot of enemies."

"Several lifetimes ago, Jimmy."

"But it was personal." His normal smile absent, Jimmy looked tired. "People are like elephants when it comes to that shit."

I let my thoughts travel back in time. "Yeah, some things you just can't forget."

Jimmy reached for my hand, which I gave to him across the seatback. He squeezed it hard, as his eyes bored into mine. "Do you remember?"

"Like it was yesterday," I whispered, half-afraid that remembering would make it real all over again. "It was the same bomb, Jimmy. Put in the same place. Too coincidental to be anything other than intentional. Somebody's sending you a message." We stared at each other for a moment, connected by a memory.

"Boogie's back." Even though a long time had passed, I felt it in my bones. I grabbed my phone, hit a familiar number, then pressed it to my ear.

The Big Boss's phone rang and rang.

No one answered.

CHAPTER TWO

$\mathcal{A}$GAINST ALL odds, me and my little band of Musketeers made it to my office without being jumped by a pack of roving reporters. Breathing a sigh of relief, I let Dane pull open the door. Jimmy motioned me in front of him. Unaccustomed to such chivalry, I wasn't above appreciating it when presented.

As was customary, my assistant, Miss P, didn't look up when I entered. And yet, despite not getting a visual, somehow she knew it was me. "Lucky, where the hell have you been? The phone has been jumping out of its cradle. For some reason, every reporter in the state wants your comments on some explosion. Why would they..." Her voice trailed off when she looked up. For once, she was speechless.

"I had a front row seat, which could explain some of their enthusiasm."

She jumped up. "Are you okay?"

"The doctor's at UMC seem to think so. Either that or they did all they could and sent me to work to die."

Jimmy took a chair against the wall of windows overlooking the lobby below. Sometimes, I loved to stop and look through the window—my day being reoriented watching all the happy people.

Today would take more than that, so I didn't bother. Dane disappeared into the kitchenette in the back. Thankfully, as late as it was, the bird, our foul-mouthed office mascot, had been covered for the night—one less strident voice to grate on already raw nerves.

I propped a hip on the corner of Miss P's desk. One glance at the huge pile of messages in my box left me on the verge of apoplexy. On the theory that actually picking them up conferred responsibility, I waved my finger at the stack. "Can you give me the high points?"

"I'll take care of them."

That took my breath. "Wow, really?"

"That's what you pay me for." She raised an eyebrow—I couldn't tell whether it was a statement or a challenge.

"And here I thought I paid you to give me a hard time." We grinned at each other. Why did all of my relationships use the dialect of obfuscation—a dance around saying what we really meant? Since I was the only common denominator, I guessed the path to the answer started in my backyard. However, I wasn't in the mood for playing in that sandbox, so I shelved it...until my next life.

Miss P cleared her throat. "There is one thing." Her eyes didn't hold mine.

"What? Something you can't handle? Oh goody."

"Flash is in your office." This time, her gaze, open and pleading, held mine. "Short of calling security, I couldn't stop her. She breezed in here without a word. And I didn't think you'd want her thrown out."

"Not today. Well, not yet anyway, but the jury's still out." I really did not need to deal with Flash right now, I thought as I teetered on the precipice of self-pity. Dane came to my rescue when he returned with a tumbler full of amber liquid. "Is that what I think it is?"

My hand shook as I reached for the glass, which probably

should have worried me. But my worry-plate was full, so I shelved that also.

"A medicinal dose of Wild Turkey 101." Bowing slightly, he handed it to me.

I would have kissed him but, given our checkered romantic history of thrust and parry, that would've been supremely stupid…even for me. Instead, I grabbed the glass and tossed back half of it in one gulp. The fact that it was a Flintstone jelly jar made me look like more of a lush than I am—at least that's what I told myself.

The liquid burned a fiery path all the way to my stomach where it burst in an explosion of warmth. My pride having long since abandoned this sinking ship, I sighed. Thus fortified, I dared a glance into Dane's emerald eyes. "Thanks. I've got to get busy putting out fires."

He took the hint, motioning to Jimmy. "Come on, I'll buy you dinner."

Marshaling my thoughts, which was a lot like collecting fire-flies on a still summer evening, I waited until the door had closed behind them before I divvied up the responsibility pie with Miss P. "I'll deal with Flash. You tell security to keep the rest of the riff-raff out. When the ATF guys show up, buzz me. But don't let them in until I'm ready, okay? Oh, and get the beautiful Jeremy Whit-lock on the phone—here in person would be even better. How is he at finding the scent on a trail that's gone cold?"

"The best." She grinned. Of course she'd say that. Fifteen years her junior, Jeremy had stolen her heart trading his in return, so her opinion was highly suspect.

FLASH SAT AT MY DESK, HER FEET PROPPED ON AN OPEN DRAWER, her phone tucked between her shoulder and her ear as she scribbled notes, nodding occasionally. One stylish pink stiletto dangled from her foot as she wiggled it. Her bright red curls were pulled back from her face and corralled with a neon orange scarf. In jeans and a t-shirt stretched over her ample chest well beyond the boundaries of good taste, she looked like a woman trolling for a fat wallet—which, of course, was a ploy. Behind the bimbo façade lurked a woman with more IQ points than an Ivy Leaguer. Giving me a quick glance, she raised a finger. As she wound up her call, I sunk into one of the chairs across from her and nursed the rest of my whiskey.

Flash had peeled back the plastic tarp covering all the furniture when she'd set up shop in the construction zone I called my office. Caught in the throes of unbridled optimism, I'd given Miss P a promotion—she was now what I used to be. Unfortunately, as the 'me' I used to be, she hung out where I used to hang out—my old office.

We'd knocked out a wall to make room for a workspace for me in an adjacent storage room. I had no doubt that my little corner of the universe would be a nice place to store my stuff—if it was ever completed. Two workmen with one hammer had been at it so long and made such little progress, I was seriously considering adopting them.

Now, tarps protected all the furniture. The only light was a weak circle cast by a lone light bulb dangling from a wire. A hole in the outer wall—my future private entrance—necessitated us locking all the important stuff in drawers and filing cabinets. To be honest, I wasn't there that much, so the whole thing never rose high enough on my priority list to actually do anything more than whine about it.

"I've phoned in my story on the explosion," Flash announced as she slammed the receiver in its cradle, then set her feet on the floor and kicked the drawer shut with one foot. Leaning across the desk, she fixed me with her most serious, investigative-reporter stare. "My deadline is almost here, and I'm still a little thin on details. That's where you come in."

"I'm fine, thank you for asking."

She waved away my grousing. "Hell, it was just a little bomb. You're walking and talking. How bad can it be?"

"Besides a blistering headache and a scar on my forehead?"

She opened her eyes wide. "Oh, I hope it's a lightening bolt like Harry Potter."

"And add Voldemort and the dementors to the list of people after me? Why not?"

"If you include some vampires, zombies, and maybe a were-wolf or two, you could sell your story and make billions." Flash, her pencil poised, morphed back into reporter mode. "But if a bomb is all we've got, we'll have to make due. What can you tell me about the explosion?"

"More than you can imagine, but some of it has to be off the record, at least for now. I need your help." I took another sip as I tried to figure out how much to tell. Flash and I went way back—all the way to our time at UNLV where she worked to keep our names out of the paper and I kept us out of jail. A match made in Heaven. We'd had each others' backs ever since. I'd trust her with my life—normally a figure of speech, but this time I might have to for real.

"I'll give you the skinny on Jimmy G's—at least enough to make you a hero with your editor. In return, I need to tell you a story that's totally between you and me."

She chewed her lip, then nodded once.

I settled back and opened the door to a time long ago, to memories I'd protected myself from for a lifetime. "When I was a kid, Jimmy had a place over on D.I. east of the Strip. The Danger Zone. Everybody went there. Late at night was the best. The entertainers would gather there after their last act. Often they'd play the piano and sing, just for the fun of it."

"I've heard of that place. There was something about it." Flash's face was open, her eyes intense. "Didn't it burn down?"

I shrugged. "Sorta. I was there." Memories washed over me. "It was late. The place was almost empty."

"How old were you?"

"Four."

"What were you doing in a joint like that late at night at that age?" Indignation tinged Flash's voice, which I thought was cute—naïve, but cute.

"Please, it was Vegas...old Vegas. And I was there with my mother. She was nineteen at the time and not long on good judgment." I leaned over and grabbed a paperweight off the corner of my desk—a golden cockroach in Lucite—a gift from the employees after dealing with one of our more creative guests. Turning the weight over and over, I stared into it as if looking through a window to the past. "Apparently, Jimmy was the go-between for my parents. He gave them a safe place to meet. Of course, I didn't know the Big Boss was part of my family then."

Wallowing in visions of the past, I paused for a moment. It's funny, I opened the door to the past, walked inside and it seemed so crisp and clear, un-diluted by the passage of time. "We were waiting at the bar. Dean Martin was piped in over the loudspeakers. Mona was having a ginger ale." I looked at Flash with, I'm sure, a bewildered expression. "Why would I remember that?"

"The mind has weird coping mechanisms."

I nodded even though I had only a vague idea what she was alluding to. "Actually, that could explain a lot but we won't go there. Anyway, my father was a no-show, which wasn't normal for him. Mona was ready to leave, but I needed to go to the bathroom before we left. Those sixty miles back to Pahrump took longer then."

"A bumpy blacktop, I remember," Flash said with a grin. "And a great place for alien abductions as I recall."

I felt a smile bloom across my face. "You remember that guy?"

"He had the whole city goin' with his story."

"Fun while it lasted." I adjusted myself in the chair. Aches and pains I didn't know I had whined for attention. "But as I recall, by the end we were all ready for the aliens to come back and get him."

"He got way more than his fifteen minutes." Flash nodded, then turned serious again. "So back to Jimmy G's, you went to the bathroom..."

I captured her eyes with mine. "The story was the place burned—a grease fire."

"That's not true?" I shook my head. "It was a bomb."

"Shit. No way."

"I saw it, but I didn't know what it was." I paused as a shiver chased down my spine. Or was it up my spine? Who knew? "Thank God I mentioned it to my mother."

"The place was leveled, wasn't it?"

I nodded, remembering. I was running, Mona pulling me...the explosion. "What little was left burned. The building was a total loss."

"But nobody died."

"No."

"Thanks to you."

"No, thanks to my big mouth and a boatload of guardian angels." Placing the paperweight back on the corner of my desk, I pretended to be consumed with getting it in just the right spot while I gathered myself.

Flash didn't leave me alone with my thoughts for long. "You think the two are related?"

"I haven't a clue, but I have a real bad feeling." I glanced at her. "The bombs were identical."

She raised her eyebrows, then made a quick note. "Okay, so what do you want from me?"

"Keep that bomb part on the Q.T. for now—I've got to chase a cold trail and I don't need the bright light of public scrutiny chasing my moles back underground."

"That's all?" Flash's words dripped with sarcasm.

"I always do right by you so quit grousing. And I want you to do what you always do: chase down witnesses and put together pieces. Give me a better picture of the whole story surrounding the original bombing."

"You got it." She tapped her pencil on her notepad. "But I got a story to beef up and, if I'm gonna' sit on what you just told me—which, by the way, will blow the town wide open—for that, you need to give me enough to get me the friggin' Pulitzer."

LIKE A RACEHORSE AT THE BELL, FLASH CHARGED OFF FULL OF investigative zeal and I turned to meet the day. Feeling the need to make myself a little more presentable, I grabbed a new outfit from my old office closet—jeans, a sweatshirt, and Nikes. After wiping off the worst of the grime—a shower was beyond my current capabilities—I touched up my face then called it good.

Curiously, my debriefing at the hands of the ATF had gone quickly. The questions were few, and I was able to give them only what I knew, keeping what I feared to myself. I called Romeo to give him my suppositions, though. As I knew he would be, he'd been a bit skeptical. But he assured me he'd look into it, though, from his tone, I knew he had about as many ideas as I did about where to start. Zip point doodle. The Big Boss could shed some light, but he still wasn't answering his phone. I tried to be calm—if Mona wasn't concerned, then I shouldn't be...at least that's what I kept telling myself. It didn't work. Even with the clock ticking into the third hour of a new day, I was wide awake, hyped on worry.

Before heading off to slay dragons, I glanced in the small mirror hanging on a nail in the wall next to the door to Miss P's office. I brushed my hair even though it didn't need it, as if outer order would bring inner order. It never worked that way—I knew that—but I couldn't resist trying. Squinting, I gave my face a good going-over. High cheekbones and blue eyes were the high points. The Steri-Strips covering the sutures in my forehead and the blooming dark pool of blood collecting under my right eye were definitely the not-so-high points. Overall, 'presentable' appeared to be aiming a bit high.

Desperate for food but feeling pretty good about myself despite my appearance, I stepped out of my office and ran head-long into Miss P, the Beautiful Jeremy Whitlock, and my second assistant, Brandy, who was younger than I ever remembered being and prettier than I had ever dared hope. Actually, I ran into their asses as they huddled around the phone with Miss P holding the receiver in the center of the group so they all could hear.

"Anything I should know about?"

The three of them jumped as if I'd fired a gun over their heads. Miss P slammed the receiver back in its cradle. Each of them busied themselves with some feigned task. No one met my eyes. And no one answered my question. I just stood there, waiting.

Finally, Miss P broke.

"It's Teddie," she started but, at my glare, she clamped her mouth shut, her lips forming a thin line. Narrowing her eyes, she seemed to debate the wisdom of continuing. Apparently she spied a chink in my armor, so she bolted through. "That man has it bad...he leaves twenty or thirty messages a day for you...one of these days, you're going to have to cut him some slack and call him back," she said in a breathless run-on, as if rushing the words would lessen the blow.

"When the fountains at the Bellagio freeze over." I enunciated each word trying to shut her down.

"You know, ice was a real problem when they first opened. Something to do with water pressure..." Brought up short by my narrowing eyes, Miss P retrenched. "But back to Teddie."

"A very bad time for this topic—magnanimous would not be an appropriate adjective for my mood at the moment. Besides, I've moved on."

"Perhaps, but you must deal with the past before you can embrace the future."

I would've laughed if I thought it wouldn't hurt my bruised ribs. "You know how I feel about your platitudes—pabulum for the easy-answer crowd."

"Grown from a kernel of wisdom." Apparently willing to risk bodily harm, she put both hands on her desk and her life on the line as she leaned closer. "I know he left. I know he hurt you. I think he finally realizes what he had."

"And what he turned his back on." I glanced at Brandy and Jeremy, unsure whether I really wanted an audience for this conversation—when contemplating homicide, leaving witnesses is not considered wise, or so I'd been told.

Caught in the act of paying attention, they quickly dove back into whatever task they were pretending to do. Hooding my eyes to shield my sorrow, I sunk into a chair across from Miss P's desk. My self-satisfaction dissolving in a mist of memories, I tried to bury the pain but, like a trick candle, it kept flaring.

The truth of it was, Teddie had broken my heart. No, he'd shattered it. And, almost worse, I'd lost not only a lover but my best friend. "Someday I might find it in my heart to forgive him, but I don't know how to ever trust him again."

"Maybe this will help." Despite Jeremy vigorously shaking his head, Miss P punched the button on the message machine. I wanted to run but, barely breathing, I couldn't move, a bystander transfixed by the carnage after a devastating wreck.

The message beeped. I heard random musical instruments in the background, like a symphony warming up before a show, and mingled voices. Then Teddie's voice. "Lucky, this is for you. I wrote the melody a while ago. The lyrics... well, I've been doing a lot of growing up lately. Listen. I hope you'll understand.

Although still pretty rough, the song has heart…my heart. I titled it *Lucky for Me.*" The strains of a song started, then his beautiful, smooth voice cutting my heart wide open.

"Fuck." I buried my face in my hands. Music, the language of love—Teddie could wield it like a weapon.

"Do you want me to stop it?" Miss P asked, concern replacing her scolding tone.

I shook my head. I'd listen. In her own way, Miss P was right—the sooner I faced him, the sooner I could put him behind me.

Naturally, the song was brilliant. A song of regret, of longing, of being on the road and wanting to come home. Teddie could pluck my heartstrings like an angel with a golden harp.

But where did the act end and the real guy begin?

Happily ever after was such an illusion.

Silence filtered in around us as Teddie's song came to a close and the machine beeped, signaling the end. No one said a word. What was there to say?

"Wow," Miss P finally whispered as she straightened and patted her skirt down. She reached over and squeezed my hand. "Love sucks."

"A ringing endorsement." I flashed her a tentative smile. "I don't even want to know what that implies about those of us who keep diving in, hoping the waters are deep enough that we don't break our necks." I would've jumped to my feet and started pacing, but given the current state of my body, I decided against it despite the fact that unspent nervous energy usually made me dangerous. Miss P reared back as I pushed myself to my feet. Apparently she had taken my hollow threats to heart. I liked it. "Time to get this day under way. What do we have?"

Leaning back, she ran a hand through her short, spiky hair. "Honey, you may be amped on adrenaline or whatever they gave you at the hospital, but the rest of us are ready for some shut-eye."

"Oh," I glanced at the other two. The whole lot of them looked like their go-juice tanks were pegged on 'E'. "Sorry. My clock is all messed up. Go home."

Miss P retrieved her purse from a desk drawer. Brandy did the same, then Jeremy stepped over my outstretched legs and opened the door, holding it for the two of them.

"Oh, hang on, I almost forgot." I tried not to be bothered by the fact that thoughts of Teddie made thoughts of bomb-making idiots on the loose flee like animals before a forest fire. "Jeremy, can you try to track down a guy named Boogie Fleischman? He paroled out of Indian Springs about eighteen to twenty years ago, I think."

"Boogie? Is that his given name?"

"Probably not." I thought back. Had I ever heard him referred to by another name? If I had, I couldn't remember, but I knew who would. "I can get you that info."

He flashed his dimples. "No worries. Finding his real name won't be the hard part."

"Hey, if it was easy, what would we need you for?"

"If it was easy, then I could retire and try my hand at stripping at Olympic Gardens. I hear they make real money."

I swallowed hard, clamping my mind shut to that visual.

"Over my dead body," Miss P announced as she hooked her arm possessively around his waist. "Come on, stud bucket, time for some rack time."

"Woman, I thought you'd never ask." He let himself be pulled through the door.

"What are you going to do?" Brandy asked as she stepped over me, following the others.

"Take a dose of French medicine to cure what ails me."

MOST OF THE CASUAL DINING RESTAURANTS AT THE BABYLON WERE round-the-clock establishments—the Burger Palais was no exception. Even though the dining hour had long since passed, the restaurants would be gearing up for the post-gambling, post-clubbing crowds. And I hoped a certain French chef would still be manning his grill—burgers being the perfect antidote to too much alcohol.

In fact, Jean-Charles Bouclet was the perfect antidote to all of my excesses, including adrenaline.

For some reason, I decided to take the stairs from the mezzanine to the lobby below. Halfway down, my body groaned like a gear frozen under decades of rust. Holding the handrail, I eased down one step at a time, then gingerly pushed through the fire door at the bottom.

As I knew it would be, the lobby was quiet. Only a few couples wandered hand in hand, lingering next to our version of the Euphrates—a flowing stream that wound its way from reception and into the casino beyond. Spotted with arched bridges and lined with flowering plants, the water was a nice oasis. Home to fish and fowl, it was one of the Babylon's signature features, along with the ceiling of blown-glass birds arced in flight and an indoor ski slope on the far side of the lobby covered with man-made snow now being groomed for tomorrow. Marble floors inset with multicolored mosaics, brightly colored cloth in varying vivid hues tented over the reception desk, and groves of palms, subtly hinted at the Persian theme so exquisitely amplified in other parts of the hotel.

At reception, I angled to the left heading under the arch announcing the Bazaar, our singular collection of high-end purveyors. Here you could buy anything your heart desired, from Ferraris to French couture and jewels worthy of a sheik's first wife. Many of the shops were shuttered at the moment. Even the lights had been doused in the Temple of Love, our wedding chapel, and Samson's, the hair salon and spa where a staff of buff and beefy Samson look-alikes awaited to ply each guest with

Champagne and attention. I didn't care. All I wanted was a French burgermeister.

In the interest of full disclosure, Jean-Charles Bouclet was so much more than a burger man. The owner of a chain of eponymous eateries around the world, he was the toast of the gastronomic set, and a coup for the Big Boss when he'd lured him to Vegas to open a high-end restaurant in our new property, Cielo. Technically, the new hotel was my pet project, so I could arrange my day to have the Frenchman perpetually near—not a bad plan. Especially since he had...well, *we* had, leapt the boundaries of professionalism and taken our relationship into personal territory. So new, we were still feeling our way. I grinned at the pun— puns were the least of my many vices. And I flushed a bit at the memories. His lips on mine. A jolt of heat where skin touched skin. The smile in his eyes. The sound of his voice. So perfect. Of course, there was Jean-Charles's son, Christophe, to complicate things. A very small boy, he was a very big concern. I had yet to meet him, but he would be arriving soon. My skills with men were bad enough. But little boys? I was flying blind.

Needing a hug and a smile, I hurried through the wide corridors, dodging a random gaggle of twenty-somethings. The young women, sheathed in tiny tubes of Lycra and balancing on impossibly high heels, held tightly to the arms of young men, stylish in their t-shirts, velveteen blazers, and French jeans. Laughing, the group rocketed on a high-octane mix of alcohol and youthful enthusiasm. For a moment, I felt the bite of jealousy, then came to my senses. I wouldn't go back there to save my soul. At my age, I no longer had the energy to handle all that desperation, which was probably a good thing. I had a sneaking suspicion the wisdom that supposedly came with age was really apathy resulting from an inability to muster enough ergs to care. If true, it was one of life's many cruel jokes. But it didn't really bother me... apparently that whole apathy thing had come home to roost. Was that a good thing or a bad thing? Somehow, I didn't care. And as simple as that, the whole question had become a tautology.

The double wooden doors bracketing the entrance to the Burger Palais stood open. Delicious smells of onions sautéing, bacon frying, and grass-fed beef sizzling over a charcoal fire beckoned all those who passed. Salivating in earnest now, I ducked through the doorway. The hostess stand was empty, so I breezed on in. With knotted wooden floors, exposed brick walls, green leather chairs, and banquettes and checkered table cloths, the place was elegantly casual, invoking the customers to relax and enjoy—or so said Jean-Charles, and I wasn't one to disagree. Brass sconces exuded a subtle light, adding to the welcoming ambiance. An ornate wooden bar from Scotland arched from the right-hand side of the dining room. Dotted with stools, also in green leather, it called to me. Another medicinal libation sounded like what the doctor ordered. However, since I had no idea what or how much the staff at UMC had plied me with, I decided to forego, at least momentarily. Besides, drinking alone had such negative connotations—not that that got in my way very often.

Instead, I angled to the left, toward the kitchen. Behind a wall of glass, a variety of culinary types carried out their tasks to the rocking sounds of Coldplay. Standing behind gleaming stainless steel workstations, replete with requisite shelving behind and refrigeration below, they juked to the music as they sliced and diced. If I tried that, I'd be minus a few digits in no time.

Casting my glance wider, my heart fell. Rinaldo, Jean-Charles' right-hand man worked the grill—Jean-Charles' normal position. A mountain of a man with curly black hair, a round face topping at least three chins, and hands the size of salad plates, he beamed when he saw me. Motioning toward the back of the kitchen with his spatula, he raised his voice to be heard above the music. "He's back there. But he's not real sociable—something about bad crabs."

I bit off the obvious reply as clearly in poor taste.

Apparently my appearance finally registered with the big man as his eyes grew worried, wiping the smile out of them. "Hey cutie, you okay?"

"Dodged a bullet."

"Seriously?"

"No, that was just a shallow attempt to get attention and sympathy." *And sidestep the question*, I thought, but I didn't say that part. Apparently it worked as he moved aside to let me pass without further elaboration.

Using the term 'office' to describe Jean-Charles' workspace was a bit optimistic. A battered, wooden, French schoolboy table tucked into a corner and a three-legged wooden stool hardly qualified, at least in the American vernacular of office excess. Functional with a bare bulb on a flexible metal stand clamped to the side of the desk, the only piece of envy-worthy equipment was a brand new 24-inch iMac. With the French being the world's arbiters of cool, it made perfect sense my chef would be a Mac man.

His back to me, Jean-Charles hunched in concentration as he straddled the stool, his feet hooked in the legs. He didn't notice me until I bent and placed a kiss just below his right ear. Pulling air in through his nose, he straightened. "Ah, Lucky. How did you know I've been missing you?"

I couldn't resist nibbling on his ear, taking delight in his shiver before I stepped back. "I didn't know, but I was hoping."

Still seated, he turned on the stool to face me. Grabbing me, he pulled me onto his lap, then leaned back to get a good look.

I tried not to let him see that he took my breath. Even with a pair of cheaters resting on the end of his nose, his blue eyes going all serious and dark as they roamed over my face, his full lips thinning into a line of concern, and weariness deepening his laugh lines, he was by far the best dish in the house. Looping an arm around his neck, I wove my fingers through his hair which, to my delight, he wore a trifle long. A medium brown with a slight curl, I found playing with the tendrils that drifted over his collar irresistible. His thighs, long and lean, felt solid under me. His chest was a hard, comforting backdrop to lean into. What was it people said? Never trust a thin chef? I wondered if that meant only his culinary skills or his character also. One way or the other, I didn't care.

With the back of the fingers of his right hand, he touched my cheek. Then he ran his thumb lightly over the cut on my forehead before kissing it. "You will tell me about this day."

"Yes." I maneuvered my weight off his lap, fearing that if I stayed there any longer, I would cut off blood flow in his legs. "Perhaps over dinner? Although I've been told you are dealing with bad crabs."

I tried to keep my expression passive, but I must've failed.

"*Oui*, but why are you looking at me this way, like it is some joke?"

"Oh, it's one of those American slang things." I grabbed his hand, pulling him up. I didn't step back. Instead, brazen hussy that I am, I stepped into his embrace. "I'll explain it another time." Why did having his arms around me feel better than anything I could imagine? Well, almost anything, and that involved him as well, but we hadn't gone there…yet.

"I will prepare your favorite, if you will open a bottle of wine." He released me momentarily, then grabbed my hand leading me through the kitchen. Apparently the word had gone out that the captain was on the bridge—someone had lowered the music. "There is a very nice Malbec that I've been saving for us. I think it will go nicely with sliders prepared as you like." He glanced back at me. "How do you say it?"

"Fully loaded?"

"This is it, yes." He took the spatula that Rinaldo proffered. With a practiced glance at the few orders listed on the screen inset in the backsplash, he dove in. "The wine is—"

"I know, in our cabinet behind the bar."

He smiled but didn't look at me, his concentration now captured by the task at hand. With Jean–Charles, food was serious business.

We were so compatible that way.

~

DINNER HAD PASSED IN EASY CHATTER AND THE COMFORT OF THE developing warmth between us. Even though I think he knew that I'd only given him the high points, Jean-Charles had let me off easy. I mean, what was there to say, really? I was in a building when a bomb exploded. Wrong place, wrong time.

The sliders had been as advertised—fully loaded and delicious. I'd stopped counting after my third, but I had taken notice when we'd popped the cork on the second bottle of wine. That had been two glasses ago.

Jean-Charles leaned across the table, capturing my hands in his. "This city, it is more dangerous than they say."

I gave him a sheepish shrug. "It just seems that way. I have a particular knack for sticking my nose where I shouldn't."

His face clouded. Idioms were indecipherable to him—I kept forgetting that.

"If there's trouble, I usually can find it," I added.

"You will have to fix that." He looked serious.

"Right after I solve global warming, bring peace to the Middle East, and a stable economy to the EEU." A glow suffused me as I looked at our entwined hands, then I shot him a rueful half-grin. "Besides, finding trouble is one of my best things. God knows I have far too few skills to abandon even one."

"Then you will be careful. I do not want to lose you." He leaned closer. I met him halfway. A jolt of fire, the kiss singed every nerve ending and seared every synapse. Reveling in the connection, I lingered, savoring. As he pulled away, little aftershocks chased

through my body, then coalesced into a ball of warmth somewhere deep inside.

Taking a deep breath, I closed my eyes. I felt a smile tug at the
corner of my mouth. Then my heart stopped as my phone sang
out at my hip. Actually, it was the Black Eyed Peas singing *I've Got
a Feeling*. Either way, the shock was a cold jolt of jump-juice to the
heart. I grabbed the thing and pushed-to-talk. "What?"

"Lucky?" My father didn't sound happy. "I'm at your place. We
need to talk. *Now*."

CHAPTER THREE

"*C*HRIST ALMIGHTY," I said as I burst through the door to my apartment on the top floor of the Babylon's west wing. "Why have you been so hard to find? Where have you been?" All the lights were off, but I could see my father standing at the window, silhouetted by the lights of the Strip streaming through the wall of glass. "And why the hell are you standing here in the dark?" I stopped a few feet from him.

He didn't turn. Instead, he stood there as still as a statue. He didn't respond. Unsure what to do, I considered checking his pulse—after all he wasn't exactly a spring chicken.

Finally he rescued me from my quandary. "Will you get me a drink?" he asked. His voice, low and emotionless, had a hard edge to it. "Then join me."

"With your recent health scare, do you think drinking is a good idea?" He didn't answer, not that I expected him to. I didn't know what to think as I walked to the far wall and pressed a panel. The wall slid back exposing a fully stocked bar. I decided on a fifteen-year-old single malt for him and club soda with lime for me—I'd exceeded my legal limit already. Besides, keeping my wits about me would probably work in my favor. While I didn't know what he had to tell me, I knew it couldn't be good. Pouring the drinks into Steuben double old-fashion tumblers, I added a couple of cubes of ice, then returned to his side with drinks in hand.

He took his glass without question or acknowledgement, then took a long sip. "The Glenmorangie?"

"Hmm." I took a tentative sip of my soda, then wrinkled my nose at the tickle of the bubbles. Although I'd tried, I never had developed a taste for tasteless beverages. Was that even possible, I wondered? The lime helped, as did the bubbles. But still, they just effervesced the boring.

The ice tinkled in my father's glass as he lifted it to his lips. "The eighteen?"

"No, the fifteen. A bit more fire-in-the-belly action. I like that from a Highland dram."

That got a snort out of him. "Lucky, I swear, you're the best son a man could have."

"As a card-carrying member of the boy's club, I'll take that as a compliment."

"As well you should." He cleared his throat after another sip. "You may be tough and know your way around, but there's folks tougher than you."

"No doubt." The lights of the Strip flashed below us, an ever-changing neon display that could be seen from the International Space Station, or so I'd been told. To me, they were magic, a tangible reminder of all that is Vegas—the fun, the food, the shows...the money. And where there was money, like blood-hounds on a scent, the bad guys lurked in the shadows. But I didn't linger on that—they weren't part of my Vegas. At least not until they started detonating bombs around town. "You gonna tell me about that note you got?"

Startled, he glanced at me out of the corner of his eye. "It's nothing. I can handle it."

"But it's upset you. I can help."

"Not this time." His tone held a subtle warning. I didn't care.

"When the shit really hits the fan, you can count on family. Isn't that what you tell me?" The stern set of his jaw told me I was being stonewalled, big time. I didn't like it. All it did was ramp up my worry-meter. "Mother—"

"Your mother and her hormones." My father bit off each word like a rabid dog tearing into a carcass. "She's seeing boogiemen in every corner."

"Boogiemen...an interesting word choice. And do I need to remind you that *you* wanted to talk to *me*?" I analyzed his profile as he turned to stare out the window again. Tension hunched his shoulders slightly, bunching the muscles underneath his jacket. The skin stretched tautly over his cheekbones, his mouth drawn into a thin line. His chin set at a defiant tilt, inviting someone to take a swing. Mona was right; something *was* going on. And being a man who solved his own problems, the Big Boss wasn't going to give it up. So like him. I'd have to outflank him somehow. "So, you think I should be scared of Boogie Fleischman?" I wiggled my glass, trying to work up an enthusiasm for a non-alcoholic beverage. It wasn't working. "Boogie's gotta be like, what...seventy?"

"Careful."

"Hey, he may be tougher than me, but I'm sure I can outrun him."

Out of the corner of my eye, I caught my father fighting with his smile. "Lucky, I swear..."

"Go right ahead if it feels good, but I'm too old to change." My arm circled his shoulders and I gave him a squeeze. "Okay, just for you, until this thing blows over, I'll check the women's bathroom before I sit down...for a meal."

"Small comfort." He handed his empty glass back to me. "I'm trying to give you a warning."

"Did anyone ever find Boogie's stash?"

"His stash?" I had my father's interest now.

"I'd been told that back in the day, the bomb makers all had hiding places for their...ingredients."

"That stuff'd be damn old by now." My father's eyes snapped to mine as realization dawned.

"Precisely." I lifted the glass with an eyebrow raised in question. "Another?" At his nod, I headed toward the bar but kept talking. "So did they find his stuff?"

"Not that I'm aware of, but I wasn't in that loop."

I almost snorted in disbelief but decided it wasn't consistent with my strong desire for self-preservation.

"Lucky, this just adds more weight to my warning."

"A warning. I heard you. But really, you know as well as I do, I couldn't do my job if I had to be afraid of every reprobate wishing to knock me down a peg. Truthfully, fear isn't my strong suit—I come by it naturally."

When I returned to his side, my father took his glass and sipped. He swished the scotch around his mouth before swallowing. "I'm trying to tell you this time is different. Boogie being back. The bomb. Just stirs up a bunch of old grudges—wrongs to be righted."

"Great, a bunch of old farts all tilting at windmills." I threw back the rest of my drink, then almost choked. I'd been prepared for whiskey, not fizzy water. "Just what we need for the Fourth of July."

"You really aren't going to take this seriously, are you?" My father sighed, a hint of frustration in his voice.

"Father, I was four when Boogie the Bomber got his balls busted. I can't imagine what beef he has with me. Besides, it's not me Boogie is after."

"Jimmy can handle himself."

"Not Jimmy." I waited until he turned to look at me. "There's someone else Boogie has a beef with, at least according to Jimmy."

"Who?"

"You."

"Me?" My father shot me a half-assed smirk. "Tell him to take a number."

"My point exactly."

AFTER MY FATHER LEFT, I LINGERED AT THE WINDOW, THIS TIME with a glass of Wild Turkey. Perhaps it was a delayed life-passing-before-my-eyes experience in the wake of a near-death experience, or maybe just the echoes of emptiness pinging off the walls of my heart, but demons assaulted me. And what was that whole weird thing with my father? Usually not one to beat around the bush, he'd left me with the feeling so much had been left unsaid—that I'd gotten only one piece of the whole picture. He expected me to read the subtext when he knew better than anyone that I was a big-print kind of gal.

So how did one protect themselves from unknown evils? Who knew? The whole thought left me curiously defeated. A Pollyanna to the last, I'd always lived each day, seized each moment. When had that changed? If I was honest with myself—not one of my best things—I'd probably have to say the whole down-in-the-mouth Lucky showed up when Teddie left. The fact that he had so much power over me should probably disgust me. But that's what happens when you give someone your heart, right?

Short on answers but long on questions, I succumbed to the bone-bending weariness washing through me. Tossing back the last of my drink—this time getting the anticipated high-octane hit —I put the empty glass on the bar, then headed toward the bedroom. While it was a nice place to sleep, it wasn't home. All my things were still packed away in the boxes stacked against the wall.

A metaphor for my life.

I wondered what I was waiting for.

∾

T‍HE F‍OURTH OF J‍ULY IN V‍EGAS—A GIANT CITYWIDE PARTY.

To be honest, it was my favorite holiday—even above New Year's Eve. Less structured, less controlled, the Fourth allowed for a bit more individual expression. All the major properties on the Strip participated. Some had private fireworks shows choreographed to a headliner concert. Some had public displays of pyrotechnic excess. All had pool parties with celebrity hosts. And for those of us riding herd on the whole thing, sleep would be at a premium.

Somehow, I was the first to arrive at the office. The ongoing construction in my new corner of this command center obviated the need for a lock and key. Anyone could step through the gaping hole that would someday be an appropriate private entrance—or so they promised, but I had my doubts. Flicking the lights on as I wandered into my old office space, I found myself still curiously wired even after only four hours of fitful shut-eye. Bucked with life, I stuffed my Birkin in a drawer, then locked it and pocketed the key.

Before I lost my nerve, and bracing for the always colorful greeting I knew would be forthcoming, I whisked off the cover on the large birdcage in the corner next to the picture window overlooking the lobby below.

Newton, my multicolored, foul-mouthed Macaw didn't disappoint. "Bitch! Slap you! Slap you bad!"

"Glad you remember me, Bird." I grabbed a slice of browned apple from the plate next to the cage and stuck it through the bars, taking care not to offer the bird any of my delicate flesh—he had a hard time discerning between the tasty and the tender.

After eyeing me, he slid warily across the bar toward the delicacy. With a "Fuck you," he snagged the morsel, then promptly retreated to the other side of the cage to savor it. At least my relationship with the bird was straightforward—I fed him, he tolerated me, sorta like a lot of marriages I'd witnessed. Maybe that explained my difficulty with commitment.

With the bird fed and mollified for the moment, I busied myself with coffee preparations—Don Francisco Vanilla Nut, my caffeine delivery vehicle of choice. Cupping my hands around the warm mug, I inhaled the aroma, then took my first tentative sip as I wandered into the war zone. After flipping on the light, I peeled back the plastic sheet protecting my desk and chair, and settled in.

I was still anticipating my second jolt of java when an angry male voice shattered my *joie de vivre*. "Lucky, you damn well better be in here!"

Coffee flew as I jumped at the shout. Thankfully, I managed to avoid staining my white shirt and slacks, but the papers on my desk took a direct hit. Grabbing a paint cloth, I dabbed at the liquid pool.

Xavier Sang, all five feet and a couple inches of wiry male, stuck his head through the doorway. "You and me, girl, we gotta chat."

With his straight hair dyed an unnatural shade of bright red and hanging across his forehead, the clean flat planes of his face unmarred by even the hint of a beard, his eyes dark and slanted to give him just the hint of exotic, Xavier looked more like a kid heading to UNLV than the master miracle worker he was. The latest in a long line of a very prominent Chinese family who made their fortune working magic with gunpowder, he was my big bang expert. I'd always wanted to ask him about his name— Xavier wasn't exactly a common choice for the Number One Son —but I'd never worked up the nerve to be that rude.

"Oh good," he remarked as he stepped over a paint can, then plopped down in a chair across from me—he didn't bother removing the tarp. "You really *are* here."

"Not yet fully caffeinated, that would be overstating." I dabbed at the last of the coffee-stained papers—something about a new fire ordinance in effect for the upcoming celebratory displays.

After the fire at the Monte Carlo, we'd had one heck of a time getting the county to once again allow fireworks from the rooftops.

Xavier steepled his fingers as he pressed them to his lips. "What's the other guy look like?"

"What?" I tossed the rag in a box that served as my trash bin.

When he lowered his hands, I could see his smile. "That's quite a shiner you've got. I hope you gave as good as you got."

"Have you ever known me not to?" I raised a finger, putting him on mute for a moment, and grabbed my now empty mug. My body squealed in protest as I pushed myself to my feet, but I ignored it. "I'll be right back. You want some?"

He shook his head. "I've already had enough to throw a lesser man into A-fib."

"No worries. I passed my last CPR course with flying colors... on the third try. I only broke a few ribs on the dummy." After refilling my cup and getting reestablished behind my desk, I took a sip, bracing myself to dive into the day. "Okay, what's got your knickers in a twist this morning?"

"You know how we carefully count and report all the major explosives we have?" He paused.

I guess he expected a response. "Yup."

"And you know how we're supposed to report anything that's missing?" Again a pause.

"Yup."

"Like to the ATF?"

This time I didn't wait for the prompt—I'm a quick study. "Yup. Can we get to the point?"

"Some big stuff has gone missing."

I set my mug down. "What?"

"I need to show you."

~

THE SUN WAS JUST HIGH ENOUGH TO BATHE THE ROOFTOP IN LIGHT, which was a good thing. Normally a minefield of knee-knockers, pipes, and electrical boxes, rooftop navigation was much less perilous in the daylight, especially now with all the mortar racks and wires as we busily prepared for the fireworks display tonight. Each individual tube would launch an aerial shell, some of them almost two feet in diameter, with precisely timed fuses. This year, the whole thing would be choreographed to the current hit by the Sewer Rats—the latest 'new, hot thing' and our entertainment option for the weekend. Xavier's team of experts scurried mounting shells, running wires, testing fuses. Precisely timed, intricately planned, tested, then retested, the show would be controlled from an electrical console that looked like the cockpit of a 747. Loudspeakers mounted on stalks behind the command center would pipe the music in so the operators could check the display timing. As I looked at the whole setup, all I could think of was if God had a sense of humor, all she had to do was get a wild hair and rain on my parade. Precip wasn't in the forecast, but this being July, a rogue monsoonal flow could strike at any time.

Woefully inadequate in the weather-control department, I abdicated responsibility for the weather. Simple mundane human problems were proving to be taxing enough as it was.

On the far side of the roof, an empty electrical shed had been converted into a secure housing for the pyrotechnics. The door hung on one hinge. The latch, with the lock still through it, was bent and mangled.

Bracing my hands on my hips and squinting my eyes against the assault of the summer sun, I surveyed the damage. "You didn't touch anything, did you?"

Xavier stood at my shoulder. "No, just poked my head inside."

"And the police and the ATF? Are they on their way?"

"Not yet."

Closing one eye, I tried to get a bead on him. "Why not?"

"We have a bit of a problem." He shifted from one foot to the other as he avoided my eyes.

"Lay it out. How big?"

"Class A." He ducked through the doorway and motioned me to follow.

I knelt next to him in the far corner. "You guys had Class A explosives up here? What the hell were you thinking?"

"The dynamite wasn't ours. I didn't even know the sticks were there until they were gone."

My voice stepped back from the edge of hysteria. "Dynamite."

"Old stuff, too." Xavier pointed to several dark spots on the concrete floor. "The nitro's leaking out pretty good."

"If you didn't know they were there, how'd you know they were gone?"

"One of my guys told me. And I thought about you being up close and personal with some similar stuff. Too much to be a coincidence." Xavier grabbed my arm and leaned in. "Find Frenchie Nixon. He'll rabbit once the Feds start sniffing around."

"Frenchie Nixon?" My voice rose an octave or two. "You hired that clepto?"

My bang man shrugged. "When it comes to rigging, he's the best in the business. Besides, he paid his debt to society. How was I to know he'd pinch some bang sticks and store them here?"

SOME DAYS IT JUST DIDN'T PAY TO BE ALIVE.

Today was shaping up to be one of them. I'd left Xavier to handle Romeo and the ATF guys, which wasn't all that nice considering the bang man had given me a head start.

Frenchie Nixon.

Under normal circumstances, that slimeball was someone I'd rather see through a long-range scope mounted on a rifle with my finger on the trigger and no witnesses. You see, Frenchie has a problem—he likes to steal stuff.

Our paths had crossed when I'd been head of housekeeping at one of the Big Boss's first properties downtown. Frenchie had been on the engineering staff. While he'd been a whiz at fixing stuff, he also had been really good at swiping it when we weren't looking. Televisions, radios, light fixtures, you name it. Even if it was nailed down or screwed into the studs in the wall, he'd take it. When he was caught, he had three or four huge storage units full of the stuff. And that was the real curious thing—he didn't take it to sell it. No, he took it to just have it.

But I knew he wasn't above unloading it when the heat was on.

And sitting on a cache of Class A explosives had to be a hot seat, especially in this day and age where folks saw terrorists under every rock. I'd just bet Frenchie was sweating bullets. In fact, I was banking on it.

Dane caught me striding across the lobby. "You have that look in your eye." He fell into step beside me.

"You mean bordering on the brink of homicide?"

He shot me a grin that lit his eyes. "Care to elaborate?"

"If you want to join me, I'll fill you in on the way."

"Not fair. You know I can't resist an invitation to a future crime."

The Ferrari was waiting at the curb, engine running, top down. The valet wiped away a drop of drool as he grinned and opened the driver-side door for me with a flourish. Men used to drool over me, now it was my car—I tried not to be bothered by that. Of course, I was well beyond wanting to turn the heads of nineteen-year-olds. At least that's what I told myself.

With several axes to grind, I stomped on the accelerator and squealed down the drive, then turned north on the Strip.

Dane had a white-knuckled grip on the handhold. "Feel better?"

"Not yet." I took a left on Sahara and tried not to look at the shuttered hotel by the same name. I guessed there were heydays for each of the properties, but I hated it when one had run its course and was relegated to a memory. Wheeling onto the north on-ramp to the 15, I let the horses run, savoring the hit of speed-induced adrenaline.

"If you weren't such an awesome gal, I'd still be tempted to hang with you just for your Italian iron."

I shot him a narrow-eyed look. "This is probably not the time to jerk my chain."

"It's the only time—you're unarmed."

Shielding my bruised ribs, I fought the laugh burbling up inside me. Losing the fight, I winced in anticipatory pain but relished the joy.

Life, a constant struggle to find the balance between happy and sad, good and bad. But heck, if it was easy, everybody would do it.

"You want to tell me where we're going?"

"Payless Pawn shop."

Dane swiveled to look at me. "Payless? Why would anyone take their junk to a place that advertises they pay less?"

"I'm guessing that, in an attempt to appeal to the retail side, they didn't consider the wholesale side. These guys aren't rocket scientists." The wind whistled past us bringing tears to my eyes. The engine behind my shoulders growled and vibrated, resonating through me. I smiled because I couldn't help myself.

"And why are we going to a pawn shop?" Dane still clutched the handhold, but he looked a bit more relaxed.

"I'm looking to score some dynamite."

CHAPTER FOUR

"*T*ODAY IS shaping up to be a real blast." Dane flashed me with a smile.

"If you can't do better than that I'll—"

"What?" His grin held a challenge.

I just smiled as I floored the accelerator, pressing us both back in our seats as we flew through the mousetrap, staying to the left and onto the 515 which would take us to the east side of town.

The Boulder Highway used to be the heavily trafficked main drag between Sin City and Boulder City, home to the Hoover Dam. Now the 515 Bypass to the east and the 215 to the south siphoned the traffic and the prosperity with it, relegating the Boulder Highway to has-been status. Home to smaller, local casinos, gun stores, dives, hotels that apparently took pride in their low hourly rates, and pawnshops, the whole area clung to the tattered memory of bygone riches—its hopes fading along with the aging-colored awnings bleached by the assault of the sun. That's not to say hope was completely gone—there were pockets of economic revitalization along this long stretch of asphalt. However, hunkered between a flophouse and bar called Balls to the Wall, which advertised in blinking neon an all-nude review, Payless Pawns wasn't in one of the sections on the upswing.

I eased the Ferrari into a tight space next to a couple of motor-cycles—the skull and crossbones insignias did little to inspire confidence. Today would have been a good day to stuff my Glock in my Birkin. I smiled at the incongruity—the Hermes hit woman. It had a ring to it. A career possibility if this casino exec thing went down the slop chute—and just one more way to shoot myself in the foot. Biting down on my weakness for punniness, I tried to channel 'tough' as I filed the idea away.

I may have missed the boat on the gun, but I'd brought the next best thing—Dane.

He unfolded himself from the car, then looked down at me as he eased the door shut with an appropriate reverence. "You always introduce me to the nicest places. First Smokin' Joe's and his XXX videos, then your mother and her girls, now the Balls to the Wall which, come to think of it…"

I burst out laughing.

He tried to ignore me. "If I didn't know better, I'd think you were trying to soften me up." His grin flared as he realized the setup he'd just handed me on a platter. He held up both hands. "Don't go there."

Then he dropped his head when I said, "If that was my goal, I'd say my choices were a bit misguided, wouldn't you?" Following his lead, I too unfolded myself, then shut the door behind me. Putting the top up would be asking for someone to slit it, so I didn't bother. "After all, you guys have the hard part."

Looking up, he shot me a grin. "Do you ever do as you're asked?"

"I have authority issues, deal with it."

"I'm trying." He squinted an eye shut as he glanced around. "I can't decide whether to come inside to protect you, or stay out here and protect the car."

"The car, for sure." Somehow I kept the grin off my face and out of my voice. "You'll get more pleasure out of it in the long run."

"Probably true." His lust thinly disguised, his eyes raked the car then returned to mine. "Seriously, how do you want to play this?"

"Give me five minutes. I'll go in alone. Frenchie Nixon's sister owns this place. Last I heard, Frenchie still runs home when he finds his ass in a crack, and this is all the family he's got."

"I won't even ask what you want with someone named Frenchie. I hope I get points for that." His eyes flicked over my shoulder—a habit of my ever-watchful, former Army MP. "And after five minutes?"

"You'll get to do your whole Texas chivalry, saving-damsels-in-distress thing."

"I'm a little rusty." He didn't like the idea—I could see that—but he always was good about letting me hang myself.

"A knight in rusty armor—*now* you tell me." I pressed my nose to the storefront window but couldn't see anything through cracks in the mirrored film.

Four latches, each with a heavy-duty padlock hanging from it, had been opened and folded back from the door. Four? The necessity that required all the locks, plus the bars on the windows did little to inspire confidence. I took a steadying breath and hoped my black eye gave me a hint of badass. With more bravado than I felt, I threw my shoulders back and pushed through the single glass door. A bell dinged somewhere in the dark recesses.

After the bright sunlight, the interior murkiness was impenetrable. As the door closed behind me shutting out the sun, I paused allowing my eyes to adjust. Only three of the canned lights in the ceiling had working bulbs, which cast thin, milky light. Smoke and the acrid tang of desperation hung in the air.

Finally, light filtered in and images hit my retinas. Musical instruments hung from the ceiling. A nice maroon Harley Springer Softail sat in the middle of the floor. A knight in full armor kept watch in the corner. Power tools hung from hooks forming an intricate pattern against peeling, puke green paint on the walls. A phalanx of bicycles stood in rows to my left. High in each corner, video cameras, their red recording lights staring like Gargoyles' eyes, captured my every move. Glassed cases filled with the high-end stuff formed a barrier in front of the back wall, protecting the lone entrance to a section marked 'private.' Snippets of a laugh track from some television show filtered through the closed door.

"Hello?" My voice, not exactly as strong as I wanted, was swallowed in the depths. I cleared my throat and tried again. "Anybody home?"

This time, the swinging door moved inward a few inches, just far enough to allow a side-by-side barrel to poke through, the business end pointed at my chest.

"Go away."

I recognized the voice, husky from decades of unfiltered Camels. "Gracie? You know why I'm here."

"He ain't here."

"Then he ain't far." I tried to look mean as I stared into the dark, evil holes of the shotgun. "He's probably next door drinking himself into the next life. But I know when he's in a heap of trouble, he hides in your skirts. And this time, Frenchie's brought trouble with a capital 'T' to your doorstep."

She lowered the gun and eased through the door. After breaking the gun, she held it over her forearm. The shells didn't eject, so she could slap the thing closed and be locked and loaded in a jiffy. Not a happy thought, being on the receiving end and all.

A tough woman forged in the fire of a hard life, Gracie was small and thin to the point of painful, with gray hair that hung in greasy waves down past her shoulders. Her face, long with hollowed cheeks, held deep-set, lifeless eyes and the slash of a mouth defined by thin lips. A few faded tattoos decorated her creped skin beneath the short, tattered sleeves of her white shirt, now yellowed with age. "I know his story. What's yours?"

"Your brother pinched some dynamite. I need it. And it would go a long way toward lowering the heat if he could tell me where he got it. I can tell you that, after a good grilling, the ATF guys will want to fry his ass. Probably yours, too," I bluffed. "I need something to douse the flame."

"He don't have no dynamite. He's just got himself a blistering headache, nothing's put a dent in it. I'm thinkin' maybe he's got a tumor or something."

"Or a nitro headache."

She shook her head. "Yeah, that boy ain't smart enough to hide from hillbillies. No way would he have thought to use rubber gloves when handling..." Her eyes grew wide when she realized what she'd said. Finally, after a moment of vacillation during which I held my breath, her face fell, laying bare the soft spot she had for her brother.

I went for the kill. "They'll throw him down a hole, Gracie, then bury him."

"Hell, his ass is a grape anyway. Might as well talk to you. Can't hurt him none. That boy's gone and done it now." She fingered a cross hanging from a gold chain around her neck. "He means well, know what I mean?"

Unclear as to how his proclivity for the ten-finger discount supported that statement, I said nothing.

She stopped fiddling and slapped me with a stern look. "You can help him?"

"I'm the only friend in his corner. I'll do what I can, but he's got to help himself first."

With one quick jerk, she flipped the shotgun closed. For a fraction of a second, I thought she'd use it on me. Instead, she leaned it against the wall. As she ran her finger around the barrel holes, she thought for a moment. Then she gave me a half-grin that lifted one corner of her lips exposing stained teeth. "Pretty tough, aren't you? You didn't flinch." Then she turned and shouted over her shoulder. "Frenchie, get your ass out here."

I thought about telling her there was a fine line between tough and stupid, but I didn't want to undermine my illusion of badass —it might still come in handy.

Just as Frenchie pushed through the back door, biting off the corner of a Pop-Tart, Dane walked in through the front, letting squint-inducing sunlight in with him. Apparently Dane was a bit more clever than I gave him credit for as he took stock of the situation with one glance. Then, he pretended not to know me as he sauntered over to the Harley. Gracie stepped around the counter to help him, leaving me alone with her brother.

An androgynous carbon copy of his sister, Frenchie sported the same painful thinness, the same long, stringy hair, the same tats. But instead of Gracie's closed, wary look, Frenchie's face was open, approachable—childlike in a way. And while his sister decorated herself with a shotgun, Frenchie wore a simple tool belt slung low on his hips with screwdrivers, vice grips, and wrenches hanging from the loops—ready to fix or filch.

"Hey, Ms. O'Toole." His eyes, clear and blue, met mine. If he was scared, he had me fooled. "You wanna sit? Look's like life's slapped you around a bit." With one hand, he lifted a stool from behind the counter and handed it to me as he bit off another bite of the Pop-Tart, which looked like a strawberry one. My stomach growled—I'm a slave to the siren call of food.

Grateful, I shot him a smile as I took a load off. Behind me, Dane peppered Gracie with questions about the motorcycle, keeping her occupied. "Heard you got a bit of a headache."

His expression turned quizzical. "Yeah, a real pounder. Been poppin' Aspirin like it's Blue Bennies, ya' know?"

Thankfully, I didn't know, and I don't think it mattered. "Caffeine."

"No shit?" He looked doubtful.

"Caffeine is a vaso-constrictor. It counteracts the dilating effects of the nitro."

"Well, I'll be damned." Frenchie set the remaining bit of his pastry on the filthy counter making me cringe, then turned to push through the door to the back. "Hang on a sec. We got a fresh pot on the burner. Want some?"

I shook my head. When he returned with both hands gripping the mug as if it were a lifeline, I started in again. "Tell me about the dynamite. Short and sweet, okay?"

"Me and Flea were wampin' around the desert north of here, out the 95, messing in some of the old mines and stuff." Flea was the leader of the motorcycle gang that had taken Frenchie in, probably as a pet or mascot. He didn't have enough macho to scare anyone, so what use would he be to the gang? I had no idea. Amusement? I looked at him as he snagged the remaining bit of Pop-Tart, polished it off, then licked his fingers one at a time. If he was their amusement, they were desperate.

"We found a crate of the sticks in one of them," Frenchie continued after swallowing, wiping his hands on his jeans.

"Anything else?"

He gave me a quizzical look. "Nothin' of any value."

"Why don't you let me be the judge of that? One man's trash, another man's treasure." I glanced around the pawnshop. "You should know that better than anybody."

"Okay, there were some old clocks. You know, those wind up things that you can't even get rid of at the flea market?"

I nodded. "Anything else?"

"Some little tubes filled with some silver liquid, blasting caps, an old briefcase with some papers in it...nothing important."

"What did the papers say?"

Frenchie shrugged. "Impossible to tell—they'd pretty much fallen apart."

"So all of this was pretty old stuff?"

"Yeah, the dynamite was leakin' like a sieve." He snorted. "Not worth much. I thought I'd scored big when this suit offered me a couple of c-notes for three sticks."

"Three?"

"Yeah. The guy was a nutcase, all twitchy-like. And stupid. Those sticks didn't have much pop left in them. Hell, half the nitro had soaked into the wood."

My heart fell. Three. I knew what had happened to two. It was anybody's guess where the third one would turn up. "Oh, those sticks still delivered."

Frenchie's eyes widened. "No shit?"

"Pretty much leveled Jimmy G's place."

Frenchie blinked rapidly as he tried to absorb that. "Anybody hurt?"

"Only me."

He backed up a step. "Shit, I'm sorry, man. I thought I was sellin' that dude a dud, know what I mean?" Wrapping himself in a hug, he started shaking. "I never thought..."

"The guy you sold the stuff to, have you seen him around before?"

"No. He had that out-of-town look to him—three-piece suit, five bill shoes."

"Can you describe him?"

Frenchie stopped shaking as his eyebrows snapped into a thoughtful frown. "A thin, white guy, tallish like you. Dark hair. Mean eyes. And always looking down his nose—talking down like I'm trash, you know?" Frenchie's eyes met mine. "I didn't like that, so I charged him double what I woulda took. Fool paid it."

"A man on a mission." I eased off the stool. "How old?"

"Like you."

I didn't want to ask him what age he thought that might be— I'd established the guy wasn't seventy, so he wasn't Boogie. "How'd he find you?"

"It was real weird, you know? He was out on the highway. Goin' for a drive, he said. He flagged us down when he saw us comin' out of the mine."

"Really? What'd he say?"

"He said some of his folks way back when had been miners in

the area. He wanted to know if we'd found anything. We'd already stashed the sticks on the four-wheeler, so we didn't give out. We don't go givin' without gettin', you know? Besides, we didn't know this guy and he looked like trouble, all mean and angry-like."

"I see." I pursed my lips and tried not to act surprised. "So how'd the same guy end up with the sticks? You're sure he was the same guy?"

"I'm gettin' to that part." Frenchie nervously picked at a scab on his arm. "Here's the creepy part. The guy shows up later that day at the shop looking for me."

"The shop? You mean here?" At Frenchie's nod I asked, "How'd he know your name and where you worked?"

"He said he read it off my work shirt I had on when we met him on the highway. The shirt with my name on the front and the pawnshop info in big red letters on the back. My sister about shit when she heard I was wearing it out in the desert—those things ain't cheap."

"Apparently he didn't believe your story about not finding anything."

Frenchie's eyes flicked to mine. Thankfully he stopped picking at that scab. "The guy flashed a wad and I got greedy, told him what we had. His eyes really lit when he heard about the sticks. He wanted it then, but I didn't have it."

"No, you'd conveniently stashed it on the top of my hotel. I should break you in two for that."

He paled then hung his head with a sigh. "Probably should. Anyway, I had to get to work and it was convenient. With all the other stuff up there I didn't think anyone would notice. I agreed to meet the guy the next day, yesterday morning, to complete the sale. The rest is history."

"Did he take anything else?"

"Couple of clocks and the liquid things. I gave it all to him in the briefcase." Frenchie rubbed his arms as if he was suddenly chilled. "Funny thing though, the guy, the way he looked at me after we did the transaction, you know...it gave me a real bad feelin'."

Yeah, unfortunately I did know. If the guy had anything to do with Boogie Fleischman, then Frenchie and Flea were lucky they'd run into him out in the open, on a well-traveled highway and again in a public place. "Look, I'll do my best to lower the heat on you, but I need you to do a few things in return."

"Just say the word."

"I need all the dynamite you've got left, and then I want you and your friends to try to track down the dude you sold the stuff to. If you find him, don't kill him. Bring him to me. Promise me."

"You got my word." He banged his chest with a closed fist— some sort of secret salute or something, I figured. I thought he might break a rib. Then he pushed through the doorway to the back. A few moments later he returned with a weathered wooden crate, which he thrust at me. "This is all of it."

Carefully, I grabbed it and looked inside. The wooden box held nine sticks, paper tubes really, each oozing a dark, gooey substance. Old and unstable. Great. I gave Frenchie the sternest look I could muster. "This is serious shit. You swear this is all there is? Your friend, Flea, he didn't take any?"

He shook his head. "Swear."

"And there's no more of this stuff on top of my hotel?"

"Promise."

Dane and Gracie's conversation was winding down behind me. I felt sure that, after we left, she'd have to wipe his drool off the bike. "Why'd you break the lock on the shed?"

"Work was crazy. By the time we knocked off, someone had buttoned-up the joint. I broke the lock and took my property. When I was offsite and out of reach, I called Xavier."

"You don't happen to know anything about the guy who bought the stuff besides what he looks like, do you? Like his name? Where he's from? What kind of car he was driving?"

"Don't know any of the particulars, but he was sportin' a hot piece of iron, just like the one you got out there." Frenchie nodded toward the parking lot out front.

It was my turn to be surprised. "A Ferrari?"

"Yeah, local plates and a Babylon emblem."

"You mean he was driving one of *our* Ferraris?"

~

"DID YOU JUST OFFER THAT WOMAN A NIGHT WITH ME IN EXCHANGE for the Harley?" Dane asked me as I carefully lowered the crate into the space behind the seats.

We both settled into the car and belted up. I punched the start button and the engine growled to life. "I wanted to know what it would be like on the other end of that kind of transaction for once." I grinned at him with more humor than I felt. "I almost had a deal, too."

"You think you're cute, don't you?" Dane tried to act angry but he couldn't pull it off.

"No, just having fun at someone else's expense. Not a particularly proud moment." I eased the Ferrari into traffic, this time at a much more sedate pace. "You wouldn't happen to know anything about the decomposition of dynamite, would you?"

"You were serious? You weren't just jerking my chain when I asked why we were headed to a cheap shop on the wrong side of town?" Dane's eyes widened, letting in a bit of light, apparently. "Don't tell me that's what's in the box."

Keeping my eyes on the road, I nodded. Besides, I didn't have to look at him to know he rolled his eyes and then glowered at me. He unfastened himself and squirmed around to take a look, then he repositioned himself. "You got a big problem."

"I have many, could you be more specific?"

"That's really old stuff. Probably made sometime in the late fifties, early sixties before they switched to ammonium nitrate."

"I know that much," I said in my 'brave' voice. "And all those

Westerns I watched as a kid where they blew everything to kingdom come with the stuff. And that bit about one jolt setting it off? That was Hollywood, right?" I accelerated onto the 515.

"Not really. This stuff is prone to unplanned explosions." Dane's voice got all quiet and serious. "I've heard of this stuff blowing when the sun hit it."

One glance told me was serious. Careful to avoid any jarring, I quickly downshifted, decelerating to make the next exit, Flamingo Road. "Change in plans. Call AFT. Have them meet us in the parking lot at Sam Boyd Stadium. If we blow, I don't want to take anyone else with us."

"If we go," Dane said as he grabbed his cell and started dialing, "it'd be a real waste—this car is a work of art."

Dane and I had just circled the wagons in the vast lots surrounding the stadium at a point that I thought was the furthest from human life, when the bomb squad rolled in sirens blazing. I let Dane give them the skinny as I found a curb to sit on, well away from the car. The fact that we were very close to the site of a rocket fuel plant that had exploded, leveling a huge area of Henderson surrounding it, was sort of ironic. I hoped it wasn't an omen. I grabbed my phone and began making calls.

THE DAY HAD EXPIRED, BUT THANKFULLY NO ONE ELSE HAD. Defusing the nitro situation had taken far longer than I'd imagined. Of course, not only did we have Metro to deal with, we also had the Feds. Despite the widely held opinion that most branches of the government were masters at making big goddammits out of hangnails, the ATF was anything but. They dealt with serious shit and a bomb really lit their fuse. Using a crane, they'd lifted the box of dynamite, then burned it in a far corner of the parking lot far away from humans. The whole thing would've been fun to watch, except one missing stick of volatile dynamite kept my feet to the fire, prodding me to action. Time was slipping away.

Firmly in the clutches of nightfall, Dane and I motored back to the Babylon. With no threat of immediate immolation, I once again let the horses run. This time, Dane didn't feel the need to hang on. Tonight, the lights of the Strip didn't hold their normal magic for me. Instead, they reminded me how hard it would be to find a dynamite needle in this huge haystack. Clearly I needed to narrow my search.

Bert, my Ferrari man, was waiting for me in the dealership when I returned the car. "Lucky, I'm sorry I wasn't here when you called. I'm working the late shift tonight—in fact, I just punched in. When I'm off, I turn the cell off. I work hard, but they don't own me."

"Clearly I'm not as adept as you at establishing boundaries." I admired a new, shiny red car turning on the dais under a lone spotlight. "The new California?"

"Sweet machine. You'd look fine wearing one."

"Nice try." I wandered over to the car, running my finger run down the hood as I admired the new lines—a compact departure from the normal Ferrari. "Did they tell you what I wanted?"

"Yeah, something about the name of a guy who had one of our cars yesterday." He pulled a white envelope out of his back pocket and extended it to me. "We had six cars out, all rented by males. I pulled the list for you."

The list was short, names and addresses, not much else. "This really doesn't help." I bit my lip as I looked inside the California and tried to think. "I need some way of narrowing the list down."

"Tell me what you know."

I gave him Frenchie's description of the dynamite buyer.

Bert blew out some air. "I could ask around, see who might've rented a car to a guy looking like that, but it could take awhile."

"Time isn't something I have a lot of." I hoped he didn't ask me why. I didn't want to elaborate—nothing like a potential explosion to create a panic— and I didn't want to lie.

"You don't happen to know where the car went, do you?"

I stopped ogling the California, turning my attention to Bert. "I have an address. Why?"

"Give it to me." Bert didn't wait. Instead, he stepped behind the counter and logged into the store computer as his mouth kept motoring. "I don't need to tell you how much dough we've got tied-up in these cars. If one went missing, well, insurance would give us a huge hassle. It would be better to recover the car." He looked up at me expectantly, a twinkle in his eye. "So we put GPS trackers in all of them."

I punched up Jimmy G's place on my phone, highlighted the address, then handed it to Bert. "Try this one first. I have another route he took out the 95 toward Tonopah."

"We'll overlay the address with the tracking system." He bent his head in concentration.

On the theory that the whole watched-pot-not-boiling thing was true, I resisted leaning over his shoulder as he worked. Instead, I turned my back. Putting my elbows on the counter behind me, I surveyed all the toys in the dealership. Nervous glances at the clock on the far wall marked the glacial passage of time.

Ten minutes had passed and my nerves were jumping when Bert said, "Bingo."

I whirled around in time to see him circle a name on his list.

"Here's the guy."

"Albert Campos. Does he still have the car? Can we see where he is now?"

Bert checked his records. "No, he turned the car back in yesterday."

I knew that was asking too much. "Anything you *can* tell me?"

Bert fell to work once again, his fingers flying over the keyboard. When he stopped, his eyes widened.

"What?"

He turned the monitor to face me. I leaned in to read where he pointed. I read it twice, then looked up. "You sure?"

"Yup." Bert said. "Your Mr. Campos was personally recommended by the Big Boss."

STILL REELING, MY LIFE ON TILT, I PAUSED IN THE LOBBY TRYING TO regain balance by absorbing some of the normal flow of nightlife in Vegas. Social creatures being primarily nocturnal, nightfall heralded an increase in activity. Tonight was no exception. Couples and herds of momentarily unattached hipsters, spiffed for the evening in their five-hundred-dollar jeans with holes in them, gathered in clusters or strolled. Five hundred bucks for something I used to make with a pair of Wranglers, a shotgun, and a washing machine.

Casual observers eyeing potential attachments, or the already attached clutching each other in a show of ownership, they all not only partook of the magic of the Babylon, but helped create our aura of coolness as well, a perfectly symbiotic relationship. And it seemed to be working.

Except for one strident note. Several teams of beefy guys checking every nook and cranny caught my eye, dispelling some of my elixir of self-satisfaction. They were *so* inconspicuous in their tight t-shirts with ATF printed in six-inch letters across the back and holding onto their bomb-sniffing German Shepherds. It wasn't going to be pretty once the Big Boss got wind of it, but there wasn't much I could do. Self-preservation dictated a flak jacket but Kevlar just wasn't part of my fashion-forward style.

Thankfully, nobody seemed too alarmed, if they even noticed the sniffers at all. One bullet dodged.

Registration was not particularly crowded—most folks coming in town for the Fourth already had arrived. Stepping to the counter, I caught the eye of Sergio Fabiano, our front desk manager, and motioned him over.

A trim man, dark and swarthy, with chiseled features and a body like those immortalized in marble by ancient Italian sculptors, Sergio attracted female attention wherever he went. If he considered it a burden, he shouldered it well. His dark hair, long and straight, obviously tickled his eyes as he kept flipping it—a habit I found a bit irritating. After finishing with the couple he had been dealing with, he moved down the counter stopping in front of me. "Ms. O'Toole, how are you this evening?" His brows creased into a slight frown. "Raw steak or cold cucumber will help that eye."

"Thanks, but I'm a moving target—ducking and weaving—no time for home remedies. But you can help me with something else."

"Your wish." He shot me a grin—how I wished it was infectious.

"Do we have a guest by the name of Albert Campos registered here this weekend?"

"One moment." He bent his head and began scrolling through screens in the hotel reservation system. He pursed his lips as he worked. Before he looked up, I knew the answer. "It doesn't appear there is an Albert Campos staying with us. I'm sorry."

"Not nearly as sorry as I am." I tapped the counter as I let my eyes wander over the crowd's reflection in the large mirrors behind the desk. "Thanks anyway."

"By the way, I love your song." Sergio clasped his hands, his eyes bright. "So romantic."

My eyes snapped back to his. "What?"

"*Lucky for Me*. Teddie is so talented—I never knew." My employee gave me a warm look. "And he must love you so. You are a lucky woman, Ms. O'Toole."

"How do you know about that song?"

Sergio looked at me like I'd crawled out from under a rock,

which apparently wasn't far from the truth. "Honey, everybody knows about that song. Teddie's been on every talk show in the Western Hemisphere. The world does love a love story. That tune is riding up the charts with a bullet."

A bullet. I could think of one tight-assed little songbird I'd like to shoot with that bullet.

Sergio's smile faded when his eyes met mine. "This song is not a good thing?"

"Nothing I hate more than a private drama on a public stage."

FLASH'S CALL CAUGHT ME STANDING IN THE MIDDLE OF THE LOBBY unsure who to kill first. "I hope you got something."

"Hell, I wouldn't be calling if I didn't." Flash didn't sound all that happy. "But don't get all woozy on me, I'm still just tickling leads. I've got a bunch of rumors, but nothing solid…yet."

"Give me what you got." I closed my eyes and took a deep breath, squelching homicidal urges. Sticking one finger in my open ear, I pressed the phone tightly to the other, focusing on her voice. The noise of the lobby faded away. Too bad the silence amplified the hurt in my heart. And the noise in my head.

"Well, I went back through all the police reports surrounding the first bombing at Jimmy G's."

"How'd you get those?"

"One of the detectives I used to hook up with back when I was young and stupid. I knew some stuff, so I did what I always do —blackmail."

"Nice."

"Some guys just got it comin'. Know what I mean?"

My eyes flew open. "*You* were the one bangin' Crayfish Crider!" My voice was louder than I intended. When I saw some people look my direction, I tried to modulate myself, but I lack a revulsion-squelch knob. "Why didn't you tell me he was into cock stuffing? What the hell is that, anyway?" Now I had the attention of most of the folks in the lobby. I headed toward the casino, seeking privacy under the cover of noise.

Flash didn't say anything for a moment. "How'd you know about that?" She actually sounded pained—a first.

"Serendipity. It's not common knowledge, so don't go Googling hara-kiri."

"Hell, I wouldn't go sticking a blade in *my* stomach. But if Crider is crowing about private matters, I'd be more than happy to start carvin' off some of his parts." There wasn't even a hint of shame in her voice.

I needed some of that moxie. "More on that later. Don't think I'm letting you off without getting the whole story. But back to the police reports, you were going to tell me something?"

"Right." She picked up steam again. "Anyway, two interesting tidbits. All the way to the slammer, Boogie claimed he was setup, that he didn't place that bomb."

"The timing was a bit off, really." I thought back. "The stuff between the Union and the holdouts had sorted itself out by then."

"Exactly," Flash agreed. "And if you think about it, with his rep, Boogie was the perfect scapegoat."

I ducked into a far corner of the casino, hopefully away from eavesdroppers. "Convicted because everyone knew he was guilty of something—maybe not the bombing at hand. Okay, assuming that's true, who planted the original bomb?"

"That's where the trail goes cold. Boogie turned into a clam. Just from reading the reports, I got the feeling he was taking the fall for someone."

"Who?"

Silence.

"Okay." I filed it away as something to hit the Big Boss over the head with. Either him or Jimmy—one of them had to know. "Anything else?"

"Yeah, it's about your father and it supports Boogie's position."

"Really? How so?"

"Your father told the police he got a call as he was on his way to the restaurant to meet you and your mother. Someone claiming they worked at the hotel—he didn't say which property, but I can get that for you—called and said he was needed, that there was an emergency. He said he knew the person who called by name but would not have recognized the voice."

"So he was deliberately called off?" To be honest, I was glad to hear that. It was far better than being left with the thought he stood us up. I don't know why it mattered after all this time, but it did.

"That's what he told the police."

"Was there really an emergency?"

"Not one that hit the papers."

"And it was a woman who called him?"

"Ah, you *were* listening." Flash laughed, her voice returning to her normal bantering tone. "What do you think?"

"I think it's time to have a father–daughter chat."

MY MOOD WAS HEADING SOUTH. THE WOUND IN MY FOREHEAD starting to throb when the private elevator deposited me in the middle of the Big Boss's living room. A huge expanse of hardwood floors, leather-covered walls, hand-knotted silk rugs, and furniture fashioned with exotic woods and the hides of African animals, this apartment had been the closest thing I had to a place I called home—except for a whorehouse in Pahrump called Mona's, which really didn't count. The Big Boss and I had broken bread countless times, with me none the wiser at the secret he kept—he hadn't told me he was my father until recently...when he thought he might die. Apparently the man was pretty adept at harboring secrets.

With the overhead lights off, the only light to hold back the

DEBORAH COONTS

darkness shone from the pinpoint lights illuminating the artwork on the walls—lesser works by the Grand Masters—and the lights of the Strip filtering in through the wall of floor-to-ceiling windows.

A figure silhouetted against the window turned as I strode further into the room. Not the Big Boss.

Mona.

"Lucky!" Worry nagged at the edges of her voice. "Just the person I wanted to see."

I hurried toward her, propelled by the worry in her tone. "Mother. Are you okay?"

She motioned to a small side table. "I'm trying to read this note. I need your help."

I leaned over it and squinted in the half-light. "This has been burned."

"I *know* that." Mona sighed as if barely able to shoulder the burden of having a stupid child. "That's why I'm having trouble reading it."

"Where did you get it?" I kept my voice even—Mona was *not* going to get under my skin. Not today, anyway. I needed to focus.

"I found it smoldering in that moveable fire pit thing your father has." When she looked at me, her eyes had that deer-caught-in-the-headlight look to them. "I think it's the note he got the other day."

"Really?" This time I looked at it more closely. The sheet was almost intact—only one corner was missing. "Bring me a spray bottle, some water, and some glycerin."

"Glycerin?" Mona tried to frown, but her brows wouldn't move.

"Check the medicine cabinet. A lot of treatments for constipation use glycerin. Maybe we'll get lucky."

Without a further question, she charged off across the room.

"If the Big Boss gets wind of this, our collective asses are grapes," I called after her, knowing she'd ignore my feeble attempt at humor. At least I amused myself.

"I'm not really worried about that right now," Mona said as she disappeared into the hallway leading to the private rooms. "Besides, that man is putty in my hands." She tossed off the line with bravado that had a hollow ring to it.

Mother never did have a firm grip on reality, but now was not the time to point it out. Besides, she'd just argue. I tried to make out the writing as I waited, but it just looked like dark squiggles, tightly woven on the crinkled paper.

Amazingly, Mona was back in a flash and with the items I'd requested. "What are you going to do with this stuff?"

I busied myself combining the water and glycerin in the spray bottle, then tightening the cap. As I shook it to combine the contents, at least briefly—water and oil weren't known to stick together long—I glanced at her. "You know all those notes from admirers you used to burn in that barrel behind the house?"

Mona gave me a narrow-eyed look. "You didn't."

"It was Miranda's idea, actually." Miranda, once my closest friend, had gone on to a stellar porn career and now made boat-loads by producing the trash. Just thinking about it made me sad. "We were just kids. It was something she saw on that TV show, *MacGyver*. We tried it. It worked."

Mona stepped back as I began spraying the paper with the mixture. "And you've been using it ever since."

"I'm a woman of many talents." After wetting the ashes, I care-fully tried to smooth out the paper. In theory, the water made it easier to flatten and the oil held it together. "Turn on that lamp." I nodded my head toward a reading lamp bending over the back of the couch.

Mona scurried to do as I asked, then stepped out of the way. Carefully, I eased the now flat paper off the table, holding it up. Amazingly, it stayed together. Holding it up to the light, I worked to make out the writing. The ink or pencil lead, whichever, was not soluble, so it would stay dark.

Unfortunately, I could only make out a few words. "It looks like a name," I said, thinking out loud.

"What is it?"

Chewing my lip, I narrowed my eyes and concentrated through the headache pain. "Eugenia, I think." I rested my eyes then looked again. "Yes, Eugenia. Eugenia Somebody. I can't read the last name. And something about a... " I lowered the paper and looked at Mona.

She paled and sank to the couch, a hand clutched to her chest. "Oh my."

Alarmed, I paused in my reading—it took a direct hit to rock Mona back on her heels. "Are you okay?"

She nodded, then appeared to regain composure. "Keep reading. Something about a what?"

"A child."

"A child," Mona whispered, her face ashen as she sunk further into the couch.

I lowered the paper and sat next to her. "What is it?" I grabbed her hand. It was cold and clammy.

With a trembling hand, she brushed at a tendril of hair that had escaped and now tickled her eyes. "I need to talk to your father."

"Okay." Unable to think of anything that would help, I patted her hand. "Where is he?"

When she looked at me, she didn't try to hide the fear in her eyes. "That's the problem. Your father has disappeared."

CHAPTER FIVE

*B*ACK IN my office, I rallied the troops. Miss P, Romeo, Flash, Brandy, and Dane perched expectantly on the meager furnishings, all of us gathered around Mona. Jimmy G leaned against the wall in the corner.

"Where's Jeremy?" I directed the question at Miss P.

"On his way. He said he had to pick up a package first."

The question quieted the group.

Jerry, our head of security, poked his head in through the makeshift doorway, then stepped inside. He took the other arm on the chair holding Dane. At my glance, he shook his head. "The Big Boss is not on the property."

"His cars?"

"He took Matilda." Matilda was his beloved fire-engine red Bentley.

I started to tell Romeo to put out an all-points bulletin, but the kid was a step ahead, speaking quietly into his phone.

I glanced around the group. Everyone waited expectantly. Even Mona sat quietly, looking as worried as I felt. "Okay." Pressing my palms to the top of the desk, I leaned forward. "Mother, the floor is yours. Give us everything you know."

She worried with the end of a peach scarf tied jauntily around her neck. "Your father…" Her eyes held mine, seeking comfort. I gave her a warm smile. "He hasn't been himself since he got that letter. It dredged up a lot of very old memories. All the way back to when he was a young man on the town, before he met me."

"Who was Eugenia?"

A gasp of surprise escaped Jimmy, and Mona gave him a look I couldn't quite read. "Eugenia Campos?" he whispered like he was summoning a ghost.

Mona gave him a curt nod that had 'shut up' as the subtext— even I caught that.

"Eugenia *Campos*?" I asked anyway. "That last name sure rings a bell."

"Let me continue," Mona said, not even trying to hide her exasperation. "She was a cigarette girl at the International," Mona explained. "Young, beautiful, the 'complete package' the men used to say. And she had a nose for money."

"And a knack for extortion," Jimmy G added, his voice flat and hard.

"You knew her?" I asked him.

"We all passed her around." His eyes skittered from mine. He looked uneasy as he stared at the floor.

"Passed her around?" My voice was as cold as the meat locker in the basement.

Finally, he took a deep breath. When his eyes met mine, they held. "Yeah, we each took our turn with her, until she met your father."

I leaned back. Surveying the group, I couldn't shake the feeling I was about to learn something I didn't want to know. "And then…?"

"They coupled up pretty good." Jimmy glanced at Mona.

She delivered the punch line. "Until he met me."

"You broke them up?" I asked.

Mona looked uncomfortable. Jimmy came to her rescue. "It

186

wasn't like that. Your mother didn't really know. But once Albert caught sight of Mona, he was done. There hasn't been anyone else for him since."

"How did Eugenia take all of this?"

"Not well," Mona said, eliciting a whistle from Jimmy G.

"That's an understatement. She threw a holy shit fit." Jimmy ignored Mona's pleading look and forged ahead. "Threatened all kinds of things. Made your father pretty hot under the collar, I can tell you that. He was just a punk starting out. She coulda derailed him big time."

A cold dread bloomed in the pit of my stomach. "I see. Did she happen to be pregnant?"

"Oh, she claimed she was. But it was an act of desperation, we all thought so."

"So nobody believed her?" I looked at both Mona and Jimmy G. They glanced at each other and shrugged. "Sorta coincidental we're dealing with a bomber named Albert Campos, isn't it? And Albert? Interesting choice for a first name, don't you think?"

"That doesn't mean the Big Boss is his father," Jimmy pointed out.

"No. But that's easy enough to prove. And it certainly indicates young Albert's mother thought so, or wanted us to think so, anyway. What happened to Ms. Campos?"

"She left town," Jimmy stated.

"Anybody know where she went?" I glanced between the two of them. "Did anyone hear from her after the fact?"

Silence.

I fixed Mother with my best stare. "I need an honest answer here."

"Honey, believe me. I wish I could tell you someone did." From the panic in her eyes, I could tell Mona and I were reading from the same page. "But as far as I know, she just disappeared."

"There seems to be an epidemic of that going around, doesn't there?"

Jimmy gave me a lopsided grin. "Hey, it's Vegas."

I didn't think he was funny.

All sound seemed to be chewed up in the gristmill of overactive imaginations, leaving an uncomfortable silence. Vegas lore was replete with stories of 'disappearances', of finding bleached bones in the desert decades later. What if the Big Boss... No. Not possible. A cool draft, as if a ghost whispered in my ear, sent chills racing through me. I didn't like it—in fact, I didn't like any of this.

"Anybody have any ideas?" Uncomfortable with my own thoughts, I threw out the question.

Seven sets of eyes stared at me.

No ideas. No plan. The Big Boss had disappeared. And his self-proclaimed son wandered Vegas with a stick of dynamite, the knowledge necessary to put it to use, and an axe to grind. Silence echoed as I presumed we all pondered the imponderable.

All heads turned as a raised voice, angry with a hint of fear, echoed in the hallway outside my office. "Careful. I paid a hundred bucks for this suit."

"You won't be needin' it in the pokey, bloke." Jeremy! "But if you keep causing me trouble, I'm gonna shove this boot up your ass."

Jerry sprang to his feet and bolted through the door—misbehaving was part of his bailiwick.

Miss P shot me a grin. "He has a nice way with people."

Before I could even cogitate on a clever retort, a man staggered unceremoniously into our group as if he'd been shoved from behind, which I suspected was the case. Jeremy loomed in the doorway behind him with Jerry bringing up the rear.

Surprise flashed across the Aussie's face as he realized he had an audience. "Convenient that you're all here." His eyes singled me out as he gestured toward the man he held. "I brought you a present."

"My birthday is coming up. Thanks for remembering. But what should I do with him?"

I leaned my head sideways trying to catch the man's eyes, which remained fixed on his shoes. Short, balding, in a hundred-dollar suit that had brown stains splattered down the front, but with an expensive watch and shined shoes, he had a trying-too-hard air about him.

Jimmy G pushed himself from the wall and stepped toward the man who now stood in the middle of the room, encircled by all of us. "Boogie? Is that you?"

The man raised his head. As he did so and we got a good look at him, a collective gasp filled the room. The man had been savagely beaten—one eye was black-and-blue and swollen shut, the other, only slightly less damaged. His lower lip, twice it's original size and marred by an open red split, oozed blood, which he nervously licked.

"Jeremy?" Miss P asked, her shock evident.

"I found him this way."

"Boogie, it *is* you." Jimmy G had stepped in front of the man, putting them nose-to-nose.

"Yeah, it's me." Boogie Fleischman growled in a voice that was far deeper and resonant than expected from such a small human.

Jeremy prodded Boogie's shoulder. "You want to tell them what you told me?" Even though it was framed as such, it was not a question.

"Look, all I did was get to telling stories."

Jeremy shot him a look. "Start at the beginning."

Boogie started again. "Okay, maybe I talk too much, okay? The kid got me talkin' about old times, remembering like."

"And...?" Jeremy prompted.

Boogie waffled for a minute as I held my breath. From the intent looks around the room, it seemed everyone else was hanging on his words as well. "Okay, I got to bragging a bit."

"And...?" Jeremy clearly had more patience than I did.

"We got to rigging explosives, like I used to do." Boogie ground his toe into the hardwood flooring.

"We?" I asked. "We who?"

"Me and the Campos kid."

"You son of a bitch!" Jimmy shouted as he launched himself at Boogie. The two men fell in a tangle of limbs with Jimmy on top. He reared back, as if in slow motion, then launched a haymaker at Boogie's head. Pulling his arms protectively in front of his face, Boogie shielded himself.

With one fluid movement, Dane launched himself, straddled the tangled men, grabbed Jimmy by the shirt collar, and lifted him off Boogie. With a practiced motion, he set him on his feet, then held him there. "Enough, big guy."

Jerry helped Boogie to his feet, then put himself between Boogie and Jimmy G.

"But he blew up my place," Jimmy spluttered.

"Not personally but, in a manner of speaking, you're right," I said, finally finding my voice. "You wouldn't happen to have mentioned the location of your old stash of bomb parts to the young Mr. Campos, would you?"

Boogie ground the toe of his shoe into the carpet. "I said a lot of stuff."

I took that as a yes. "And the papers in the briefcase?"

"Letters Eugenia had given me. She wanted me to get rid of all of it."

"Why?"

He looked up. When he answered my question, he didn't look at me. Instead, he stared at Mona. "They proved Albert Campos wasn't the Big Boss's kid."

Something tight loosened inside me. "Truth. Such a hindrance to blackmail." But Albert had to know that these days DNA could solve that issue pretty easily."

"Crazy people do crazy things." That bit of wisdom came from Boogie—he should know.

"It doesn't add up. Something's bothering me, but I can't put my finger on it." I looked at Mother. "We may know the truth, but Albert Campos is still operating under his mother's lies."

"You gotta believe me! I had no idea he would do any of this." Boogie didn't even try to keep the beg out of his voice. "When Jimmy's place blew, I had a real bad feeling. I was on my way here to shut the kid down when that...guy," he tilted his head toward Jeremy, "waylaid me."

"Why were you coming here? To warn the Big Boss?"

Boogie looked at me like I'd lost my mind. "Albert? Of course not. I was coming to warn *you*."

I leaned back as if I'd been slapped. "Me?"

"This is the second time a Campos has tried to kill you." Boogie's eyes—okay, the open one—bored into me. "With you out of the way, he thinks he's Albert Rothstein's only heir."

Mona gasped. "Kill Lucky?" Then her hand flew to her belly. It wasn't hard to read her mind.

"Mother, relax, I don't think that's his game. He knows he's not the Big Boss's son, and he knows it would be easy to prove. No, he's after something else." I tried to see the whole puzzle—it was there—but I couldn't. "High math isn't my strong suit but, given Mother's age when she met Father, and my age when the first bomb blew, Albert Campos is only five years older than me, six max. I don't know too many nine or ten-year-olds who have the bomb making skill set. Do you?"

"It wasn't the kid who tried the first time." Jimmy G glanced around the group. "It was his mother." His eyes locked on Boogie. "Tell 'em, Boogs."

After a moment of vacillation, Boogie dove in. "Eugenia played all the angles." Dane rose and offered Boogie his seat, which I thought was gallant of him. Boogie did look a bit worse for wear. He accepted Dane's offer with a nod, then a cringe. Once settled in the chair, he began again. "Her best play was gettin' guys over a barrel, and then squeezing their balls until they screamed."

"A real peach," I groused. "The Big Boss would never fall for that."

"His first and last time," Jimmy G added. "He always did learn things the hard way. Guess we all did."

"Boogie, finish your story," Mona prompted.

He shifted uncomfortably in the chair. "As I was sayin', Eugenia could get pretty much anybody to do pretty much anything."

As I looked at him, the light dawned—just a glimmer, but it was there. I leaned toward him and lowered my voice. "You taught her how to make that bomb, didn't you?"

Boogie's eyes wouldn't meet mine. A bead of sweat trickled down the side of his face.

"You taught her, then you took the fall. Why?"

Finally, he looked up. Licking his lips, he glanced around the room. "I loved her."

"Even when she loved someone else?"

"Hey, love ain't some two-way street you know."

"Pretty profound for a two-bit hood," I spat, I don't know why.

"Life has a way of grinding stuff into you." Boogie pulled himself up, regaining a bit of bravado. "I loved her. And back then, I wasn't above letting her erase my competition. I'm not proud of it. Stupid and shortsighted, I know. Love does crazy things."

I couldn't keep the sarcasm out of my voice. "This is like a B movie."

Mona reached over and patted my hand. "Honey, back then, Vegas *was* a B movie."

"Boogie may have tried to kill you, sorta secondarily-like, but he had noble motivation," Jimmy added, as if love was an exoneration for attempted murder which, between you and me, was an interesting premise. If it was, the gene pool would be whittled down significantly.

"And that makes everything fine," I countered. "So no one

knows what happened to Albert's mother?" I caught a glance between Jimmy and Boogie.

"What? Tell me."

"Eugenia had the baby while Boogie was in jail," Jimmy explained, his voice strong with the story. "She hung around for awhile, but ten years was a long time to wait."

Boogie jumped in. "Eight. I got out early on account of good behavior."

"So she took her shot at killing Lucky or Mona—either one, I don't think it mattered." Jimmy continued after silencing Boogie with a look. "Then she took the kid and disappeared. She'd taken a shot at Albert Rothstein. She wasn't no fool. She ran and she ran fast."

"Did you try to find her?" I asked Boogie.

"I thought about it. But if she'd wanted me to find her, she woulda told me where to look." Heartbreak hung heavy in every word.

God help me, but I felt sorry for him. "And young Albert? How'd he come into your life?"

"About ten years ago, he came knocking on my door."

"Just like that?"

"Yeah, weird, isn't it?" Boogie tried to grin, then thought better of it when the skin on his lips stretched the split already there. "I took him in. No questions."

I glared at Boogie. "And you filled his head with stories...and instructions."

His smile fled. "Like I said, the kid got me talking."

I leaned back and closed my eyes, trying to think—pretty hard to do when all I saw was red. The past—no matter how far you run, it'll always catch you and bite you on the ass. But if all this was true, it supported the facts Flash had ferreted out of Crayfish Crider. Opening my eyes, I surveyed the group. "So Albert is from a short line of petty hoods and extortionists who want me out of the way so he can move higher on the food chain. How clichéd."

"Honey," Mona said, in that irritating, placating tone she sometimes adopted. "It's Vegas."

"Would you people stop saying that? It is *not* Vegas, at least not the Vegas I know." I looked around the group for support. Finding a few nods but little else, I forged ahead, building steam. "Look, the bottom line is, we need to find Albert Campos before he blows up something, or someone else."

"We know he's after you," Dane added quietly.

I knew he would only offer me as bait if no other alternative presented itself, so I didn't hold it against him. From where I was sitting, I thought we were out of options, too.

Boogie nodded as his eyes bored into mine. "He's right. If you want to find Campos, I'd be looking over my shoulder, if I were you."

"Lucky, where're you supposed to be tonight?" Dane asked, his eyes intense, his voice hard.

"On the roof with the VIPs." Like a kill shot from a sniper rifle, the ordinary part of my real life hit me between the eyes. "Shit, what time is it?"

"Almost nine," Miss P answered with a worried edge to her voice. "You better hurry."

"Sending me into harm's way?" I kidded.

"You'll do it anyway. Arguing about it would waste time we don't have." She turned and grabbed Dane with one hand and Jeremy with the other. "If anything happens to her..."

"Boogie," Mona said, her voice soft. "Who did that to you?"

"I had it comin'." Boogie squirmed as he looked at her.

She cocked an eyebrow at him. "No doubt. But I need to know."

"Your husband, ma'am."

"The Big Boss did this to you?" I don't think I kept the awe out of my voice.

"He doesn't cotton to anyone comin' after his own." That was probably a gross understatement, but I didn't think I needed to point that out.

Mona swallowed hard. Her internal struggle bloomed across her face when she looked at me. "He'll kill him, Lucky."

"Over my dead body." Okay, perhaps that wasn't quite the quip I was reaching for, but I didn't have time to correct it. I squeezed Mother's shoulder as I moved to step by her. "Don't worry. We'll both be fine. And I won't let him kill Albert Campos." *If I could find him in time*, I thought, but didn't think Mona needed to hear that part.

I didn't make the same promise about myself.

Jerry's security walkie-talkie jumped to life. "Sir, Mr. Rothstein is back on the property."

Jerry grabbed the device and pushed to talk. "Location?"

"Service elevator six. He's headed to the roof."

I glanced at my watch. Almost nine.

The fireworks were just about to start.

A SYMPHONY OF VOICES—A MELODY PITCHED ON AN UNDERCURRENT of excitement—greeted me as I strode out of the elevator and into the crowd gathered, drinks in hand, in Babel, our rooftop club. The Big Boss was up here somewhere. His presence was a sure sign Albert Campos was also wandering among the crowd of innocents. But where?

My gaze swept the crowd in front of me. The heat of the day had yet to fully yield to the refreshing temps of night in the high desert. Daylight, caught in death throes, fractured into vibrant oranges and pinks on the horizon, just above the dark outline of the Spring Mountains. With Dane and Jeremy sticking close, I moved to the bar and rounded up the staff as quickly as I could.

Our head bartender, Sean, could tell it was serious with one look. His grin vanished and he rallied the staff out of earshot of the partiers. God, had I really bemoaned all those bomb-scare drills we'd suffered through? Never again.

Surrounded by the staff—really just kids in too little clothing —I went into my spiel. I remember the bomb squad guys telling us that maintaining calm was the key. That and maybe not throwing up. God, if a bomb went off... I slammed my brain closed on that visual and focused. "Listen up, folks," I said, trying to keep my voice low yet loud enough to be heard. "This is not one of those drills. This is the real thing. You know what to do. Clear the area. Move everyone downstairs. Use the service elevators as well, just like we practiced. Got it?"

They filtered into the crowd.

I grabbed Dane and Jeremy. "You two make sure all the guests are out, then escort all the employees to the ground floor." I looked at first one, then the other. "I'm counting on you."

They both nodded. I could tell they wanted to argue, but they didn't.

Romeo with the SWAT team was guarding all exits—I could hear him giving orders through the earpiece I had stuck in my left ear. He'd thought it wise that I could keep track of his where-abouts, which was out of character. Wise to his games, I wasn't fooled—he wanted me listening so he could give me orders. But I could talk back. Not only could I hear, but I could communicate through a tiny mic on a stalk extending from the earpiece around toward my mouth. "Romeo, you there?"

"Right here."

"Dane and Jeremy will be coming down with the employees after all the guests are out.. I want you to keep the two of them there. Neither you nor I want a couple of Lone Rangers riding into this showdown."

"You got it."

I could hear him give instructions to his officers.

The bomb squad was waiting in the wings for...well, for a bomb—although I caught sight of a few teams of two agents, each team with a dog. The sooner we found that dynamite, the better for my blood pressure. I'm sure I wasn't alone in that.

And I needed to find the Big Boss. Campos had lured him up here, of that I was sure. Campos also knew I'd be up here manning the fireworks display. Guess the guy had picked his O.K. Corral—a showdown, which had its upside. If I was right, then I had time to clear the roof. As Jimmy G had said, this was personal.

Jerry would be leading several details of security personnel up through the staff elevators onto the roof outside the confines of the club. Although I couldn't see them, I knew they would be there, searching just like me as I made my way toward the dais near the command module for the fireworks. I strained to catch a glimpse of the Big Boss through the crowd as it oozed toward the exits. Xavier materialized out of the crowd that was moving reluctantly toward the elevators. "Lucky, girl. Where the hell you been?"

Surprise brought me up short. I hadn't seen him. Apparently my eyes were tracking higher. "As if you didn't know."

"What're you talking about?"

Okay, maybe he didn't know. I grabbed his shoulder, wheeled him around, and propelled him back toward the control console for the fireworks as I filled him in on the missing dynamite.

"One stick of dynamite. Not enough to even dampen enthusiasm around here," said the man used to playing with things that went boom.

"But enough to get someone's attention." We stopped at the console. "Xavier, tell your men to leave. You should get out of here, too. It's not safe."

Xavier nodded at his men who had overheard. They silently filed past, heading toward the service elevator. We both crawled around the dais looking for any evidence of a bomb. We didn't find one. Damn.

With the all clear, Xavier stepped up onto the dais, manning the console. With the sun now below the horizon, natural light faded fast. We'd killed the breaker to the lights up here so no one could accidentally trip the switch and ruin the show. In retrospect, that probably wasn't a great idea. My eyes were adjusting, but it was hard to penetrate the growing darkness. Even the dim glow from the fish tank under the Lucite dance floor had been killed.

With one hand shielding my eyes, I peered into the gloom. "I can't see a thing."

Strains of music—the score to our fireworks show—filtered through the speakers.

"I can give you light," Xavier said, raising his voice to be heard as the music swelled, building toward the first salvo. "Intermittent, and only thirty minutes of it."

We'd established that the Big Boss wasn't in the club. But service elevator six came up to this wing of the rooftop. He had to be somewhere shrouded under the cover of night. I scanned the far reaches of the roof, trying to penetrate the darkness. "Go for it."

Xavier turned his attention to the console in front of him as I stepped to the railing separating the club from the rest of the roof, climbed over, and eased into the darkness.

The first shell exploded out of its mortar with a huge boom, jolting me to my core. Then a few seconds later, it burst overhead in a shower of light. Instinctively, my eyes shut in defense against the assault. I forced them open, scanning the rooftop in the dissipating light from above, my eyes tearing.

Nothing. No movement. The glow faded as I moved carefully further out onto the rooftop. Vaguely, I became aware of the music and the muted noise of the crowd lining the Strip far below.

Stilling my body, I prepared for the next launch. This time, the sound didn't make me jump...much. Desperate to make each second count, I forced my eyes open, waiting for the light. The second boom high above thrummed through me, then a tear-inducing brightness. Through narrowed eyes, I tried to calmly scan the rooftop, focusing a few seconds on one ten-degree quadrant at a time out of the 180 degrees in front of me.

This time, I thought I saw movement. I stilled and tunneled my vision.

Yes. Two figures. One tall and lean. On short, hunched over. As if in pain. Moving away from me.

The embers burned out and darkness once again engulfed the rooftop.

I waited. My heart pounding. Then I whispered into my mic. "Romeo. I got them." Breathlessly I explained, using as few words as possible. "Campos has the Big Boss. And I think he has a gun."

"I'll send some guys up in the service elevator."

"Tell them subtle, Romeo, okay?"

"Lucky, it's my job."

"Romeo, it's my father."

Another launch out of the tube behind me caught me off guard and I flinched. The music grew louder. Nothing like a techno-pop soundtrack as my life played out in flashes of light and spikes of adrenaline. Had I been picking the music, I would've thought of a better song than *Thanks for the Memories* redone by someone who sounded a bit like Nicki Minaj—and who had the same potty-mouth.

Prepared, I moved quickly through the burst of light, this time a kaleidoscope of colors. Adrenaline appeared to be the antidote to bump and bruises. My body didn't give me any lip as I stepped lightly over various pipes and around small electrical junction boxes, closing the gap. The light once again faded. I paused, gathering myself, then launched again into the next explosion of light. Through a few more cycles, like a stop-and-start dance, I weaved my way, drawing closer.

Crouching behind some electrical thing, I eased my head around in the fading glow. Albert indeed had my father...the other Albert. The young man pressed my father down, forcing him to sit on one of the many boxes similar to but smaller than the one I hid behind. I guessed the young man had summoned the Big Boss, then jumped him. Whispering, I gave the location to Romeo. Although he didn't respond, Jerry would be listening in as well.

Mentally following the chatter in my ear, I tried to visualize where Romeo wanted everyone.

"Lucky, I know you're out there," Campos called out.

A body hurtled in next to me, crouching to remain hidden. A hand grabbed my arm. Then a woman's disembodied voice whispered. "Don't say anything. Not yet."

My heart leapt into my throat, strangling any reply I might have had. "Who the hell are you?" I managed after my heart dropped back down to beat a rhythm in my chest.

"Sophia Denton." She sat on the ground, her back to the box as she whispered a few things into her own mic. When she finished, she turned her attention to me. "Romeo sent me. I'm a hostage negotiator with Metro."

"I don't negotiate." I adopted a similar position, my shoulder pressed to hers—the box was pretty small to cover both of us.

"Give the bad guy anything he wants, then give him a bullet?" Darkness hid Sophia, but not the smile in her voice.

My heart still galloped. The breeze cooled the sweat that had popped out everywhere, sending a shiver through me. "Pretty much."

"That's why Romeo sent me. You want your father back in one piece, don't you?"

"Right now, I'm on the fence on that one." I closed my eyes and took a deep breath. When I opened them again, a bit of calm returned.

"Really?" Sophia sounded like she was starting to think I might be part of the problem and not a part of the solution.

To be honest, I wasn't sure about myself either. "As far as I'm concerned, you guys can perforate the bad guy all you want, as long as you avoid doing that to my father. I reserve that privilege."

"Using force is the last resort, at least on our side of the equation." Sophia chuckled. "We'll do our best. Do you have a gun?"

"No."

"Good. Romeo said to ask."

The kid knew me too well. "You wouldn't have one I could use, then?"

Sophia snorted. "Not on your life. They'd have my badge."

I wanted to argue, but thought better of it.

"All righty then." Sophia's voice held a hint of respect along with a dose of caution. "It's show time."

A shell hadn't exploded over our heads for a bit. "Wonder what's up with the fireworks?" I peeked my head around but couldn't tell whether Campos and the Big Boss were still there or not.

"I asked him to give us three minutes to get everyone in place. They should start again any second now."

As if Xavier was privy to out conversation, a mortar whooshed to life behind us, launching another ball of fire.

"Lucky! Answer me." Albert's voice had a cold, calculation to it —not ruffled at all.

Sophia chuckled softly. "Cool customer. Good."

"Good?"

"At least he's not hanging on the ragged edge. Those guys, they're pretty unpredictable. I bet this guy wants to talk, tell us his story. And that's the goal: keep him talking, focused on you. Shouldn't be too hard; he hates you already."

"Great." I wasn't sure how I felt about that. I glanced around the electrical box at my back. Campos and the Big Boss were still there, half-hidden in the lee of a larger box—a condenser for the air conditioning system.

"Honey, we're known not only by the friends keep, but by the enemies we make." Sophia squeezed my hand. "We got a sniper on the roof over there." She pointed to the east. "The goal is to take him peaceably. If we can't…"

"I'm really not in a peaceable mood," I groused. And for once, I was telling the God's honest truth, completely unvarnished by even a thin coat of smart-ass.

"Try it my way, first. Keep him talking. Be non-confrontational. Draw him out. Romeo filled me in, but we still don't know exactly what he wants—besides killing you, I mean."

Like a shot, the firework exploded high above. My heart skipped a beat—someone ostensibly wanting to kill me was still a bit new and I hadn't totally adjusted. "I'm here, Campos," I shouted into the cascading light, waiting for it to reach the rooftop. "I understand it's me you really want."

"You don't understand nothing."

"Draw him out," Sophia whispered, then she turned to speak in hushed tones into her mic. "Let him tell his story."

"You're right about that. Why don't you tell me what I don't know, then?"

"Lucky, girl," my father said, his voice strained as if filtered through a mask of pain. "Get the hell out of here. It's gonna—"

"Shut up, old man," Campos growled.

Peeking around, I saw the kid raise his arm, then bring it down in a vicious swipe. A grunt. Then silence.

Instinctively, my muscles bunched. Sophia's hand on my arm stopped me from charging. "No."

"Fuck." I leaned back and tried to focus. "Campos, I know you're angry. Can you tell me why?"

"Our old man killed my mother."

Darkness once again oozed into the corners, closing out the light and wrapping its tentacles around my heart. The Big Boss a killer? Was it possible? I forced the thoughts away—I so didn't want to go there. And his last words had sounded like a shout of warning. But of what?

"Did you hear me, Lucky?" Albert Campos' voice sounded as taut as a piano wire.

Sophia nudged me with an elbow. "You can do this."

The urgency in her whisper drew my focus like a sharp stick in the side. "Why do you think the Big Boss killed your mother?"

"The guys told me she was shaking him down. Then she disappeared. Later, when I was old enough, I put two and two together."

The light dawned. I started breathing again—funny, I hadn't been aware that I'd been holding my breath. "What pieces?"

"I was eight when my mother disappeared. I can tell you the foster system isn't a good place to grow up."

"Where was she when she disappeared?" I kept asking the logical questions even though the conclusions to be drawn scared the hell out of me.

"She'd come back here, to Vegas. I remember her telling me she had a score to settle. And that was it."

"You never heard from her again?"

"No."

"And her body?" I braced for the answer I knew was coming.

"Never found," Albert's voice turned hard, but with a hint of pain. "She just disappeared."

"Did somebody go to the police?"

That got a laugh out of him. "Half the force was on the take. One old guy did finally tell me that word had filtered down from some big shot, and they'd closed the file and buried it."

I didn't want to know what Albert had done to the "old guy" to get him to spill. If I was a betting gal, I'd put my money on the old guy now being just another nameless body buried in the desert. "And you assumed it was our father?"

"He seemed the best candidate."

Sophia leaned in as another mortar exploded behind us. "Don't argue with him. Go along."

I shot her a look even though I knew she couldn't see it, then raised my voice so Campos could hear. "I can see where you're coming from. It sure looks bad."

"Bad?" Campos' voice rose. "I should shoot him right now."

I whirled and peeked around the corner. The kid grabbed my father by the collar, pulling him around. He still slumped like a rag doll, but I thought I saw hints that he was coming around. Tough old bird.

"If you kill him, then you'll never know for sure, will you?"

The kid paused.

"Can you tell me why you planted the bomb?"

"Good," Sophia whispered.

Campos laughed. "I knew it would stir things up. And if I killed you, so much the better. I wanted your father to know what it felt like to lose someone important."

"Okay, I get that. I understand why you did that. And nobody was hurt. That's a good thing." I paused, thinking.

"Negotiate," Sophia urged.

"Albert, we're sort of in a difficult spot here. You want your story out. You want to get to the bottom of who killed your mother. Boy, I understand that. And I promise, we'll turn over every stone to find the truth. But I need something from you."

"Perfect." The edge in Sophia's voice dulled just a touch.

"If we're going to get the truth, we need our father." The words stuck in my throat, but I choked them out. "I need you to put the gun down. Kick it to the side, then take your jacket off so I can see you're not hiding anything. When the next dose of light hits us, put your hands behind your head, step away from the Big Boss, and then drop to your knees."

Another mortar exploded behind us. Interminable seconds of silence followed.

"It's the only way you'll know, Albert. The only way your mother can rest."

The shell exploded overhead.

"How do I know I can trust you?"

I leaned back trying to think of something to say.

"Tell him…"

"You don't," I said, taking a flier. It's the truth he wanted. I hoped he could recognize it when he heard it.

He laughed. "You are a ballsy broad."

All things considered, I wished folks would stop telling me that, although I thought I detected just a hint of respect, but I might have imagined that part.

"Okay. Your word, Lucky."

That's what he'd wanted all along—to put me where he was. To cause me the pain of losing someone so important. But even more, he wanted me to be responsible for my own loss.

I knew what I had to do. As the reality washed over me, I think my spirit died just a little. "Albert, you have my word." Then I lowered my voice and whispered into my mic. "Romeo, keep your guys hidden. Let me do this."

Sophia stiffened beside me.

"Lucky…" Romeo's voice held the hardness of an order.

"This is my show, Detective. He doesn't know you're here. No need to alarm him. Besides, it's me he wants." Rising, I stepped into the light to face one of my worst fears.

CHAPTER SIX

I TOOK two steps and stopped. I tried not to look at my father slumped at Albert's feet. My eyes met his and held. "I promise you, I'll get to the bottom of this."

For a moment, I wasn't sure what he would do. Then, keeping the gun trained on me, he worked one arm out of his jacket, then switched hands and shrugged out of the other sleeve. Making a show out of it, he dropped the cloth, then moved it in my direction with one foot.

I couldn't read his expression, couldn't tell how he was feeling. But with a gun pointed at my chest and nothing to protect myself with, I sure knew how I was feeling. The dot of a sniper sight targeted his chest, blood red on the white of his shirt, making me feel a bit better.

Romeo's whispered order sounded in my ear. "If he so much as twitches, shoot him."

My heart pounded as I tried to appear calm. My muscles tightened, coiling. "Don't you need to know, Albert? I know I do."

Finally, his shoulders sagged as the fight leaked out of him. Lowering himself, he set his gun on the ground and kicked it to the side, away from the Big Boss. Then he moved forward and dropped to his knees, his hands behind his head. The police swarmed, pressing him down, then securing his wrists in handcuffs. He didn't fight.

I rushed to the Big Boss, falling to my knees next to him. "Father?"

He groaned, a good sign.

The trickle of blood oozed down his forehead. Circling his shoulders, I drew him to me. "Don't move."

A figure dropped down next to me, opening a familiar black box. I looked up into the dark, serious eyes of Nick the paramedic.

"I'll take it from here." He gave me a reassuring smile as he fell to work.

Rocking back on my heels, I pushed myself to my feet, giving him some room.

The Big Boss's hand snaked out and grabbed my ankle, stopping me.

He struggled to say something.

I dropped to a squat, balancing on the balls of my feet as I strained to hear. "Don't talk. Rest." A perimeter of lights sprang to life making me blink against the brightness.

My father gripped me tighter, his fingers digging into the soft flesh of my lower leg. "Don't," he wheezed.

I bent toward him. "What?"

"Don't." He struggled to pull breath into his lungs. "Briefcase."

"Briefcase?" I asked, a cold dread surging through me. "What briefcase?"

"Would this be it?"

I turned in time to see a young Metro officer pick up a worn, leather case by the handle.

My father wheezed. "Ten seconds."

Motion timer! I glanced at Campos as the police lead him away. He threw me a look and I knew. Pushing myself to my feet, my legs were already in motion. I reached the cop in two strides. In one motion, and never slowing my pace, I grabbed the brief-

case. The edge of the building wasn't far. I counted in my head...
Three one thousand. Four one thousand. Planting my forward
foot, I reared back, my arm arcing behind me, coiling, with the
briefcase held firmly by the handle. I forced myself to pause—
timing would be everything.

Five one thousand. Six one thousand. Seven... With all my
weight behind it, I hurled the briefcase as high and as far as I
could. "Everybody down!" I shouted as I watched the case arc into
the night. Then I fell on my stomach, covering my head with my
arms.

Eight one thousand. Nine...

The air shattered as the dynamite ignited.

After the concussion passed, I raised my head and looked over
my shoulder. The others were moving.

From below, I heard the roar of the crowd.

A cheer for the grand finale.

I rolled over on my back and stared at the stars..

As Romeo peered down at me, I started to laugh.

LIKE BIRDS PECKING AFTER THE FOOD WAS GONE, SEEMINGLY HALF
of Metro scurried around the rooftop. With the excitement over,
there wasn't much left to do but fill in the gaps. The Big Boss sat
on a chaise by the pool, his normal vitality clearly at an ebb. He
chewed his lip, squinting one eye against the pain as Nick taped
his ribs. In the half-light of the perimeter floods, the bruise
blooming across the right side of his face was highlighted by the
gash left by the gun Albert had clocked him with. Apparently, the
gash wasn't that bad—his only needed one Steri-Strip where mine
had needed several. Either that or Nick was running low on the
things—there'd been a run on them lately.

Easing myself down next to my father, I grabbed his hand then
leaned my head on his shoulder.

He sighed, briefly touching his head to mine. "I can always count on you." There wasn't even a hint of disbelief in his voice, just a quiet assurance that that's how it would be between us. I liked that.

"After all these years and the things you've done for me, I figured I sorta owed you."

Drawing strength from each other, we shared the comfort of closeness for a moment. When he spoke, he spoke haltingly as if searching for the words or stumbling over the emotion. "The past. You can never out run it."

"Our past is part of who we are." That sounded profound, especially for me. When I had stepped into the deep end?

I felt my father stiffen. "You need to let the Campos matter go." His voice held a plea of conviction.

"Tell me about Eugenia Campos," I said, sidestepping.

"I'm sure your mother brought you up to speed."

"Yes, as far as she knew. But I have a feeling there's more to the story. Like what happened when, after eight years, she drops into your lap again?"

My father sighed, buying for time. Finally he said, "She claimed the kid was mine. She wanted money, wanted him to share in 'my empire' as she called it." He chuckled. "It was far from that at that time, I can assure you."

"If you don't have two nickels to rub together..." I stopped, suddenly defeated. I didn't want to know any of this. With knowledge came responsibility, and I wasn't ready to shoulder that burden.

"Of course, I wanted proof," my father continued. "Even though DNA was pretty rudimentary, she agreed. I told her if the kid was mine, of course I would claim him."

Now *that* sounded like the Big Boss I knew...and loved. Was sentiment affecting my discernment? Of course it was, but I am who I am. "And then?"

"Nothing."

"What do you mean 'nothing?'"

"She didn't show for the test."

I felt the stirrings of hope…and the hint of disbelief. "She vanished?"

My father's eyes met mine and held steady. "Yeah."

"So on the eve of getting what she wanted, assuming you were the father, she split?"

"I'm not saying that. To be honest, I don't know what happened. I got my suspicions, but I wasn't going to push it. My problem had been solved. Besides, I was hip-deep in building the Lucky Aces. I had more than I could handle already."

"I see. And the police?"

His eyes flicked away from mine. "What about them?"

"Did you ask them to bury the file?"

"I might have." His hand reached out and covered mine. It felt cold.

"I promised Campos I'd look into his mother's death."

"He fooled you into it."

Knowing they would be a dagger to his heart, I weighed my next words. "I need to know."

He took a sharp breath as if absorbing a blow. I'd been right. The thought made me sad. "She's dead, Lucky."

"How do you know?"

"I just know."

On complete overload, I needed time to myself. I'd left the Big Boss under the watchful eye of Mona, who'd been hovering around like a mother bird protecting a fledgling that had fallen from the nest.

Separating from the crowd, no one noticed me leaving or, if they did, they were kind enough to understand. I rode the elevator down to the lobby as thoughts whizzed through my brain at hyper-speed, impossible to grab and hold. A wall of sound hit me as the doors opened at the bottom, shattering the cloud of discomforting musings like a bazooka shell exploding a barn. People filled every corner, excited chatter poking holes in my bad mood.

The magic of Vegas. Folks from every corner of the universe gathering to have some fun, shrug off the burden of daily worries and responsibilities—recharging so they could handle the vicissitudes of life. As I pushed into the crowd, I breathed deeply, absorbing. A glimmer of hope bloomed deep inside.

Was the Big Boss right? Did Albert Campos' manipulation excuse me from my promise to find the truth? What is it the lawyers called it? Fraud in the inducement? Lawyers, I shook my head. So clever, taking simple concepts and obscuring them with obtuse language. Now we all believed we couldn't survive without an attorney on retainer, thereby ensuring their survival.

Survival. Interesting word.

Unsure where I really wanted to go, I wandered through the crowd. Survival. The word hit my heart. The lengths we all go to ensure our own survival. What would I do? What had the Big Boss done? Was it my place to judge? Was it wise to dig up old skeletons?

And who was I really worried about? The Big Boss? Or myself? I'd just found my father, was I ready to have him taken from me once again? Then again, did I want a murderer for a father?

Lost, I wandered through the casino only half-aware of the games under way, the music filtering through, the siren call of the slots, the shouts of joy, the groans of disappointment. Glasses clinked, wheels spun—I felt safe, cocooned in the familiar. Leaving the noise behind, I ambled into the relative quiet of the Bazaar, spurred on by a primal need. Human contact. The comfort of a hug.

As if hearing my silent plea, Jean-Charles met me halfway. Before I could say anything, he wrapped his arms around me pulling me tight to him. My arms pinned by my side, I let him hold me. Nuzzling into his neck, I breathed him in.

"You are okay," he whispered against my hair. It wasn't a question. Instead, it sounded more like an answer to a prayer.

My heart swelled as I nodded against his shoulder.

"I am hearing these things about something bad on the roof. About you and your father." Still holding me, he leaned back to look at me. "A bomb?"

"It's over now." I didn't want to explain. I couldn't find the words. I avoided the emotion.

Somehow he understood. "Yes. It is over. And the angels brought you back to me." He dropped one arm, keeping the other one around my shoulders so we both faced in the direction I'd been heading. He urged me forward. "Come. I will feed you, if you like. Or I have wine...or perhaps something stronger. A good Cognac to settle the nerves." He chuckled, a deep rumble that hit my core with warmth. "Your nerves and mine."

A line snaked from the entrance to the Burger Palais, which we bypassed, making me feel guilty. Every table was full but, amazingly, a couple sitting at the bar had just paid their check, and they relinquished their stools to us. Jean-Charles made sure I was comfortable. Normally I didn't like anyone fussing over me, but tonight it made me feel good, chasing away the demons of the unknown. Stepping behind the bar, he put his hands on the counter and leaned toward me with a smile. "What'll it be?"

I looked at all the bottles on the shelves behind him. Everything from sipping vodka—Tito's was my favorite—to Napoleon brandy, to the stuff in the Baccarat bottle that cost a king's ransom for a couple of sips—I didn't have the palate nor the ego to go there. After a moment of thought, I met his clear blue eyes that held undisguised emotion. Was this what love looked like? "You know, I'd really just like a super thick vanilla shake."

He shot me a grin, then reached over and squeezed my hand as if he could see into my heart and understood. Then he stepped out from behind the bar and disappeared toward the kitchen.

Staring at my reflection in the glass behind the bottles, I realized I didn't look half as bad as I felt. The shiner made a bit of a statement, but the rest of me looked somewhat normal, which didn't feel at all...normal. My life was still on tilt, but from the looks of me, it was hard to tell. I guessed that was a good thing.

The conversation of the couple next to me captured my attention. "That song. My God, it's wonderful," the lady said as she bent to sip a pink drink through a straw.

I listened to the tune playing in the background and my heart fell.

"*Lucky for Me*, I think it's called," the lady continued. "I saw the guy on *Good Morning America* this morning. He wrote it for a lady who works here." She turned to her male companion who looked bored. "I wonder who she is? She could be sitting right here and I wouldn't know it."

The lady glanced around, catching me staring. "It could be you," she said.

I gave her a weak grin. "What are the odds?"

She reached out and tapped me conspiratorially on the arm. "Wouldn't it be grand? I mean, to have someone love you like that?" Then she sighed as she pressed her hand to her heart.

"Mmmm," I answered with my usual erudition. When she turned her attention back to her partner letting me off the hook, I almost sighed out loud. Listening to the strains of music, to Teddie's soulful voice, I had to admit the song was wonderful, perfect even.

Except for the whole broken-heart thing.

I pulled my iPhone out of my pocket—a new acquisition, I wasn't used to the whole app thing yet. But I did know how to work iTunes. I searched the store, found the song, and downloaded it.

There it was, *Lucky for Me*, in my library. Then the phone asked me if I wanted to make it my ringtone.

Without thought, I hit yes.

THE END

Thank you so much for going on a Lucky adventure with me. I hope you enjoyed the ride.

As you may know, reviews are SUPER helpful. They not only help potential readers make a choice, but they also help me win coveted spots on various advertising platforms.

So, if you would please, do me the favor of leaving a review at the outlet of your choice.

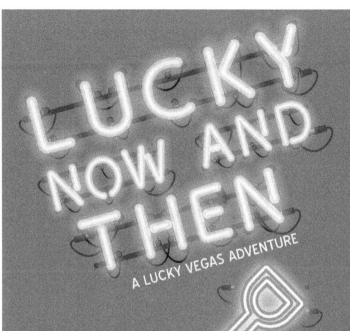

LUCKY NOW AND THEN

A LUCKY VEGAS ADVENTURE

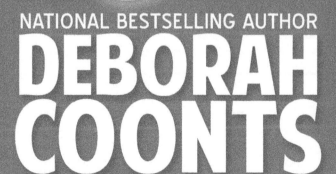

NATIONAL BESTSELLING AUTHOR

DEBORAH COONTS

PART I

PROLOGUE

Summer 1982
Downtown Las Vegas

*A*LBERT ROTHSTEIN *rarely abandoned himself to sleep. Tonight was no different. After a couple hours of fitful tossing, he'd donned his corporate monkey suit and fought with his tie, then wandered down to the building site.*

Little more than a hole in the ground, The Lucky Aces, his first Vegas hotel, was inching its way from dream to reality. He'd made more than a few enemies along the way—necessary risks in this town that didn't tolerate fools and gave little ground. He could shoulder the burden of putting his life on the line, but Mona complicated things. Just the thought of her in the crosshairs made his stomach clench. They also had a daughter, Lucky, but nobody knew she was his—a secret he and Mona had decided to keep for a lot of reasons, her safety being but one.

Vegas was long on secrets.

He took a deep breath and shrugged off the worry—any chink in his resolve would be a death sentence.

Vegas rewarded those with steel balls.

Standing on the sidewalk along Main Street, Rothstein hooked his fingers through the chain-link fence, then rested his forehead on his hands as he visualized his future.

Floodlights illuminated the iron-beam skeleton rising from the deep hole, casting surreal shadows. Four floors had been erected and half of the fifth. Cranes stood at the ready like sleeping giraffes, their long necks arced, ready, waiting. Still hours from sunrise, the construction crew had yet to show. They'd be here soon though, building dreams. Rothstein liked that. Building dreams. Yeah, that's what Vegas was all about.

Lost in thought, Albert Rothstein didn't hear the man creep up behind him.

"You need to come with me." The voice held the sharp edge of a threat. And a hint of familiarity.

"Boogie? You fucking son of a bitch!" Rothstein started to turn but froze when the man jabbed the barrel of a gun into his side.

"That's right. Don't turn around. Don't do nuthin' other than we're going for a ride, like I told you."

Rothstein paused for a moment, his body coiled, ready to spring, his hands itching to close around the wart's neck. Boogie Fleischman. What that two-bit hood wanted with him was anybody's guess. Of course, he could take him right now—the guy was a loser—but it might be more interesting to play along, to see who wanted what from him. 'Cause Boogie didn't have the balls nor the smarts to be anything other than somebody's stooge.

"Sure, okay, Boogie. Just keep the piece outta my side."

Knowledge was power and Albert Rothstein hungered for both.

At thirty-five, he'd put in his time, learned the ropes. Now it was his turn. Vegas was his for the taking, he could feel it. And nobody was going to get in his way.

A black sedan eased to the curb next to him and someone inside pushed the rear door open. Boogie pressed the blunt-nosed handgun a bit harder, encouraging him to move. "If you know what's good for you..."

He left the threat hanging. After enough hesitation to keep Boogie thinking he was going unwillingly, Rothstein stepped to the car and ducked his head inside. With a foot in his back, Boogie shoved him all the

220

way in. Caught off guard, Rothstein fell across the seat. He saw the raised hand holding the gun a fraction of a second too late. The metal connected with his right temple. Pain exploded then rippled through his head, tunneling his vision.

As his vision tunneled, he caught a glimpse of the passenger leaning over from the front seat—a hard, cold face. A badge. The realization hit him that he had grossly miscalculated. Then his world went black.

~

CONSCIOUSNESS RETURNED SLOWLY. WHAT THE HELL HAPPENED? Where am I? Albert Rothstein eased open his eyes but remained motionless. Pain kept his right eye half-closed—the thumping headache made it hard to think. He was in the backseat of the car...alone. From the rhythmic thump of the tires passing over the joints in the road, he assumed they were on the highway, most likely heading south toward California. There was nothing out there but open desert and death. As the car passed through the anemic glow cast by random lights, Rothstein could see the men in the front seat...two of them. Boogie manned the steering wheel, the other one rode shotgun. Boogie was a lightweight, always hanging with some wise guy who was bigger and tougher, absorbing some swagger while safe in his shadow.

Moving slowly, trying to not attract any attention, Rothstein pressed the heel of his right hand to his temple, then probed with his fingers. Blood matted his hair. He winced when his probing met tender, torn skin and a growing goose egg. An hour, not much more, had passed, he guessed.

He felt the car slow. Pressing his feet against the door, he held himself against the turn. The car bumped off the highway leaving the lights behind. In the darkness, Rothstein moved, testing his limbs, his strength. Other than the bomb that had exploded in his head, he seemed unhurt. The car jounced and rolled over the rutted road.

He needed to do something fast. This was a one-way ride to nowhere.

He'd heard stories about bones bleaching in the desert. And that wasn't part of his plan.

The car wallowed over the rough surface for a few minutes more. Rothstein braced himself, biding his time. He'd get one shot, if he was lucky. Finally, the car slowed to a stop. Boogie killed the engine but left the lights on. The silence of the desert closed around them like a warm, stifling cloak, muffling the world.

No one said anything. Rothstein could feel his heart pounding, the trickle of sweat wilting his shirt. Slowly he worked his hands above his head, finding purchase on the door. Then he flexed his knees. Coiled, he worked to steady his breathing, clear his thoughts.

"There they are. Looks like there's two of 'em." Boogie sounded bored but tense, feigning bravery. "Late, as usual. Assholes."

Rothstein caught the faint dancing glow of light as it flashed through the interior of the car. Another car, headlights illuminated, must be bouncing over the same rutted road. More trouble, but he couldn't be worried about that right now.

While the other guy remained where he was, Boogie popped his door open, then levered himself out of the car. Stepping around to the rear passenger door, he grabbed the handle and pulled.

When he heard the latch release, Rothstein braced with his hands, then kicked the car door with all the force he could muster. The door flew open catching Boogie Fleischman off guard, hitting him in the chest. The small man flew backward into the darkness, grunting when he hit the desert floor. His gun arced into the night, out of sight...and out of reach.

With the ferocity of an animal sensing weakened prey, Rothstein pushed with his arms propelling himself, then scrambled the last bit through the open door. In the diffuse edges of the cone of light from the headlights, he saw the shadowed outline of Fleischman, hands in the dirt as he pushed himself to his knees. The little asshole.

With a growl, Rothstein launched himself. Fisting his hands in the shirt on the bastard's back, he drove a knee into the soft flesh of his side, doubling the small man over. Standing, Rothstein let loose a savage kick, catching Boogie in the stomach, lifting him. For a moment he seemed *suspended, then he dropped, curling his knees to his chest, his arms a ring of protection around his legs.*

Rothstein whirled, looking for the passenger. Nobody. He thought about diving after Boogie's gun, but he didn't. If they'd wanted to kill him, they would've done that already. So he waited, looking for movement. Wondering. What did they want from him?

He hadn't seen anyone get out of the second car...yet. Or maybe he'd missed them. He dropped his hand and squared his shoulders. Fighting to slow his breathing, he eased around a full three hundred and sixty degrees. If he looked directly into the headlights his night vision would be shot, so he cast around the edges of the light.

"What do you want?" He hoped his voice sounded strong.

Nothing moved. Through the smell of the sage and the heat of the long-absent sun, a stale tinge of fear hung heavy in the stillness. The night air pierced his damp shirt, bolting a chill through him.

Still breathing hard, now more from adrenaline than exertion, Rothstein gathered his breath and shouted, "Come on, you bastards. Show yourselves. You want me, you gotta take me." He swiped at his nose with the back of his hand. Clenching then unclenching his fists, he waited. "Chicken shits," he muttered. Anger still pulsed through him as he fought for control. God, he ached for a fight—this one had been too short—but he didn't think a fight was what these jokers were looking for.

A bright light bolted out of the darkness. Another set of car lights, the high beams. Blinded for a moment, he squinted against the assault. He couldn't see how many of them there were. Boogie had said two.

"That's enough, son." The voice was low, heavy, thickly accented. Boston maybe? Or New York? Rothstein wasn't sure.

He braced himself, ready. Shoulders hunched, he took a couple of steps toward the voice. The click of a hammer being pulled back stopped him.

"That's far enough." The man behind the voice stepped into the light. Tall and lean with a nose mashed to one side, thin lips and dark, hollow eyes set too close together, the man had the look of someone hope had abandoned. Rothstein had seen that look before, once. He had a scar from

a .22 slug to remember it by. *This man also had a gun, but he'd come better prepared. This one looked to be a .45. "I've been looking for you, son. You're a hard man to find alone."*

"Who the hell are you?" *Rothstein kept his eyes moving, keeping track. He was outnumbered. As far as he could tell, the odds were three to one against him—not good, but not impossible. He heard the door on the car he had been delivered in open. He backed up and angled so he could keep all the players in front of him. Boogie's passenger got out of the car but didn't move toward him. Backlit by the headlights, his face remained in shadow. A flash of familiarity—something about him—but Rothstein couldn't place him.*

Boogie groaned, then crawled over to a Yucca and puked. Rothstein didn't allow himself to smile.

"Your uncle sent me," *the man with the gun said. Flat and cold, his voice lacked even the hint of an inflection.*

"What?" *The statement caught Rothstein off guard.* "My uncle? I've got nothing to say to that piece of trash."

"That don't mean he ain't lookin' for you."

"Tell him to go to hell. He chose which side of the line to stand on." *Rothstein worked to even his breathing, to act casual, but the last thing he needed was some two-bit hood claiming blood relations. Especially with his application for a gaming license pending. After the last round of purging, one almost needed a fucking letter from God and dispensation by the Pope to be blessed by the Gaming Commission.*

"Now that ain't very sociable."

"Fuck you."

The man chuckled, a low, evil rumble. "You're like one chip off that block, you know that? Your uncle sent me to give you a message. He said he'd be watching you. And someday soon, you'll be expected to pay what you owe."

"I don't owe him." *Rothstein spat the words.*

"Kid, he staked you."

His blood ran cold. "I paid him back. Every cent plus interest."

"This here's a surcharge, for going above and beyond and all."

"Fuck him."

The man paused. Lowering his gun, he stared at Rothstein, his eyes cold holes to hell. "You got a kid, right?"

"A kid?" Rothstein snorted and let his arms fall to his sides. "What? I look stupid or something?" He forced a casual, derisive tone, but the fight balled into a cold hard spot in his stomach.

The man paused. Albert could sense him weighing his words. "All's I know is you got a tasty bit of trash you've been banging for a good long time. And she's got a kid. Whose it is don't really matter. That's the thing about bangin' whores, you don't really know, do you?"

Rothstein almost lost his war with self-control, but he didn't. He adopted a nonchalant stance. "An advantage by my way of thinking."

The man's laugh was cold and cruel. "I can see why your uncle wants you on a short leash." He took a few steps closer.

Rothstein thought he could smell garlic.

"Think about this, kid. That piece of ass...Mona, isn't that her name?" The man didn't wait for a response. "She's nineteen. If the kid is yours, even if she isn't, you do the math."

Rothstein's heart jumped. "What?"

"Fuckin' minors. Hell, even in this backwater, that's a felony." The man lowered the hammer on the .45 with his thumb, then flipped on the safety and tucked the piece in his belt at the small of his back. He made a point of straightening his jacket and buttoning the middle button before he leveled his gaze at Rothstein. "Gotta treat your family nice, kid. You never know when you might need some help, you know? Secrets, they have a way of not bein' so secret anymore."

He turned around and walked slowly back to his car. Stepping to the passenger side, he bent and opened the back door. Squinting into the headlights, Rothstein couldn't make out what the man was doing. A moment passed, a seeming eternity to Rothstein, his heart banging a staccato rhythm in his ears.

Finally the man stepped back into the light, dragging something. Rothstein squinted one eye trying to make it out against the glare. A man. He staggered and groaned as the man in black shoved him into the light. With his arms pulled behind him, the passenger staggered a few paces, then dropped to his knees. Hanging his head, he moaned.

Rothstein couldn't make out the man's features. Nothing about him seemed familiar.

"Here's your package," the man said to the passenger who had been riding in the car that had brought Rothstein. "We're square."

Then he pulled out the .45, thumbed off the safety, pressed the barrel to the back of the man's head, and pulled the trigger.

Albert Rothstein stared in horror. "Christ Almighty. You fucking killed him!"

The man brushed his coat aside and replaced his .45 at the small of his back, then let the cloth fall back into place. "And you're an accomplice. That guy there is a witness." He tilted his head toward the passenger who hadn't moved, hadn't uttered a sound. Then he turned on his heel and climbed back into his car.

Rothstein watched the car retreat toward the road, the cone of its headlights knifing through the night. The lights winked out as the car crested a small ridge then edged over, dropping from view as it descended below the horizon. Boogie Fleischman groaned behind him. Rothstein whirled around. He grabbed the small man, hauling him to his feet in one jerk. "What the hell is going on? And who the hell was that guy?"

Fleischman reeked of puke. In a weak gesture, he wiped his mouth on his sleeve. Rothstein let go of him with a shove of disgust.

"I can give you some insight." The voice behind him was quiet, calm...assured.

Rothstein whirled to face the man who had been riding in the passenger seat next to Boogie. "That would be so...unexpected." Wit was his only defense since he'd decided having a gun was just a temptation to use it. Right now he was rethinking that whole premise. "Who the fuck are you?"

"Name's Crider." He stepped into the light as he adjusted his belt—it was a county-issued gun belt, his piece still holstered.

Rothstein squinted. The guy wore a sheriff's department uniform. They had him. They had him good. If he went to the authorities with his story, the other two would weave a tall tale with him at the center, and it would be two against his one. "All of this was to get me over a barrel?"

"Not really, it just presented a good opportunity. You see, me and Fleischman had been hired by the union to provide some...enthusiasm... for some holdouts to join."

"You bombed their joints." *It wasn't a question. Rothstein knew the answer.*

"Fleischman did the heavy lifting. I just provided cover." *Crider shouldered the weight of the admission easily. He dipped his head toward the body.* "That guy was the head of the Culinary Union."

"So what'd you want with the union chief? And why is he dead?"

"He didn't pay." *The man smiled. It sent a chill to Rothstein's heart— it was the smile of a dead man.* "The guy whacking him was a stroke of luck."

CHAPTER ONE

Summer 2012
Las Vegas

*O*NE STICK of dynamite had not been enough to kill me.
Although it was sufficient to put a dent in my day.

Of course, I'd been lucky. I didn't even smile at the pun, which was unusual for me. You see, Lucky is my name, Lucky O'Toole to be exact, and I'm the V.P. of Customer Relations at the Babylon, one of the primo properties on the Las Vegas Strip. Usually my duties include diffusing the average domestic dispute, not bombs, but life had been…well, a bit more explosive lately.

When the elevator doors opened and I stepped out onto the rooftop of the Babylon, I was returning to the scene of the crime, drawn by a primal need, a curiosity I didn't understand but felt powerless to resist. A survivor, I was lured by the inexorable pull of reliving my incredibly close call. The police and the bomb squad were finishing up. Like wraiths, they moved silently in the half-light, in and out of shadows, gathering clues, looking for answers. Just like me. Although, as I stepped to the edge of the roof crossing my arms against the slight chill on the night breeze,

I suspected my questions were a bit different, my answers more difficult.

"What are you doing here?" Detective Romeo's voice was a soothing salve to my raw nerves.

I turned to find the detective in the shadows. "You see me, right? I'm, like, really here?"

A sympathetic smile ticked up one corner of his mouth, as he stepped in next to me. "I don't see dead people, if that's what you mean. Well, I see dead people—all the time, in fact—but they don't talk to me." He shook his head as if tossing one of those snow globes, trying to realign the snowflakes of words and thoughts. "Well they talk to me, but, well, not like you mean..." Trailing off, he looked as confused as I felt. With a sigh, he put a hand on my arm and squeezed. "See, you're not dead."

"To be honest, I'm sort of ambivalent about that right now." I meant it as a joke, but I didn't pull it off. My recent bout of melodrama was getting a bit tiresome—it was so not me, the normal me, anyway. Of course, my life had been turned on its head recently: my lover had abandoned me, I'd moved, and now had almost been killed. I would guess, coupled together, those would rank me as a strong candidate for a meltdown—if I allowed myself that sort of thing.

Romeo didn't respond. I could see him fighting the urge to run. Typically male, all of his flight tendencies were triggered by a woman on the verge of histrionics. To his credit, he held his ground.

Could my father be a killer? Assaulted by the possibility, I tried to shake off impending panic. And with my armor worn thin by the spinning wheel of a life out of balance, it took all the strength I had to cling by my fingernails to the ledge of logic.

Resolutely I pushed away the thought and returned to one of my favorite views: Vegas at night. Like a blanket snapped out full, the lights of Las Vegas unfurled at our feet, covering the valley floor in every direction. Several hours had passed since the conclusion of the annual 4th of July fireworks display, launched from the rooftops of seven major properties and choreographed to the second. The bomb I had tossed in desperation off the top of the Babylon had been a bit of ad-libbing, but I doubted anyone noticed.

The lights from the huge signs lining both sides of the Strip to the south painted our perch in a shifting kaleidoscope of color and alternating shadows as they flashed their messages to the world. Someone told me once the lights of Vegas could be seen from space. I didn't doubt it—the folks in charge around here would accept nothing less.

Vegas, as quintessentially American as apple pie and baseball; but while the others exuded wholesomeness, Sin City had an ugly past.

That happy little thought led me right back to the line of thinking I was trying to avoid: my father's past.

When my father had begun his climb up through the ranks, Vegas had been a rough-and-tumble town run by the Mob. Born of nothing, he had clawed his way to the top of the heap. As the owner of the Babylon, he was one of the men who had made Vegas what it was today. And as a player who had gotten his start in the rough-and-tumble Vegas, then made his mark in the corporate Vegas, he was an enigma. To be honest, I didn't know many details of his past. I'd never thought to ask. What can I say? I'm sort of a big-picture kind of gal. Besides, Vegas was like that...nonjudgmental.

A city of second chances.

Just about everybody who came here was running from something, so nobody asked and nobody cared. Which fit my father like a tailored suit. To him, the past was the only thing in life that couldn't be changed, so it wasn't worth much thought or discussion.

But as a man in the public eye, a member of the Vegas elite, his silence created a vacuum of conjecture.

Could he have something to atone for? I shook my head in self-recrimination and chewed on the inside of my cheek. Guilty until proven innocent might be the battle cry of the Internal Revenue Service, but it wasn't mine. However, I wasn't stupid. Men had done much worse for a lot less.

I shivered in the cool breeze—probably not that cool, really, but the disparity between the triple-digit sizzle of the sun on your skin and the tickle of a slight wind in the dark usually peppered my skin with goose bumps. The pops of distant fireworks from the suburbs sounded like gunshots. Like summer clouds, puffs of smoke eerily lit by the city lights below drifted on the breeze, most likely remnants of the fireworks...or a bomb. A couple sticks of very old dynamite, a 12V battery and a fairly clever motion trigger...

Life...what a crapshoot.

This had all started with the appearance of Albert Campos.

"Care to share?" I asked the detective at my shoulder. He appeared almost as shaken as I felt. When we'd met, he'd looked all of twelve. Now, less than a year later, he looked a decade older, which wasn't that bad when I thought about it. But if his job kept taking its toll at the same pace, he'd soon be old before his time. Dealing with death and despair day-in and day-out, some of it was bound to rub off. Tonight his sandy hair ruffled in the light breeze, his cowlick at the crown standing like a flagpole, tall and defiant. His eyes, normally a vibrant blue, now held the faded hue of color too long in the sun. His clothes hung on his slender frame —the kid needed several good meals and some serious R and R. I felt the tug of guilt; it's not like I was helping or anything. And I did feel sort of responsible for him.

"I don't know jack." He gave me a sideways glance as he pulled his pad and pencil from an inside pocket. "But I bet you can fill me in."

"What makes you think I have any answers?"

"Experience," he noted with a wry smile.

He had me there. "I'm assuming you heard Campos claim to be my father's illegitimate son?" At his curt nod, I started in, "Apparently Boogie Fleischman tutored him in bomb making. Not only that, but the creep told Campos where to find his old stash of materials."

"Boogie Fleischman." Romeo's voice held a hint of awe. "Man, he really knew how to blow. He took out a bunch of non-union joints back in the day."

"Kid, he's not a rock star." Why the world held a fascination with the old, Mobbed-up Vegas was beyond me. Boogie and his ilk came after that, though. During an unsavory period when the Mob was on its way out, leaving a power vacuum, the Culinary Union had valued his skills, using them to sway holdouts to join up.

"To hear him tell it, this whole thing with your father started over some woman." He gave me an impish look—at least that's what I thought it was. "That's so trite it's a cliché, isn't it?"

I cocked an eyebrow at him. "Everything good begins with a bad woman."

He shrugged and I knew he was blushing even though I couldn't see it in the half-light. "In this case, the bad woman was Eugenia Campos, Albert's mother."

"So you know that part of the story?" The detective had clearly done his homework.

"Yeah. She was quite a looker. I've seen pictures." Romeo ran a finger around the inside of his collar, tugging at it. "She ended up pregnant, had the kid, never pointing the finger at the father."

I nodded. "That's not the whole story. To hear Boogie tell it, he took the fall for something she did. When he was sent up, she hung around for a while, then split."

"What did she do that got him sent to prison?"

"Tried to kill Mona and me."

Romeo's head swiveled in my direction, his hand poised in his note taking. "Really?"

"So Boogie says." I squeezed my eyes shut against the memories. "A bomb. Jimmy G's first place, the one on Flamingo."

"Wow. How come you weren't killed? Didn't the bomb level the place?"

"Just lucky, I guess." I rubbed my arms, chasing away the shiver of murder. "I really don't remember much."

Romeo paused. I could see the questions bubbling inside him. Thankfully he didn't press me for details. "Okay, so Boogie gets sent up, Eugenia Campos has her son, but she never names the father?"

"Not until she comes back eight years later and fingers my father."

"Why then?"

I shrugged. "Beats the heck out of me."

"Why'd she leave?"

"Would you stick around if the rumor mill had you tied in with trying to kill Albert Rothstein's family?"

Romeo exhaled sharply.

"My point exactly."

"Boy, I sure would like to talk to her," Romeo added wistfully, as if asking the Universe would make her appear.

"Wouldn't everybody."

"Any idea where she might be, assuming she's still around?"

"I've asked and nobody knows." I turned. Finding Romeo's eyes I held them with my gaze. "She disappeared."

"What do you mean 'disappeared'?"

"Gone. Vanished. Without at trace."

"Whoa." Romeo let the word out in one long sigh, his imagination clearly galloping off, leaving rational thought in the dust.

I could almost see the visions of bleached bones in the desert dancing in his head. I did not want to go where he wanted to take me, but it was hard to deny my father had motive, means and opportunity.

However, there was no body—which sorta shot a hole in the whole murder theory...for now.

But accusations were funny things: once planted they tended to grow. Watered by our access to instant information and fed by immoral media outlets, simply pointing a finger and laying blame was often enough to tarnish even the most unassailable reputation.

Somehow I needed to diffuse this situation before too many fingers started pointing in my father's direction.

Before the paramedics had led him off for stitches and x-rays, my father had leaned into me, his mouth close to my ear, his voice hushed and strained as he'd whispered, "Leave the Campos matter alone, Lucky girl. It's history. Best not to disturb old bones."

His eyes, when they'd met mine, had had a hint of beg in them.

And Albert Rothstein never begged.

Was it a confirmation? A warning? When I'd pressed him for more, he'd clammed up.

My worry was compounded by the possibilities lodged as a cold ball of dread in my stomach. I rubbed my arms again—I couldn't get warm—and contemplated my city. Enigmatic, Vegas was a city of contrasts. A city of hope. A city of despair. A city of desperation. A city of untold riches.

I blew at a lock of hair that tickled my eyes. My father knew better than anyone that I was a black-and-white kind of gal who struggled mightily living in a world cloaked in shades of gray. Before tonight, I'd thought my father was one of the white hats. And he was...is. But was he always?

I had no answer.

Now what? Could I tolerate the unknown? Even when the unknown could turn out to be the unthinkable?

Romeo tucked his pad and pencil away, then brushed down his jacket, which must've been a subconscious move—there was no way a simple smoothing would erase the wrinkles. "Better go. Gotta put the thumbscrews to Albert Campos."

Fighting with my own demons, I stared out at my city and nodded. "If you get any answers—"

"—you'll be the first to know."

After he'd left, the night filled the space he'd abandoned, like air rushing into a vacuum when the seal is broken, closing around me in the comforting press of solitude.

My peace didn't last long.

I felt a presence at my shoulder, then a soft hand on my arm. Her perfume identified her—a scent I'd known my whole life. Normally a thorn in my side, my mother rarely added comfort to my day, but tonight, for some reason, she did. As she snaked an arm around my waist, I rested my head on her shoulder.

"You okay, honey?" Fear and fatigue modulated and softened her normally strident tone. Of course, being very pregnant and besieged by hormones might have had something to do with this nicer, more nurturing version of Mona. History dictated it wouldn't last, but I'd ride this pony as long as it would run.

"Oh, a bit shell-shocked, but I'll rally."

"Of course you will, dear."

"You know, you could clear all this up if you would just tell me what happened to Eugenia Campos. You had a vested interest back then, and you were right in the center of the action."

"So were you."

I lifted my head off her shoulder and gave her a stern look, which she refused to meet. "I was four."

"I wasn't much older...and clearly not very wise." She gave a subtle shrug but didn't offer any more. Even with a shadow hiding her face, I could see she was scared and tired, and more than a little angry.

My mother, tossed onto the streets at fourteen, had made her way as best she could. With her tall, lithe yet lush figure, high cheekbones, full lips that often curved provocatively, and soft brown hair that brushed her shoulders, she had found taking money for sex to be child's play. I frowned at that word choice—

LUCKY NOW AND THEN

perhaps not the best. I glanced at her. Time had not diminished her subtle, forceful beauty and pregnancy seemed to have enhanced it, giving her a softness, a rounding of her hard edges. If only it had the same effect on her often-acerbic personality, but I hadn't seen much of that.

At fifteen, Mona had become a mother. Even though my father knew I was his, he and my mother had kept that a closely guarded secret—my father had enemies and could ill-afford any vulnerability. Meeting my father had altered my mother's trajectory in incalculable ways, beyond the obvious. They'd both thought they had the world by the tail, had covered every contingency.

But Mona had lied. When he took up with her, my father thought she was nineteen, so he couldn't really be faulted for bedding a minor. However, ignorance was no defense in the eyes of the law. Nor apparently with the Vegas power brokers. Nothing like a felony rape charge to get everybody all hot and bothered and derail a bright future. Somehow it always struck me as funny that cold-blooded killers had a moral code. And despite it being as riddled with holes as a body after a hit, that moral net that captured my father.

Anyway, the threat had been made, a sword hanging over my father's head. Of course, it never came to an arrest or anything— the threat was enough. Even though their marriage was thwarted, my parents had carried a torch for each other through the decades.

I didn't know any of this until recently when my father, thinking his end was near, came clean. Both of them had left me hanging for decades, letting me think that my conception had been the product of poor protection and that my mother didn't even know who my father was. To be honest, I hadn't totally forgiven either of them for the subterfuge.

And when my father didn't meet his maker, he'd gotten all rash and weepy and married my mother, thereby terminating my illegitimacy—a fact I was conflicted about. Now to all who weren't in the know, I appeared to have had a normal upbringing instead of having been raised by a single madam in a whorehouse in Pahrump.

The truth just had more panache.

The truth. There I was, back to that. Did I really need to know what had happened to Eugenia Campos? Did I need to know whether my father had killed her? Could I live with not knowing? Could I live with the truth?

Lost in the labyrinth of our respective thoughts, Mona and I stood there as we always had, shoulder-to-shoulder, the two Musketeers against the world and the forces of darkness. A few bottle rockets spurted in the distance—too far away for the sound to reach us.

A subtle clearing of the throat sounded behind us and I turned to face one of the paramedics—Nick, I think his name was. Gorgeous and Greek, he didn't even register on my libido meter— I must have been more out of sorts than I'd realized.

"I'm sorry to bother you, but we're all done here." His white teeth flashed in the darkness as he shot me a smile. "You and your family have kept us pretty busy today."

"Just want to keep you on your toes." I don't think my smile matched his in wattage, but I tried. "And the Big Boss? How is he?"

At Nick's quizzical look, I clarified, "My father. We call him the Big Boss around here. It's sort of a joke, a clichéd term of respect."

"Gotcha. A couple of broken ribs. A pretty good headache. He'll be hurting for a bit, but he'll make a full recovery." Nick tilted his head toward the elevators. "One of my guys made sure Mr. Rothstein got back to his apartment okay. Are you two ready to go? It's pretty dark up here."

His concern was nice—unnecessary, but nice. "We'll be fine, thank you."

He nodded and turned to go, although I could tell he wasn't happy leaving us there. He had no way of knowing that this rooftop was my backyard...literally. The Babylon—my father's hotel—was home. Actually, the three of us lived at the hotel, my parents in one apartment, me in a smaller one next door. While I liked the convenience—my job kept me on perpetual problem-solving duty—it had pretty much driven a nail in the coffin of my life. Of course, my former life had pretty much been torched anyway.

Teddie—a one-man firestorm.

He had lived in the apartment above mine in the Presidio, a high-end apartment building not far from the Babylon. A tower of steel and glass, it would be visible from my current perch, if I chose to look. I didn't.

Teddie and I had leveraged a best friendship into a love affair. I knew it had been a mistake from the beginning, but I'm easily led astray by love. The short of it is, it was great, then it was gone. Teddie left, vanishing into a life as a touring rock star and leaving nothing but memories. It still hurt like hell.

"She just disappeared."

"What?" I turned back to my mother, my thoughts having a hard time regrouping. "Who?"

"Eugenia Campos." My mother darted me with a quick scowl. "Were you thinking of someone else?"

I ignored her jab. I'm sure she could tell she had scored a bull's eye—she just had that knack. "Disappeared. That's what everyone says. But a mother of a small child doesn't just willingly vanish, leaving her child."

"She was a conniving, heartless bitch." The venom in my mother's voice went beyond jealousy. No, there was something way more powerful there. "Just because she gave birth doesn't mean she was a doting mother."

"Point taken. Did Father demand a paternity test?"

Mona pursed her lips as if this was the first time that idea had been broached. "Not that I know of."

"I wonder why?" I shelved that thought for later and shifted gears. "Let's say your assessment of Ms. Campos's character is accurate." I tugged at the shawl that had slipped off one of her shoulders, securing it around her. "By all accounts, Eugenia was on the cusp of getting everything she wanted. Father was willing to support both her and her son, to treat the boy as his legal offspring. If that was the case, why would Eugenia leave with nothing?"

"She got scared?" Mona offered the weak explanation, but even I could tell she didn't really believe it herself. "She tried to kill us, remember?"

"How could I forget?" A bomb...exactly like the one that had nearly killed me today.

"I always thought there was something about that day you never told me."

I recoiled in shock. "Really? Like what?"

Mona looked at me: her eyes were troubled. "I don't know. For weeks after, you had terrible nightmares. Everyone said that was normal, a natural effect of the trauma. But it wasn't like you." She waved her hand in dismissal. "Maybe I was just seeing ghosts. Vegas was like that then, dangers lurking in corners, behind parked cars, everywhere. Probably my imagination running wild. That's what your father always said."

I cast back in time. Hazy memories, diffuse, like looking through a thin veil, I couldn't find any clarity. "I don't remember —not the explosion, not the dreams, none of it."

"You were pretty traumatized. You fainted. I remember that—scared me to death. And when you came back around, you remembered nothing. The doctors all said it was a normal type of amnesia."

"Coming within a whisker of death can have that effect." I've been close enough to death a couple of times to feel the Grim Reaper's breath on my neck, so I knew what I was talking about.

"They said you just needed the right trigger to bring the

memories back. Something is blocking you." Mona's simple observation raised a host of possibilities.

But did I really want to know?

1982
Las Vegas

ALBERT ROTHSTEIN STOOD, FEET PLANTED SHOULDER WIDTH APART, *hands on his hips, fighting worry and his growing anger as he looked out his office window. He'd been a fool to let them take him last night...an arrogant fool. Now he had more problems than a wet spring and a delayed building project.*

Boogie Fleischman. A wart on the world's ass. Rothstein ached to kill him, but he had to think. Crider and the trigger man—they were serious complications. But every problem had a solution. He just had to find it.

Then there was Mona. Fifteen when Lucky was born? That couldn't be true, could it? If so, that little complication might prove a bit more difficult.

He tried to park his worry for the moment. From four stories up, the view out his office window allowed him to survey the entire project. Behind schedule—thanks to a wetter than normal spring—they'd starting pouring the foundation only last week. Despite the gaping hole and only the bare bones of a structure taking shape, Rothstein could picture the building rising in front of him.

The Lucky Aces. His dream. His future.

Goddamn it, he'd done it. And he'd be damned to an eternity in hell before he let them take it from him.

All those years of fighting, of scratching out some respect, of trying to play the game but keep his nose clean, fear had been his constant companion. Fear of a bullet in the back of his head if he stepped on the wrong toes. Fear of being caught in the Kefauver net and thrown in with the wise guys he'd had to do business with. But life had played out for him, and somehow he'd convinced Mr. Thomas and his bank to lend him the money. That along with a serious dose of junk bonds, a new financial instrument. He was about as far from a Wall Street suit as it was possible to be, but Rothstein had done his research. Although sounding too good to be true, apparently junk bonds were the real deal. A risky deal, but one with odds well within his tolerances. A betting man, he understood odds. The hotel was all that mattered. Albert Rothstein shook his head and pressed his lips together. For a kid from the wrong side, life was really looking up. Or it had been until his little trip to the desert. They thought they had him. They always did. But they'd underestimated him before.

He glanced at his watch. 4:14. He'd better hurry if he wanted to be on time. Grabbing his jacket off the coat tree in the corner, he took one last glance around, then flicked off the lights. He still wasn't used to running his own show...and his office was bare bones compared to the lush digs he'd had as Operations Manager at the Desert Inn. But this office, with its metal desk, chairs he'd pulled from the curb in front of one of his neighbor's houses, and an old couch with a couple of busted springs even Goodwill didn't want, was his...all his. With a worried glance at the photo of Mona— the mother of his child and the love of his life, her head thrown back in laughter—he pulled the door behind him. Those guys in the desert couldn't be right—if she'd been underage, she would've told him. The hint of his returning smile lifted the corners of his mouth as he shrugged into his suit jacket. His family, his hotel. Who would've thought it?

Jimmy G's Bar and Grill wasn't far. Mona and Lucky would be waiting. And Jimmy would make sure their secret was safe.

Matilda, his secretary, stopped him on his way through the vestibule. Her hand over the mouthpiece of the telephone receiver, she extended it toward him. "It's for you." Her lips, painted red, pursed in seriousness. Her bleached blond hair piled on her head and teased within an inch of its life just screamed former Strip dancer, which was true. What Matilda lacked in office skills she more than compensated for with ambition and a desperate need to better herself. Albert Rothstein could identify. So *there they were, two unlikely allies in the mad scramble up the ladder of life.*

"Not now. I'm late." He buttoned the middle button, then reached for his fedora.

"She says it's important."

CHAPTER TWO

Summer 2012
Las Vegas

*M*OTHER AND I found Father exactly where the paramedic had told us we would: in his apartment, propped up on the couch, with what I guessed to be a triple dose of single malt clutched in his right hand. Shirtless, his torso tightly bound in thick white surgical tape, he looked ready to spit nails...or shoot somebody. Not that I was surprised or anything—the day hadn't been without its challenges.

Despite looking a bit tattered around the edges, with the butterfly holding closed the cut over his cheekbone and the bruise blooming underneath it, he still oozed a masculine appeal. Handsome, with chiseled features and a body to match, salt-and-pepper hair cut short, and eyes that could shift from warm to deadly in a blink, he emanated a vital, virile force, like a lion winged by a hunter's bullet.

Not killing him had been Albert Campos's first mistake.

Although I'd long ago grown accustomed to his presence,

today I recognized something new—something feral—something I hadn't allowed myself to see before. Wearing blinders, especially where loved ones are concerned, was one of my best things. Of course, I'd always known my father was a man who solved his own problems, but I had never seriously contemplated exactly what that might mean.

"Where have you two been?" His gravelly growl lacked its normal force. Those broken ribs probably put a bit of a crimp in his bluster, and thankfully, they would keep him moving slowly so he couldn't do anything rash. Not that he would, but I'd learned long ago it was never wise to underestimate the lethal capabilities of a cornered animal.

Mother rushed to his side. As she lowered herself to sit on the edge of the couch next to him, he winced but still managed to look happy to see her. His wife clutched at his free hand, holding it tightly for a moment in both of hers. Then she extricated one of her hands and reached to touch his face lightly before smoothing his hair—normally every follicle would be in place, but today his hair looked as ruffled as I felt. "Oh Albert, what a day." Her simple words carried a whole conversation, pregnant with unspoken emotion.

My father lifted my mother's hand, pressing the back of it to his lips as he shut his eyes for a moment. When he opened them, love had replaced the hint of feral I'd seen there. Like an evil spirit banished by an exorcist, his tension fled and his posture eased as he settled back into the pillows under his shoulders, holding her hand in his lap.

"Are you comfortable?" I asked, feeling like an outsider.

His eyes swiveled to me as he took a sip from his glass. "I've been better. You?"

"There's an epidemic of that going around." I stepped to the bar and poured myself a liberal splash of Wild Turkey 101. As I raised the glass to my lips, I was surprised to see my hand was shaking. I sloshed the liquid around my mouth, savoring the heady aromas, then swallowed as I glanced at my reflection in the mirrored wall behind the rows of bottles. Other than a smudge of soot on my cheek and a red scrape on my chin, I looked like myself: light brown hair touching my shoulders, side-swept bangs that tickled my blue eyes, which, come to think of it, were a trifle larger than normal. High cheekbones and full lips bracketed by smile lines completed the me I knew myself to be. Somehow I found that comforting—a constant in a world that was shifting like sand under my feet.

Needing a dose of normal, I let my eyes sweep around the vast room—three thousand feet of high ceilings and burnished hardwood floors, dotted with bright colored, hand-knotted Persian carpets made from the finest spun silk. The walls were either painted a warm peach or were upholstered with leather and featured lesser works by the Grand Masters from the Big Boss's large collection, which was housed in a special gallery in the Bazaar, the Babylon's row of exclusive shops. Brass sconces and appropriately focused spotlights lent comforting light and subtle accents to the art. Clusters of chairs, sofas and tables made from hides of various beasts, exotic woods and leaded glass occupied the carpets making the vast room warm and somehow homey. This being July, the movable fireplace remained unlit and tucked into a corner, but I had known the Big Boss to lower the temp on the air conditioning and light the fire. "Vegas, it's all about setting the stage," he used to tell me. I smiled at the memory.

A bit calmer now, I turned and wandered back, rejoining my parents. I took a chair near the end of the couch. The three of us said nothing for a bit as we took in the view out the wall of windows. A runway of neon, the Strip stretched away from us. No matter how many times I looked through this glass, I never tired of the Strip.

Vegas, my town...my home. I belonged here and I wasn't about to let anyone, alive or dead, mess with my magic.

I kept my eyes on the view. "Consider the Campos matter closed. As you said, no use disturbing old bones." Only after I had said the words did I allow myself to look at my father. I waited until his eyes met mine and I was sure I had his undivided attention. "There's something between you and Boogie Fleischman. I don't know what it is, and I don't want to know. But it isn't good, that's easy to see. So I'm telling you to take your own advice: let it go. If you can't do it for you, or for Mother, do it for me. By my way of thinking, you owe me that much."

That got a grudging half-grin out of him. The set of his jaw and the tick that worked in one cheek hinted that the bad blood ran deep. After a moment, he lifted his glass to me. A simple gesture seemingly lacking in appreciation—I'd pretty much saved his ass today, after all. But between us, gratitude and thanks were inappropriate.

No, the Rothsteins took care of their own.

It was just what we did.

1982
Las Vegas

EUGENIA CAMPOS TUGGED THE HEAVY EARRING OFF HER RIGHT EAR. THE gold veneer of the cheap trinket had worn thin in spots, exposing the pot metal underneath. She sneered at the bit of junk as she placed it next to the phone, then dialed the number she knew by heart with her knuckle— she wasn't going to spoil a great nail job, not even for Albert Rothstein.

Her heart hammered. Her life depended on getting this right. Boogie had said so and she believed him. Closing her eyes against the memory of his fingers digging into her arm, the dead look in his eyes, the booze on his breath, she filled her lungs with air, then let it out slowly, summoning a composure she didn't feel. But she could fake it...hell, she'd been faking everything for so long that she'd forgotten what was real.

She pressed the receiver to her ear when she heard the number ring-

ing, tapping one perfectly manicured fingernail on the chipped Formica countertop as she waited. Pretty soon she'd have real gold—lots of it—no more the cheap stuff. No, she was done with cheap: cheap jewelry, cheap hotels, cheap men.

Eugenia Campos was moving uptown.

After several rings, a woman answered. "Albert Rothstein's office. May I help you?" Eugenia sneered. That uppity Matilda Delacroix.

"Put him on." Eugenia didn't waste party manners on people who didn't matter.

"He's on his way out the door and he's in a hurry." Matilda's voice turned chilly.

Eugenia squared her shoulders, pulling herself together. "It's important. Real important. I got news he's gonna wanna hear."

She heard muffled voices as Matilda's hand covered the mouthpiece. Then Albert's voice boomed over the line. "This better be good. Make it quick."

"You really should treat people better, Albert." Eugenia kept the tremor out of her voice. "You kick a cur, they'll bite you."

"You're getting your cut." Eugenia could almost picture him as he propped his butt on the corner of the desk and shifted the phone to his good ear. "Now, what's so important?"

"The attorney general, he wants to meet."

"Davis? I just had lunch with him yesterday. He didn't mention anything."

"At the club, I know." She could hear the irritation in his voice, the dismissal. She bet he was tugging at his tie—he'd started wearing them every day now that he was hitting the big time, owning his own place and all, and he hated the things. Like a noose just asking for someone to pull it tight. Makes it damn easy for someone to string you up. His words, not hers, but they'd made her smile, as if he could glimpse his future. "This ain't exactly something you want thrown around at the Las Vegas Country Club, is it?"

Silence signaled the point was hers.

"There's some trouble from back east. Like I said, the A.G. wants to meet."

"Fine. When?"

"Now."

"Not possible."

"Well," Eugenia cooed. "You know those big shots are busy people. Davis had a moment in his schedule where he was free from his handlers. You understand why he wants this to be...private."

Silence once again.

Eugenia felt a bead of sweat trickle between her breasts. She reached a finger down the crevice and flicked it away. Sweat stains on her best dress wouldn't do...and satin stained worse than anything. Davis had told her she looked just like Jackie O. She wasn't sure who he meant, but he'd made it sound like a compliment so she'd taken it as such. "He said it would be quick." She cringed as her words rushed out making her sound flustered and hurried. Nervously, she reached for her other earring, tossed it on the counter with its mate, then shifted the phone to her other ear.

"Where?"

That one terse word made her relax—he'd taken the bait. She shifted the phone, then cooed, "Mama Farino's. The booth in the back."

IGNORING THE DRUNK HUDDLED IN THE CORNER, ALBERT PAUSED IN THE doorway of his office building to admire the framework of Lucky Aces. Yes, it was coming along nicely, and once it was pretty far along, he'd turn the wrecking ball on the office building. The location was perfect for a multi-level parking garage.

Slapping on a pair of Ray-Bans, he strode with purpose the half block to Fremont Street. Thankfully, the traffic was thin, although the sidewalks were filling with folks looking for the evening's action. The neon signs blinked at him: Binion's, the Horseshoe—Glitter Gulch they called it. The sign he planned for Lucky Aces would put them all to shame, and it would be right on the corner, exposed to not only Fremont Street traffic but the cars on Las Vegas Boulevard as well. He could close his eyes and see it. It had to be the best...the biggest and the best.

His car, a ten-year-old Olds Cutlass convertible, cherry red with a white top and interior, waited on the surface lot behind Binion's. As he stuck the key in the lock and opened the door, rusty hinges squealing, Rothstein grimaced. The biggest, most gaudy neon sign, then a new car... once he got the money guys off his back. A red Bentley ragtop with real leather seats...yup, that would be the perfect step up. With a whispered prayer, he turned the key. After a couple of false starts, his prayer was answered and the 445 growled to life. He loved the thing. Bold with power to spare, it was the metaphorical Vegas car—and, if he'd thought along those lines, a metaphor for himself.

With a wave to Tommy, the attendant, he motored out of the lot and into the flow on Fremont Street. He glanced at the clock on the sign at the corner. He still had half an hour, but with traffic and sucking up to Davis Lovato, he'd be late. Mona would be worried, but she'd wait.

Besides, there wasn't anything he could do. They had him over a barrel and he had to play their game, at least for now.

Summer 2012
Las Vegas

WITH A GLANCE OVER MY SHOULDER AT MY PARENTS SILHOUETTED together in front of the wall of windows and backlit by the lights of the Strip, I stepped into the maw of the elevator, turning as the doors slid silently closed. I pressed the button with the well-worn 'C' on it, then took the few moments of solitude to check my messages on my new iPhone as I descended to the casino. Scrolling through them, I noted more than a dozen from Teddie.

Teddie.

I ran a hand through my hair as I stared at the list on the screen, silently counting. Yup, fifteen to be exact.

Teddie. A romantic tsunami that had left my heart shattered when the surge of emotion receded.

The pain, searing and so unexpected, still flared at the memory of him. For a few moments in time, I'd had all I'd ever wanted—or I thought I had, at least. But if his love had been so tenuous, so insignificant, that he could abandon it at the first opportunity, then I hadn't really had all that I wanted. No, I wanted way more than that.

Of course, Teddie hadn't bolted frivolously—he had traded our love for his dreams, so he wasn't quite the toad I'd like to think he was. Hating him would be so much easier. He had always dreamed of being an international singing sensation—and I was the only thing in his way.

Well, he effectively solved that little inconvenience.

Lost in my memories, I wasn't prepared for the assault of revelry that hit me when the elevator cushioned to a stop and the doors slid open. Just after midnight, the casino ran with the throttles wide-open. With no destination in mind, I stepped out of the elevator and paused, drinking in the energy. Throngs three deep circled every table. The slots spun and whirled and sang out an occasional song. The recent change to players' cards had silenced the clinking and clanking of real coins running through the machines—music to the ears of every old timer in the casino business, including me. So ingrained was the concept that noise equaled profit, I still panicked at bit at the relative silence. Of course, my nerves were a bit singed.

The Babylon's Persian motif carried trough the casino. With dark walls, carpet in rich-hued mosaic patterning, towering palm trees and loops of bright fabric marching across the low ceilings, the casino looked like a den of iniquity straight out of Ali Baba. Subtle light flickered from wall-mounted sconces fashioned to resemble bundles of burning reeds, a glass cylinder on the end capturing the open flame, enhancing the illicit, Arabian feel.

Turning left, I headed toward the lobby. I hadn't made it three paces before I felt a hand on my elbow. Paxton Dane fell into stride, leaving his hand on my arm.

"Some excitement tonight, huh?" His voice, deep and Texas timbered, flowed like sap in the spring, which to be honest, was a pretty good analogy for the long, tall drink of Lone Star charm. "Glad you weren't blown into little bits."

Stopping, I turned and shot him a half-grin. "Why cowboy, your concern has me all a flutter."

"Hey, I call a spade a spade. No use sugarcoating the truth, as my grandmother used to say." A bit of impish delight fired in his emerald eyes and a grin split his face in a flash of white teeth. All angles and planes, his face, along with those amazing eyes and the wavy brown hair with flecks of gold, combined into a work of art designed to bring the female half of the population to its knees.

Although he had let go of my arm, my skin was still warmed from his touch. What was it with me and men lately? Throw a half-decent one across my path and I turned into a slathering dog. Other than the paramedic, Nick. For some odd reason, he hadn't flipped my switch, an anomaly I probably should pay attention to given my recent less than stellar choices and run of abysmal luck in the game of love—a game with no rules and apparently no time-outs either. Was I trying to fill the hole in my heart? Who knew? I hoped I was smarter than that. That sort of self-medication was just a quick fix at best, with little possibility of long-term upside.

I tried to match Dane's bantering tone. "So what keeps you wandering the casino at his hour? Chasing someone's wayward husband or addicted wife?" The Texan had recently joined forces with the beautiful Jeremy Whitlock, Las Vegas's primo P.I.

Dane's eyes turned all dark and serious, and his smile vanished. "Seriously, you scared me to death grabbing that bomb and throwing it off the roof. You've got one hell of an arm, though. When the thing blew, it didn't even so much as crack a pane of glass. But really, what was up with that bit of stupidity?" He held up his hand silencing me as I opened my mouth to speak. "Rhetorical question. I'm pretty wise to your act by now."

"Gosh, I'm touched." I turned, continuing toward the lobby.

"More like touched in the head," he groused as he fell into step beside me.

Out of the corner of my eye, I glanced at him, taking in the rest of his appearance. Several inches taller than my six feet, he made me feel less like an Amazon—I liked that. Tonight he'd decked out his lean and lanky frame in a starched peach cotton shirt which hadn't wilted—a fact that told me he hadn't spent any time outside today in the 115-degree day, or he was smart enough to keep a change of shirts handy—and creased 501s that hugged his body perfectly—tight, but not too, leaving a bit of room for imaginations to roam. A flash of gold at the wrist and snakeskin kickers completed the picture of studied Texan perfection.

I liked the guy, I really did. But there was something... I couldn't put my finger on it. Even though all the females I knew disagreed, I still felt he worked hard to lull you into complacency with his aw-gee-shucks act. Then like a shifty rodeo bronc sensing a weakness, he'd dart out from under you leaving you flat on your ass in the dirt. I'm sure my assessment wasn't particularly fair, perhaps even a bit cynical, but I couldn't shake it. However, even mired as I was in self-delusion, I was aware my feelings probably said more about me than they did about him. But I didn't want to dig any deeper into myself. Not now anyway. Besides, it was so much easier to attribute my shortcomings to someone else.

"Are you okay? Really?" Concern dripped from his every word.

I could feel his eyes boring into me like a diamond-tipped drill into granite. "Never better."

"Right." Once again, he lightly touched my elbow as he shifted subjects. "Are you going to take in the implosion tomorrow?"

The Lucky Aces. I'd forgotten. "I don't know. I have a hard time with those sorts of things, and that one in particular... a bit of our history reduced to rubble, then scraped away and erased like it never existed."

"The Lucky Aces was the Big Boss's first property, wasn't it?"

"Yeah," I sighed. "The realization of a dream."

"Bet it was something."

"Something is right." I smiled as I replayed the memories. Of course, I'd been so young that the past was more like a series of disjointed snapshots rather than a newsreel.

My father took his first baby step, then Steve Wynn one-upped him four years later with the Mirage—the start of the mega-resort explosion on the Strip. Most people had thought he was nuts moving away from downtown and pouring so much money into the place. Caesar's was the most extravagant property at the time; Mirage eclipsed it by many, many multiples and created the concept of "destination properties." My father thought Wynn was brilliant, the wave of the future. He'd been right, of course. But the Lucky Aces had been where it all began.

1982
Las Vegas

MAMA FARINA'S OCCUPIED WHAT HAD BEEN A BUSTLING CORNER AT *Eastern and Desert Inn. For years it had been the beating heart of the best part of Vegas, but Howard Hughes was changing the landscape. He'd bought the Desert Inn and a whole bunch of the desert north and west of town. A bold move that many thought was crazy, but Albert Rothstein had learned to watch the men who'd made money...watch and learn. Then follow their lead.*

Now, the smart money was moving to the west side of town aban-

doning Mama's as easily as a two-bit hood abandoned his conscience. But Albert drew the line at abandoning Mama's. By his way of thinking, if you forgot where you came from, the folks who extended a hand and pulled you up the ladder, then you were no better than when you started —and perhaps you were worse. You'd just changed clothes, trading workingman's clothes for a suit. But the suit didn't make the man.

And this man had been made in the kitchen at Mama's. Albert still had the scars.

Heavy wooden doors with solid brass fittings and small, stained glass windows, the glass now opaqued by the grime of too many years and too little attention, guarded the entrance. Albert grasped the iron handle and pulled, then stepped through the doorway and back in time.

The casino people needed a home away from home, and they had picked Mama's. Albert remembered sitting at the bar listening to all the big acts on the Strip play pickup after their shows. Various members of The Rat Pack had been regulars. He'd liked Sammy Davis the best... well, him and Dean Martin—both were classy guys. Sinatra was a jerk who loved to push around the nobodies. That had raised Albert's hackles. But the guy had stood up for Sammy Davis when the nice joints were closed to the Coloreds, earning Albert's respect...not that Sinatra cared.

Mama's hadn't changed in thirty years or more. Flocked wallpaper still covered the walls, faded now and almost obscured by the multitude of framed black-and-white eight by tens. The waiters still wore black velvet jackets, black shirts and pants, red ties, and spats that made Albert cringe. The wooden floors creaked with memories, and the walls reeked of garlic. The kitchen still turned out the best Italian food in town, cooked to exacting standards according to Mama's family recipes from the Old Country. Albert didn't know which country was the 'old country,' and he'd been smart enough not to ask. The illusion of authenticity was often enough in Vegas—a lesson Albert Rothstein had tattooed on his heart.

After his eyes had adjusted to the dim interior, Albert turned right into the bar. Striding through, he headed for the last booth on the right—

it had been Davis's booth for as long as he could remember. No one else dared to sit there.

Sal, the head waiter, met him at the booth. "You want I should get you the regular, Boss?" Sal loved to act like he was from Sicily, but Albert knew he really was from Boston, and his father had run a bunch of fishing boats out of Gloucester. But give them the air of authenticity and people would buy the fiction.

"Just some fizzy water and a lime, Sal." Albert slid into the booth. He was the first to arrive.

Albert sat facing the door with the rear wall at his back—one of those Vegas habits of survival. "I'm meeting my ladies in a bit. Don't want them to think I stepped out on them."

"Gotta keep the ladies happy. Yes, sir." Sal stepped behind the bar. "How is Mona? Such a pretty lady. And her kid, Lucky. How is she?" He chuckled and shook his head as he scooped a couple of ice cubes into a tall glass, then filled it with a shot of soda. "That kid is going to be a ball-buster, mark my words."

Albert smiled as Sal set the glass in front of him, then disappeared through the double swinging doors into the kitchen, leaving him alone.

Davis was late. It wasn't like him.

Something wasn't right.

Summer 2012
Las Vegas

WHEN LIFE GOT THE BETTER OF ME, WHICH IT HAD BEEN DOING A lot of lately, I usually sought solace at the Burger Palais, a high-end burger bar in the Bazaar. Today was no exception. While finishing out his eponymous restaurant in our new boutique hotel property, Cielo, Jean-Charles opened this burger joint...just because he wanted to experiment with the American staple.

Having him virtually underfoot complicated my life enormously, not that I was complaining or anything

The cork exploded from the bottle with a bang. I flinched.

"You're as jumpy as a flea on a hot griddle," Dane teased, then turned a cool eye on the chef, Jean-Charles Bouclet, who had popped the cork and was now mopping the overflow from the sides of the bottle.

Jean-Charles grinned at me as he leaned across the bar and filled the flute in front of me. The smile didn't reach his eyes—the normal robin's egg blue deepening with concern. "You have had the day, no?"

"A bit more excitement than usual." I tried to lighten the tone as I raised the glass to my lips and savored my first long sip of happiness. Having Dane next to me was a bit awkward. Both men had charged into the breach when Teddie bolted. A two-horse race for my heart with Jean-Charles the frontrunner by a wide margin. I'd pretty much told Dane as much, but he wasn't one to give up without a fight. While that might be thrilling to other women, it left my nerves all raw and jangled. Of course, the events of the day might have also contributed just a touch.

Jean-Charles tossed me one of his patented Gallic shrugs—he knew they made me smile. I complied, grateful he was keeping the tone light. And to be honest, his presence alone lightened my mood. Tall, and trim, with a square jaw, full lips and brown hair, which he wore a trifle too long for my father's taste but I thought was perfect. Today he wore his kitchen whites and black-and-white striped pants to match. Most chefs I knew had their name stitched on their right breast. Jean-Charles did not, which spoke volumes. I'd yet to see him without a scarf knotted around his neck—today's was blue to match his eyes.

Dane cleared his throat. Guess I wasn't paying him enough attention to suit his delicate ego. Any woman who wanted to be fought over by two men ought to seek psychiatric care.

"So what are you going to do about this Boogie Fleischman thing?" Dane's green eyes challenged me over his bottle of Bud as he tilted it back and took a long pull.

I half expected him to wipe his mouth with the back of his hand before setting the bottle on the bar. I was glad he didn't. "What Boogie thing?" Perhaps if I acted coy he would forget the whole thing. I so didn't want to discuss this now.

No such luck. Dane wasn't buying my act...not that he ever did. "Although that Campos character took the fall, Boogie was behind it."

"How do you figure?" I took a sip of the Champagne, letting the effervescence tickle my nose. Alcohol delivered in little bubbles of perfection...brilliant.

"Well, it was awful convenient that Boogie not only taught the kid how to make the bomb, but also told him exactly where he'd stashed all the components years ago." Dane let that little verbal bomb hang while he took another swig of his beer. "And if you think about, Fleischman had the biggest axe to grind."

"I don't want to think about it."

"Perhaps it would be wise for you to think this way? He could be dangerous, this Boogie person," Jean-Charles chimed in.

Fighting a grin at the absurdity—Dane had seen Boogie Fleischman, a tiny septuagenarian and hardly a menacing threat—I glanced back and forth between the two of them. "You guys are like the Greek chorus in a bad melodrama. Don't you think you might be overreacting?"

Dane waved his empty bottle at Jean-Charles who turned and grabbed a fresh Bud out of the cooler behind the bar, popped the top, then set it next to the empty. "This thing just doesn't pass the smell test," Dane continued. "Think about it. Boogie takes the fall for a bomb he didn't plant—a bomb that almost killed you and Mona. That reeks of a setup."

I shot him a narrow-eyed glance. I knew what was coming, but I didn't want to hear it.

"You know your father wouldn't let that one alone. That's not how he rolls."

I couldn't argue, so I didn't even try. Instead, I threw back the rest of the Champagne, eliciting a wide-eyed look from Jean-Charles when I motioned for a refill. "To hear Boogie tell it, Eugenia Campos, Albert's mother, planted the bomb. He loved her, so he took the fall."

"And you believe this?" Jean-Charles's eyebrows shot upward.

"I really want to."

"So where is this Eugenia?"

Dane leaned back and let the Frenchman take the lead.

The Champagne was doing little to settle my nerves. "That's the kicker. She disappeared." At his quizzical look, I continued. These two weren't going to let me off the hook, and I didn't have any more fight left. "The short story is this: Eugenia had been the Big Boss's plaything. Then he met Mona, and Eugenia was out. So licking her wounds, she took up with Boogie. Hanging around a bomb maker had its advantages; she got pretty good at rigging the things herself. And in keeping with the whole 'hell hath no fury' thing, she tried to take out the competition—Mona and me."

"I'm sure the Big Boss was a bit peeved." Dane smiled at his own understatement.

"Boogie took the fall. And with no one to protect her and the Big Boss on the warpath, Eugenia split."

Dane's eyebrows crinkled into a frown. "With the kid? How old was he?"

"A bit older than me? I don't really know, but Eugenia had tried to shake down my father by claiming Albert was his son."

"I wonder how he took that bit of news," Dane said quietly. His eyes met mine in the mirror behind the bar.

We both knew the Big Boss would not have taken that well.

"So," Dane said, and from the tone in his voice, I knew I wasn't going to like what was coming. "Eugenia, free and clear with everybody thinking Boogie planted the bomb, and with the Big Boss over a barrel, and with a child of her own to care for...with all of this, she disappears?"

"Well, when you say it that way..." I groused. "I know it looks bad."

"Bad? Lucky, the worst lawyer on the planet could take that little story to a grand jury and walk out of the room with an indictment."

"Not here." I sipped from the flute, relishing the Champagne, trying to conjure the nicer side of life. "This is Vegas, and it's my father we're talking about. No one would dare."

Would they?

CHAPTER THREE

1982
Las Vegas

*D*AVIS LOVATO *ran his finger along the edge of his four iron as he worked the shaft into his golf bag. Ben Hogan blades, they'd been made especially to fit his tall frame and flat swing. And they had the reputation of being the hardest clubs to hit. Lovato liked that. Today's round hadn't been spectacular, but an 82 wasn't anything to be ashamed of either. Especially since he'd taken the attorney general job and his course time had become severely limited. But in the dog days of summer, his schedule opened up a bit and a round or two of golf a week became a possibility—a reality, if he didn't mind the heat.*

Davis Lovato had never minded the heat.

Not the blistering temps of the summer in the Mojave, nor the heat of battle in a courtroom or on the political stage. That's why the citizens of the Silver State had elected him attorney general. Of course, his imposing height, strong jaw, quick wit, ready smile and uncanny ability to remember not only the names of people he met, but also the names of their associates and family members, had helped. If you're going to play the part, you gotta look the part—one of the primary rules of any game, or so his father had taught him. His father had been the patriarch of one of the oldest ranching families in Nevada, a legacy his son used to his advantage whenever possible.

Lovato popped the top off the last beer in the cooler and took a long pull, draining half the bottle.

"You all done, sir?" The young man dressed in caddie overalls stepped over to the cart, then stopped, leaving a deferential distance between himself and the Attorney General. "May I clean your clubs and put them away?"

"All done." Lovato reached into his pocket and pulled out a twenty, which he handed to the kid. "Put some good luck on them this time, will ya'? And the five iron could use a new shaft."

"A new shaft, sir?" The kid's eyes widened just a bit.

"The old one somehow got wrapped around the trunk of that damned pine tree on number seven."

To the kid's credit, he didn't smirk. Instead, he nodded in understanding. "That tree's eaten a couple of my shafts as well." After unstrapping the bag, he shouldered it and disappeared into the cart barn.

Lovato turned toward the clubhouse anticipating tossing back a couple more beers with his friends in the grill.

The head pro met him as he pushed through the doors. "There's a call for you, sir. You're welcome to take it in my office."

The Attorney General shook his head with a rueful grin. "What happened to the sanctity of the golf course?" He kicked the door closed and lowered himself into the oversized chair behind the pro's desk. Putting his feet on the polished mahogany, he tucked the receiver between his ear and shoulder and punched the blinking light on the phone. "Lovato."

"How was your round, sweetie?"

The smile evaporated from the Attorney General's face. "Eugenia, fuck. I told you never to call me here."

"Well, I wanted to talk to you. And I didn't think you'd be wanting me to call your house. I mean, what if the beautiful Mrs. Lovato answered...well, then, what would I say? That would be sort of awkward, don't you think?"

Lovato ran his hand over his eyes and glanced around to see if anyone was watching him through the wall of glass separating the office from the pro shop. No one appeared to be taking an unusual amount of interest. "What do you want?"

"Honey, I just want you." Eugenia's voice held a plaintive, seductive tone.

Lovato used to find Eugenia Campos alluring—she was a damn fine package, no one would say otherwise. He'd let his pecker pick his path, not that that was such a sin. Having a piece on the side was sort of expected for someone of his stature, but times were changing. Lovato had a lot to lose, and these days, everyone seemed to expect their public figures to smell like a rose. And if you slept with a whore too often, eventually the stink would rub off on you. Eugenia Campos was not worth the risk. Besides, his wife would be hurt, and his three daughters would be disappointed. And his son...well, he didn't want to think what Daniel might say—the kid had gone all sanctimonious recently. Guess he got that from his mother.

To be honest, the Attorney General couldn't believe he'd been so stupid. And now Eugenia was getting bolder, more possessive. He could see where this was going, and he didn't like it one bit. "Let me finish up here, honey. Then I'll meet you at the usual place."

Something needed to be done, he thought as he slowly recradled the phone and his mind worked through the possibilities.

Summer 2012
Las Vegas

THE MORNING SUN STREAMING THROUGH THE OPEN SHADES assaulted me. Without opening my eyes, I groaned and rolled over. A headache pounded behind my right eye; a bit too much bubbly last night. Jean-Charles had warned me, but I hadn't listened. He had been kind enough to walk me to the elevator, but I'd made the final trek to my bed alone. Casual sex made me twitchy. With sex came connection...and commitment—at least where I was concerned. And I'd had more than enough of both lately to develop a healthy distaste for more.

I sneaked one eye open. Yes, it looked like my apartment—boxes stacked everywhere. Although I'd been in residence several months, I'd yet to unpack fully, treating my apartment like a way station rather than a home, which was a pretty good metaphor—my life on hold. Clearly I was waiting for something, I just didn't know what.

A trail of clothes stretched toward the living room, but that was as far as I risked looking. If I moved my head, I was rewarded with a stabbing pain that felt like an ice pick in my eye, so I quickly decided to keep my head immobile. Taking a deep breath, I searched for the aroma of coffee, the cure for everything that ailed...well, everything except the broken heart thing—apparently that wasn't a quick-fix deal.

No coffee. Programming the damned thing clearly fell outside my skill set, so instead of providing coffee, the machine just delivered a dose of humility. That coffee pot was not long for this world...provided I could figure out how to move without having my head explode.

From behind a copy of *Billboard* magazine, Miss P glanced at me as I pushed through the office door. "Teddie's song "Lucky for Me" is in the top five pop tunes this week." She shrank a little at my glare and folded the paper, placing it in her bottom drawer. "Just thought you would want to know."

"You thought wrong." I hated that Teddie considered it to be a good idea to trot out our checkered love life as fodder for the masses. If he was angling to get my attention, he succeeded, but I don't think unabated fury was the reaction he'd hoped for.

Miss P trailed me into what would be my new office—if the construction guys ever decided to show up and finish it. She stopped once to grab a mug of coffee, which she pressed into my hand as I sank gingerly into my desk chair.

Closing my eyes, I savored the medicinal hit of the first sip of caffeine. Don Francisco's Vanilla Nut. Miss P clearly was attempting amends for the blindside.

"He is trying, can't fault him that," she offered in a conversational tone.

I refused to be drawn in. When I finally opened my eyes, Miss P perched on the edge of the chair facing my desk, looking at me with a mixture of concern and irritation. With short, spiky blond hair, subtle makeup that highlighted her large eyes and a pouty yet prim mouth, she looked a decade younger than she had before Teddie's makeover.

Teddie...I blinked a few times batting away the memory. For once I was successful.

Miss P, in her cool, pale pink silk blouse and white slacks, looked every inch the casino executive she was. Until recently, she had been my stalwart assistant. Now as the Head of Customer Relations for the Babylon, her job was to support the new V.P. thereof, which would be me. So even though we both had moved up in pay grade, nothing had really changed...other than she had my comfy old office and I lived in a construction zone.

A single lightbulb dangled from its cord in the center of the ceiling—a temporary fixture, which cast a circle of light that illuminated my desk but left the corners of the room shadowed. Probably just as well. I didn't want to see the buckets of paint and all the other junk piled there—it just made me angry. But really, how much could two guys with one hammer do? I tried to adjust my expectations lower, but it was impossible...they bounced off the bottom as it was.

With my right hand, I arced through the thin layer of dust that whitened the burled, black walnut of my desk and tried not to scowl. Everything in my life seemed to be under construction.

"Quite a day you had yesterday," Miss P remarked, her voice modulated to an emotionless monotone.

I snorted, then instantly regretted it. I was pretty sure if I did it again, part of my brain would ooze out my nose. "Do you think Denny Mix could help me remember stuff I've forgotten?"

"Denny Mix?" Miss P's voice remained steady, matter-of-fact.

While not perhaps in the top tier of hypnotists in town, Denny still had a good reputation for bringing in a crowd...and he was cheap. Personally, hypnotists scared the hell out of me—abdicating control over my behavior to implanted suggestions from a modern-day snake oil salesman wasn't even close to my comfort zone. But if the clue to getting to the bottom of the Campos mess was buried somewhere in the deep dark recesses...well, it seemed like a small sacrifice to keep the whole bomb thing from happening again. Assuming, that is, that Dane was right and Albert Campos was merely a stooge. And assuming Mona's assertion that I knew more than I remembered proved to be accurate. *And* assuming Denny Mix could help me remember. Several very huge assumptions.

As she gave me the once-over, Miss P's eyes widened slightly, but that was her only reaction. "How much *did* you have to drink last night?"

I shot her a disapproving look. "I can remember last night, well, most of it anyway. I'm pretty sure I have a mild case of PTSD or something, but that's not what I'm talking about." I pushed at a Lucite paperweight holding a few papers on my desk. A golden cockroach encased in the clear plastic, it had been a present from the staff after I had a run-in with a guest who had smuggled thousands of the beasts into the hotel. "I need to access repressed details from an event that happened when I was four."

"I don't know... stuff that happened before the earth was cool might be more difficult."

"Or at least more pricey." I gave her a grin—I could rally, even when the chips were down...and someone was jackhammering inside my skull.

"The deeper you dig—" She left it hanging there, earning my eternal gratitude. "That bomb...you could've been killed."

I just looked at her while trying to think of something clever to say, but the truth sort of deflated me.

Luckily I was rescued by a voice emanating from the front office. "Hey, doesn't anybody work here anymore?"

Miss P looked alarmed, which made me smile. The voice belonged to Flash Gordon, my best friend and the top investigative reporter for the local rag, *The Review-Journal*. She had the loyalty of a Labrador retriever, the smarts of a border collie, and the bite of a pit bull...and she made Miss P all twitchy, which was her best trait.

"Work?" I raised my voice ignoring the jolt of pain, which was quickly abating—caffeine, a miracle drug. "Of course not, we're management."

Flash appeared in my doorway, took one glance around, then plopped on the couch along the wall behind Miss P, forcing her to angle her chair to the side.

Today Flash sported faded jeans with strategic holes, for which I'm sure she paid a King's ransom. Her ample figure filled a hot-pink tee shirt to the bursting point. Her red hair fell in a cascade of messy waves, and along with her slightly full lips and bedroom eyes, it gave her the look of someone who had spent the night abusing some hapless lover, which was probably closer to the truth than I could handle at this early hour.

"So girlfriend, how're you holding up this fine morning?" Flash's tone telegraphed concern—a rare occurrence. "To be honest, you're looking a bit owl-eyed and green around the gills."

Imagine, Flash going all motherly on me; I must have looked as bad as I felt. "Thanks for stopping by to make me feel better."

"Feel better?" Flash scoffed. "Hell, I just wanted to see what was left."

"Preside over my demise? I knew I could count on you to sift through the remains."

"The lengths I have to go to for a story." She gave me an exaggerated pout.

My face must've sobered as I saw a reflective, anticipatory sobering in hers. "There is something you can do for me."

"Name it." She leaned toward me.

"I'm trying to piece together the details of the bombing at Jimmy G's when I was four. Can you go through what you've put together so far?"

Flash blew at a tendril that hung in her eyes, then chewed on her lip for a moment as she culled through her mental database. She rose, then plopped a butt cheek on the corner of my desk as she glanced between Miss P and me, bringing us both into her gaze. "Short and sweet?" She paused, giving me a questioning lift to one eyebrow, then continued at my nod. "The police reports were pretty specific. The Big Boss was late meeting your mother and you, which was unusual. No one could remember him being anything but early before."

I stared at the wall behind Flash as my eyes lost focus, searching for clarity in the murky past. "Mother was worried, I remember that. She had a box, something for my father." I refocused on Flash. "Was there any mention of that in the reports?"

She shook her head. "No, the only thing your father said was that he'd received a phone call just as he was leaving the office. Something about a problem at the site he needed to deal with."

"Did he say who called?"

"No, just that the voice was female."

"No mention of a name attached to that voice?" I leaned back in my chair, fully intending the question to be rhetorical.

"Not yet, but I've got a lead for you." Flash paused, giving in to her penchant for melodrama.

I didn't give her the satisfaction of showing my surprise. "And?"

"I was pumping Crayfish..." She shot a sideways glance at Miss P whose face remained impassive. "For more info. He was still wet behind the ears back then, but that bomb was one of his first big cases."

Crayfish Crider was one of Flash's more nauseating forays into casual sex—he was old enough to be her grandfather, and he had a penchant for weird sexual...devices. I tried to close my mind to the visuals. "And he remembered something?" I pushed.

"He sorta went all wonky on me when I pushed him too far. But he did say to ask Matilda, that she knew more than she'd let on."

Great. My day had just gone from as-bad-as-it-gets to worse.

Flash must've seen the look on my face. "You know who Matilda was?"

"Is...she's my aunt...sort of. It's a long, sordid tale." I leaned back, placing my hands palm down on my desk, and stared at my two friends. "Aunt Matilda, how does she fit into all of this?"

1982
Las Vegas

ALBERT ROTHSTEIN RACED OUT OF MAMA FARINA'S, HIS HEART pounding, a cold sweat gripping him. Davis Lovato was never late—tardiness was one of his pet peeves. No, this whole thing reeked of a setup. The guys from the desert hadn't made their move—he'd been waiting for it. But would they really go after his family?

The Family had its rules, its code of conduct, and killing women and children was considered bad form. But that had been before, in the old Vegas. The new blood came with new rules. Albert's heart constricted as he jumped into his car, turned the key, then floored it, racing out of the parking lot with a squeal of rubber.

Jimmy G's wasn't far.

MONA, DRESSED IN SHORT SHORTS, A HALTER TOP AND A SMILE, perched on the stool at the bar nearest to the front door. After two washings and fifty strokes of the brush, just as her mother had taught her, her deep mahogany hair with copper highlights shone as it cascaded past her shoulders. Large, dark doe eyes, high cheekbones, and a neck to rival Audrey Hepburn's, Mona pretended to be oblivious to the heads she turned. Even though she was Albert's, she still liked to preen for the men. As she waited, her long thin legs crossed, she dangled a flip-flop from her foot, bouncing it as her excitement grew. She looked all of sixteen, which wasn't too far from the truth, although she kept her age a closely guarded secret. Even Albert didn't know. Her smile dimmed.

"Mom?"

Mona's smile returned to its former wattage as she gazed at the young girl squirming on the stool next to her. Only four, Lucky was as lean and lanky as a colt.

Barely beyond childhood herself, Mona never dreamed that being a mother could've been the one thing to save her. "What, honey?"

"I need to go to the bathroom."

Mona reached down and brushed a strand of dark hair out of her daughter's eyes, securing it behind her ear. Lucky had her father's eyes, blue as the summer sky just before sundown, which made Mona smile. "Go ahead then."

Lucky sidled off the stool and galloped toward the back of the bar. Usually Mona would go with her, but this was Jimmy G's place; nothing bad would happen here, at least not at this time of day—still a bit early for the real rowdies. A glance around confirmed her assessment; the only people in the place were the local drunks, and they'd probably been there all day. Mona felt sure they were past caring about a little girl, or if not, too drunk to do much about it.

Mona reached into her fanny pack tethered around her waist, extracting the small, hinged box. Cradling it in both hands, she thumbed open the top. Nestled in silk rested a ring—a man's ring, with two initials, an 'A' and an 'R,' framed in gold and filled with pavé diamonds. She'd been saving for months. This was to be her present to Albert to commemorate Lucky Aces.

He'd worked so hard, had come so far.

"Whatcha got there?" Jimmy angled into the bar opposite her, wiping a beer mug with a rag that looked a bit dirty by Mona's way of thinking, but she didn't say anything. "You want a refill?"

"It's a surprise." Mona showed it to him, then smiled at his appreciative whistle.

"Quite a bauble."

"I've been saving forever." Mona snapped the lid shut and set the box on the bar. Albert would be here soon. She eyed her empty mug. "Yeah, I'll take another hit. Thanks."

"Better go easy on that fizzy water, the bubbles can go right to your head." Jimmy winked at her as he refilled her ginger ale. A short man, he had the wiry build of a boxer coupled with a ready smile and easy manner

Probably not a bad combination for a bar owner, thought Mona as she watched him top off the mug, then reholster the soda gun.

"Your man is late. That's not like him." Jimmy wiped his hands on his rag and gave her a wink. "He's usually pacing back and forth waiting for you two."

A frisson of fear flashed through Mona as she took a sip of her drink, but she dismissed it. "He'll be along. Just like every Thursday. That's our day, you know."

Jimmy smiled, then excused himself with a nod to attend to a new customer.

Mona chewed on her lip as she glanced at the front door. It wasn't like Albert to be late. Every Tuesday she drove in from Pahrump, and

Albert would meet them at Jimmy G's. Then they'd go off on an adventure. It was their day. Albert would be there. But she wondered what could be keeping him.

"Mom." Lucky's voice, serious and low, pulled Mona back.

The girl was standing next to her. Mona hadn't heard her return. She brushed down the child's hair. "What is it, honey?"

"There's something wrong... in the bathroom." Lucky didn't scare easily; growing up in a whorehouse, she was used to the unusual—a realization that worried Mona, but she pushed it aside. She had no choice. Life was what it was, and she was making the best of it.

Mona eased off her stool and grabbed Lucky's hand. "Show me."

On all fours, mother and daughter peered behind the toilet in the last stall. Mona tried not to grimace; the floor was filthy.

"There." Lucky pointed, her eyes large and round, her expression serious. "See it?"

Mona bent her elbows, leaning her head to the side. Her heart stopped.

The device was small: two sticks of dynamite, a battery, a clock, a few wires. Although she'd not seen one before, Mona knew what it was instantly.

As she scrambled backward out of the stall, she grabbed Lucky's arm, tugging the girl with her. "Hurry."

They ran into the bar. Mona pushed her daughter toward the front door. "Run, baby. I'll be right behind you." She took a moment to watch Lucky bang through the door and be swallowed by the sunlight. "Jimmy." Mona raised her voice to get everyone's attention. "Get everyone out of here. Hurry."

Jimmy shot her a look, then did as she ordered.

Mona raced after her daughter. Once outside, the assault of the sun brought tears to her eyes. She blinked furiously trying to adjust. Squinting, she searched the gathering crowd for her daughter. There she was, separating herself from the throng. Mona's heart stopped when she realized what the girl was doing.

"Lucky, no! Don't! Come back. Oh my God!"

CHAPTER FOUR

Summer 2012
Las Vegas

*T*HE LUCKY Aces called to me. Time to say goodbye. I felt a song coming on and smiled at the odd associations my mind made when under stress. At least this goodbye wouldn't be accompanied by the too-often-played Andrea Bocelli track. At least I didn't think it would be, knowing the Big Boss as I did. Besides, the Bellagio ran that track to death with the whole fountain thing.

To be honest, I sucked at goodbyes, and I'd resisted this one as long as I could. The cab dropped me a couple of blocks away so I could stroll down Fremont Street. The canopy of programmed dome lights high above, known as the Fremont Street Experience, sheltered the crowd from the midday sun. Still, the air hung heavy, sultry—stagnant with the putrid smell of stale beer and the rotting remnants of last night's 4th of July citywide picnic. It fit my mood.

Easing into the crowd, I let the flow of people propel me along as I rode the current of memories; memories that would soon be buried under a pile of rubble, then swept away as if they'd never existed.

Vegas, the city of reinvention.

Most days I liked the bright, clean, shiny-penny land of opportunity. But not today. This was my history—my heritage—that would be reduced to rubble, then extinguished, banished to the history books.

As I rounded the corner at Main Street, reality sucker punched me. The Lucky Aces, all signs of brightness and life removed, sat hunkered down, a tired, old hulk, stained, dated...abandoned. Tattered curtains—faded strips of cloth—waved in surrender from broken windows. Wires dangled from holes in the concrete, reminding me of snakes writhing to escape death. Clean spots on the now-dirty gray concrete marked the locations of signs that had blinked their come-ons in multicolored neon for as long as I could remember. I guessed they'd gone to the Neon Boneyard, a museum housing famous landmarks, bits of Glitter Gulch magic. I didn't want to think about paying a fee to see signs that no longer beckoned anyone. That was too sad to think about.

A chain-link fence cordoned off the property. Signs announced the demolition and the danger, warning everyone away. In the wee hours before tomorrow's dawn, like a death row executioner, someone would pull the switch and extinguish the Lucky Aces. But truth be told, her heart had stopped beating years ago.

One lone figure, his hands above his head, his fingers laced through the fence, his forehead resting on his entwined hands, stood staring at the old hotel.

The Big Boss.

He glanced at me as I stepped in beside him. He didn't look surprised.

"A trip down memory lane?" I asked, because I didn't know what else to say. I didn't have the words.

"A lifetime of hopes and dreams..." He trailed off as his voice caught. Apparently words failed him as well. "A lot of secrets inside those walls."

His words surprised me. *Secrets?* I shot him a grin. "A few skeletons in those closets?"

He didn't smile.

1982
Las Vegas

*I*F THE DEFINITION OF ARROGANCE WAS "CONFIDENCE WITH NO *foundation," then Boogie Fleischman was an arrogant man. Small, wiry, not particularly bright, he had one skill: he could blow stuff up. Loyal to the highest bidder, he made a living out of playing both sides of the fence —a particular lack of character he shared with Eugenia Campos. Somewhere deep inside resonated the knowledge he was overreaching with her —she had her sights set on bigger fish—but he couldn't help whom his heart picked. And he was patient. For now, he'd take the crumbs she offered him, but one day...yes, one day she'd come around. He'd make sure of it.*

Eugenia's apartment building was classy—all thick carpet, marble floors and staff that bowed and scraped. He wasn't sure who was toting the load on the lease—God knew Eugenia didn't have that kind of smack —but it must be somebody important. Boogie didn't belong there, he knew that, but he tried to act like it didn't matter.

The security guy, a mountain of a man with a scar on his chin and arrogance in his eye, nodded to Boogie as he passed. Boogie didn't nod back. That was how the rich did it. He fidgeted as the elevator lifted him toward the top floor. Of course, Eugenia had the penthouse—only the best for her.

She answered before he had time to knock; she must've been waiting. His heart skipped a beat.

"Oh." Her face fell when she saw him, then she turned her back and walked away. "What are you doing here?" She threw the words over her

shoulder like morsels for a stray. "I'm expecting someone, so you can't stay."

In front of the window, she turned to face him.

Her beauty took his breath but not too much—Boogie knew it didn't run deep. "Fine." His tone was brusque to hide the hurt. "How'd it go down with Rothstein?"

"He bought it. He should be waiting at Mama Farino's." Eugenia frowned.

Boogie might've misinterpreted it as a flash of conscience, but he knew better. He also knew that she had it bad for Rothstein. "You know the rule..."

"Never fall for the mark, I know." Eugenia worried with her pearl choker. "But you're not going to hurt him, right? Just scare him."

"Sure, sure."

"I don't want nothing bad to happen to him," Eugenia said, letting her veneer slip a little.

Boogie gave her a smirk. "Not even to the bitch and her kid?"

A flicker of doubt flashed across her face as her mouth curled slightly at the corners.

"That's what I thought." If he understood anything, he understood creating competitive advantages—his stock-in-trade.

Eugenia turned her back in dismissal and stepped to the window. "You gotta go. I'm expecting somebody."

Boogie stepped to the small table next to the couch and picked up the phone, holding the receiver to his ear. "Gotta make a call, then I'll be out of your way." After he checked to make sure she wasn't paying attention, he palmed the single gold earring sitting next to the phone and pocketed it.

Summer 2012
Las Vegas

AFTER I LEFT MY FATHER ALONE WITH HIS THOUGHTS, I DROWNED

my worries in the sea of problems swirling at the Babylon. The amount of mischief three thousand guests could find at any moment in time never ceased to amaze me. Seeing Matilda was on my list of things to do, but she never agreed to see anyone, even extended family, before midnight at the earliest. So I had some time to kill. And some courage to find. A visit to see Matilda required extra fortification—and a bottle of cheap gin.

My staff and I scurried through the rest of the day, all of the evening and into the night handling a variety of complaints ranging from a very drunk man attempting to jump from his balcony into the pool, to several couples wanting to get married, to two high-end call girls working the tables, to...well, it was a pretty normal night, but like everything in Vegas, far from ordinary.

About an hour into the new day, the energy waned just enough for Miss P and me to sag onto stools in Delilah's. Our fancy watering hole in the middle of the casino, Delilah's sat on a raised platform surrounded by trellises of winding bougainvillea, giving it sort of a secret grotto kind of feel—if you could ignore the music and merriment filtering in from the casino. Water cascaded down the rough rock facing behind the bar. I ignored the white baby grand sitting untended at the far end of the bar. Sometimes, about this time of night when our days were drifting toward home and sleep, Teddie would sit and play a few tunes. I'd join him, enjoying the way his fingers danced over the keys, the sound of his voice, the warmth where his shoulder pressed to mine. The memories wound around my chest, squeezing. Fighting the constriction, I took a deep, ragged breath, but it caught in my throat.

Miss P placed a hand on my arm and gave it a sympathetic squeeze. "Not to make things worse, but..." She lifted her chin toward the television that hung high above the bar. "It's about time for the implosion."

"You ladies look like you need some joy juice." Sean, our head bartender stopped in front of me, his grin sparkling in his eyes. Spiky hair, a receding hairline and an easy, comfortable manner, he was one of Babylon's best assets, providing a willing ear, a shoulder to cry on, a glass of courage or anything else a patron—or co-worker—might need. Following our gazes, he glanced over his shoulder. When he turned back to us, he'd dialed down the wattage. "I hate it when they take down one of the old places. So much history there." He shrugged. "I know, making way for progress and all, but when we quit remembering where we're from, we lose our bearings. Know what I mean?"

"All too well," I said, thinking that for years, I hadn't known where I'd come from at all. Still a bit sketchy on any family details beyond the immediate, I continued to feel a bit untethered. Maybe that's why this implosion bothered me so much—the Lucky Aces was a part of my history that was already as thin as well-worn cotton.

Dragging my eyes from the pictures on the screen—thankfully someone had muted the sound—I turned my attention to the various medicinal waters lining the shelves on either side of the water feature, from countertop to higher than I could reach. The fancy stuff was way up on top. A bottle of Louis the XIII in its distinct Baccarat bottle was the most recognizable. At several hundred dollars a shot, it was a curiosity for me, nothing more. Personally, I wanted a bit more bang for my buck.

"Ah, Sean, it's a Wild Turkey kind of night." I shot Miss P a look, and she nodded. "Make it two."

"101?" he asked, as if he didn't know the answer. "Water or soda?"

"A sacrilege," I scoffed, bringing back the wattage to his grin.

As he scurried off to do my bidding, my attention once again drifted to the television. Numbers in the lower-right corner counted down—just a minute left.

I barely noticed when Sean set the tumblers of amber liquid in front of us. The first sip got my attention, burning a path of fire from my mouth to my stomach where it exploded in a ball of comforting warmth. Miss P choked a bit, which made me smile. "Grade A firewater."

Her face flushed; she dabbed at tears. "Stout," she managed to choke out. Then she took another sip. Yup, she was a gamer, and this job would make a serious drinker out of her yet. "Aren't you going to go see your Aunt Matilda?"

Unable to look away from the scene unfolding on the screen, I didn't look at her. "In theory, but it's not like the world is hanging in the balance. It's just a fishing expedition. And really, I just don't feel up to tackling her bit of crazy right now."

I watched as the numbers hit zero. Time seemed to stop. Then the Lucky Aces folded in on itself in a cloud of dust, until it was no more.

1982
Las Vegas

DAVIS LOVATO HAD WORKED UP QUITE A LATHER BY THE TIME HE RAPPED *sharply on Eugenia Campos's door. He heard her heels clacking on the marble floor, then the door swung open. Eugenia filled the doorway. Keeping the door next to her, she ran her hand up it slowly, giving him a provocative smile. She really was stunning—dark hair, full red lips, almond-shaped eyes and a figure that wouldn't quit. Today a tight-bodiced dress scooped low across her chest highlighting her assets.*

Davis pushed her out of the way, then stepped around her. "Don't leave me standing out in the hall. What if someone saw us?"

If his rudeness bothered her, Eugenia didn't show it. Instead, she glanced up and down the hallway. The man with the camera stepped out from his hiding place and gave her a nod. She smiled before closing the door. Composing herself, she turned and followed her guest into her parlor.

Davis helped himself at the bar, pouring a tumbler of single malt. He liked that Eugenia always remembered to have his favorite brand on hand—his wife couldn't be bothered. Eugenia pressed herself to his back, snaking her arms around his waist. With one hand, he pulled one of her arms away and shrugged out of her embrace, putting distance between them. He couldn't trust himself when she was that close—just her perfume alone was enough to erode his willpower.

"Honey, what's the matter?" Eugenia had taken his not-so-subtle cue and now parked herself on the arm of the couch, her long legs daintily crossed where he could see them.

Davis took a slug of his drink and swallowed. Tearing his eyes away from her legs, he tried to focus on what he had come to say. "Honey, you've been great, you really have. But we've got to quit this."

"I don't understand." She looked caught off guard, hurt flashing in her eyes. "You told me you loved me."

For a moment, Davis felt like a creep, but the feeling passed. "Honey, you've been around the block a time or two. Hell, we both have. You knew from the beginning this was just for kicks." He tried to keep the tone light.

Her eyes narrowed, and her expression hardened just a bit. "For kicks? That's what this was?"

He snorted and shot her a you-can't-be-serious look as he took another sip of scotch. "I'm the attorney general. Taking up with you publicly would totally torpedo my career. I know you don't want that."

"I wouldn't be too sure." Eugenia's voice held a threat.

Davis had been prepared for histrionics—for crying and pleading—but he hadn't been prepared for the cold calculation he saw in Eugenia's face. "Eugenia, I'm putting together a team to float the possibility of a run at the governorship. This will bring much more intense scrutiny to my personal life. I can't have them finding out about us."

"Perhaps you should've thought of that earlier," she said with a smile that didn't reach her eyes.

"How much?" Davis set his drink down and reached for his wallet. "I've got fifty grand here. That'll stake you and the boy somewhere else."

He thought he saw a softening at the mention of the boy. "You don't want the kid to get caught in the middle of this, do you?"

"You want to buy me off like some cheap whore?" Her posture rigid, she didn't move.

"Oh, you're anything but cheap." He gave a rueful chuckle as he shook his head. "I'm being nice now, Eugenia, but it won't last. Trust me, you don't want to make me angry."

"Don't threaten me, Davis. You don't hold all the cards. Seems to me that you have more to lose than I do." When he opened his mouth to answer, she held up her hand, stopping him. "My son is out of your reach. I'm not afraid of you."

Davis Lovato moved to loom over her. "You should be."

Summer 2012
Las Vegas

DETECTIVE ROMEO FOUND ME IN MY OFFICE TRYING TO JUMP-START the day with my second cup of coffee. Too much Wild Turkey, too much skipping down Memory Lane, too much Teddie and his friggin' song—it popped up all the time on the radio feeds around the property until I felt like running for cover...or shooting the pompous little songbird. My head was fuzzy, my skin sallow, my smile wan and my heart heavy. Not my best morning. Not that morning was ever my optimal time.

"You seen your father around?" Romeo didn't look happy. In fact, he looked uncomfortable. His eyes, normally clear and direct, refused to meet mine. "I can't seem to find him."

"Good morning, Detective." I added a healthy dollop of vanilla-flavored creamer to my coffee—a new obsession—then took a sip. Too hot. As I blew on the steaming liquid, I looked at Romeo over the top of my mug. The dark suit was new. So was the tie. Hermes. Nice touch; it must've been a gift. His sandy hair was a trifle longer than normal. And his expression was a bit more grim than I was used to. "It's early. I haven't seen anybody. Why?"

"You might want to sit down."

I gave him a dirty look. The kid knew full well that I could take whatever he could dish standing up. Turning and running was so much easier from this position.

He waited for a moment, then shrugged. "Suit yourself, but don't say I didn't warn you."

My heart skipped a beat at the frisson of fear that jolted through me. My head cleared. As jump-starters, adrenaline outranked caffeine any day.

"You know that implosion?"

"The Lucky Aces, sure."

"There was a problem."

"What kind?" A tickle of fear drifted up my spine. What had my father said? Something about secrets at the Lucky Aces? To steady myself, I took another sip of my coffee. Better. Even though Romeo was trying to rain on my day, I just couldn't work myself up to going to general quarters. Not yet, anyway. "The Big Boss hasn't owned that property for years."

"He built it, though. Right?"

"It was his baby." The thought made me happy and sad at the same time.

"Well..." Romeo paused. His eyes met mine and held. "We found skeletal remains in the foundation."

I paused, my mug halfway to my mouth. "In the foundation?"

"Apparently the remains had been there since the walls were erected. I'd like to talk to your father."

"I'm not sure I like where you're taking this conversation." No longer interested in my coffee, I set my mug down. "My God, anybody could've dumped a body in there. Back then, that practice was so common it's clichéd."

"All true." Romeo pursed his lips as he stepped over to the wall of glass that provided a view to the lobby below. Crossing his arms behind him, he kept his back to me. "Still, I need to talk to the Big Boss."

"I'm sure he's not hiding from you."

Romeo turned to face me. When he did, I saw the seriousness in his eyes. "I wouldn't be too sure." Romeo reached into his pocket, then extended his closed fist. He turned his hand over and opened it. "We found this next to the body."

A ring. With the initials AR in diamonds.

DENNY MIX HAD AGREED TO MEET ME IN TEDDIE'S OLD THEATER. To be honest, I wasn't really excited about being hypnotized, but I didn't see any other option, especially in light of Romeo's little bombshell. The first to arrive, I passed the time pacing from one side of the stage to the other. If Mona was right and I did know something else about the explosion at Jimmy G's all those years ago, now was a good time to find out what it might be.

Denny came out from behind the curtain surprising me. A short man with an open, honest face, shaggy dark hair and a sincere smile, he wore torn jeans, a muscle shirt, and Converse high-tops. Even though he was not yet forty, the muscle shirt was a bad idea...especially considering the hair on his back. I stifled a shudder of revulsion—what was it with hairy men and muscle shirts?

"You alone?"

"No witnesses," I managed to say with more glibness than I felt.

Denny brought a chair with him, which he placed in the middle of the stage, then motioned for me to sit. "This won't hurt."

Feeling totally out of my comfort zone, I took the chair, crossing my arms across my chest in a defensive reflex.

"Are you afraid?" Denny asked.

I thought for a moment. "No. Uncomfortable, but not afraid."

"Good. Fear makes hypnosis impossible." He squatted in front of me. "After your call, I did a little quick and dirty research on the event you mentioned."

"The explosion when I was four?"

"Right. So I'm going to get you real relaxed and take you back."

"You're not going to make me bark like a dog or anything, right?"

He smiled. "Tempting." At my stricken look, he sobered. "Kidding. This is serious, I know. We'll leave the silly games for the paying crowd. You do know that this might not work; the jury is still out as to whether hypnosis can open the door to repressed memories."

"It's worth a shot." I purposely hadn't told him the latest particulars—the body, the ring, Romeo's insinuations. Actually, I hadn't told him any of the facts I remembered. I didn't need Denny Mix to implant a memory that wasn't there.

"Okay. Just relax. I'm going to talk to you, try to get you to really relax, work your way back in time. This won't feel odd to you, really. Our brains go into what we call a hypnotic state several times a day. You'll be present. You'll be able to respond to me. The whole thing will feel normal."

Not a chance in hell, I thought, but I didn't say so. Instead, I added the rather insincere, "If you say so."

"Close your eyes."

I did as he asked and tried to relax, to let go. For once I was glad I hadn't overdosed on caffeine.

"Okay, concentrate on relaxing your shoulders." Denny's voice took on a soothing timbre. "Good, you're doing fine. Now your arms, relax them."

I keyed on his voice, letting the rest of the world and my worries fall away. I felt myself relaxing. We worked our way down my body, focusing on relaxing the muscles.

"Now your breathing. Make it slow and deep."

I took several deep, slow, conscious breaths as my mind drifted. As tired as I was, letting go was easier than I thought—my body, needing rest, overruled my fears. I let my mind wander back to that day long ago. Back to Jimmy G's. I could see Mona. So young. So happy. Short shorts, her legs swinging as she sat on the stool sipping a Ginger Ale.

Mona fidgeted; she was nervous. The Big Boss was late. Unusual. She was worried. Funny how kids picked up on those subtle emotions so easily.

Then the bathroom. The bomb.

Fear. Then running. Mona pushing me toward the door. The light...

I was alone. Scared. Then Mother followed me.

But I hadn't stayed outside. I'd gone back. Back inside.

Why? There was something else. Something important. The bathroom...the bomb with only tens of seconds left. Hurry. I crouched down. I knew what I'd come for. A bit of gold next to the bomb.

An earring? I'd grabbed it. Turned to run.

Then hands grabbed me. I looked up.

My breath caught. My eyes flew open. My hand clutched my chest.

"Oh my God!"

PART II

CHAPTER FIVE

Summer 2012
Las Vegas

"YOU WERE there." I faced down my father.

He turned his back to me and stared through the wall of windows at the Las Vegas Strip as it unrolled at his feet. My father, Albert Rothstein, the owner of the Babylon, Vegas's most over-the-top Strip property, flinched as I stepped in beside him, but he didn't look at me. Normally a vital force, he seemed to lose wattage, shrinking in on himself like a dying star.

I wasn't very happy with that analogy. Turning my back to my father, I squinted against the brightness as I took in the view. The sun drowned the neon—midday, not Vegas's most magical time. To be honest, it wasn't shaping up as my best time either. "At Jimmy G's, right before the explosion. You were there."

"I knew someday you'd remember." His voice was emotionless, pragmatic.

"I went back inside. You grabbed me." My voice caught. I couldn't say the rest, but I remembered. "You saved my life."

"Life is funny." His voice hitched as he shook his head, then angled a quick glance and a fleeting one-sided grin my direction. His gaze steadied, capturing mine as he said, "It can change on a dime."

"Why did you hide it?"

A flash of shock fled across his face, then was gone. If I didn't know him so well, I would've missed it. "Hide what?" His voice was steady, the defeat in it a memory.

"You being there. None of the police reports, none of the newspaper articles, not one mentioned you being there." I paused, trying to pull through my panic the facts Flash had told me. "In fact, you specifically told the police a phone call had delayed you."

"That was the truth." He turned back to the view out the window.

"But not all of it," I pressed. I knew I had bits and pieces, but not every detail. I sensed there was something missing—something important, riding on the edge of my consciousness like a butterfly on the wind, floating just out of reach.

"What else do you remember?" he asked. I got the feeling he was trying hard to sound as if he didn't care, wasn't worried.

"Bits and pieces, but clearly not everything." Vegas stretched toward the western horizon. My city, filled with magic...and secrets.

"It was a different time, Lucky." My father ran his hands over his eyes as if trying to rub out the memories.

We both jumped, startled as the elevator whirred to life.

"Are you expecting anyone?" I asked.

"Probably just your mother. Mrs. Olefson invited her to lunch."

Mrs. Olefson was nearing ninety and from somewhere in the Midwest. She'd lost her husband a few years ago, and time had dwindled her circle of friends until she had only her Maltese, Milo. The two of them had come to the Babylon and had decided to stay...permanently. So we gave her a nice, sunny room, and she became a de facto den mother, riding herd over our ragtag little bunch, but especially over Mona. Which, if I had any say, earned her a gilded throne and phalanx of handsome footmen in heaven.

"Those two, they've become thick as thieves." I relaxed a bit, thankful for the change of topic.

"Hmmm." My father's thoughts were clearly elsewhere.

As the elevator doors opened, Mona charged into the room like a bolt of lightning—unbridled energy that attracted attention like an atom pulling in electrons. Today she wore pink, not one of her best colors. Her cheeks flushed to match her sweater, a loose-knitted tunic that hid her growing baby bump. She wore her hair collected at the nape of her neck with a few tendrils pulled to frame her face. Her eyes were big and worried. "Albert! Albert!" she called as she scanned the room. Spying us on the far side, she beelined in our direction.

She wasn't alone.

Trailing one arm dramatically behind her, she hurried across the hardwood floors, her flats lacking the normal clackety-clack that heralded her arrival. "Detective Romeo wants to talk with you. I didn't see any harm."

My father calmed her worried look with a smile. "Not at all." He turned his attention to the two cops who had ground to an uncertain stop in the middle of the apartment. "Come, gentlemen. Welcome." My father motioned them closer.

Detective Romeo had been a total greenhorn when I'd met him not too long ago. Had it really been less than a year? Hard to believe. Now, his boyish face and sad blue eyes seemed to sag under the burden of death on a daily basis. I was glad to see that his cowlick at the crown of his skull still refused to bend under the weight of responsibility and sadness, even though his sandy hair held the hint of a recent combing. His normal jacket hung on his increasingly thin frame, making him look as if he were a boy who'd pulled his father's coat from the hall closet. And he didn't look happy, which was the first sign that this wasn't a social call. My stomach tightened.

He stopped in front of my father. "Sir, I'm sorry." His gaze flicked to me and, if possible, he looked even sadder. But, he squared his shoulders as if bracing for a storm and turned back to my father.

"You need to come with us."

1982

Las Vegas

TERROR SEIZED MONA AS SHE TURNED TO SEE HER DAUGHTER BOLTING *back into Jimmy G's. The bomb. No more time. "No! Lucky, come back!" Moving to chase after the child, Mona was a step too slow.*

Hands grabbed her arms. "No, Mona. You can't." Jimmy G held one arm in a vise.

Gripped with fear, Mona struggled and pulled. When that didn't break his grasp, she turned like a cornered puma, clawing, scratching. "Let. Me. Go," she growled through clenched teeth. "You have to let me go."

Jimmy ducked away but tightened his grasp. Another pair of hands grabbed her, helping. Male, strong, but Mona didn't turn to look at the face. "No, honey," Jimmy insisted. "The bomb..."

A huge explosion ripped through the building. The concussion lifted them, then threw them to the ground. Mona landed on her back, Jimmy on top of her. The other guy had disappeared. Glass and splintered wood rained down. Instinctively, Jimmy covered Mona as best he could; she was twice his size.

Jimmy felt the heat of the flames before he heard the roar of the fire. He held Mona with the weight of his body.

Mona must've heard it, too. She pushed weakly at Jimmy's body, most of her fight gone. "Let me up, Jimmy. I've got to find Lucky."

Sirens sounded in the distance. He twisted around and watched the fire tear through the dry wood, consuming everything. "She's gone, baby." He wrapped Mona in his arms as she started to shake. There wasn't anything else he could do. He felt the cool, wet trail of tears on his own face. "Damn that kid."

The sirens grew closer. Fueled by gas from broken and twisted pipe, the fire grew into an inferno. The heat raked his skin like sharp needles of pain. Insatiable, hungry, the fire inhaled the oxygen, leaving Jimmy fighting for air.

Still cradling Mona, he worked himself to his feet, easing her upright as well. Her legs wouldn't hold her weight, so he shouldered as much as he could. "Honey, help me. We have to move back."

He'd managed to half-drag her to a safe distance when he thought he heard a voice. He paused, lifting his head, turning to try to catch the faint sound again.

"Mom!"

He waited, his heart stilled. Could it be?

"Mom!"

Yes, louder now. He didn't imagine it. "Mona..."

She straightened in his arms and whirled toward the voice. "Lucky?"

"Mom!" The kid came whirling around the building as fast as her little legs would carry her.

A keening, primal sound escaped Mona as she knelt. Lucky launched herself at her mother. Arms wide, Mona clutched her to her chest, burying her face in her daughter's hair.

Tentatively, Jimmy reached out and touched the girl's shoulder. She was real all right. "Lucky, how the hell?" His fear coalesced into anger. "Why did you go back in there?"

Mona set her daughter on her feet but kept an arm around her. "Yes, why, Lucky?"

With one sooty hand, the girl brushed her hair out of her face. Ghostly pale under a fine layer of soot, Lucky looked at her mother, her eyes wet with unshed tears. Her lip quivered.

Mona stroked her face. "Honey, you've had quite a shock. But what possessed you?"

Lucky started to say something, then her eyes rolled back, and she fainted into her mother's arms.

Summer 2012
Las Vegas

MEMORIES. WEREN'T THEY SUPPOSED TO BE OUR SOLACE IN OLD age? As I stared at my father, I realized how wrong that might be.

"Romeo, you can't be serious. You've got nothing but some bones and a ring. Anybody could've put them there."

He cocked an eyebrow. "A ring, with your father's initials, in the foundation of his old hotel. A bit more than coincidence, don't you think?"

"You really think the Big Boss'd be so stupid as to leave his ring there?" My voice ended the sentence an octave higher than when it began.

"Lucky," my father said, his voice calm. "Don't argue. I have a feeling your young detective here is following orders—orders he can't refuse. Am I right?" He directed his question to Romeo.

"Yes, sir," he answered, then brushed me off with an "I'm sorry, it's out of my hands." To his credit, he looked as stricken as I felt.

My mother clung to my arm as we watched the police lead the Big Boss away. Then I got on the horn to his lawyer and motivated him to meet my father at the Detention Center. Then I made a few additional calls. Romeo hadn't exactly arrested my father, but I felt the noose tightening.

When I'd finished calling out the cavalry, marshaling the troops, and heading the press off at the pass, I joined my mother. Curled into the arm of the couch with the pillows pulled around her, Mona gazed out the window with an unfocused stare. I didn't have any words of comfort. She probably knew more about all of this mess than I did. But she'd clammed up, keeping her fears and memories to herself.

"Lucky, you need to do something." Mona's voice held the hollow ring of fear.

That much I knew. Energy boiled inside me, but I didn't know what else to do, what rock to turn over in this snake hunt. The Big Boss was up to his ass in alligators and allegations...or at least strong suspicions he'd committed murder. And Romeo pulling the we-need-you-down-at-the-station trump card would set tongues wagging, which was one step short of arrest on the rumor meter.

And whispered conjecture created a prison of its own, inescapable and eternal.

I needed to discover the truth...fast. Thankfully, Denny Mix had been wrong—hypnotism *could* stir up repressed memories. He had opened the door to the past, and each day it opened wider. Eventually, the past would become clear—I'd remember whether it was comfortable or not.

Closing my eyes, going back, I summoned memories I wasn't sure I wanted to see.

I'd been in the bathroom, crouched down in front of the bomb. I squeezed my eyes, concentrating. The smell, the odor of puke and yesterday's indulgences, filled my nostrils and took me back.

There was a ring...no, an earring. I grabbed it. Then my heart jolted as hands grabbed me from behind.

"Lucky! What the hell?" My father's voice—of course, I hadn't known he was my father then. With one swoop, he grabbed me. Clutching me to his chest, he turned and ran, bolting out the back door. He covered my head with his free arm. A heartbeat passed, seemingly nothing more, but it must've been. We burst out the back of the building. A few steps more, then the building exploded behind us. The concussion hit with the brute force of a tornado. Falling to his knees, he shielded me with his body. Grunting with effort, he put out a hand to break the fall as we fell forward. He covered me in the tuck of his body. Then he staggered to his feet and moved further away. His breath wheezed in my ear.

Taking shelter behind a Dumpster, he lowered me to my feet, then crouched so we were eye to eye. He looked scared, and that scared me. "It's okay, honey. Don't be afraid. Are you okay?" His hands smoothed my hair, tested my arms and legs. When he touched my face, I looked at him.

He had a black eye, purple and ugly, turning to rainbow colors. Blood oozed from the split in his lower lip. Yes, blood. There was so much blood. It had splattered and soaked the front of his shirt.

I reached for his hand. His knuckles were raised and raw and sticky with blood.

He grabbed my other hand, still fisted around the earring. "What do you have there?"

I opened my hand for him.

His face closed, anger replacing fear. He said one word, "Eugenia." He pocketed the earring. Then rising slightly to look over the Dumpster, he glanced around. Ducking back down, he grabbed me, a hand on each shoulder.

I was scared. I couldn't think. My father shook me slightly. "Honey, pay attention. This is important. Real important."

The look on his face scared me even more.

"You must forget I was here—don't tell anyone, okay?" I must not have responded quickly enough. He asked again, "Do you understand? Promise me, Lucky. You won't tell anyone. Not even your mother. Promise, Lucky. You never saw me. You have to promise."

"I promise." My voice didn't sound like mine.

"Run to your mother, honey. But," he shook me to get my attention, "they'll put me in jail, Lucky, if you say anything. They'll take me away and you'll never see me again. I won't be able to take care of you and your mother. You have to forget."

ONE THING I COULDN'T BE FAULTED FOR: I'D DONE WHAT HE HAD asked. All these years I'd forgotten everything. Nothing like a little PTSD to brighten one's day. What else had I forgotten?

Although questions filled my head and dread filled my heart, I hadn't asked Mona anything else—she was his wife and couldn't be forced to testify against her husband. I didn't have that shield. And when I saw my father again, I wouldn't ask him anything either.

If he'd killed somebody…well, there was no statute of limitations on murder.

If this thing went from bad to worse and they actually put him on trial, I didn't need him confessing to me. If called to the stand, I'd lie. My father knew that. So I wouldn't ask and he wouldn't tell.

But I knew who would.

THE FERRARI I'D PURLOINED FROM THE DEALERSHIP AT THE Babylon earned an appreciative glance from the valet as I eased to a stop under the overhang at the French Quarter. Unfolding myself from the deep recesses of the car, I grabbed the bottle of Admiral's on the seat next to me, took a deep breath, and straightened my shoulders—I could look confident even if I didn't really feel it. I handed the kid a twenty. "Keep it close, would you?"

Money up front got special treatment. Of course at the Quarter, the Ferrari was probably enough, but that wasn't how I rolled. As the VP of Customer Relations at the Babylon, I had a firsthand knowledge of the difficulties of making it as a lowly valet.

"Yes, ma'am." The appreciation in the kid's voice put a smile on my heart—the French Quarter wasn't a twenty-dollar tip kind of place. As the most profitable off-Strip property, the place was a mecca for locals looking for loose slots, loose women, a good fight card on the cheap, and old crooners willing to take twenty bucks a pop to fill the theater and boost their failing careers and flagging egos.

I pushed through the front doors and stepped into the middle of Mardi Gras on steroids. The place was packed, even at midday. Jazz thumped. High above, on tracks dangling above the crowd, a parade worthy of Bourbon Street snaked along as revelers tossed the King's beads to the throng below. I ducked and bobbed my way to the elevators, then leapt inside the next available car, sighing as the doors closed with me as the sole passenger. A precious moment of peace. To be honest, the whole Quarter experience was too much stimulation for me—especially with murder on my mind.

Let me be clear, I wasn't planning someone's demise. Although Aunt Matilda had been less than cordial when my phone call awakened her at noon, and her sharp tongue had prodded me perilously close to homicide. But I really couldn't afford to kill her, not yet...not when I needed her help.

To solve a murder.

And clear my father.

Yup, just a normal Monday in Vegas.

I paused. Was it Monday? My eyebrows snapped into a frown as I pondered my reflection in the metal in front of me. Blue eyes, a bit red, brown hair that looked a trifle limp as it brushed my shoulders, cheeks pinched with worry and my normally full lips pressed into a thin line, I looked like me...sort of...but I couldn't for the life of me be certain what day of the week it was. With a 24/7 job like mine, they all ran together. I didn't think that was a good thing, but I wasn't sure.

An all-consuming job was a good place to hide.

But that was a worry for another day. Right now I was wondering whether my life insurance was up to date—my Aunt Matilda, well, she attacked life and all who crossed her path like a rabid poodle. I'd felt her bite more than once.

The first and only female owner of a large casino property in Vegas, she was tough as an old boot and mean as a hungry coyote. But the truth was, although she scared me, I had a great deal of admiration for her. The fight she had waged to leave Matilda behind and resurrect herself as Darlin' Delacroix, her Vegas reincarnation, would've buried most women...heck, it would've put most men six feet under. She'd left herself behind—her history, her family—and had become part of mine by choice. She preferred being called Darlin', but I just couldn't.

Which brought me back to my current problem.

The elevator deposited me on the top floor. As I trekked down the long hallway, I strategized. What I needed was a snake charmer...or a handsome young man. What I had was a bottle of cheap gin, Matilda's favorite, and that would have to do.

The door opened before I had even fisted my hand to knock. The young man who greeted me was young and handsome, as expected. If I had brought anyone, they would've been redundant, so I excused myself the oversight.

"Lucky O'Toole, to see Ms. Delacroix."

"She's waiting for you in the parlor." He stepped aside motioning me past, then shut the door behind me.

His voice seemed devoid of even a veiled warning, so I took heart. Maybe, for once, Aunt Matilda would make this difficult journey a bit less so. Maybe Matilda would be less of a horror than normal, but her parlor still gave me the willies. The place was like a Hollywood whorehouse on crack, with red, flocked wallpaper, dainty Queen Anne couches covered in plush purple velvet, skirted end tables boasting lamps with fringed shades, and potted palms weeping in the corners. Normally the place would've been populated by a bevy of beautiful young men to lounge on the couches as additional decoration, but they were conspicuously absent, as was the usual sexy music.

Aunt Matilda, normally ensconced in a raised chair to offset her diminutive height—barely four feet ten on a positive day—sat cocooned in the curve of a plush sofa, cradling a mug of coffee. A terry cloth robe swallowed her. She'd rolled the sleeves several times, making her look small and fragile—only one of which was true. Even though she was sliding toward eighty, there wasn't anything fragile about Aunt Matilda...at least I hadn't thought so until today. Without her carefully made face, her ubiquitous leather jacket with the likeness of Elvis pieced out of dyed-leather swatches on the back, her fishnets and Lycra mini, and her impossibly high heels, she looked frail and almost human.

"There you are." She smiled at me. "Would you like some coffee?"

My morning had been jolted into hyperdrive by the whole murder thing, so I was still about a quart low. "Yes, please."

At her nod, the footman, who had come to attention at her side after escorting me into the parlor, disappeared through a swinging door.

Matilda patted the cushion next to her. Still a little caught off guard by this nicer version of my aunt, I ignored her invitation, choosing instead to pull a wingback chair closer.

As I took my seat, she gave me a wan smile. "You're here about your father." It was a statement, not a question. She stared over my shoulder, looking into the past. "I knew this day would come. I'd told Albert nothing good could come from what he did."

CHAPTER SIX

1982

Las Vegas

*S*TILL SEVERAL *blocks away, Eugenia Campos felt the explosion before she saw it. The reverberations buffeted the car, shaking it as if the earth itself had moved. Then a huge fireball burst skyward, exploding over the buildings in front of her. She eased the car to a stop at the corner and craned to see down the street toward Jimmy's. Buildings blocked her view, but a few gawkers huddled across the street.*

Smoke billowed, darkening the sky. Sirens sounded in the distance.

"Oh my God!" She whispered the words, afraid to say them out loud. Boogie had lied. That wasn't meant to scare somebody...no, he'd meant to kill. How could she have been so stupid? You lie with snakes, you'd better learn to crawl on your belly. *How many times had her grand-mother admonished her with those very words? A few thousand, she figured.*

With a shaking hand, she patted her hair, pressing the loose tendrils back into place as she tried to think. What was she going to do? What if someone had been killed?

Fear gripped her as she glanced in the rearview, sure someone would be following her, looking for her. *Irrational, she knew that. No one could tie her to the bomb. How could they? But what if they did? Sure as shootin', Boogie would squeal—he was stupid that way. A loose cannon as well as a loose end.*

Taking the alleyway that ran behind Jimmy's, she eased the car as close as she could, then angled it in next to a couple of Dumpsters. She'd go the rest of the way on foot.

Albert Rothstein barreled around the corner, darn near knocking her over and startling both of them. He grabbed her by the shoulders, steadying her. "Eugenia? What the fuck?" Bloodied, breathing hard, with fury in his eyes, he hardened his voice as he glowered at her. "Checking your handiwork?"

Eugenia's eyes shifted toward the building, now consumed by the inferno, then back. "Me? My handiwork?" Her voice sounded choked. She coughed and her eyes teared when the wind swirled smoke around them.

Albert didn't give any ground. He reached into his pocket, then extended his open palm. "Looking for this?"

One of her earrings! Surprised, she reached for her earlobe. Her heart stopped. Her ear was bare. "Albert, I swear..."

"Save it."

"Just tell me, was anybody hurt? Did anybody die?" Eugenia could barely get the words out as fear squeezed her throat.

He glanced back at the building. "We've gotta get outta here." He grabbed her roughly by the arm, then pulled her with him as he put some distance between them and the fire. "My ride is just around the corner."

Summer 2012
Las Vegas

MATILDA LOOKED UNCOMFORTABLE AS HER EYES REFOCUSED, THEN caught mine and held them. "It was a different time. You understand that, don't you, Lucky?"

"That's what everyone keeps telling me." Although I disagreed,

I wasn't going to argue. What would make all of this go away? As much as I complained about my lot in life, I was quite content with the issues I had.

At least those didn't come with jail time.

"We had to solve our own problems." She paused, waiting while her footman brought my mug of coffee. Actually, it was a tankard—my aunt knew me better than I'd thought.

"Milk?" the young man asked.

"Please." I glanced into the depths as he poured. "Lighten it up pretty good." After a moment I said, "That's good."

"Sugar?"

I shook my head, and he disappeared through the swinging doors, leaving me once again alone with my aunt.

She worried with the fringe on her shawl as she started in again. "I don't really know everything that went down. Albert didn't tell me all of it."

"Why would he tell you any of it?"

"I was his secretary."

I choked on the sip of coffee. As I hacked and wheezed, Matilda searched for a tissue, which she dangled toward me. I snatched it, covering my mouth with it. Finally, when I could breath again, I managed to fill my lungs with enough air to ask, "His secretary?"

A sour look pinched her features, making her look elfin. "We all have a history, girl. And history has a way of catching up, no matter how hard we work to put it far behind us."

History. Nothing like the past to mess up the present and compromise the future. "The past ... the only thing we can't change, huh?" Even Matilda knew a rhetorical question when she heard one. She stayed quiet while I fought with my demons. "Okay, you worked for the Big Boss."

"That's how I got drawn into this mess." Her face got that faraway look again. "The day of the explosion."

"The first one at Jimmy G's?"

She nodded once. "You'll need to let me finish, girl. That's the only way I can do this." She straightened her shawl and pulled it tighter around her. Then she drew her feet up under her until she almost disappeared in the cushions and pillows. "Something happened a day or two before the explosion. I can't remember how much time passed, but not much." She looked at me through red-rimmed eyes. "I'm getting old. Perhaps I don't want to remember."

"What happened?" I leaned forward, bracing my elbows on my knees and cupping my coffee mug in both hands.

"I'm not sure, but it was something bad. Your father was furious...and scared. I'd never seen him like that."

"I got a feeling I know." I stopped. I didn't want to say it out loud. That would make it real—at least if all those people who say ideas become reality were right—and I didn't want to tempt fate. When I did, it usually turned out badly.

"You can tell me." Matilda looked like she had her own suspicions.

"I think I know what happened to Eugenia Campos."

Matilda's head snapped to attention, then her expression closed down. "Really? What?"

"Before I go there, let me ask what you thought happened that day at Jimmy G's. And be straight with me. My father has a huge problem."

"Tell me what you know. I promise I'll help if I can."

I took her at her word and brought her up to speed. When I finished, she leaned back, a distant look in her eyes. "A skeleton in the foundation of the Lucky Aces? Anybody could've put it there, and your father would never have been so stupid as to leave a ring with his initials on it behind."

"Believe it or not, but I got that far on my own." I gave her a grumpy look, which didn't seem to faze her. "When Detective Romeo hauled my father down to the station for questioning, he was aware of all of this, but he did it anyway."

"The station?" Matilda snapped back to the present.

I nodded. "On orders from Daniel Lovato."

"Lovato." Although she recovered quickly, Matilda failed to hide her recognition and surprise fully.

"Does that name mean something to you?"

1982
Las Vegas

"YOU HAVE ONE HELL OF A NERVE SHOWING UP HERE," ALBERT Rothstein growled as he eased the nose of his car out of the alley just far enough so he could see in both directions. The wail of sirens split the air. They were close...too close. As they rounded the corner, he accelerated into the street, turning away from Jimmy's.

"I know what you're thinking." Eugenia Campos paused as she buckled the seatbelt around her waist.

"You have no goddamn idea what I'm thinking." His hands fisted around the steering wheel, his knuckles turning white from the effort. "Lucky damn near died grabbing that bit of gold you left behind."

"She wasn't?" Eugenia whispered. Her hand fluttered to her chest, then clenched as if squeezing her heart.

Albert shook his head.

"Thank God." Eugenia was quiet for a moment. She worried one of her rings, rolling it around and around her finger. "This was my fault. I should've stopped him."

Albert shot her an appraising glance. He was pretty good at recognizing bullshit when he heard it. "Stopped who?"

"Boogie."

Albert snorted. "Boogie? That little pip-squeak? He doesn't have the balls." But when he said the words, he knew they weren't true. Lately, Boogie had been full of surprises. "Why should I believe you?"

Eugenia found a bit of backbone and straightened. Fire flashed in her eyes. "Why shouldn't you? You and me, we go back a long way. You pulled me out of the gutter, and for that I'm grateful. You know that. Why would I plant a bomb in Jimmy's? It makes no sense." She wasn't going to tell him about the pictures, not yet. Those were her trump card, and she didn't know how this game was going to play out.

"Maybe you want Mona and Lucky out of the way." It was weak; he knew it. He and Eugenia had been hot and heavy, but that had been a long time ago. He'd broke it off. She hadn't taken it well, but they'd worked their way back to friendship—at least he was pretty sure they had.

"So, that is what you think of me? I'd risk killing others in a fit of jealousy?" She rolled her eyes. "I can be pretty dumb, but stupid? Not no more. And really, if I wanted them out of the way, they'd've been gone a long time ago." Of course, she hadn't been above trying to scare them off, but she wasn't about to mention that. Albert would jump to all the wrong conclusions—he was black and white that way, he could afford to be. But she didn't have that luxury.

"Okay. But what beef did Boogie have?"

"I don't know all of it, but it had to do with the union and Jimmy bein' a scab."

Now that rang true for sure...and it jibed with the whole incident in the desert. The timing was a bit off, but it stood to reason that if Boogie was working for the old boss, he could've made a deal with the new guy. Albert knew there was something missing, though. A connection? He wasn't sure, but he intended to find out. "There's more to it than that."

"That's all I know. I swear."

When Eugenia looked at him, he could see the truth in her eyes, hear it in her voice. "I'd sure like to know how many angles Boogie is playing...and why."

Summer 2012
Las Vegas

MATILDA AND I SAT, EACH OF US LOST IN OUR OWN THOUGHTS, AS the footman brought me a fresh mug of steaming coffee.

Nothing like caffeine to settle my nerves.

I took a tentative sip. Scalding—just right. I looked at my aunt over the top of the mug as I tried to sip without taking off the top layer of my tongue. I was marginally successful. When it became clear Matilda wasn't going to offer up what she knew without some goading, I decided a bit of gentle cross-examination was in order. "So ... Lovato. Was that who called my father when he was heading out the door to meet me and my mother the day of the bombing?"

Matilda seemed to have grown smaller under the weight of the conversation. "What?" Her voice was a whisper.

I felt badly, but I had to know. "Who called him? Lovato?"

She shook her head once. "Eugenia Campos."

My heart skipped a beat, or half a dozen, I wasn't sure. Regardless, I felt a bit lightheaded and sick to my stomach. "What'd she want?"

Matilda filled me in on the nice little triangle of Davis Lovato, Eugenia Campos and my father.

"What were the three of them cooking up?"

Matilda squirmed deeper into the cushions, as if willing herself to disappear. "Honey, if we had any suspicions, we were smart enough to keep our yaps shut. But I do know that the attorney general didn't show that day."

"Lovato didn't show?" I raised my eyebrows and sipped my coffee as I tried to lasso my thoughts, but they kept racing around like a herd of wild mustangs, until a cloud of dust obscured everything. "Somebody wanted my father not to be at Jimmy G's?"

"Plausible."

"That begs a question: who?" I had too many questions with no answers. I felt like we were circling the wagons, but I didn't know who our enemy was. "Was Eugenia Campos the go-between?"

"Always."

I leaned back into the embrace of my chair, the wingback forming a cradle of sorts—I liked the analogy, but it didn't work. Comfort proved elusive. "Anything else?" I asked the question not really expecting an answer.

"Well..." Matilda's tone focused my attention.

"Now is not the time to hold anything back."

Her eyes, filled with resolve and fear, met mine. I swallowed hard.

"I helped him cover up a murder."

1982
Las Vegas

MATILDA MANNED HER DESK IN THE VESTIBULE WHEN ALBERT Rothstein burst through his office door, towing Eugenia Campos with him. Stopping, he pulled Eugenia in front, propelling her into his office. "In there. I need to think." He watched until she did what he'd asked, then reaching for the buttons on his shirt, he turned to his secretary. "Matilda, I need you to do something for me, no questions asked." He stopped and gave her a knowing look. "Can you do that?"

Matilda's eyes widened when he shrugged out of his shirt and handed it to her.

"Get rid of this. I don't want anybody finding it, you hear? And you never saw it." He followed Matilda's eyes as they flicked toward his office. "Don't worry about her. She's got more at stake than I do."

She reached for the shirt, then wadded it up and stuffed it in her purse, closing the clasp with an audible click.

Albert reached across the desk and squeezed her shoulder. "I'm sorry to draw you into this. I'll make it up to you."

Matilda shrugged and shot him a smile. She'd done worse...but he didn't have to know that.

Eugenia sank onto the couch. Instead of joining her there, Albert grabbed a clean shirt from the closet and bent over the sink to wash up.

He needed to get rid of every drop of blood. Looking down, he realized a clean pair of pants might be in order as well. Eugenia worried the strap on her purse, quiet and pensive and obviously nervous, she waited for him to finish.

Albert gave himself a careful once-over. Satisfied that he'd removed the blood— he couldn't do anything about the bruises and the split lip— he stepped over to the window. For some reason, looking out at life going on helped him organize his thoughts, put everything into perspective. The crew hustled through the Lucky Aces building site, creating his dream one beam, one load of concrete at a time. He crossed his arms behind his back. "Any theories on how your earring ended up next to the bomb?"

"When I called you earlier, I took it off and put it by the phone. You know how I do?"

Albert could picture her. She always plucked one off her lobe before pressing the receiver to her ear. She'd said it was more comfortable.

"Just as I finished with our call, the doorbell rang. I went to put the earring back on, but I'd lost the other one somewhere. It must be in the apartment, but I didn't have time to look for it."

"Who showed up?"

"Boogie, that little creep..." Her voice trailed off.

"What?"

"Nuthin'. I just thought he was someone else, that's all."

Albert shot her a disapproving look. "Don't tell me you are still seeing Davis Lovato."

Guilt colored her features as she averted her eyes. "Why do you think he agreed to help you with your gaming license application?" When she looked up, anger snapped in her eyes. "What, you think he puts his ass on the line for nuthin'?"

Albert seemed appalled. "When I asked for your help, I didn't think you would sleep with him to get it."

"What else do you think a girl like me's got to trade?"

Albert let his breath out in one long sigh as he turned back to the view out the window. "I guess I didn't think." He stared at his hotel rising from the hole in the ground. "Sometimes you want something so bad, you put blinders on."

"Tell me about it," Eugenia whispered, but the meaning hidden in her words was lost on Albert.

Albert moved to sit beside her. Taking both of her hands in his, he didn't know what to say. "Oh God, Geenie, I'm so sorry. I would never..."

She gave him a smile that held a lifetime of world-weariness. "I know. It's really not your fault. I was in love with the guy already."

"Really?"

Eugenia gave a snort in self-deprecation. "Head over heels. Can I pick 'em, or what?"

Summer 2012
Las Vegas

MORE THAN A LITTLE SHELL-SHOCKED, I STAGGERED INTO MY office and collapsed into a chair against the wall of windows that overlooked the lobby below. Miss P's desk was empty. I stretched my legs out in front of me, then leaned my head back and closed my eyes. I needed to think, but that was proving to be more difficult than normal. Matilda had scared the hell out of me. Helped my father cover up a murder? Christ.

And she hadn't known who, or where, or really what his part had been.

"Where the hell you been, bitch?" Newton, my foul-mouthed Macaw clearly was happy to see me.

I snorted but didn't open my eyes. "Shut up, bird."

"Asshole," he sang out with conviction—it was his best word.

That got a smile out me.

"Really, talking with a bird. What will people think?" Miss P sailed into the vestibule from my old office, which was now hers.

I jumped at the intrusion—I still hadn't gotten used to the new office arrangements. "I thought we were alone. I'm not used to you being the old me."

"The old you?" She looked at me over the top of her cheaters—zebra-print today, which matched her animal-print silk blouse and loose white slacks. With spiky blond hair, large, kind eyes and just the right amount of curves to get the right attention, she was the picture of cool, feminine competence.

"You have the office that belonged to the old me." Next to her I felt frazzled. "If you could bottle that whole thing you got going on, I'd buy a lifetime supply."

"Food. Food. Food," Newton demanded as he scurried from one side of his perch to the other, bobbing his head in excitement.

Miss P took a seat behind her old desk and started rummaging through the drawers. "He's your bird. I suggest you do as he asks."

After levering myself to my feet, I did as the bird ordered. Picking up a piece of browned apple from the dish beside his cage, I stuck it through the bars. As he lunged for the morsel, I let go—I'd sacrificed a chunk of flesh more than once when I had been a fraction of a second too slow. Today, my timing was perfect. I took it as a good sign.

"You're looking a bit shell-shocked today, if I may say so." Having apparently found what she was looking for, Miss P punched the button on the phone to play the messages.

The first one was from Teddie. It was becoming a daily ritual. I shot Miss P a dirty look as I sailed past her and into my old office, looking for a mirror and a chance to pull myself together. Stepping into the small bathroom, I closed the door, shutting out the world...and Teddie.

At six feet, I had to duck a bit to see myself in the mirror. I blew at a lock of soft brown hair that had fallen into my eyes and surveyed the damage. Not too bad, all things considered. I still looked a bit owl eyed—my blue eyes a bit wider and perhaps ringed with a bit more red than normal. My cheekbones seemed sharper, the skin pulled a bit tighter.

Stress and worry—taking years off, both figuratively and literally.

Of course, a broken heart didn't help. Yes, that was Teddie's parting gift. My first and only love, he'd left a few months ago to chase international rock stardom, leaving a hole where my heart used to be. Time wasn't healing this wound. Still raw and tender, my heart needed a time-out. Of course, what it needed and what it got were usually two different things.

Pulling out a drawer filled with curious cosmetics I still didn't quite know how to use effectively, I pawed through the lot. Selecting the basics, I set about refreshing my tired face. Then I chose a fresh outfit from the closet: white jeans, gold sandals and a loose royal-blue top—light and breezy, it set off my eyes...or so I'd been told. And frankly, today I was looking for any leg up I could find.

Rejoining Miss P in the outer office, I parked a cheek on the corner of the desk and grabbed the stack of messages in my in-box. Plucking out the multiples from Teddie, I waded them up and dropped them into the trash.

"He's really sorry," Miss P started, then stopped when she ran into my scowl. "Doesn't that song count for anything? It's so romantic."

She was referring to a song Teddie had written for me entitled, "Lucky for Me." Honestly, it was a beautiful song, but he'd floated it out on the airwaves in an attempt to get my attention. Sort of understandable, since I'd been ignoring him and all. But I wasn't in the mood to cut him any slack. And he should've had enough respect to give me some space, some time. But no, he had to press the point by hitting every talk show known to man. Now our story was fodder for the masses and the song was flying up the charts.

"He knows that's just the sort of public display I hate." I pulled a couple of messages out of the stack: one from Romeo and another from my mother. The rest I put back in my box.

"Desperate measures for desperate times." Miss P had a platitude for every occasion.

"Divided loyalty?" I stood and brushed down my pants.

"I didn't know this was a war."

"Not a war, an effort in self-preservation. Once trust is broken, how do you ever repair it?"

Miss P shrugged. Apparently she didn't have an answer. Neither did I. What I did have was a murder to solve, a father to keep out of jail, and a day that was galloping off without me.

I needed some help.

CHAPTER SEVEN

1982
Las Vegas

*S*MOKE BILLOWED *from what was left of Jimmy G's when Albert Rothstein returned to the scene. Soot drifted on the wind, fueled by the inferno as it fed on any available oxygen. There wouldn't be anything left, which Albert was grateful for. Sometimes people got what was coming to them. Jimmy didn't deserve it, of course— he was just a pawn in a power play, an example...or a convenient cover.*

As he maneuvered his car between the police cars at the scene, he tried to gather his thoughts. Eugenia's story was filled with loose threads, interesting angles. Life had presented him a rare opportunity. How could he take advantage of it?

If what Eugenia had said was true...well, he had several scores to settle and things were lining up. But could he believe her? Notoriously capricious, Eugenia had always been straight with him...and they went back a long way. He'd saved her bacon so many times he'd lost count. And she'd called in more than a few markers to help him. They were sort of a mutual benefit society operating in the gray areas between bad and worse. Vegas was still that kind of place. Well-placed friends with a

questionable moral code could mean the difference between sitting on top
of the mountain, or being buried six feet under. But Albert wasn't a fool
—loyalty often went to the highest bidder. He wondered if he had the
winning number.

One of the cops motioned for him to pull the car into an alleyway.

Albert rolled down his window. As he eased to a stop, he smiled—it
wasn't a friendly smile. "Crider. We meet again."

The cop's eyes were cold, black holes in a dead face. Recognition
flashed in his eyes, but that was his only reaction. "Just park over there
and stay out of the way." He pointed down the alley.

Albert did as he said, then he wandered back and pulled the cop
aside. "We got a rare opportunity here, Crider."

Summer 2012
Las Vegas

THE CROWD IN THE LOBBY SWELLED WITH THE PASSING OF THE
hours as day stretched its last tentacles across the western sky.
Through the sets of double glass doors creating the front entrance
to the Babylon, I caught a glimpse of the brilliant oranges and
pinks in the clear, turquoise desert sky. With no humidity to
speak of, the brilliant colors of the Vegas sunset often put on a
better display than 4th of July fireworks.

Gauging from the throngs packing the lobby, cocktail hour
was fast approaching. Of course, alcohol was an all-day beverage
in Vegas, so the marking of the hour was simply an affectation us
working stiffs still clung to...even though our days often stretched
toward endless as well.

As one of the Seven Wonders of Vegas, the lobby of the
Babylon attracted a crowd regardless of the hour. White marble
floors, with brightly hued, inlaid mosaics and rich multicolored
fabric tented above the reception area along one wall, added
inviting splashes of color, as did the thousands of Chihuly blown-

glass hummingbirds and butterflies arcing across the ceiling high above.

A languid stream, our version of the Euphrates, meandered, separating the lobby area from the casino. Bordered by various reeds, rushes, and flowering plants, and arched at convenient intervals by wooden footbridges, the waterway was home to various fish and fowl.

The wall opposite registration was made entirely of clear Lucite and created a border between the lobby and an indoor ski slope made of honest-to-goodness snow. Skiers still populated the slope; schussing or snowplowing, they were all smiles...and optimism in their shorts. I cringed at the thought of bare flesh meeting the icy slopes—man-made snow wasn't nearly as skin-friendly as nature-made. But running on 80 proof, few would feel much pain...until tomorrow.

Closest to the entrance was a large portal. Arched and ornate, it beckoned everyone to partake of the riches on display in our high-end shopping arena called the Bazaar. There, for a mere king's ransom, one could obtain brilliant jewels fit for a sultan's first four wives, designer fashions, Italian automobiles and gourmet hamburgers, among other gastronomic indulgences. One could also be pampered at Samson's, our beauty salon and spa, or get married at the Temple of Love. All you needed was a credit card with no limit.

Vegas, where perceived value reaped retail gold.

Flash had said she'd meet me in Delilah's. The bar sat on a raised platform in the middle of the casino—like a queen on her throne, or an altar for offerings to the gambling gods. Feeling fresher than I thought I should, I took the few stairs two at a time, arriving at the top a bit winded. My lack of fitness was sobering to say the least.

And it called for a drink.

I claimed a club chair at a small, knee-high, round table in the corner overlooking the casino, as far away as possible from the white baby grand next to the bar. Sometimes at the end of a long day, Teddie would wait for me there, playing for the customers. I could see him, his blond hair spiked up, the planes of his face, his broad shoulders, tight ass...all that and a Juilliard-trained tenor that could melt hearts, including mine. When we'd first met, he was working at a small showroom at the Flamingo as a female impersonator. I hired him, moving him up in the world. He'd flourished and made the whole impersonator thing his own. To be honest, at first it was odd dating someone who not only stole my clothes, but looked better in them than I did. I got over it. But now I wondered, would I ever get over him?

"Girlfriend, don't go there." Flash plopped herself into the chair next to mine. Barely five feet, buxom, with riotous red hair, a quick smile and an even quicker wit, Flash was my best friend and the ace investigative reporter for the local rag, the Review-Journal. Today she sported her ubiquitous painted-on jeans, tight-to-the-edge-of-decency tee shirt, and hot-pink stilettos. The diamond-encrusted J-12 on her wrist and the sparkly hoops at her ears lent just a bit of class to her trashy. Not nearly enough, but at least she'd made an attempt to upgrade.

"Go where?"

"Honey, you spend so much time looking in the rearview, you're gonna drive yourself right into a head-on."

"Sometimes the past can offer some enlightenment."

Flash made a rude noise. "Don't you know when you stop thinking about them, that's when they show up again?"

"Ahhh, so that's how it works."

"Pretty sure." Flash flagged down a cocktail server who headed in our direction. "What are you having? I've got a real hard-on over this Rosè Champagne that's popping up everywhere." Flash's lack of personal refinement clearly hadn't degraded her palate.

"Prime stuff. I'm in. We just got in a very nice Domain Carneros." At Flash's nod, I nodded to the waitress and she charged off.

"You know, you guys really should spring for some actual clothing for those girls."

"What? You think two dish towels and some braided rope isn't enough?"

Flashed watched the waitress as she punched our order into the register. "They just look...cold. And underfed."

"Proving once again you can't please everyone." I let it go at that and waited, letting my gaze drift over Flash's head to the casino and its action beyond. I didn't want to dive into the meat of the conversation only to be interrupted by the waitress returning with our libation.

She didn't disappoint, returning quickly. Flash and I watched as the waitress busied herself with all the Champagne show. Pouring a taste into my flute, she cradled the bottle and waited. I took a sip, savoring the bubbles. A bit on the dry side, just as I liked. I nodded, then she filled our flutes, nestled the bottle in ice, placing the silver ice bucket next to the table, and took her leave.

Flash took a big swig, swishing it around her mouth, then swallowing. "Primo juice."

"I'm plying you with rare elixirs so you will do my bidding." I leaned forward, setting my now half-empty flute on the table. "I need you to do some digging."

"Righteous."

The fact that she said that word with a perfectly straight face had me worried. "I don't know who you've been hanging out with, but the experience has completely decimated your vocabulary."

"Sorry." She threw back the rest of her Champagne, then reached for the bottle and poured a new dose of the pink bubbles for herself. "Been doing the exposé on the underground music industry. Where do you want me to dig?"

"I need the skinny on Davis Lovato—all the dirt, everything you can find."

"You mean Daniel Lovato," Flash said referring to our current district attorney.

"Not the son. The father."

Pausing mid gulp, Flash raised her eyebrows as she looked at me over the top of her flute. She lowered it to the table next to mine, then pulled a notebook from her hip pocket. I waited while she rooted in her extraordinary cleavage for the pencil she always kept there.

When her pencil was poised above the paper and her attention shifted back to me, I continued. "Davis Lovato was the attorney general back when I was about four."

"So, to be clear. Davis Lovato was Daniel Lovato's father?"

"Yes, somehow my family's history seems inexorably tied with the Lovatos'." Daniel and I were grudging friends. Let's just say we had a history...and I kept close some of his secrets. First the fathers, now the offspring.

Flash shook her head as she made a few more notes. "This place is so fucking inbred." Her head shot up when realization dawned. "Sorry. I wasn't referring to you."

"If the shoe fits." I smiled at my cliché—for some odd reason I just loved those trite turns of phrase. They held all this meaning you didn't have to say.

"You say he was in office around the time you were four?" Her expression turned serious as she shifted to reporter mode. "You know where he is now?"

"Haven't a clue—he <u>was</u> a bit before my time." I refilled my flute—bubbles just made life better somehow. "Funny thing is, I don't remember anyone ever talking about him."

"Some of those guys being bigger than life, that is odd." Interest flared in her eyes. The girl knew a Pulitzer-worthy story when she saw it. "Does this have anything to do with the bombing at Jimmy G's?"

"I don't know. I'm just turning over rocks, trying to make connections."

And I shuddered at the possibilities.

1982
Las Vegas

ALBERT FOLLOWED CRIDER AS HE PUSHED THROUGH THE CROWD OF gawkers. No one said much; he firefighters had things pretty much under control now.

Catching sight of Mona, he got Crider's attention by grabbing his arm. A quick shrug in the direction of his family. Crider nodded in understanding, then kept pushing forward. Albert lost sight of him as he waved his badge and was ushered inside the perimeter the police had erected around the site.

Soot smudging her face, Mona stood facing the fire, her chin lifted in a defiant tilt. Lucky, her back to her mother's legs and held there by her mother's hands on her shoulders, had the same look on her face, that same unmoving swagger, if that was possible. As if she sensed his presence, Mona turned in Albert's direction, scanning the crowd.

He could see the trail of tears through the soot on her face. When she saw him, she didn't move, yet relief eased through her posture.

He grabbed her, looping one arm around her shoulders. "Everyone's safe," he murmured against her hair as she sagged against him. With his other hand, he found Lucky's shoulder and squeezed. As he held his family, he struggled with emotions that threatened to boil over.

This was about him. A warning, for sure ,or the worst kind of promise, but he didn't know by whom or for what. He'd damn well find out, though. Fear, anger, hate, dread...they all coalesced into a certainty: he'd kill whoever did this.

Summer 2012
Las Vegas

COCOONED IN THE SOUNDS OF THE CASINO AT FULL-BORE THAT swirled around me, I refilled my once-again empty flute with Champagne and settled back, relishing the momentary lull. With a mission at hand, Flash had launched into action, leaving me alone. Patrons filtered into Delilah's looking for a bit of high-octane fuel to power their evening. I could relate.

"Drinking on the job?" Mona eased into the club chair next to me, the one Flash had vacated. Her stomach seemed to expand as I watched.

"Drinking to survive the job." Mother never came looking for me unless the end of the world was imminent, so I sipped my bubbles and tried not to panic. To be honest, she looked the worse for wear, but valuing my life, I didn't say so.

Mona eyed my Champagne with thinly disguised lust. She'd been on the wagon since getting knocked up. I felt for her—giving up go-juice was too high a price to pay for the privilege of bringing a new life into this world, but that's just me...a die-hard hedonist addicted to my pleasures.

With two fingers, I scooted the glass over to her. "One sip won't hurt. And if it lowers your blood pressure, then that would be a net gain, I'm willing to bet."

Her indecision lasted a nanosecond. She gently grasped the thin stem of the glass between her forefinger and thumb. Reverentially, she lifted the glass to the light. Then, eyes closed, she took a sip and groaned.

"My sentiments exactly."

She opened her eyes and grinned at me—not her normal wattage, but it was start. "You have no idea."

"And I don't want to."

"Lucky, it's a gift."

"It scares me."

"It scares everybody."

For some reason that admission surprised me. I thought everybody knew how to be an adult, a parent, other than me. "Really?"

Mona pushed my glass back, then grabbed my hand and gave it a squeeze. "Honey, we all make it up as we go. Just follow your heart, that's the best you can do." She gave a little laugh, like she was laughing at a private joke. "It's all any of us can do."

"I don't think that's why you tracked me down, is it?"

Her face sobered. "Your detective didn't just want to question your father today, he wanted to arrest him."

Although that infuriated me, it didn't shock me. Surprised me, maybe...but shock? No. "Well, Romeo may be just a kid, but he's wise enough to know if you take on the Big Boss, you better have serious ammunition. But right now, unless there's something I don't know," I paused and gave my mother a pointed look, which she ignored, "he's long on supposition, short on proof."

Mother didn't respond right away. I sat back, leaving her to wrangle with her thoughts. If I knew anything about my mother, it was that she was a woman on a mission...always. The mission might vary, but she rarely wavered from her purpose. Tonight I'd drawn the short straw and ended up in her crosshairs. I couldn't wait to hear why.

As luck would have it, I didn't have to wait long. Mona leaned closer and lowered her voice. "I need your help...*we* need your help."

Although she emphasized the 'we,' I doubted the Big Boss knew she was here talking to me. "What's up?"

"The last time I saw that ring was the day the bomb exploded at Jimmy G's all those years ago...and now it turns up next to a body in the foundation of the Lucky Aces? Don't you think it's odd?"

"Very odd indeed." I bolted the last of the Champagne. "Tell me about that ring."

1982
Las Vegas

CREIGHTON CRIDER SIFTED THROUGH THE REMAINS OF JIMMY G'S

place. What the bomb hadn't leveled, the fire had taken care of, reducing the thriving restaurant to a pile of ashes. A few steel girders and I-beams remained, charred, twisted sentinels, guarding only memories. Smoke drifted upward as the embers smoldered. Crider moved the ashes around with a long stick—the coroner had told him to be careful...if there were any remains, he shouldn't disturb them. Crider didn't often do as he was told.

That Rothstein guy had presented an interesting opportunity. Crider didn't know whether to believe him or not. Oh, he'd heard of the guy. He was supposed to be on the up-and-up. But this was Vegas, and folks weren't always what they seemed. Take himself, for example. A good kid from Kansas, he'd taken one bribe, done one fairly innocent "favor," and look where it had got him. The whole thing had snowballed. He wore a sheriff's department uniform and badge, but he was far from one of the good guys. It all had gone so wrong.

Pretending to be focused on his search, he worked his way to what would've been the rear of the building. An arch of steel, scarred and twisted from the fire, marked the entrance he looked for: the entrance to the kitchen. Stepping through, he feigned a professional disinterest. A couple of techs were working in an area where broken pipe protruded from the ashes, presumably the bathrooms. Intent on their job, they didn't even give him a glance, but their presence worried him. If they knew what he was going to do...

One of the techs looked up. "You there, be careful."

Crider fought the anger. Why'd they always think he was stupid or something? "Yeah, I got it."

"The fire originated back here, so look extra hard." The guy paused, giving Crider a hard look. "You do know how to process a fire, right?"

"I took the course. Why do you think I'm here?" Crider almost laughed. He really had taken the course. He wasn't used to being legit.

The tech appeared satisfied and returned his attention to whatever he was looking at. Crider didn't know and didn't care. If Rothstein was right, it wasn't what he had come to find.

From the outline of the foundation that remained, he calculated his *position, then marked off a few paces toward the center of the room. He knew what he was looking for.*

Rothstein had told him where to look.

Summer 2012
Las Vegas

ONCE AGAIN I EASED MY CHAMPAGNE TOWARD MY MOTHER. THIS whole thing called for serious alcohol to settle my nerves, so I had replenished. A new bottle of Rosé bubbly nestled in the now-watery ice, which was perfect for holding the ideal cooldown temp. It probably should scare me that I knew something like that, but I was too worried to worry. My flute was full. "One more sip won't hurt." I felt sort of bad leading her astray and all. But I really did believe her elevated blood pressure was more of a health hazard than a bit of Champagne to bring it down.

As Mona took a sip, I searched for signs of self-loathing at her weakness. Not even a hint showed in her face, which remained passive although pinched with concern. That's one trait—probably the only trait—my mother possessed I wished had trickled down through the gene tree: her total acceptance of her decisions. No self-recriminations. No second-guessing. Just dealing, and moving on.

"What do you remember about the ring?"

When she went for another sip, I took the glass gently from her grasp. She didn't put up a fight. Instead, she graced me with a thankful smile, a small one, but it was there. Curious. I could get used to this hormone-moderated mother. "I was so excited to give it to your father. I'd been saving for practically forever. He'd worked so hard. I wanted him to have something nice, something to celebrate the Lucky Aces."

I patted her hand on the table but kept my bubbly out of her reach. "Did you ever give it to him?"

LUCKY NOW AND THEN

"No. I'd showed it to Jimmy...you'd gone to the bathroom. Then I set the box on the counter."

"Did anybody else know about the ring? Had you shown it to anybody?"

"No one. I even had it made out of town...no one could've known." She flagged the cocktail server down. "Some water, please." She waited until she had it in hand and had gulped most of it before continuing. "After I showed Jimmy, you came back full of excitement about the bomb and dragged me off to see. After that..." She looked at me with haunted eyes, remembering. Then they cleared. "I always assumed it had been lost in the fire."

1982
Las Vegas

FUCKIN' A, CRIDER THOUGHT. ROTHSTEIN HAD BEEN RIGHT. MAYBE *they really could pull this off. Huge stakes. A big gamble. But if it worked...*

Moving the ash carefully, as he'd been trained to do, Crider squinted his eyes and concentrated. They'd said fire would make a difference. Gently poking, prodding, he finally saw it.

Keeping his back to the techs, he kneeled. Pulling the plastic bag from his pocket, he sifted, collecting the pieces. There were more than he expected, and he had to be careful. The gloves made it difficult to get the smaller ones. Those he obscured into the ash.

Sweat dripped into his eyes. He swiped it away with the back of his forearm and focused on his task. He had to get it all.

"You there!"

Crider jumped at the voice. His heart hammered. What if someone saw? What would he say? Glancing over his shoulder, he feigned irritation.

The coroner gave him a stare. "What did you find?"

"I don't know." Crider shrugged. "I'm bagging it for you."

"Mark it and its location before you give it to the techs."

"Yeah, yeah. I know what to do."

The coroner disappeared as quickly as he'd come. Crider's heart rate didn't settle down quite as quickly, but he hurried now. Too much time had passed. Someone was going to take a keener interest.

Tucking the bag into his shirt, careful not to mash the contents, he resumed his search. Jimmy G's. Focused, yet nonchalant, Crider rose, trying to blend in—even though he'd found what he was looking for, he still needed to appear to be doing a job. No one paid any attention to him. Leaving the kitchen, he worked a grid that would bring him closer and closer to the opening that had been the front door.

Kicking aside some ash, the toe of his boot made contact with something solid. He bent down and brushed the residue away. Rock. No, granite. It must be the bar top. Cracked in several places, it had survived the firestorm relatively intact. Crider worked his fingers under one side and lifted, flipping the piece over.

Underneath it, wood splinters, a piece of leather from the barstools, all of it remained unburned. Crouching, his haunches on his heels, one elbow on one knee, he sifted through the dirt with one hand. Picking up handfuls and using his fingers as a sieve, he let the ash drift through. On one scoop, he saw a glint of gold. Something embedded in the dirt. Digging further he managed to pry the object loose with one finger. A ring. Gold, with the letters 'AR' in diamonds.

He glanced around to see if the techs were taking any notice. They weren't. With a smile, he pocketed the ring.

CHAPTER EIGHT

Summer 2012
Las Vegas

*A*T THIS hour, Jean-Charles would be at full throttle in the Burger Palais. Hugging my mother at the elevators, I gave her a peck on the cheek. "Go to bed, Mother. We've done all we can today."

I watched the doors close, then I turned and dove into the crowd milling around the lobby. Gawkers stopped, craning their eyes upward to enjoy the thousands of blown-glass humming-birds and butterflies that arced across the vast, coffered ceiling. Skiers careened down the indoor slope. Spectators gathered in front of the Lucite wall separating them from the winter warriors and oohed and aahed or groaned, depending on the success or failure of the particular run. Reception had quieted, only a few waited in line to check-in. Through the front doors I could see the valets running to shepherd away the thick collection of cars disgorging this evening's throng of revelers. Some dressed smartly, apparently on their way to a show. Some dressed casually, ready for a night of gambling. The hour was way too civilized for the hip and trendy club set. They wouldn't arrive for several hours yet.

Dodging and darting, I worked my way toward the entrance to the Bazaar.

Someone grabbed my elbow from behind. "Lucky, can I have a minute?"

I stopped and turned. Boogie Fleischman. I froze. I didn't know what to think or do. Should I break his nose? Should I run? I hadn't a clue, so instead, I said with as much poise as I could muster, "Sure, Boogie, what can I do for you?"

Short and spindly and bald with a thin fringe of greasy hair, which he wore too long, Boogie held a hat in both hands which he scrunched nervously as his eyes darted to mine, then away again. Liver spots dotted his weathered skin. His cheeks were sunken and hollow; his clothes dirty and wrinkled. He didn't smell all that great either. "I heard about your father."

"What about him?"

"Well..." His eyes darted in again for a furtive strike, and he scrunched that hat harder, as if wringing it dry. "You know, the police and everything."

I didn't react. If he was hoping to get some information from me, today was not his lucky day. I smiled at the pun, I couldn't help myself. At my smile, he looked hopeful, then confused. "What do you want, Boogie?"

His face closed down, his eyes turning flinty. He stopped worrying with the hat, then slapped it into form on his thigh and settled it carefully on his head. "You be careful, you hear. People can get killed messing in other people's business."

The way he looked right through me gave me a chill, but I wasn't going to let him see he got to me. As he turned to go, I grabbed his arm and squeezed, hard. I could tell I caught him off guard. I leaned down, my mouth close to his ear. "What the hell do you mean, coming in here threatening me? You've got some nerve." I pulled him closer, and he winced away from me. "Don't mess with me. I've got Rothstein blood coursing through my veins."

He tried to pull his arm out of my grasp. Good luck—I had him by forty pounds, six inches, several decades and a snootful of pissed off. "What's your bit part in this melodrama?"

He tugged once more. This time I let go. "Just giving you a friendly heads-up."

With that, he melted back into the crowd. I watched his hat bobbing along until he bobbed out the front door, into the night. I turned and eased into the flow of the crowd. Like a fish in a fast-flowing stream, I let the current carry me along. I didn't look back. Fighting with myself, I worked for control.

Threats didn't scare me. They just made me mad.

Although I was up to fending off threats, with more than a reasonable amount of sparkling wine sloshing around in my belly, I wasn't as confident that my skill set extended to resisting an amorous Frenchman. However, through my Rosé haze, sacrificing a bit of virtue for the pleasure of his company seemed like a reasonable trade.

The Burger Palais—yes, I fought to get rid of that name. I lost.

Anyway, the Burger Palais was a trifling little venture for someone of Jean-Charles's skill and reputation. With restaurants in all the major gastronomic centers of the world, it made sense that he should have his own high-end eatery in Vegas—which is exactly what the Big Boss had promised him. After some tense negotiations, Jean-Charles and I had agreed on specifics, and the crews were busy on the finish out, hopefully at a faster pace than the work on my new office. Needing to play in a kitchen while he waited, Jean-Charles took over the space of an Italian place that just hadn't made the grade. Overnight, he had transformed it into a gourmet burger joint. For some reason, the idea of a James

Beard, Michelin-starred chef in a burger joint made me smile...and like him all the more. He had told me many times he was just a cook and he liked to please. I was good with that.

The ubiquitous line of hungry diners didn't even slow me down as I sailed through the entrance, nodding at the hostess. With hardwood floors, muted lighting from brass wall sconces, rich green leather upholstery and brick walls with drippy mortar, the restaurant exuded the warmth, refinement, and openness of its proprietor. With the tables full and the air filled with yummy aromas and contented chatter, the restaurant wrapped around me like a heartfelt hug.

Halfway back on the left, behind a wall of glass, the kitchen staff danced to their own rhythm, one that Jean-Charles conducted. I found him exactly where I thought he would be: in front of the large charcoal grill. Pausing in the doorway, I crossed my arms and leaned against the jamb, enjoying the fine-tuned syncopation.

As Rinaldo, Jean-Charles's right-hand man, eased by me on his way back into the kitchen, a bottle of Sherry in one hand, he paused before jumping back into the show. "An artist at work."

"Most would not consider hamburgers an artist's medium," I commented, surprising myself—my thoughts had a habit of bypassing my filter to leap out of my mouth.

"Ah, but Chef takes everything he prepares very seriously. We all have been with him a long time—we have the scars from the lash of his words." Rinaldo smiled, not looking the least bit put-off.

"He is tough, then?" Jean-Charles had only let me see a glimpse of that side of his personality. In some ways, I was waiting for the gloves to come off.

"He has to be. It is his reputation."

We both watched the chef as he shifted fluidly between stove, grill, refrigerator, console listing orders and the finishing table where he plated the food.

"We had to learn how he moves," Rinaldo explained.

"How he moves?"

"Each chef, at least the good ones, have a way of creating—a movement pattern that is intrinsic. It is part of their artistry. As staff, we had to learn his way." Rinaldo made a sweeping motion with one arm. "Chef is the stone tossed into the water. And we are the ripples." He touched my arm. "Stay here."

Not wanting to disrupt the flow, I did as he said, watching as the big man delivered the Sherry to one of his cohorts manning a selection of saucepans on the stove, then leaned in and said something to Jean-Charles. A nod, a moment, and Rinaldo stepped into the chef's position, joining the dance with nary a missed step. Jean-Charles observed for a moment as he wiped his hands on the white towel that hung from the sash of his apron. Only when apparently satisfied did his posture relax. He turned and graced me with a smile, melting me as easily as chocolate over an open flame. Raising his hand high, he pointed into the restaurant.

I knew what he meant: he wanted to meet me at the bar. He didn't have to make the suggestion twice. Turning, I headed across the restaurant, then ducked behind the bar—a beautiful mahogany construction that arced from the far wall. Grotesquely expensive—I know because I had to negotiate with Chef Gregor, the proprietor of the previous tenant, a failed Italian place—it added a special touch of class. The bartender, accustomed to my presence, acknowledged me with a quick grin, then returned to his mixing. Crouching, I squatted in front of the glass doors of the wine cooler. Ah, a nice white blend. I pulled the bottle.

Jean-Charles straddled a barstool just as I popped the cork. "You like this wine," he said with the flat tone of a rhetorical question.

Setting one of the thin-stemmed glasses with a narrower bowl in front of him, I poured him a taste. Lifting it to the light, he swirled the liquid, then held it to his nose, taking a deep sniff. Apparently satisfied, he took a sip, then smiled.

"Most of the nuance comes through the nose," I parroted. If I had a dollar for every time he reminded me of that...well, this job would be history.

He cocked an eyebrow at me, then extended his glass for a more generous pour. "We come from the same place, you and I."

Technically, he couldn't be more wrong, but I knew what he meant, and I agreed.

Before I could respond, Flash shouldered her way through the crowd, then wedged herself in next to Jean-Charles. "Hey, cutie." She tossed the line at him, then focused on me. "Girlfriend, you are so not going to believe this."

1982
Las Vegas

EUGENIA DRIFTED DOWN THE ALLEYWAYS, DRAWING NEARER TO JIMMY G's, but hiding herself from view. She knew what to do. As a beautiful woman in a man's world, she had the advantage. Men, they always followed their dicks. Working them was child's play.

The poor metaphor was lost on a woman of Eugenia's intellect.

Eugenia's man, the one she'd had on retainer for years snapping photos for blackmail—or insurance, as she liked to refer to it—leaned against the back wall of a sandwich shop across the alley from Jimmy G's, or what was left of it. Hidden in the shadows, he escaped Eugenia's notice even though she knew where he'd be hiding. She found him on the second pass.

Casually, she ambled over to him, then ducked into the shadow to stand close. "Get anything good?" She straightened his tie in a familiar way as she sidled just a bit closer to him than normal.

He brushed her back. "You ever known me to disappoint?" He handed her a stack of Polaroids. "This is just a sample. I got the rest on regular film."

Eugenia flipped through them. Her smile grew. "Interesting."

"I thought you'd like them."

"I'll say." She touched his arm, letting her hand rest there lightly. *"Are you ready to move up the food chain?"*

That piqued his interest. His eyes met hers. "Whatcha have in mind?"

Summer 2012
Las Vegas

FLASH'S SKIN FLUSHED PINK AND HER EYES SHONE.

I knew that look—the thrill of the chase. "That was fast."

"The Internet ... you'd be surprised what you can find. I also got this remote setup where I can access the historical records at the *Review-Journal*." Planting a foot on the lower rung of the barstool, Flash boosted herself up. Then she leaned across the bar and grabbed a glass in one hand, and the wine bottle by the neck with the other. With bounty in hand, she dropped back onto the barstool with a satisfied grunt. As she poured herself a healthy dose, she gave me a look. "Lovato was easy."

"Give me the high points."

"Almost taken out in a Mob hit—"

I held up my hand, stopping her. "Let me guess, there was a bomb involved." It was a wild guess, but I had a hunch.

Flash nodded, clearly unimpressed by my powers of insight. "Car bomb. He survived, but the woman with him didn't."

"Who?"

Flash shot me a thousand-candlepower grin. "Eugenia Campos."

"Whoa!" I wasn't expecting that. To be honest, I had her figured as the bones in the foundation. If they weren't hers, whose were they?

"Yeah, creepy, huh?" She handed the wine bottle back to me, then took a healthy pull from her glass. "Lovato didn't get very far after that: failed bid for the Governor's Mansion. The whispers of philandering derailed him."

"Gosh, just think," I added. "If the electorate still had such high standards, imagine how much better the world would be." Politicians held the bottom rung on my ladder...right under lawyers. Davis Lovato had been both.

"I got more." Flash polished off her wine and pushed her glass toward me signaling a refill was in order. "That Crayfish, he's been holding out on me." She pulled a sheaf of papers out of her back pocket. Smoothing them on the bar top she motioned me closer. "Here, take a look at this."

I scanned the documents...twice. Then I saw it. "Crider worked the crime scene?"

Flash pursed her lips and nodded. "He didn't mention that. He knows something he's not telling. And he's scared."

1982
Las Vegas

MY PLACE LOUNGE WAS A POPULAR PLACE WITH SOME OF THE WISE *guys. Co-owned by Frank Cullotta, it was frequented by Tony Spilotro and most of his Hole-in-the-Wall Gang. Normally, Albert Rothstein steered clear of this kind of joint, not wanting to be thrown into the pot of public perception as one of their associates. But today, he didn't much care anymore; life had just delivered problems far more important than worrying about what people thought. Besides, they'd have to prove it, and he had Davis Lovato in his back pocket to take care of that, along with any whiff of indecision by the Gaming Control Board. He did not need his name popping up in their Black Book. Then he could kiss the Lucky Aces goodbye.*

The lounge was dark, even in the middle of the afternoon. The front had been blacked out, but once your eyes adjusted, it was bright enough. The aroma of pizza permeated the place—the bar adjoined Upper Crust

Pizzeria next door. He waited in the last booth on the left-hand side, facing the door. Nobody with any smarts sat with his back to the front—people had been killed that way. Though to be honest, he really wasn't worried. If they killed him, who would earn the money the Mob wanted to skim?

Albert grimaced as he stared into his mug of coffee, his third. He had been a fool to think he could leave his past behind. That somehow building his dream, being on the up-and-up and legit, would erase his family's well-connected history. Nothing like being born with the taint.

Rothstein had known all along that the old guard in town wouldn't take kindly to him going out on his own. They'd see it as a defection, a betrayal. Or an opportunity. Rothstein had no doubt that's what they intended to do to him: get him over a barrel, then make him pay...and pay...and pay.

He'd rather be dead.

But Vegas couldn't go on as it had, run by a bunch of hoods. No, for Vegas to reach her potential, she needed money—more money than the East Coast families could even dream of. Wall Street money. Banking money. And to get that, the city needed to be clean. Mr. Thomas and he had agreed on that, and as a banker, Mr. Thomas had been the first to put his money where his mouth was, making the first loan on a casino project. He'd taken another risk on the Lucky Aces.

Albert Rothstein had made promises. Like Mr. Thomas, he was a man of his word...a dreamer, for sure, but also one hell of a scrapper.

So the Family was on its way out, and they'd taken his defection personally—he'd known they would. But he never thought they'd come after his family. After all, that wasn't how the Family did business. There were rules.

And there was a price to pay for breaking them.

The bomb would have killed Mona and Lucky if it hadn't been for Lucky and her curiosity. His blood boiled at the memory, the realization of how close he'd come to losing everything he valued.

Revenge would be his, and it would be sweet.

But first, he needed to square things with Mona.

Even though he was still staring into his coffee, he knew the moment Mona walked into the joint. It had always been like that for him—if she was near, he could feel it. He raised his eyes and watched her walk toward him. Short shorts, long legs and a coltish stride, she moved quickly and confidently. Her long hair pulled back from her face in a tail, she looked like a fresh-faced kid. His face clouded at the thought.

Mona's smile dimmed just a hint as she slid into the booth across from him. "We almost lost her, Albert."

He smiled and covered her hands with his. "But we didn't."

"What if...?" Mona's eyes turned dark with worry. Her smile wavered, then fled as her lips trembled.

"Don't." He squeezed her hands. "I won't let anything happen to her. I haven't yet, have I? Did you leave her where I told you?"

"Yes, Matilda met us there."

Albert nodded. "Good. Now, there's something we need to talk about."

She stared at him as he talked, a lost look in her eyes. She hadn't heard a word he'd said. The tears started slowly, trickling down her face until they became a steady flow. Albert could see her effort as she fought them, but she lost the battle. He squeezed into the booth next to her and wrapped her in his arms. He kissed her hair as she sobbed into his shoulder, breaking his heart.

Summer 2012
Las Vegas

THE FERRARI HUMMED AS IT ACCELERATED UP THE STRIP, WARMING to the task. I was pretty spoiled being able to steal a car from the dealership in the Babylon anytime I got the itch. This one was white, with a convertible top. I didn't put it down. Neither a gal in an open car nor a Ferrari would be safe in Naked City. A down-on-its-luck stretch of the Strip between Sahara and downtown, Naked City had been home to most of the showgirls during the '50s and '60s. The girls used to sunbathe on the rooftops in the nude, hence the name. Of course, the tinsel had all moved uptown, and Naked City had become a rough neighborhood. Recently, refurbishment and investment had started filtering in. The pimps and dealers had been encouraged to move on, but Naked City still had a ways to go before it captured even a hint of its former glory.

According to Flash, Crider was holed up in a less-than-savory hotel. Not that there were any other-than-unsavory hotels here; in fact, there was a whole string of them, shutters hanging loose, paint peeling, plastic flowers faded under the unrelenting assault of the desert sun, hourly room rentals. Great. I slowed to a crawl as I turned in, trying to avoid the potholes in the asphalt. I didn't even want to know what an alignment on a Ferrari would set me back.

I angled into a parking place and killed the engine. As I unfolded myself from the car, I took a look around. No one seemed to be taking an interest in me or the car, but frankly, I don't know why I bothered looking—I never saw the bad, even when I looked for it.

Room 7 was halfway down on the right. Lucky 7 had been written in marker on the door. I felt like running.

As I raised my hand to knock, the door inched open.

"Yeah?" The voice sounded like forty years of unfiltered Camels. Through the crack, I couldn't see the face obscured in shadow.

"Detective Crider? It's Lucky. Flash sent me."

After a moment, the door opened. Crider hid most of himself behind the door, but I could see enough to know it was him. A girl could never be too cautious. As I stepped into the gloom, I prayed no one had recognized me and memorialized this moment with a camera phone. But of all the worries I had, that was not even on the first page.

As Crider closed the door behind me, the gloom deepened. "Christ, Crider, you growing mushrooms in here or something?"

"I'm laying low 'til this whole thing blows over."

My eyes adjusted to the dim light and the room came into focus. Dismal would be too kind. The carpet, a filthy brown, had once been another color—at the edges it lightened to a mustard yellow. I took a couple of steps further in; my shoes stuck to the carpet, which made me a bit queasy. The bent and broken Levolors on the windows leaked a bit of the outside in, enough that I could see the clunky brown table decorated with the initials of former guests carved into its scaled and cracked varnish. The television still had a tube and rabbit years. The twin beds, covered with threadbare spreads, sagged under their burden of broken dreams.

Unwilling to touch anything, I crossed my arms and planted myself in the center of the room. "Why are you holed up here?"

Crider did not present the picture of arrogance I expected from a newly retired Metro detective. He looked old and broken. His white tee shirt, threadbare and stained under the arms, stretched thin over his belly. A worn leather belt on its last hole secured his khakis under the overhang and above indecency. Several days of thick stubble covered his cheeks, making up for the lack of hair on his head. A round face with bags under his eyes that hung like deflated balloons, he looked beaten up by life. With a meaty hand, he motioned toward the bed, then clearly thought better of it. "Not much of a place to entertain a lady."

"Well then, why don't you tell me a story?" I tapped my foot and tried to not touch anything. "What are you doing here?"

"Staying out of sight."

"I bet cops really blend in around here." Sarcasm, one of my best things.

"I'm not a cop anymore."

"Once a cop, always a cop."

"You sound like your father." He made it sound like a good thing, which showed an unexpected bit of insight.

"Why are you here, Crider?" I tried to keep the impatience out of my voice. I couldn't tell if he was leading me on or just taking the long way around—I wasn't a fan of either.

He pulled a chair from the table and sat, extending his feet toward me. They were bare. He needed a podiatrist in the worst way. "I heard about that body and the ring and all."

"And...?"

"Well, your dad..." He stopped as if searching for the right words. "Back in the day, he stepped up to the plate for me. Big time. He didn't have to. To be honest, I didn't deserve his trust or his concern. In fact, quite the opposite."

That sounded like my father. I gave him an encouraging smile as I tried to corral my impatience. I desperately needed to know what he knew.

"I guess Flash told you I'd worked the fire scene at Jimmy G's back in '82?"

I nodded. She'd also told me he didn't know anything pertinent about the car bomb that derailed a future governor, but afraid to say anything that might shift him off track, I didn't mention it.

"I found that ring in the ashes." He shook his head and looked hangdog.

I felt like giving him a hug but resisted, given that I was alone in a hotel room with him and he had some interesting sexual fetishes—last time I'd seen him, he'd been in the ER at U.M.C. for one of them. I don't think he knew I knew, so I thought it wise to keep that little factoid to myself.

"It was under a big piece of stone. Came through that inferno looking like it was new."

"So how did it end up in the foundation of the Lucky Aces next to a dead body?" That was sort of redundant, but for the sake of expediency, I didn't correct myself.

"I can't tell you that."

"Can't...or won't?" My voice turned hard, and I let loose my impatience.

"Can't." He sighed heavily, which sounded more like a wheeze. He leaned forward, clasping his hands together between his knees. "I'm real ashamed of what I did—your father going out on a limb and all."

My heart stilled. "What *did* you do?"

CHAPTER NINE

1982
Las Vegas

*T*HE TREMORS *wracking through Mona's body subsided until they became intermittent spasms. Holding her tight against him, Albert stroked her hair and murmured to her, "Honey, it's okay. Everybody's fine."*

Finally, she pulled away. She dabbed at her eyes with a napkin, then ran her fingers through her hair. "I must look a fright."

Albert went back to the other side of the booth so he could look at her. "You are always a vision."

Her smile lacked some candlepower, but at least she managed it.

"Now, I need to ask you something." Albert's voice turned serious, chasing away Mona's fledgling smile.

She fidgeted with the napkin, clearly uncomfortable. "What?"

"Mona, honey, how old are you? Really?"

She swallowed hard. "Nineteen."

Albert's heart stopped. They'd been right. Nineteen. That meant five years ago, when he'd first taken up with her... "Fuck." Albert stared at Mona and tried to think. Nineteen now, which meant she'd been fifteen when he had knocked her up. A felony in every state, including Nevada. She'd looked so much older. He'd believed her lies when she'd told him she was twenty. Maybe he'd just wanted to believe. Regardless, the deed was done.

And the East Coast guys were putting the pressure on.

"Mona, honey, why'd you lie?"

"I was on the streets; I had no choice. Nobody wanted a fifteen-year-old." Her eyes were clear despite being puffy from crying. Strength returned to her voice. "What did you want me to do, Albert? When I met you, I thought you were just another john."

Grudgingly, he admitted she was right. He had behaved badly—and he wasn't particularly proud of himself. She'd been so beautiful...even more so now. He'd fallen under her spell pretty quickly, but he did understand. Her choices had been limited. "You do know this makes life a bit more complicated, don't you?"

Her surprise seemed genuine. "Why?"

"Having sex with an underage person is a felony."

Mona's hand fluttered like a butterfly riding a breeze. "Oh, that. I'd never press charges."

That made Albert smile. Mona, the street-wise hooker, could be so naïve...part of her charm. "I know that, honey. But the D.A. might not feel so magnanimous."

"He can bring charges without me?"

Albert nodded.

Mona looked stricken as she lapsed into silence. Finally, she looked up. "What are we going to do?"

"I haven't a clue. I know there is an answer, I just don't know what it is right now."

"You'll think of something. You always do."

Killing Boogie Fleischman would be a good start.

Summer 2012

Las Vegas

MY HEART POUNDED AS I WAITED FOR DETECTIVE CRIDER TO FESS-up, still straddling the fence as to whether I really wanted to hear what came next or not. "So what did you do?"

"That ring, it was good as new, an expensive bit of junk. I should've given it to your dad. But seein's how I was gonna take the high road from then on, if he got my ass out of a crack as he promised, I was gonna have a severe cash shortage—the county pays civil servants slave wages." He glanced at me and gave me a one-sided grin. "I know it's an explanation, but not an excuse."

"It's history." I tried to prod him forward.

"I pawned the thing," he said, his voice heavy with guilt, yet bright with confession.

That wasn't what I expected. "You pawned it?"

"Yeah, took it over to that shop on Main. You know the one? It's gone now."

"Joey Bone's place? Sure, I remember it. Didn't the Feds eventually close it down?" My mind shifted into overdrive.

"There was some talk it was a front for the Mob and some numbers thing," Crider said. "I investigated, but I never could prove it."

"Who else knew you pawned the ring?"

"Hell, coulda been a buncha guys. Bones was hooked in with all the petty hoods and wise guys."

Another dead-end. Great. "What happened to the place?"

"I heard Bones retired a wealthy man. He went south. The Caribbean, I think. He got a little press when he donated the whole kit and kaboodle to the Mob museum. Last I heard of him. For all I know he's still sittin' on a beach somewhere."

My wheels were spinning but the hamster was dead—I just couldn't make sense out of any of this. Lotsa beads, no string to thread them on. I looked around the room. "So this is where hope goes to die, huh?"

Crider glanced around. "Nothin' here but despair."

"So what are you doing here?"

When he looked at me, his face had gone slack, his eyes hollow. "I know what your father can do when he's angry."

1982
Las Vegas

"RECOGNIZE THIS?" ALBERT ROTHSTEIN PLACED THE EARRING LUCKY *had found next to the bomb at Jimmy G's in the middle of Davis Lova-to's dinner plate. It rolled into the empty carcass of a lobster tail.*

Davis plucked it from his plate, then held it up, rolling it between his thumb and forefinger. He didn't glance at Albert; he didn't need to. They knew each other well. "What the hell are you doing here?" His voice was a low growl—he hated being disturbed at dinner.

Rothstein pulled out a chair, flipped it around then straddled it, crossing his arms across the high back. Thankfully, Davis was a late diner and a man of habit. Tuesdays always meant the lobster special at Villa d'Este, 9 p.m. That day and time were by design—the restaurant would be virtually empty. Tonight that proved true, a fact that Rothstein was thankful for. Leveling a steady gaze at the attorney general, he waited.

When Davis moved to pocket the bit of gold, Albert shook his head and said, "Oh, no, no, no." He extended his hand. "I'll need that back."

The attorney general's gaze locked on his. Davis's eyes were windows into a haunted soul. Albert had thought Davis smarter than that. Playing both sides of the fence could get you killed...or worse. Was stupid an inherited trait? Or was it made? Perhaps a bit of both.

He took the bit of jewelry from Davis's wavering hand and pocketed it, in an inside pocket. "Evidence."

"Of what?" Davis waved him away. "The chain of evidence is broken anyway."

"We don't stand on that kind of pretense now, do we?"

"I don't know what you mean." A light sheen of sweat glistened on Davis's brow.

Albert glanced around looking for eavesdroppers. Finding none, he leaned in a bit closer. "I know all about Eugenia and her...condition."

"What the hell are you talking about?" Davis's eyes flicked around the room as he swallowed nervously.

Albert pulled the Polaroids Eugenia had given him out of his pocket and put them down in front of Davis. He waited while the attorney general flipped through them. When he looked up, his eyes were hard. Albert didn't object when Davis pocketed the photos. "Keep them. There are more, lots more. She's squeezing you, isn't she?"

A tic worked in Davis's cheek. Albert could see murder in his eyes.

"Look, you've got your ass in a crack." Albert rolled his eyes at the ceiling in self-deprecation. "You aren't the only one. But I've got a plan."

Summer 2012
Las Vegas

"Who do we know that can get me into the Mob Museum at this time of night?" I asked Miss P, who manned her desk as I breezed in through the outer office and into my old one...her new one. I knew she'd be there—we'd been together long enough that we could pull the vibes out of the ether when one of us needed the other.

In her peach sweater and flawless makeup, she looked fresh as a daisy. If I didn't love her, I think I'd hate her. Why did all the women in my life make me feel like a schlump?

"Mayor Goodman." She creased her brow. "Of course, it's a bit late to call."

The whole Mayor Goodman thing had gotten confusing with Oscar, Mr. Goodman, bowing out because of term limits and the lack of a statutory basis upon which we could elect him emperor. In grand Vegas fashion, Mrs. Goodman, Carolyn—equally qualified in her own right, if not moreso—was elected to fill his shoes. "Oscar?" I asked, to make sure we were thinking along the same lines. At her nod, I said, "Perfect! Call him. He's a night owl—reads until darn near dawn."

Miss P picked up the phone and dialed as I stepped into the private bathroom to make a halfhearted attempt to repair the day's damage. Squinting at my reflection, I was happy to see that I looked better than I thought, although my appearance was far less than I hoped for. Typical.

The theme song to life these days.

As Miss P made arrangements with the former mayor, I set about touching up my face.

I heard the outer door of the office open but couldn't summon the energy or the interest to tackle whatever problem had let itself in.

"Anybody here?" Detective Romeo.

Oh joy. He was in the top three on my shit list. "Back here. Old office," I called, keeping my voice as low as possible to not interfere with Miss P.

"Thank you, sir," she said, then recradled the phone. She didn't give Romeo a glance as he stepped into the room and sagged onto the couch. Instead, she lowered her head, and looking over her cheaters, she focused on me. Peeling the top sheet off the notepad, she extended it to me. "Here's the code. He said go around back— there's a keypad by the door. Let yourself in."

"Where're you going?" Romeo asked. He rubbed his eyes.

I got the distinct impression he was avoiding looking at me. "I got a bone to pick with you." I stood in front of him, looming, with my hands on my hips.

He looked up. "Was that pun intended or just casual brilliance?"

The kid was trying to butter me up. Good luck with that. "Okay, let's start with the bones first. You got an I.D. on the body in the cement casket?"

"No." He took a deep breath. "I probably shouldn't be telling you this, but I sorta owe you one. We didn't really find a body, just a bunch of bone fragments. All pretty damaged by fire, which is making the DNA analysis darn near impossible."

"Gender?"

He shook his head. "That's all I know. Had to send the fragments up to Reno to the crime lab. They're working on it." He rushed on, his words flowing together, "I'm really sorry about hauling your dad away like that. I did it for his own good."

I cocked one eyebrow in disbelief. "His own good?"

"There's just a lot of chatter on the streets."

"What kind?"

"Old scores to be settled." He glanced up at me. "But I couldn't have avoided hauling your father downtown if I'd wanted to. The order came from someone way above my pay grade."

"I know, the D.A."

"You got any idea what Daniel Lovato wants with your father?" Romeo bent forward, resting his arms on his knees, and lowered his voice. "If you got a theory, I'd sure like to hear it...before someone gets hurt."

"It's just a hunch, but I'm willing to bet it had to do with his father and mine back in the day. I have this feeling the two of them were up to their asses in alligators, along with Detective Crider. I just don't know exactly what went down." And for the record, I wasn't a hundred percent sure I wanted to know—not if it threw my father into a bucket of boiling water.

Romeo sighed, then belched. "Sorry, my stomach is killing me. This job is going to kill me yet."

I didn't know what to say—the kid did look a bit green around the gills.

He gave me a weary look and fought to hide another belch. "It gets worse."

I gave him my full attention. "What?"

"Albert Campos made bail today."

"You mean our bomber is on the street?"

"Footloose, fancy-free, with a score to settle." Romeo stopped my heart with a hard look. "Your father posted his bail."

1982
Las Vegas

AFTER ALBERT ROTHSTEIN LEFT HIM ALONE WITH HIS NOW-COLD dinner, Davis Lovato pushed his plate away, his hunger having fled. Leaning back, he pulled a new Cohiba from his inside suit jacket pocket. The latest in a long line of storied Cuban cigars, the Cohiba wasn't for sale yet. Davis had acquired his through some well-placed friends in the I'll-scratch-your-back-you-scratch-mine world. When he'd started as a lowly assistant D.A., he never could have imagined the trajectory his professional life would take. If he'd had a glimpse, he would've been a bit more careful about the friends he cultivated along the way.

Holding the tightly wrapped tube between his thumb and forefinger, he rolled it as he held it to his ear, listening. Hand rolled...only the best. Fumbling in his pocket for the cigar tool he kept on his keychain, he pulled the tool out and went through the ritual.

The waiter jumped in and flicked his BIC. Davis stuck the cigar into the flame, taking a couple of quick pulls to get it started. After a final long pull, he sat back, waving the waiter away. Then he blew a long plume of smoke toward the ceiling as he savored the nicotine hit.

Rothstein was a clever fellow. Perhaps too clever for his own good.

Summer 2012
Las Vegas

"YOU COMING?" I ASKED ROMEO, WHO SAGGED ON THE COUCH looking like a puppet with severed strings had been severed. I extended my hand. He took my offer, and I pulled him to his feet where he wobbled a bit.

"My blood sugar is in the tank." Sweat popped on his brow.

From our stash, Miss P tossed me a candy bar, which I handed to the kid. "Here you go, Detective. You're no good to me if you faint on the job."

He inhaled the sugar as if he was one toke over the line. After I had gathered my belongings, he looked a little bit brighter—a hint of pink blushed his cheeks. He trailed after me as I stepped into the hallway and headed toward the elevator. "Where're we going?"

"To talk to some old ghosts."

1982
Las Vegas

ALBERT ROTHSTEIN OPENED ONE EYE. HIS OFFICE. HE'D SLEPT ON THE couch. For a moment, he allowed himself to linger. Then he unfurled and pushed himself to his feet. Stretching, he grinned...it wasn't a happy grin. Today would propel him toward his dreams or give him a permanent home at the will of the government.

A gambler at heart, he'd put it all on the table. Today would make him or break him.

He glanced at the clock on the wall. Time to get this show on the road.

Summer 2012
Las Vegas

THE MOB MUSEUM, A PET PROJECT OF THE FIRST MAYOR Goodman, my buddy Oscar, occupied the former Las Vegas Post Office and Courthouse, built in 1933. A huge stone edifice, it now boasted three floors of exhibits including the courtroom from the Kefauver Hearings in the early '50s, to the bloody wall where the St. Valentine's Day massacre occurred. Beautiful, accessible, endlessly entertaining and enlightening, the place gave me the creeps...in a good way. To be honest, I didn't need a reminder of how ugly Vegas could be, but the tourists loved it.

Romeo stood guard behind me as I used my phone to shine a bit of light on the keypad by the rear door. For some odd reason, I'd memorized the numbers. The light in the hallway was on when we pushed open the door. "Looks like they wanted any intruders to think someone was home," I said just to be cute. Glib wore better than scared.

"Are you sure we're supposed to be here?" Romeo whispered.

"You're a cop, what difference does it make?"

"That makes it worse. We don't have a warrant."

"We have permission."

"Oh yeah." Romeo rubbed his eyes again. "You know, I'm not feeling too good."

"So you said. It's going around." I pressed the back of my hand to his cheeks and forehead. He felt clammy but cool. "You want to wait here?"

"And miss all the fun?" He shot me a weak grin, which faded quickly. "By the way, what exactly are we doing here?"

"Looking for a needle in a haystack."

1982
Las Vegas

ALBERT ROTHSTEIN TAPPED HIS FOOT AS HE LEANED AGAINST THE FRONT *wall of My Place Lounge, surveying the parking lot and trying not to look nervous. His stomach clenched but time slowed—it always did when he was under pressure. At this early hour, the die-hards were stoned to the gills inside, but the parking lot was virtually deserted. Breakfast wasn't the most popular drinking time, even with the shift workers and the minor muscle—they'd catch a few winks and be in around noon.*

By then, Albert's fate would be sealed.

He knew almost instantly when the big Lincoln eased in off the street. Davis Lovato was right on time.

Lovato angled the big car across three spaces. Albert noticed he left it idling as he opened the door and walked in Albert's direction. Albert pushed himself off the wall and met Davis halfway. Ducking, he glanced around Lovato through the driver's open door. In the passenger seat, Eugenia Campos touched up her lipstick in the mirror on the back of the visor in front of her. She didn't acknowledge him.

Albert straightened and gave Lovato a cursory assessment. He looked calm.

The attorney general pulled a manila envelope from his inside pocket. He extended it to Albert. "Your turn."

Glancing around, Albert satisfied himself that no one was around to see. He then took the envelope, opened it, pulled the papers out and scanned them.

"It's all there: your gaming license, all the right signatures. You're legit."

Albert took a deep breath and looked over Lovato's shoulder. Eugenia had stepped out of the car and now looked in his direction, a dainty hand shading her eyes against the morning sun. Albert nodded a couple of times as energy surged through him. He was legit! The smile he'd kept contained burst through, and he laughed out loud.

"Now earn it, kid." Lovato lowered his head and gave Albert a stern look from under the shelf of his brows. "You're playing in the big leagues now."

After stuffing the papers and the envelope in his pocket, Rothstein slapped Lovato on the shoulder. Then he sobered. "My turn."

As Lovato turned to go, an explosion ripped the air. The concussion threw both men against the wall behind them.

Albert was the first to roll to his hands and knees. Fighting for the breath that had been torn from him, he hung his head and gasped. Finally, he was able to stagger to his feet. Hands on his knees, he waited until the world steadied.

Lovato lay crumpled against the wall. Albert dropped to his knees *beside him. With one hand, he gently rolled him over. Lovato groaned. Dots of blood marred his face and a jagged cut bolted across his temple, disappearing into his hairline. It oozed blood. Albert helped him to a seated position, then dropped down beside him. They both looked at the burning frame of what had been a very nice Lincoln.*

No one rushed out of the bar. Albert had figured right—most of them were drunk beyond caring. Finally, a bartender poked his head out the door. Gray headed, he obviously had been around—in the old days, everyone knew that rushing toward a car bombing was a great way to walk into the line of fire.

"You guys good?" His eyes widened in recognition when they landed on the attorney general. "Shit. They try and take you out, sir?"

Albert nodded. "But he's okay. Did you call the authorities?"

"Not yet."

"Might not be a bad plan."

The man ducked his head back inside.

"Fuck." Lovato hurled the invective at no one in particular. Then he brightened. "Man, I can really spin this. This is going to be great."

"Eugenia," Albert whispered, then dropped his head into his hands.

Summer 2012
Las Vegas

THE MOB MUSEUM WAS CREEPING ME OUT. THIS LATE AT NIGHT, surrounded by silence and the recitation of death, I was sure I could feel the ghosts stirring. The thin streetlight filtering in through the occasional window didn't help, but Romeo's Maglite did. Waving the thing back and forth in front of me with Romeo trailing behind, we followed the cone of light. I closed my mind to the dark corners and what might be lurking there—clearly my imagination was working overtime. I wished it would clock out and go home.

The young detective and I stayed together as we searched each floor for Joey Bone's stash of Mob memorabilia. We hit pay dirt on the third floor. A clever designer had fashioned walls out of glassed-in towers of old files and drawers stuffed with scraps of yellowed paper: receipts, notes—curiosities obviously deemed unimportant to the overall depiction of Mob shenanigans.

Oh, how I hoped they were wrong.

I inched through the chute formed by the glass walls, eyeing the collection inside with a critical eye. Stopping in front of one display, then cocking my head to the side, I thought I could make out the logo of Joey Bone's pawn shop. Hope surged through me. "Hey, Romeo, I found something."

No response. Romeo wasn't behind me.

"Romeo?" Retracing my steps, I found him huddled on the floor, clutching his knees to his stomach.

Sweat glistened on his face. "Man, my stomach is killing me," he managed through gritted teeth.

He still felt cool to the touch. Shivers twitched his arms and legs.

"When did you eat last? I mean, before the candy bar?"

"I grabbed a taco at the stand out front of the Babylon."

"There's your first mistake. Vegas isn't known for its street food, although the new food trucks are changing that." His groan stopped me. "Sorry. We need to get you to a doctor."

Tucking the flashlight between my arm and my chest, I grabbed his elbow and tried to haul him to his feet. He couldn't help me much. Giving him another tug, I felt the flashlight drop. It hit the floor, then rolled away in a splash of light. Like a spotlight, it lit the walls as it rolled.

As it arced across the far wall, the light caught the figure of a man. Then it fell back into darkness. My heart leapt. My pulse quickened. He'd been holding a gun.

Nothing moved for a moment. Then I shrugged. Just part of the display, I guessed, and chided myself for being such a wuss. My heart had just settled a bit, and I'd managed to get Romeo standing but leaning heavily on my shoulder, when a voice from the darkness stopped me cold.

"Find what you were looking for?" Boogie Fleischman strode into the glow from the flashlight. I'd been right—he had a gun. And it was leveled at my chest.

My heart leapt into my throat. Anger surged through me. I wanted to throw myself at him and beat him to a pulp. But staring into the cold black eye of the barrel, I thought better of it. I considered asking him what he was doing here, but that seemed stupid, so I waited.

Romeo wasn't as patient. He grabbed the front of my shirt and whispered in my ear, "He was at the taco stand."

My eyes snapped to Boogie's as I tried to process.

"Yeah, the kid had no idea I was following him." He gave a little self-satisfied chortle. "I could see he was puttin' some of the pieces together."

I resisted going for his throat. "What'd you do to him?"

Gently, I lowered Romeo to a seated position—I couldn't hold him up much longer. As I did, he whispered, "Backup weapon."

He kept a Glock 9mm in a holster at the small of his back. He made a big show of grabbing onto me as he slipped down my body to the floor—a nice bit of distraction that allowed me to find the gun and transfer it to the waistband of my slacks. The playing field was almost level.

Straightening, I stepped away from Romeo.

"Careful." Boogie shook his gun at me.

"What do you want?" I glanced around looking for an advantage, something...anything. The gun was cold against the skin at my waist. I itched to use it, but Romeo's life, and perhaps my father's freedom, depended on me playing out this whole scenario the right way.

Boogie called behind him, "Kid, I got 'em."

Albert Campos materialized at his side. He didn't seem to be armed, but the odds had changed. Tweedle-dumb and tweedle-dumber.

"You guys are barking up the wrong tree."

"Your father killed my mother," Albert growled.

"No," I shook my head slowly, buying time. "Your mother was killed in a car bombing." I let that little tidbit hang there. My mind whirled. Davis Lovato's son, the D.A., and my father both had a hand in young Albert making bail...for attempted murder. I felt for my pocket.

Boogie waved the gun. "Easy."

"You think I got a gun? Wouldn't I have used it by now?" Reaching in, I pulled out a crumpled piece of paper. "This what you're looking for?"

"What's that?" Boogie tried to sound disinterested, but he didn't pull it off.

"A receipt from Joey Bone's shop with your signature, showing you bought that ring of my father's...the one found next to the body."

His eyes shifted to my hand. Momentarily focused on the slip of paper, he stepped toward me...and I ran. Diving behind a glass wall of files, I rolled and pulled the gun from my waistband. Pulling back the slide to chamber a round, I ducked as a shot exploded the glass over my head. In a shower of crystal particles, I dove for the stairs and tumbled down to the second floor. I heard a second shot. Bouncing to my feet, I pounded on. I knew just where I'd wait.

His steps were quiet, but his labored breathing gave him away.

I stilled myself. For a moment I closed my eyes, gathering myself. Then I opened them and assumed the pose, gun at the ready. There was just enough light from the glow of the illuminated exit signs to see movement.

Like a shadow passing in front of another, Boogie eased out of the stairwell and moved in my direction. "Lucky, girl, I know you're not leavin' your cop friend here. So where are you? Show yourself. We can talk. Negotiate. I get that paper, you get the kid."

Where was Albert Campos? This was the only way down that I knew of—at least the only one close. The fire escape was on the far side—too far to come into play.

I held my breath as Boogie moved closer. When he looked in my direction, my heart damn near stopped. But his eyes flicked over me, then moved on. He kept coming. A few more steps...

"Lucky, I know you're here." Right beside me now. He could reach out and touch me.

One step. Two. He moved past me.

Another few steps and I spoke. "I'm right here, asshole."

He whirled around and raised his gun. A body hurtled out of the darkness, leaping between us.

The sound of the gun shot reverberated in the small room.

CHAPTER TEN

Summer 2012
Las Vegas

*U*NIVERSITY MEDICAL Center. How I hated hospitals. But as all things go, this trip wasn't that bad. Leaning against the wall, I watched with a smile the cluster of friends gathered around Romeo's bed. Propped up with pillows, he looked thin and wan, but alive. Brandy, my assistant and his main squeeze, clutched his hand with both of hers. Her face was pinched with worry, but a smile lit her eyes. My father, Miss P and her hunk, the Beautiful Jeremy Whitlock, were there, too...even Dane. Jean-Charles had called. He was on his way. I'd phoned the story to Flash, and she was working to pull it together before her deadline. So life had settled back into some semblance of normalcy. Mona was the only one missing—Father had left orders that she stay in bed.

"You got him here in the nick of time." The attending ER doc stepped in to hold up the wall with me.

"That's all that matters. And Albert Campos?"

"He's in surgery. The gunman only winged him; he'll be fine."

The doctor gave me a half grin. "You want to tell me how you managed to plug up the gunshot wound and hang onto the gunman until the police arrived?"

"I was raised in a whorehouse—I can handle myself."

"Remind me not to make you mad."

"Save my friend over there, and you're golden."

The doctor politely bowed out when my father stepped away from the gaggle around Romeo and joined me at my wall. "Are you going to go first or am I?"

I shot him a wry look. "Since I've got a feeling you and Daniel sprung Albert so he could save my bacon, I'll start. You just tell me where I'm wrong." I told him what I knew; it didn't take long. He didn't interrupt me.

After I finished, he said, "Do you have the receipt from Joey Bones?"

"Hell, no. We'll have to tear the place apart to find it, if it's even there."

"You always were the best bluffer." My father shook his head. "Hell of a risk."

"It was the only play I had. And it worked. Romeo heard Boogie say he bought the ring...if not those words, close enough. Should be good enough to get you off the hook and Boogie Fleischman a one-way ticket to the Big House."

"Oscar will be happy to hear we don't have to tear his place apart looking for a scrap, then." He gave me a warm smile. "I'm grateful for all that you did."

"You want to tell me what all this was about, exactly?"

"Not really. Some secrets are best left unknown."

"Secrets. They have a way of biting you on the butt. But I don't think I need your help—I've got most of this figured out." I looked him full in the face. "The whole thing started with you. Somebody from back east was putting the squeeze on you. I got a feeling the bones in the foundation are, well, maybe some muscle or something. You'd had a hell of a fight with somebody at Jimmy G's when you saved me from the bomb."

"How so?"

"The blood on your shirt was fresh and too much to have come from the split in your lip, which was still oozing. You also had a puffy eye."

"Coulda been a fight somewhere close by." My father eyed me, his face passive. But he wasn't near the poker player I was.

"But it wasn't. The guy died in the fire. Then you moved his bones to the foundation of the Lucky Aces." I gave my father a long stare. "You owe me the truth. It's going to come out anyway."

"He was alive when I heard someone running. I followed the sounds to the bathroom where I found you. I had a choice: I could only grab you or the guy...not both."

"I understand." I linked my arm through his and looked over at Romeo who was fielding questions from the group. All of them were too engrossed and too far away to overhear, so I continued, "Crider worked the scene after the fire. He collected the remains, didn't he?"

My father nodded. "But he gave them to me. I buried them in the desert—just me. No one else went with me, no one else knows."

"Who was the guy?"

"Some ugly-ass muscle my uncle sent to shake me down."

"Uncle?" That was the first I'd heard of family.

My father shrugged, then sighed. "Yeah, our family is well connected. My uncle was in the family business, if you get my drift. I'd left them all behind, but had been stupid enough to take a stake from him when I moved west. I'd paid it all back, but once you're in, they never let you out. The muscle followed me to Jimmy's. And no one would've believed that I didn't kill the guy...not then. I was the one with everything to gain by that guy dying."

"And Crider helped because he'd gone to the dark side, and

getting rid of that guy sent a message back east. Crider went good after that."

My father pursed his lips and nodded. "Go on."

"Okay, here's where it gets a bit thin. If you were having trouble from back east—a family connection would've derailed your gaming license application. I'm guessing that Davis Lovato was greasing those skids." I glanced at my father.

He gave me a solid stare. "You're batting a thousand."

"Rumors of philandering derailed Lovato's bid for the governorship, and that just reeks of Eugenia Campos. So maybe she had him over a barrel." I kept going, clearly on a roll. "And back to Crider...not only did he hide evidence for you, he also found the ring with your initials." I paused to make sure I had my father's full attention. "Which he pawned..."

My father's eyes turned flinty.

"Oh, don't be too hard on him. Going straight took a bit of adjustment, time to break old habits. And that bomb that darn near killed you and Davis Lovato? And the unidentified woman who died in the explosion?"

"Eugenia Campos."

"But she didn't die, did she?"

My father looked shocked.

"I'm thinking you don't kill people, even to save your own hide. So you got rid of Eugenia for Davis Lovato. But she'd been doing you favors all along...so you got her away, probably gave her a new name, a new start, somewhere else."

He grinned and shook his head. "Yeah, the two of us, Eugenia and me, we had it all worked out. She set the bomb. While I kept Davis's attention, she turned and ran out of sight. She plated the bomb and she knew how to blow it. Boogie had taught her. Then Davis put the fix in, sold the story. We didn't have a body in that car. I was always worried some reporter or something would go messing through the files. I'm sure they did, but the tracks were covered pretty well. Story held up anyway."

"What I don't get is why she came back here eight years after all of this and tried to hook you in to paying for her kid."

"Who told you that?"

"Boogie," I started. Then it hit me and I snorted, "He lied."

"He didn't know. When he got out of prison, he came back here trying to pick up her scent. He knew how the game was played, and I don't think he ever believed she'd died in the car bombing—it was a trifle convenient. Anyway, we floated a bunch of stories trying to put him off. In truth, Eugenia married a real estate mogul who made a mint investing in Orange County. They had a couple of kids. She died last year...cancer."

"Mother?"

"She doesn't know. She was just a kid back then, and the fewer the number of people who knew, the better chance we had of keeping all of this under our hat. Lives depended on it. There were all kinds of rumors floating around, Davis Lovato being so high profile and all. Some folks thought Eugenia had gone back east, some believed she'd died in the explosion, some never believed that—you know how people are. But we all worked very hard to keep the story airtight—to keep the truth hidden. Eugenia deserved that. She wasn't bad, just in way over her head." My father looked sad. "There's a consequence to every choice, Lucky." He sounded tired. "Without her and Davis...hell, without all of them, we wouldn't have gotten a clean start; I never would've been able to put my family history behind me and carve a new future."

"And they all got what they wanted. Well, except Davis."

My father smiled. "You know, that's the funny thing about life. We all think we know what we want, but sometimes we get something totally different. And years later, when we look back, we can't imagine our life any other way than it turned out. Davis's story is like that. He wanted to be a big shot. Instead, he came home to his family, repaired his marriage, raised some fine kids and spent a happy life flying under the radar, but helped to make

Vegas what it is today." He tugged on my arm that was looped through his, pulling me closer. "I'm sorry to keep you in the dark."

"I had no need to know. Not until they found those bones and your ring."

"Boogie, working every angle. He used to tell me I'd be sorry one day. I had no idea what he was talking about."

"Matilda is an interesting angle. Your secretary. And in return for helping you and keeping her mouth shut, you set her up with the French Quarter."

"Hell, I just opened the door. She took the bit and ran with it. Best investment I ever made." My father shook his finger at me. "Don't ever cross that woman. Not if you value your hide."

"She is a force." I grinned just thinking of all that conviction in that tiny little body. "And young Albert?

My father's eyes turned dark and serious. "The only casualty, really. He's Boogie's kid. Boogie was supposed to deliver the kid to Eugenia once she got away. He didn't—young Albert was his trump card to keep Eugenia quiet. She had some photos of Boogie planting the bomb at Jimmie G's. He hid the kid away, told him his mother had died. You know the rest. You faced him down on the roof of the Babylon. You heard his story." The Big Boss sighed. "Darn near killed Eugenia, but there wasn't anything we could do."

"And how did he end up trying to track Boogie down tonight?" I held up my hand, stopping him before he could say anything. "You and Daniel told him the whole story when you made his bail."

"Enough of it."

In a way, I felt sorry for young Albert. And he'd been partially right: my father had orchestrated the events that lead to young Albert being taken from his mother. But the decisions hadn't been my father's alone. "So if the bones in the foundation don't belong to your uncle's muscle guy or Eugenia Campos, then who?"

"Jimmy Hoffa?" My father shot me a tired grin. "Seriously, I haven't a clue."

"Burned fragments aren't much to go on," I allowed.

"Then I guess we'll never know. Life has a way of working out. Vegas could be rough, but justice got her due in the end." My father put his arm around my shoulders. "Let's go home."

THE END

Thank you so much for going on a Lucky adventure with me. I hope you enjoyed the ride.

As you may know, reviews are SUPER helpful. They not only help potential readers make a choice, but they also help me win coveted spots on various advertising platforms.

So, if you would please, do me the favor of leaving a review at the outlet of your choice.

A LUCKY VEGAS NOVELLA

NATIONAL BESTSELLING AUTHOR
DEBORAH COONTS

CHAPTER ONE

FLASH

*P*ISTOL FIRE popped as the Fremont Street Experience's final pounding, pulsing crescendo of overhead lights exploded in color. The music reverberated in my chest. Or maybe that was my heartbeat. Who needed paddles to jump-start the old ticker? A .45 unloaded in the general vicinity usually did the same trick.

The Saturday night crowd packed in under the lights tighter than cattle at a feedlot—smelled sorta like them, too. I waited. They shifted. A few oohed and ahhhed. But nobody fell. Nobody screamed. This seemed like a good thing, although the jury was still out.

When Johnny Pismo had bolted off the stage in the middle of the show at the Desert Breeze Casino and I'd followed him, I'd known we were both leaping headlong into trouble. I'd made the leap before.

My name is Frederika Gordon; folks who know me call me Flash. No, I won't tell you why, but I will say I'm an investigative reporter for the Las Vegas Review-Journal, the local rag that, despite the flight to the Internet and the fact none of the visitors in town read anything longer than the list of porn channels on their in-room feed, was still hanging on

But that's beside the point, except when my rent is due. Right now, I had agreed to chase Johnny Pismo, a perpetual musical mediocrity. Not my normal prey.

So tonight, like most nights, I was chasing a story. But unlike most nights, this story had just gotten interesting. Gunfire had a habit of piquing my interest.

Between you and me, I hoped whoever was jerking on the trigger had perforated Johnny Pismo's hide. That'd dispatch one problem. But, in my experience, problems were a lot like Medusa's heads—hack off one, three more took its place. Besides that, my pal Lucky would be pissed. Apparently she had some business with Johnny Pismo, though I couldn't fathom what a high-and-mighty corporate exec would want with that lowlife.

Narrowing my eyes, I scanned the crowd again. I was either the only one aware of tiny lethal projectiles hurtling through the air or the only one smart enough to panic. Of course, I had been listening for gunfire. Even then I'd had to strain to hear it.

I swiveled it in a methodical sweep, like radar seeking a ping. On the second pass I caught the faint pops of another round of shots. Turning toward the sound, I began pushing my way through the wall of people all looking skyward. Still, nobody seemed alarmed.

"Excuse me." I elbowed aside a tourist couple dressed in the usual cliché—Bermuda shorts, white socks, loud shirts, cameras. They gave me a collective glance that succinctly conveyed their irritation—I was impressed—but they moved so I could pass. At barely five-feet, I usually have to push the issue to get anyone out of my way.

With the show over, all the craned necks resumed a normal posture, and the crowd started oozing along Fremont Street. Still, nobody had raised an alarm so I assumed no blood had been spilt... yet, but the night was young. Johnny Pismo could tap into the milk of human kindness like a wildcatter with a nose for oil, draining it dry.

I increased my pace, feeling like a salmon fighting a strong current. Lowering my head, I moved as fast as I could. I didn't even bother with eye contact and niceties—I just bulled my way through. Finally, when I glanced up, I saw the man I was looking for: Johnny Pismo.

Okay, I saw the back of him. "Johnny, you little creep, stop right there!" I shouted at his retreating back.

Much to my amazement he did. Of course, so did everyone else. The crowd was looking for a show, any show, and, if my hunch was right, this one was going to be a doozy. The mass of people moved back until they'd circled around Johnny Pismo, giving him room. If he was smart, which I knew would be a huge stretch, he'd pass a hat—Saturday night had aged sufficiently that most folks were feeling generous.

Instead, Johnny Pismo looked stupid-scared.

All twitchy, he shifted from one foot to the other, managing to look like a rat ready to run. Dressed in a red-and-white-check-ered blazer with wide lapels, orange pants and a splash of purple sock where his pants failed to meet the tops of his white bucks that coordinated with his lavender shirt, he looked every inch a throw-back. Or a throw-up, but I tried not to judge. Permed in tight curls, his hair was dyed an unnatural flat black. His eyes, narrow and dark, flicked over the crowd. Finally they landed on me. I thought he looked relieved to see a friend, but that was probably a figment. Last time I'd seen him had been ugly. This time wasn't shaping up any better.

Bad men. Bad times. And a nose for bad news. My epitaph.

But, the one bright spot was I didn't see a gun in his hand.

"What *are* you doing here?" He snarled, trying to mask the tinny high-tones of fear. He'd been a singer; well, that's what his press release said anyway. He'd fancied himself Frankie Avalon's successor—a rather grand vision for a guy with a thin voice, an average mug, a less than average bod, and no Annette Funicello. Lucky told me he was mounting a comeback, hoping to struggle out of obscurity to his former position smack in the middle of mediocre. Personally, I thought he was overreaching.

But nobody really cared what I thought. Lucky asked me to find him. What she did with him from here was her business. "Trying to keep your ass in one piece." I gave him some attitude—it had always worked before.

He kept his eyes moving. When they passed back over me, they paused. "They're trying to kill me."

Even though I couldn't imagine anyone taking the trouble to actually kill Johnny Pismo, I could tell he believed it. I thought I could smell his fear from where I stood, but that may just have been a gas leak. "Who's trying to kill you?"

He shook his head, taking in the onlookers with a glance. "Not here."

I took a deep breath and stepped into the circle. A few in the crowd murmured in surprise as recognition dawned. I sorta had a rep around town—I wasn't exactly the wallflower type—and this little standoff would make great water-cooler chat tomorrow. They crowded in closer. "Fine. But let's get you out of here."

Johnny looked receptive but rooted to the spot by fear or indecision, so I took a step toward him, intending to prod him along.

His narrow shoulders sagged a bit, allowing his chest to sink into his paunch. In the fight against physical decline, Johnny Pismo didn't appear to even be mounting a battle.

Shouts arose from somewhere deep in the crowd behind me, to my right. I whirled, but not before I saw Johnny stiffen.

The crowd parted as two huge black men forced their way through.

My heart sank. One of them I recognized, one I didn't, but I knew bad news when I saw it. "Wrong guys, Johnny. So wrong," I whispered.

Pounds of gold hung in ropes around their thick necks. I'm not one to do that whole racial profiling thing, but I felt like shrinking back into the crowd—these guys looked like they meant business, and, if the word on the street could be believed, they could bring it. Broad and bulky where it counted, lean and mean where it didn't, like ex-NFL types, their gold grills flashed with reflected glow from the lighted canopy high above, giving their smiles a weird rainbow effect. Dressed in tight white tees, black jeans slung low across their hips, unlaced Timberlands that looked fresh out of the box, they postured. Putting the bad in badass.

They lowered their heads to glower at Johnny Pismo, who quaked liked a sapling in a hurricane.

The one bright spot? The guy with the gun tucked it into a holster under his arm.

The downside? He still had a gun, and, from the sound of gunfire I'd heard, he wasn't afraid to use it.

Busta' Blue, the biggest of the man-mountains, stepped toward Johnny Pismo, shaking his head like a parent scolding a misbehaving child. Busta' was a big dog in the local gangsta rap scene. He'd even gotten some national play, but was still working his way up the food chain—I didn't even want to imagine what that might entail. A bright smile flashed, then faded, leaving his eyes hard. "You got something of mine, Pismo. I want it back."

Johnny tilted his chin. "Possession is nine-tenths of the law."

What do you know? Johnny Pismo actually had balls.

Busta' Blue gave him a chilling smile. "Fine. Then you won't mind if I just relieve you of my property." He uncrossed his arms and motioned to his muscle to follow as he stepped toward Johnny Pismo.

Johnny reached around to the small of his back. When he brought his hand back into view, it clutched a gun. At first I thought it might be a toy, but I decided to act like it was real on the off chance I was wrong.

Johnny Pismo pointed at the men, who stopped, frozen. I

guessed guns really did have a chilling effect. "Don't come any closer." The gun wiggled despite his two-handed grip. "I'll shoot you, I swear."

Frankly, I'd put the odds of him hitting either of the two men at less than one in ten. But the odds of him hitting a bystander, one of the hordes of gamblers who make it possible for Nevada to resist a state income tax on its residents, were better than even. As a potential taxpayer, I had skin in this game.

As if reading my mind, the crowd scattered.

"Johnny Pismo. Don't be a fool." The minute the words escaped my mouth I cringed—that was like asking a fish to quit pulling oxygen from water.

Johnny Pismo ignored me, which men did only at their peril. He knew that. But his reaction did solidify my disinclination to risk bodily harm to save his tiny, white ass.

Busta' grinned, his eyes fixated on Johnny Pismo. "If that piece is all you got, white boy, you better start running. That little popper won't do anything other than piss me off."

Johnny nodded toward me. "She's my backup."

All three of the men turned and looked at me. I raised my hands, open palms toward Busta' and his muscle, and gave them a smile and a shrug. "I'm sure we can work something out."

This time Busta' laughed as he started confidently toward Johnny Pismo. His man followed, licking his chops, a predator hoping for scraps.

I saw the little twerp's arms tense. "Johnny! Are you nuts?" I shouted.

He closed his eyes and pulled the trigger.

CHAPTER TWO

LUCKY

"WHERE'S JOHNNY Pismo?" I asked my best friend, ace investigative reporter and Vegas know-it-all, Flash Gordon. We huddled in a dark alley, the only illumination a spitting street lamp dying a slow death. I tried not to see it as a metaphor. Even though well past an acceptable hour, I had no trouble finding Flash—apparently she had not only discovered that it was possible to dress head to toe in Day-Glo orange, she owned it.

Before we get too far, I ought to introduce myself. My name is Lucky O'Toole, and I am the Vice President of Customer Relations for the Babylon, Vegas's primo Strip property. This is a fancy way of saying I'm the chief problem solver, hence my being on the Strip at an ungodly hour, chasing down some has-been at the behest of my father, who is also my boss.

Flash tossed her mane of red curls as she gave an exaggerated head tilt toward the rear of the hotel across the alley. Fronting the prime section of the Strip, surrounded by much grander properties, it was finally undergoing a facelift. Unfortunately, right now the whole thing was as dark as a mobster's heart and surrounded by an eight-foot chain-linked fence. From the other side of the abandoned hotel, I could hear the hum of traffic, occasional twitters of raucous laughter, shouts of joy, the thump of bass woofers as carloads of young men cruised the Strip looking for mischief—the party known as Saturday night in Vegas.

The glow of the multiple marquees that sprouted along either side of this section of the Strip—a blinding display of competition between the properties—lit the sliver of night sky above the abandoned hulk like a multihued sunset. Unfortunately, it did little to illuminate my present location or brighten my mood.

I pulled my sweater tighter against the night chill.

"Pismo shinnied up that tree." Flash dropped that little tidbit with a condescending tone, as if I should've known that. Like everybody picked a tree as a hiding place.

The trees stood like a line of weary soldiers, listing and sagging but still standing guard because it was their duty, even though they no longer had anyone to protect. I eyed the drooping palms, their fronds a dead shade of brown. It always surprised me how quickly the Mojave could suck the life out of abandoned flora and fauna. "Which tree?"

"Third one down." Flash spoke out of the side of her mouth as if worrying somebody would figure out what we were talking about.

I sent furtive glances into the impenetrable shadows. Though it wasn't hard to imagine all manner of nasties lurking there, as far as I could tell we were the only fools in the alley—besides Johnny Pismo. The smell of over-ripe garbage and countless nights of overindulgence were effective deterrents. "Why are you talking that way? And how the hell did you find him?"

Flash hitched one hip and put a hand on it. Bey-girl, Queen B, attitude. "Why am I talking this way?" She lowered her glance and her voice. "Because I've been chasing this half-wit has-been around this silly burgh for the better part of the night trying to keep him from shooting somebody or from getting shot himself."

"He still have a gun?"

Flash shook her head.

"He shoot anybody?"

"Not that I know of."

Relaxing a bit, I crossed my arms and leaned against the light pole. "So how *did* you find him?"

Flash let out a long sigh as her smile faded, then her eyes skittered from mine. "I know all his secrets."

"How?"

"I—We—"

Wow. Flash at a loss for words. The Emperor without his clothes.

Then I connected the dots. "You *dated* him?"

"You don't have to shout it to the world."

I tried hard not to laugh, I really did. But I failed...miserably. If Flash had one downfall it was her consistently abysmal choices in men. Of course, I'm not one to brag, but we aren't talking about me right now. "He has a habit of hiding in trees in back alleys?"

Flash let me have my fun. "You don't want to know, trust me."

"Oh, but I do. Every tiny, embarrassing, enlightening detail. But, I'll let you off the hook...for now." Fighting a serious case of the giggles, I tried to adopt a serious tone. "I appreciate your finding him, I really do. You've saved me from a huge headache. But now, with all your knowledge of intimate details regarding Mr. Pismo, do you think you could come up with a way to get him *out* of the tree?"

She held out her fist for a knuckle bump. "I got your back, girlfriend."

I ignored the knuckle thing. "Glad to hear it." Flash and I went all the way back to college days at UNLV. We knew so much about each other that blackmail was an inevitability. "Now, about getting him down from there."

"Couldn't we just leave him? I mean, no loss, no foul, right? He's not exactly the caliber of entertainer you'd book for the Babylon, is he? What's all this about?" Flash could sniff out a story before anyone knew there was one.

At her question, a faint alarm sounded in my deep recesses. "I'm not really sure. Something's going down and Pismo is in the thick of it." He'd been nothing but trouble from the get-go. This was the Big Boss's fault.

Sometimes being right wasn't as much fun as it should be.

And being the chief problem solver was a pain in the ass.

Unable to conjure much meanness, I leveled my tired gaze on Flash. "I don't think you can tease anything salacious out of this, sorry."

She gave me a look. "You think not?"

I didn't like her tone. It was too... hopeful. "Okay. What *don't* I know?"

Flash glanced toward the tree that ostensibly hid Johnny Pismo. "Well, it's complicated."

"Give me the short-and-sweet version. It's a three-day weekend that somehow I have off. They've worked me raw, and I'm in desperate need of me-time away from this crazy place."

"Really?" Flash turned big eyes my direction. "Three days? You'll never be allowed off the corporate leash that long. Unless... " Her eyes brightened. "Are you going somewhere?"

I nodded.

"Someplace cool?"

I nodded again. "Uh-huh."

"Where?" Flash warmed to the story. I could just see her writing a headline. "I bet the Big Boss gave you the corporate jet, didn't he? So, where to? Cabo? San Francisco?"

"Even better."

"Paris? Rome?" She tugged on my arm. "Oh, please tell me you're going to Rome. Those Italian men... I'm so down for that."

For a moment I thought about pointing out a rather interesting interpretation of her word choice; but I was too tired to keep playing, so I gave it up.

"Flash," I couldn't keep the tired out of my voice. "I'm going to bed."

She pursed her lips. "Typical. But it still could be fabulous depending on who you take with you."

"Which is none of your business. Now," I put my hands on my hips and turned my attention to Johnny Pismo's perch, "how the hell do we get him out of there?"

"I bet it's Jean-Charles."

Flash goaded me. Jean-Charles Bouclet, a rather dishy French chef, had been worming his way into my life, not that I objected or anything. Of course, my former lover, Teddie, had just reappeared complicating things and increasing the odds that I would shoot him and end up in jail with no conjugal visits. So I'm not sure any of it mattered. "Pay attention. Johnny Pismo? The tree? I'd really like to wrap this up and go home, not that it hasn't been a laugh a minute."

Her face clouded as the fight left her. "There's a problem." She avoided my eyes.

I got one of those hollow feelings in the pit of my stomach. You know the ones. The ones that make your mouth go all cottony right before you hurl. "A problem? Of course there is. He's hiding in a friggin' tree." I leveled my best dirty look as I pulled myself to my full six feet. Nothing really intimidated Flash, but I was desperate enough to pull out every stop. "What. Is. The. Problem?"

"He shot somebody." Flash avoided my gaze.

I snorted in disbelief. "Johnny Pismo? He doesn't have the balls."

Flash gave me an unenthusiastic shrug. "Well, I saw him aim and pull the trigger. After that, things got a bit sketchy. I heard a yelp; then the crowd erupted like a swarm of bees prodded from the hive—ready to attack but all flutter with indecision. Johnny

Pismo took off like a scalded dog. Since he was my target, I took off after him."

Under pressure, I switched to automatic problem-solving mode. My heart rate slowed, my vision sharpened, my brain jump-started. "Did you see who he fired at?"

Flash squared her shoulders. "You are sooo not going to like this." She stared over my shoulder, avoiding eye contact.

"I already sooo don't like this."

"Busta' Blue." She took a step back awaiting my reaction.

She got one. I flapped my arms and stomped around as my blood ran cold. "Great! Just what we needed. Now I've got to save his pansy ass from the gangsta and gun crowd. Terrific." Then a thought brightened the night. "Did he kill him?

Flash tightened her lips into a thin line and shrugged. "Like I said, I didn't hang around. From the reaction of the crowd—women didn't faint or anything dramatic—I figure he just winged him, but I don't know for sure."

I didn't know whether that was a good thing or a bad thing, not that the answer really mattered all that much. It just defined the rules of the game and who the players would be. Of course, I was ignoring the fact that it probably mattered a whole lot to Busta' Blue. And—not that I cared—it also factored greatly into Johnny Pismo's longevity. But, dead or alive, damage had been done. And retribution was required by the Code. "I wonder if Johnny Pismo appreciates his position. He's just started a turf war with the toughest guys around."

After Tupac got gunned down on the Strip, that whole part of the music scene had been a powder keg ready to blow. I glanced up and down the alley with a new sense of urgency. "We'd better get him out of that tree and someplace safe before someone else finds him. Any idea what his beef with Busta' Blue is?"

"I heard Busta' say Johnny Pismo had something of his and he wanted it back."

"What?"

Flash shrugged. "It wasn't exactly a good time to wring details out of anyone."

I gave her that as I tried to think.

"When he scurried up that tree, I tried talking to him, but he's pretty shook," Flash continued. "He was talking a mile a minute. I couldn't understand a word. Maybe you'll have better luck; he's scared of you. But," she put a hand on my arm as I started for the tree, "he's armed."

Something in her tone sounded off, but I blew by it. "He still has the gun, I know."

Holding on to my arm, Flash squeezed tighter. "No, he traded the gun." Her lips pursed, and seriousness clouded her eyes—I caught it all in the glow of a streetlight nearby.

I gave her my full attention. "He traded the gun? For what, a bazooka?"

"No, a tiger."

I looked again at the tree. "A tiger? He's got a tiger in the tree?"

Flash fought a grin—a hint leaked out, curling her lips on one side. "I told you, I only lost him for a few minutes. Next thing I know, he's got a tiger. I don't exactly know how."

"How big?"

"Siegfried and Roy big."

I gave a low, appreciative whistle. "How'd he get it up a tree?"

"He tossed a chunk of something up there, and the tiger went for it."

I mentally squashed the other questions burbling up—they could wait. I tipped my head toward Johnny Pismo's hiding place. "Let's talk him down. The longer we wait, the better the odds of increasing our problems. Busta' and his crowd aren't stupid. They'll find Johnny Pismo sooner rather than later."

Lights arced across the back of the building as a car turned down the alleyway, its engine idling. Flash and I ducked back into the shadows. A figure leaned out the passenger-side window and flicked on a powerful light, the kind that reminded me of the ones used to spotlight corner girls.

"Shit." Flash, still squeezing my arm, pulled me close to her side. "You're like some friggin' prophet or something."

The car eased in our direction as the light flashed around the alley. "Just once, when it comes to this sort of thing, I'd love to be wrong."

"What should we do?"

"You wouldn't have a gun, would you?" I asked Flash, even though I knew she hated the things.

"You think I have a gun? Seriously?"

"A passing spark of unbridled hope. But, for the record, they do come in handy from time to time." I took a deep breath. "This would be one of those times."

"Point taken."

The car idled closer.

Feeling powerless, I tried to think. A couple of garbage cans, a few empty bottles, not much in the way of firepower. "Be still. Maybe they won't find him. Or us."

"They knew enough to come down this alley," Flash whispered.

As the car kept inching closer, we pressed further back, squatting behind the shelter of a dumpster. Its top open, it reeked of the rotting detritus of dreams. Johnny Pismo had reeked of it. And desperation made stupid people do seriously stupid stuff. If I ever got my hands around his neck, I'd toss the twerp in the thing and leave him there—after I figured out what the hell was going on.

I held my breath and ducked out of sight as the car rolled past, so close I could smell the sweet stench of its over-cologned occupants combining with the already bilious fumes from the dumpster in a truly nauseating olfactory overload. When I saw stars, I deigned to breathe again. My breath escaped in a long, silent sigh as the car eased past out hiding place without stopping. Thinking they'd had time to move away, I ventured a peek around the dumpster. Brake lights painted the shadows an eerie red. The spotlight still probed the darkness. The car pulled even with the first tree. Leaning over me as I crouched, Flash put a bracing hand on my back as she craned for a better view. I don't think either of us took a breath. I know I didn't—not until I saw stars.

The fronds of the first tree, an impenetrable tangle of dead brown and hopeful green shoots, tossed the light back. I dared a shallow breath as the car kept moving.

Two more trees until Johnny Pismo would be out of the woods.

The noise of the Strip faded as every molecule of my being became focused on the car. The idle of the car's engine faded until there was nothing, as if time had stopped, pausing life. Silence filled all the spaces around us.

"They have guns?" Even though my positive thinking was often dashed, I clung to it. One of these times I had to be right... right?

Flash leaned down, her mouth close to my ear, and whispered, "Hell, these guys accessorize with the latest calibers."

A shot split the night.

Flash and I both jumped. "Now you're the friggin' prophet," I hissed.

"You had to ask." Flash's voice lowered into a growl.

But hers wasn't the only growl. Echoing down the alley came the distinct, low rumble of a Tyrannosaurus Rex. Or may of a pissed off, overly large feline.

I let my head drop. If we heard it...

Sure enough, when I hazarded another glance, the light now probed the third tree, Johnny Pismo's tree. Brake lights flashed on. Doors opened, then shut. Three shadowy figures gathered under the tree. The light was too weak for me to make them out perfectly, but, from their posture, they had meanness on their minds.

A voice snarled, "Pismo, get your pansy ass down from there. You got some answerin' to do."

Still with a balancing hand on my back, Flash leaned down again. "Busta' Blue."

I'd gotten that far on my own.

"Guess Johnny's aim is as bad as his act," Flash continued.

The urge to spring to his defense coiled inside me. Why all of a sudden I felt the need to go bounding to his rescue beat the hell out of me. It was a knee-jerk thing, not a thought-type thing—sort of a save-the-world character defect. I opened my mouth to object.

Busta' Blue beat me to it. "You and me got a score to settle, Pismo."

Silence. The night stilled as if it too was afraid of Busta' Blue. Even the hint of a breeze that had raised goose bumps on my arms had fled, although the goose bumps remained.

In the weak light, I saw one of the men raise his arm and point toward the tree. Metal glinted in the light. A gun. Both hands on the grip, he took aim.

Damn. Why did men always seem to bring a gun to the fight when fists would solve the problem?

Without a thought, I pushed myself to my feet, apparently catching Flash off guard. She yelped as I hit her chin, slamming her mouth shut.

"Sorry." I threw the word over my shoulder as, legs churning, I ran. "No!" One small word wasn't much defense against three big dudes with a gun, but fresh out of ideas, I was winging it.

At my shout, clearly surprised, two of the men turned. The third one, the one I was interested in, didn't flinch as he focused on his target.

A shot split the air. Then another shot. The muzzle flash seared white in the darkness so bright it left a light shadow in my field of vision, half-blinding me for a moment. I cringed against it, but kept running. I stumbled, then caught myself, staggering to regain first balance then forward momentum.

Johnny Pismo, if he was in fact in the tree—a fact we had yet to truly establish, remained silent. A body didn't fall, so I assumed he also remained unhurt… or absent.

"Stop shooting!" I shouted again.

This time the shooter turned to look at me, then swiveled to point the gun at my chest.

Okay, so I didn't think this through. Nothing more dangerous or foolish than action without a plan. A wing and a prayer, that's my M.O.

I skidded to a stop. The four of us, wait…Flash skidded in beside me… the five of us stood there in some sort of an O.K. Corral moment.

"What do we do?" Flash whispered.

"Don't ask me. Dark places and angry men are more up your… alley."

"Cute," she said but didn't argue. Instead she squared her shoulders. "Busta', whatever Johnny Pismo's got, I'm sure we can negotiate a trade."

"Being up a tree isn't exactly a strong bargaining position." Busta's voice was low and menacing.

Before Flash could counter, the fronds of Jonny Pismo's hiding place shook as something moved, shifting positions. Then a low growl, starting soft then amplifying into a roar. Primal and menacing, it hit every visceral flight-nerve I had. Every hair on my body stood at attention. A flood of adrenaline accelerated my heart as a sheen of perspiration popped. My breath came in short, shallow gasps. Flash clutched my arm. Indecision rooted us to the spot.

The men froze, clearly using the deer-method of dealing with danger—if you don't move, they can't see you—which was a problem for the deer but not for any of the creatures that viewed them as dinner. We all watched in dread as the fronds moved again, scratching against each other, like the tiger was sharpening its claws.

Like something out of a Siegfried and Roy show, the big cat leapt from its perch in a graceful arc, landing without a sound. Little cat feet. Make that big cat feet.

In one easy leap it pounced on the shooter, who crumpled beneath it with a whimper. The cat batted at him. But no blood-curdling screams, not blood that I could see. A big cat playing with an even bigger mouse. The cat looked up like it was just getting started.

"God Almighty, don't one of you fools have a piece?" Busta' whispered, his voice tight with fear. Apparently the guy under the cat was the only one with a gun.

"You're the badasses," Flash reminded them. "Three idiots and a gun." That last comment, said out of the side of her mouth, was meant for me.

"How many gangstas does it take to stop a tiger?" So helpful, I know, but I couldn't think of anything else to say. Panic tends to loosen the bonds of my brain cells, freeing random associations.

Busta' and his one upright buddy remained rooted, transfixed as if unable to comprehend the danger. The cat returned its attention to the third man. Gave a tentative pawing. The man gave no response. Curled in the fetal position, either he was playing dead or it wasn't much of an act.

Big cats without their handlers made me wary, but not too much. This being Vegas, although the tiger was still at heart a wild animal, it would be very accustomed to humans. Christ, Johnny Pismo had led the thing on a merry chase through the back alleys then had gotten it up the tree without incident. I watched the tiger and I could tell it was playing.

Finally, the big cat apparently decided what to do with its catch. It cuffed the man like a mother grabbing a wayward child—hard enough to ensure attention, but soft enough to not hurt—then the cat leapt for Busta's other companion. The man crumpled beneath the big cat who gave him the same treatment. Both men whimpered as they clutched their knees to their chest.

Still standing over his prize, the cat turned its head to stare down the last man standing, Busta' Blue.

Looking the cat in the eye finally galvanized Busta' to action. He grabbed at the door handle behind him. He struggled with it, darting panicked looks at the cat, who eyed him, then snarled. The cat bounded toward him.

Taking off at a dead run, he headed my direction. As he passed by me through the weak glow of the street lamp still sputtering above, Busta' Blue shot me a wide-eyed look of terror but kept running. He had a slash across his upper arm that trickled blood—why I noticed that, I don't know.

Last I saw of Busta' Blue, he was hightailing it around the corner, the tiger in loping pursuit.

Flash ran and pounced on one of the prone men. One step behind her, I took the shooter. The smell of urine was strong. I'd probably piss myself too if a tiger jumped on me, so I tried not to judge. A cursory pat down revealed he was unarmed except for his handgun, which I kicked out of reach. Unbuckling his belt, I then pulled it free. "Cross you wrists."

Eyes white with fear found mine, and he did as I asked. "Where's the tiger?" he whispered.

"Waiting for me to give the word to eat you alive."

The guy actually bought that line. "What're you tying me up for?"

"Not what. Who?"

"The cops, I know," he said, showing he had a few brain cells. "But what'd I do?"

"Discharged a gun in the city. Hell, I don't know. Picked the wrong guy to hang with? Guilty by association. I'm sure that's a crime somewhere." Not in Vegas, though. If it was, half the city would be in the slammer, including me, but I didn't say that. I secured his hands behind him with the belt. It wouldn't hold him for long, but hopefully long enough—especially with the tiger threat. As an afterthought, I tied his shoelaces together. "One thing I do know: you and your friend are not my problem. Metro can deal with you two, so save your whining for them." Metro is the local nickname for our fearless protectors, the Metropolitan Police Department, many of whom I held in rather low esteem. Through the years they'd worked hard to be held so low, so who was I to refuse to grant their wish?

With her guy flipped onto his stomach, his arms wrenched behind him and a knee firmly in his back, Flash had been watching me as I secured Busta' Blue's buddy. When I'd finished, she used the same technique on her guy.

Now certain the two men wouldn't go anywhere anytime soon, I pushed to my feet, then grabbed my phone from its holster at my hip. As I hit the Emergency button that would auto-dial 911, I growled at Flash, "Get that ass Johnny Pismo out of that damn tree, and keep him out of my reach for now. I'm not feeling too charitable at the moment."

Flash grinned—she knew I was 90 percent bark, 10 percent bullshit.

After a few moments of heated conversation, I managed to convince the dispatcher at the Metropolitan Police Department that this wasn't a crank call, that there was indeed a tiger in hot pursuit of a rap star, both of them headed toward the Strip. It defied logic that she seemed so unconvinced that something this absurd could happen in a city where the absurd was common-place, but then, again, we are talking about Metro—the place where the lower your I.Q. the larger your weapon was not only a rule, it was a mandate.

When I finished my call, I joined Flash underneath Johnny Pismo's tree.

"Come on, Johnny honey," Flash cajoled. "I swear they're gone."

"Last time you sweet-talked me I ended up naked, smeared with honey, and dumped on the Strip without a shred of clothing."

I looked at Flash with a raised eyebrow.

She shrugged. "But I rolled you in birdseed covering your... shortcomings, so I left you with some dignity intact."

"Not after the pigeons found me." He didn't sound angry, which wasn't a surprise. Johnny Pismo's career path had taught him if not to enjoy public humiliation, at least to tolerate it.

"Pigeons?" Flash's voiced cracked a bit. I couldn't tell whether from laughter or pain. I didn't dare look at her.

Johnny Pismo's feet appeared, then his legs, followed by the rest of him as he chatted. "Actually, the pigeon's weren't so bad." He wrapped his legs around the trunk of the tree and shinnied down. Landing on both feet, he brushed himself down as he turned and locked eyes with Flash. "But the crows? Damn, those buggers are nuthin' but feathered flesh-eaters."

Open-mouthed, I stared at both of them. Words deserted me. Flash clearly suffered from the same affliction. Sirens sounded in the distance, faint at first, then growing louder. A cruiser squealed into the alley followed by an unmarked, high-beams on, the light bar on top of the cruiser strobing like flares igniting. I winced and squinted against the light. The cars screeched to a halt. With my pupils still pinpointed by the bright lights, I heard but didn't see the doors open and boots hit the ground.

"Hold it right there," someone barked.

Still blinking furiously, my eyes tearing a bit, I rolled my eyes —we hadn't moved.

"Stand down, officer." A calm voice that made me smile— Detective Romeo. He and I went way back, and he was perhaps the only member of the force that I would invite to dinner in my home. A trusted friend and ally against the silly, the stupid, and the lethal.

"Lucky, are you okay?"

His worried face appeared through my tears. Still looking all of twelve, except for the worry lines bracketing his mouth and the dark circles offsetting the bright blue of his eyes, he stared at me intently, his concern evident.

"Christ almighty, Romeo. Your lights are making me feel like I'm having a near-death experience."

As I talked with Romeo, Flash drug Pismo off to the side. I'd let her have her fun.

That got a relieved snort out of him. He turned to his men. "Lower the wattage, guys." It took them a moment, but they did as he asked, leaving light to see by but not enough to coerce a confession during an interrogation. "Now, get these two in the cruiser." He turned his attention back to me. "So what's this about a tiger?"

I filled him in. Embellishing the good parts, I had him in tears as I ended with a flourish describing Busta' Blue's ignominious departure.

"You and me keep learning the same lesson over and over." He swiped at his eyes with the back of a hand.

"Bullies—nothing but big sissies if you push back."

"Or have a tiger," the young detective added as he sobered just a bit. "So where is this... what's his name?"

"Johnny Pismo."

"Right." Romeo took his notepad out of the inside pocket of his ubiquitous crumpled overcoat, pulled the pencil from the spring binding, then flipped it open and started scratching a few notes. "Where'd he get that name? From that Brazilian liquor?"

That stopped me for a second. "No, that's Pisco. Pismo's a beach in California."

Romeo shrugged, clearly unconcerned about his poor grasp of useless details. "Whatever. Let's get this over with; sleep's a wasting."

We joined Flash, who had Johnny Pismo up against a fence. A lapel in each hand, her face inches from his, she was giving him the what-for.

Romeo stepped in to break it up. "Down, girl. I'll take it from here."

Flash whirled with a scowl, her hand still fisted in Johnny Pismo's jacket. Her face brightened when she recognized Romeo. She let go of her handfuls of cloth and stepped back, making a sweeping gesture toward Johnny Pismo, like a matador taunting a bull with a red cape. "Sure, detective. He's all yours. For the record, he likes it rough."

Wide-eyed, Romeo stared at her for several blinks, then turned his peepers my direction.

"Don't let her scare you; she respects the uniform."

Romeo glanced down at his civvies.

"You know what I mean."

Released from Flash's grasp, Johnny Pismo stood a bit taller as he brushed at the wrinkles in his lapels with little effect. The tattered cloth, thin with age, held every crease. "You guys got a smoke?"

"Haven't you learned?" Flash asked. "Three packs a day. That stuff will kill you."

I thought Busta' Blue posed the more immediate threat to Johnny Pismo's longevity, but I didn't want to get into that conversation.

A bit twitchy and reeking of fear, Pismo put on a brave face as he glanced from the detective to me, ignoring Flash. He glanced over Romeo's shoulder and seemed to relax at the sight of Busta' Blue's muscle corralled in the back of the squad car and guarded by several officers. "Look, this is all a big mistake."

Romeo sighed and readied his pencil over a new page in his notebook. "It always is. So start at the beginning, and if you leave out any pertinent facts, I'll bust your ass."

I crossed my arms and smiled—my young detective had added a gravelly growl to his repertoire. Nice.

That knocked a bit of the jaunty out of Johnny Pismo. "Look, I didn't steal it. I just borrowed it."

I'd seen bad acts before, but Johnny Pismo's truly sucked.

"I'm going to give it back. Really."

"Of course you are." Romeo sighed and gave me a tired look of disgust. "If I had a dime for every two-bit has-been who tried to entertain me with me that song and dance, I'd be a rich man. Just give whatever it is to me."

Johnny Pismo glanced around weighing his options from the looks of it. "Okay, but I gotta have it back. It's important." He reached into his jacket pocket and pulled out a huge ring festooned with an impressive square-cut diamond.

"Liberace's ring? And a good fake, too." I asked, narrowing my eyes. I knew that ring pretty well, had held it one several occasions.

"Why do you think it's a fake?" Romeo asked.

Flash pulled out her pad and started scribbling.

"The real one belongs to the Big Boss." As I said it, some of the tumblers in my head fell into place. So this is what the Big Boss wanted with Johnny Pismo. "It's one of the centerpieces of the music collection in the museum at the Babylon."

Johnny Pismo nodded. "This one used to belong to Liberace."

Flash whistled. "Serious?"

Johnny nodded. "Stole it myself."

"From the Babylon?" I asked, still not connecting the dots.

"No, from Busta' Blue. That's why he's pissed. He's a big fan of Liberace."

"Liberace." I allowed myself a moment. The face of Vegas when I was young and impressionable, I'd met him numerous times, even going to his house with my mother. Nobody new could hold a candle. I focused on the bauble. "That's got to be a fake." The security at the Babylon, while not impenetrable, was damn solid. I couldn't imagine one of these bozos pinching the ring without sounding all kinds of alarms.

"This one is the real one," Johnny Pismo gave me a knowing look. "You got the fake one in your case."

My disbelief must've been written across my face.

"Look," Pismo continued, warming to the story, "the Big Boss put you on my tail, right?"

So now I knew why the Big Boss sent me after the half-wit—it wasn't Pismo he was after. It was the ring. He should've given me a heads-up. I'd try to remember that when I gave my boss a piece of my mind, assuming I had any left after all this. "So you tell the Big Boss your story about the ring, that Busta' Blue has the real one and the Babylon has been insuring a fake. He doesn't believe you. And you decide to prove it by stealing Busta's?"

Johnny nodded. "And a good plan, too. Well, until Busta' Blue came home unexpected. But I knew the Big Boss would keep an eye on me, just in case. I'm sure he probably will get the ring in his case checked, maybe might have put that into gear, but things with me sorta escalated pretty quick. I just talked to the Big Boss a few hours ago." He glanced at Flash. "I didn't know I'd end up with the second-string though."

"Delegation, it's what I do. And you were darn lucky to have her chasing you all over town. Had it been me, I would've wrung your sorry neck and been done with it." I held out my hand, and, swallowing hard, Johnny Pismo dropped the ring into my palm. I hefted it a couple of times. It felt real. But you could say that about most of Vegas; that was the sleight of hand. "Liberace," I sighed his name. I longed for the old days, when the Mob kept the peace, everyone knew the rules, and the entertainers were exactly that, without fancy mixing and huge productions, and near-naked backup performers to compensate for the headliners who were long on charisma and short on everything else.

"You're not helping," Romeo said out of the corner of his mouth.

"This is Vegas. He was a god."

Romeo held out his hand. I shook my head. "Belongs to the Big Boss."

"It's evidence."

Reluctantly I handed it to him. "Lose it, it's your ass."

He knew I was half-joking. Without even giving it an appreciative look-see, Romeo dropped it in an evidence bag and pocketed it. "You took this from Busta' Blue?" Romeo's voice held a hint of awe. "You might not have much, but you got balls."

Johnny managed to look slightly incensed. "He stole it first." He put his hand out, palms down as if pressing on an invisible table, or tamping down escalating emotions. "Look, I can't prove it, but there's some guys in town, they're stealing the real stuff replacing it with fakes. Nobody's the wiser."

"How do you know that?"

"Pawnshop downtown. I tried to fence a piece I lifted from the storage room at Hard Rock." Like I said, Johnny Pismo wasn't the brightest bulb.

Romeo looked amused. "Busts usually aren't this easy."

"You're going to arrest me? Hey, I put it back," Pismo squeaked, a post-pubescent reaching for the high note. "Besides, I'm on a case. Yes, that's it; it's all part of a scavenger hunt."

"And gunfire on Fremont Street, according to these ladies here." He motioned to Flash and myself. "Patrol confirmed reports of gunfire."

Johnny Pismo waffled. "I didn't mean for that to happen. I was shooting for the stars, in a manner of speaking."

"On a case?"

"Well, in a manner of speaking."

"You a PI now?"

"In training."

"He's all yours," I said to Romeo.

"What is it you think you know?" Romeo's voice was flat, angry with a hint of exhausted.

"The competitors were given a list of cool music shit. Stuff that belonged to some of the greats. The harder the stuff is to grab, the more points we earn. The one with the most points wins."

"Wins what?" I asked while Romeo scribbled in his notebook.

The uniforms had secured the men in the back of the cruiser and now stood guard in a bored sort of way—this sort of thing was probably routine and therefore boring to them. On the other hand, Flash seemed riveted as she too took notes in what I knew to be her own personal version of Sanskrit—illegible to most and unreadable to all unless they had access to her mental Rosetta Stone.

"The winner gets a recording contract. Dig Me O'Dell of Smooth Sound Downtown Records is offering a one-year contract, a shot at opening for one of their big acts, promotion… you know, the whole enchilada."

Scribbling stopped as all eyes landed on Johnny Pismo. Unused to the scrutiny, he shrank into himself.

"You mean we have a bunch half-crazed wanna-bes running all over town, taking things that don't belong to them, to try to win a shot at the big time?" Romeo sounded incredulous.

Personally, even though the scheme sounded ill-advised, it didn't seem all that far-fetched. "You got a list of the icons you're looking for?"

"Not on me." Johnny patted his pockets. "It's like a treasure map; I've got it stashed where nobody can find it."

"I'll take you to get it, then you're coming downtown with me."

Pismo didn't argue. Considering Busta' Blue wanting to put a heap of hurt on him, jail probably seemed like a safe place to hide.

"How many contestants are there?" I asked Johnny Pismo.

The crooner shrugged. "Who knows?"

"What happens to the items that are stolen?"

"Here's the deal," Johnny leaned in, lowering his voice. "I can't prove it or nothing, but the items get returned to their rightful owners—in theory. But I'm thinking that's how they pull the switch, giving the owners back the fakes."

I couldn't shake the feeling that Pismo's story held about as much water as a sieve. Time to move up the food chain. The Big Boss had some explaining to do.

CHAPTER THREE

FLASH

a BIG part of being an investigative reporter involved keeping my mouth shut and my ears open. So I'd stayed in the background while all the excitement died down, letting Lucky and Romeo untangle Johnny Pismo's story. Romeo had tucked Pismo into the back of his unmarked—there still was that whole shooting into a crowd issue to be dealt with, along with the possession of stolen property thing. Lucky had staggered home. Between you and me, she needed less real world and more role play.

Bondage has been known to bring back the near-dead.

My friend Fabian would be just the man to whip her into shape. His little House of Horrors was just what the sex doctor ordered. Of course, talking Lucky into the fur-lined handcuffs would take some doing. I wrote that onto my mental to-do list for tomorrow. The handcuffs were essential.

But right now I wasn't thinking about sex, an unusual state. Well, okay, I was thinking about it, just not for me. And I was thinking about Johnny Pismo's tall tale. Yeah, that's right, I didn't believe a word. Okay, maybe under the stench of all that bullshit lingered a hint of the sweet smell of the truth, but I couldn't shake the feeling Johnny Pismo had layered the compost on pretty dang thick. Something was going on. I could feel it.

Right now I needed more info—this whole scavenger hunt thing. What could possibly be in it for Smooth Sound Downtown Records? I'd leave the big shots to Lucky and Romeo. After years on the streets combing through the trash for stories, I had my own strategy. While Lucky started at the top and worked her way down, I cut straight to the lowest rung on the ladder.

Ralph "Woodstock" Winslow was my go-to guy when I needed the inside skinny on the music biz.

LIKE A RAT, I KNEW EVERY BACK ALLEY IN VEGAS, SO IT DIDN'T TAKE me long to get to the Babylon, saunter up its grand curved drive, then push through the gold–and-glass front doors. Even at four in the a.m. the place was packed, the vibe just hitting the peak of the evening. Every time I stepped foot in Lucky's place it hit me like a peak sexual experience, leaving me weak-kneed and tingly all over. I don't know what it was—maybe all that white marble inlaid with mosaic tiles in every bright color imaginable. Or maybe it was the multihued cloth tented above registration. Or maybe all the plants and little bridges over the stream complete with all sorts of waterfowl that made rabbits look like pikers in the breeding game. Or maybe it was the indoor ski slope behind a thick wall of Plexiglas across from registration. Or maybe it was the handsome servers in their tiny uniforms that left practically nothing to the imagination. Yes, handsome servers—at the Babylon, the fiefdom of cocktail wait staff had been gender-integrated at Lucky's insistence, God bless her.

Never one to ignore eye candy, I ogled a few of the hunks passing flutes of Champagne as I strode through heading toward the casino.

A couple of them triggered a spark of recognition. Where had I seen them? Fabian's? Everybody there wears a mask which made facial recognition iffy. Most of the other defining physical attributes were not presently on display—Lucky and the Brass at the Babylon would frown on that. Maybe I'd seen them at the Green Door? I hadn't partaken of the sexual free-for-all in a while, so I doubted that was it. Whatever. Vegas had an abundance of handsome, willing young men—if one left the game, there were always two to take his place.

A couple stood in a passionate embrace tangled together at the apex of the small bridge over the Babylon's version of the Euphrates. Intent upon each other, they seemed oblivious they were stopping traffic both coming and going. Other folks nicer than myself rerouted to one of the other nearby bridges. I, on the other hand, put my head down and charged up the slight incline. At the top, I poked the guy on the shoulder. It took a couple of pokes to get his attention.

"What?" He gave me a bleary eye. His hair a mess. Red lipstick smeared across his mouth, he didn't smile.

"You're blocking traffic, dude." I didn't back down. "Why don't you and your lady get a room? I hear they have some nice ones here."

"She ain't mine." He winced, prodded by that painful point of reality.

I wanted to say she didn't look much like a lady either with her breasts popping out of her tight corset and her pussy skirt—so named because, with no underwear, that's exactly what oglers got an eyeful of—but who was I to judge?

"Well, take it somewhere else then."

"Who are you to tell me…" His eyes shifted over my shoulder and widened a little.

"Let the lady pass."

The couple beat a hasty retreat.

I smiled, but didn't need to turn to know who was behind me.

"Hey, Renny. Didn't know you were in the business of rescuing damsels in distress." I turned and recoiled in surprise myself. "Shit."

Renny Mitchum, fondly known as Renny the Reefer, because of his fondness for a certain tripointed leaf, looked like himself, except for the gruesome makeup, pirate scarf tying his salt-and-pepper locks back, one long earring dangling from his left earlobe, and a large snake coiled around his neck. "Honey, I've never known you to need rescuing."

"What're you doing here, with...that?" I put a hand to my throat as I nodded at the snake who eyed me with lifeless eyes.

Renny adjusted the weight of the snake on his shoulders. "Me and Christine...you know Christine, right? The girl with the chicken show," he prompted, his eyebrows raised.

I thought for a moment. "Oh, the show where the chickens play tic-tac-toe against anyone willing to risk a ten-spot?"

"Yeah, that's the one. She's my friend, and I stopped to watch her do her thing." His face clouded and his eyes grew misty.

"What happened?" Before I remembered Renny didn't like to be touched, I gently squeezed his arm. Renny was running on a high double-digit I.Q., but he held his own and got by better than most, but he struggled in social situations.

He flinched but didn't pull away. "Jake here..." Renny scanned the area like he was looking for a place to hide. "I forgot to feed him, alright? And when Jake gets hungry..."

I bit down hard on the inside of my cheek, bringing tears to my eyes.

Renny's eyes drifted from mine as he became focused on his shoes, Converses with no laces.

"Did Jake eat one of the chickens?"

Renny nodded, still looking down. "Her best rooster."

"And Christine?"

"She was okay, nice even." Renny looked up. "She's my friend.

DEBORAH COONTS

And she's got lotsa chickens, although she says they're not too smart so they're hard to train."

Training a chicken—now there's a concept. "I know some pansy-assed men who could benefit." Renny gave me a narrow-eyed look. I shrugged. "My point being," I continued, "chickens we can find. The training is up to her." I gave him a good once-over. The look in Jake the snake's eyes left me no doubt he considered the chicken nothing more than an appetizer. Renny looked a little gaunt himself. "Why don't you and Jake come with me? I got to find a friend at Pandora's Box, then maybe we can catch a bite in Neb's." Neb's was the Babylon's twenty-four-hour buffet fit for a Sultan and his harem. "Whaddya say?"

"I'm tapped out. That's sorta why Jake went after that chicken. Usually he has better manners, but he's not so good at going without."

"This one's on me."

Renny brightened. "Jake, too?"

"As long as security doesn't kick us out, Jake." I had no idea what a snake would want, but, whatever it was, I felt sure the Babylon would have it.

Renny followed me off the bridge and through the arched entrance to the casino. This late in the evening the vibe was still going strong; patrons ringed most of the tables three deep. Occasional shouts erupted, a few groans, lots of laughter and clapping, chants of encouragement. Even if folks weren't staying at the Babylon, they came to gamble here—which was like the pot at the end of the rainbow where gaming establishments were concerned.

There was just something about the place. I'd tried to figure it out, but I still couldn't put my finger on it. But I knew Lucky and her father, the Big Boss, had themselves the Vegas equivalent of a printing press, churning out C notes like they were bits of taffy at the fair.

The casino with its thick mosaic-patterned carpet, deep purple walls, open flames under glass providing subtle, low-light ambiance, palms softening the spaces, and bright fabric looping from the high ceilings was a welcoming, comfortable, classy yet cool place.

Everybody wanted to be seen donating money here.

Renny dogged my heels a bit too close for my comfort. At any minute I was sure he'd step on the backs of my shoes, but I didn't bother asking him to not walk so close—he'd never had been able to grasp the concept of personal space. In fact, Renny didn't understand a lot of things, but he got by. He had no family that we knew of and we tried to fill that void where we could. Renny lived in the storm drains. He kept a very neat space next to Crazy Carl Colson, one of Lucky's biggest fans, so Renny was in good hands.

I ignored the startled looks thrown our way and headed directly for Pandora's Box. The line of youngsters still waiting to get in filled the space against the wall behind the velvet ropes. Most of them were male—the unescorted young ladies all got in pretty quickly on the theory they were the bait to attract the young men who would shell out a shitload hoping to get lucky. From the looks of it, the theory held plenty of water. Bottle service and a small ringside table started at ten grand. How these kids got that kind of money… "Must be nice to be sperm privileged," I muttered. My dad was a dealer…blackjack, thank you very much, and my mom was a waitress. Kinder folks you'd never know, but privilege wasn't in our genetic line.

"What ?" Renny leaned forward, bringing Jake a bit too close to my earlobe for comfort. This time he stepped on my heel. He didn't say he was sorry. In fact, "sorry" wasn't a word I'd ever heard him use.

"Nothing." I spied the man I was looking for.

Thumping electric dance music blared through the open doors as Ralph, the bouncer at Pandora's Box, stepped through and assumed his position at the head of the line. A couple of willow young things presented their reed-like arms for his perusal. They must've had the right stamps indicating they had already been inside as Ralph nodded and pulled open one side of the double doors for them. As he did so, music blared. But when he pushed the door closed behind them, the sound disappeared. Pretty serious soundproofing. And classy, too with the thick red leather upholstery riveted to the doors with gold nails, like some secret, hidden hideaway. Ali Baba's Den of Thieves sprang to mind. Not that Lucky would mind the analogy. She'd be the first to admit Vegas hadn't been built on a bleeding heart.

Ralph's face brightened when he saw me. A look darted across his face as his grin widened even further. "You didn't have to bring the snake. I woulda let you in anyway."

I hooked my thumb over my shoulder. "You know Renny, right?"

Ralph nodded. "A course. How're they hanging, dude?"

"Righteous," Renny said solemnly. Like I said, his social skills needed some nuance.

Ralph smiled as kindness softened his sharp features. He wasn't as tough as he was big. With his dark hair gelled into a Mohawk, his pale skin with just the hint of a heavy beard showing, his bent nose, the scar under his right eye and the multicolored tat of an eagle, its wings spread across the back of his neck, Ralph played up the scary part. But, in counterpoint, his suit was pure Italian, his shirt Egyptian cotton and tailor-made, his loafers Gucci, and his watch Heublot, which said more about his personality than his flat expression and hard eyes. I should know; we'd been friends since grade school. He was a softie resorting to confrontation as a last resort—that's why Lucky had hired him. She was smart that way—hiring someone quick to rough up the young glitterati could have a chilling effect on business.

"What're you two doing here at this hour? You know after four a.m. those over thirty turn to dust."

"What makes you think I'm over thirty?" I pretended to be all huffy, then I remembered we were both the same age. "You know age is a state of mind."

Ralph leveled a look at me. "Then you're too young by a long shot to get into this place."

"Good thing it's you I need to talk to."

As a gaggle of giggling girls wiggled their way out of the club followed by a bunch of guys trying not to trip over their tongues, Ralph nodded to a threesome of guys waiting in line. He glowered at them as he held the door open. They seemed oblivious—males on the scent of willing females are the personification of stupid... but tons of fun to toy with. Alas, not tonight. Tonight I had smaller fish to fry.

"You still playing drums in that band?"

"You know me, music is in my blood." Ralph smiled like it was a joke, but, in truth, he had the soul of songwriter and a soft, smooth tenor that could make the ladies weep. And, knowing Ralph, he always had his fingers on the pulse of the local beat.

"So what's the deal with this scavenger hunt and a recording contract?"

His face snapped into a frown. "Bunch of idiots chasing all over town. Lookin' for music artifacts, they say. Man, I heard a couple got busted trying to take a booth out of the Golden Steer on account Sinatra put his fancy ass in it at some point."

"And I just took a big sparkler off Johnny Pismo. He swore it had belonged to Liberace."

Ralph whistled. "The King of Kitsch. Ring's probably fake."

"Not everything about him was smoke and mirrors."

"Nope. Personally, I loved the guy."

"Anything else you can tell me about this scavenger hunt thing? I don't understand why Dig Me O'Dell would get involved in something like that. It's just asking to be a big splash of the wrong kind."

"You can't fix stupid," Renny said.

I gave him a look. It wasn't clear exactly who he thought was stupid and I didn't feel like asking, so I nodded. "Right you are."

"There's some weird shit going down, though," Ralph added as he churned through what I'd told him.

"Could you narrow that down a bit for me? It's late."

"It's nuthin' I know for sure." He unhooked the rope and waved another gaggle of stick-thin prepubescents into the club. "But, you know, they got music memorabilia stashed in odd places all over town. I love that shit. But folks who have it don't pay it the proper reverence, know what I mean? They treat it pretty casual."

I didn't. To me old shit was old shit, but I was smart enough to play along. "Totally."

"Well, that stuff is low-hanging fruit to the properly motivated sticky fingered."

"So Dig Me O'Dell offered the golden egg to a bunch of no-talent wannabes willing to overlook the whole legal thing. He's actually gonna sign one of them. At least according to my source. What I don't get is what's in it for O'Dell? Sweet Sound Downtown Records is one of the big players." The whole thing sounded far-fetched to me.

Ralph seemed to have suspended disbelief. "Well, desperate times call for desperate measures and all that shit. Digital downloading took a chunk of green away from those guys, and Sweet Sound hasn't had a winner in a long time."

"Man, a lack of money hits a guy where it hurts. Right in the ego."

Ralph nodded. "Follow the money, you'll find your answers."

I thought for a moment. "I'm a journalist with my finger on the pulse of the happenings here in Sin City. If Dig Me O'Dell wanted to make a big splash with this scavenger hunt thing, don't you think it's odd I didn't know about it?"

Ralph's face sobered.

"How'd you find out about it?" I asked him.

"Somebody floated it on the grapevine."

"Who?"

"That no-talent dude with the seriously bad wardrobe." Ralph thought for a moment then shook his head. "Can't remember his name."

"And therein lies his problem. Unremarkable and forgotten. The name Johnny Pismo, ring a bell?"

His face lit with recognition. "That's the dude."

Now I knew Pismo was lying. The question was why.

CHAPTER FOUR

LUCKY

TEDDIE PEELED himself off the wall as I stepped off the elevator and into my living room. A gal just couldn't catch a break.

"How'd you get up here? You need to know the secret handshake and have the secret code."

He flashed me his patented dimpled grin. That, along with his tight ass, bright baby blues, and a voice as smooth as 20-year-old whiskey, could probably pry the secrets out of Forrest, our former NFL defensive end turned security dude, if he had to, but he didn't.

"Oh, yeah, you live here." I reached for the back of the couch, steadying myself as I shucked a shoe, then repeated the process for the other. I would've sighed in ecstasy, but Teddie would've found encouragement in that. "Correction, you don't live here; you live upstairs."

"With a back staircase to you kitchen."

"One I'm seriously considering boarding over."

"But you haven't."

He had a point, one I didn't want to think about right now. "What if Jean-Charles had been with me?"

"He's asleep in your room."

"What?" My mind froze, but the rest of me overheated. If I could ever get my body parts in synch, life would be so much simpler. Then the cold shower of rational thought filtered through the hormones on high alert. "I just talked to him. The kitchen is swamped. He won't be done for hours."

Teddie shrugged. "Wanted to see your reaction. Do you love him?"

Always the pragmatist, and having been so recently burned, I'd been asking myself the same thing. "When I see him, my heart soars. At odd moments during the day, I think about him, trying to picture where he might be. At other times, I am overcome with a joy so deep it infuses every part of me. When he is not with me, like now, I crave his touch. I want to be the me I see when he looks at me."

Teddie recoiled as if I'd slapped him, which I guess I had. I didn't feel particularly good about that. Actually, he'd asked, I'd answered. What I didn't like was how I felt delivering the blows. I could be cruel. I could enjoy inflicting the hurt, not something to be proud of.

Teddie regained his equilibrium. "None of that changes that I feel exactly that way about you."

Disappointed in myself, disappointed in him, I felt defeated and sad. "There was a time I returned that love."

"We could get back there."

"No, I fell in love with the man I thought you were. You proved me wrong. You are not that man."

Another blow. Was I being honest or vengeful? "We need to stop talking about this. I'm not liking myself much right now."

"I'm not liking myself much either." Teddie's eyes held a sadness I felt. "We all make mistakes."

"Yes, but once trust is broken..." I let the thought hang there. The Harvard boy could fill in the blanks.

I stepped close to him and touched his face. For a moment I let myself remember, then I scooped up my shoes and sailed by him. Comfy clothes were in order. "Don't be here when I get back."

My bedroom, my sanctuary, welcomed me. I stood in the large room, still shaken by the encounter with Teddie. Why did he have such an effect on me still? When would the hurt go away? I disrobed, finding my sweats on my bed where I had left them. I half-hoped Teddie would ignore me and stay, and I despised myself for feeling that way.

Sweats donned, socks on swollen feet, I went in search of comfort—first Wild Turkey, then food, if I had any. Teddie leaned on the counter in the kitchen, a tin of cookies open in front of him. He popped one in his mouth and gave me a tentative grin. He hurt, too.

His comfort with his vulnerability made him irresistible...well, except for the whole love me then leave me episode. A broken heart had a definite chilling effect on the libido. Thank God he hadn't chosen this moment to park himself behind the baby grand and sing my song, *Lucky For Me.* That'd tear my heart in two. And I didn't think half a heart would be sufficient for either Teddie or Jean-Charles.

Jean-Charles...

"I thought I told you to leave." I peered into the fridge, pretending to be absorbed. What I really wanted was for us to go back to how we were before we'd slept together—best friends. I missed that part so very much.

"If you're looking for anything edible, you won't find it in there. Only thing in there are a couple of interesting lab experiments and some seriously wonky vegetables."

The door eased shut on silent hinges. "That drawer in the bottom is mislabeled. It's not a crisper, it's a rotter."

"Everything dims with time, even hurt."

That subtext hit me right in the heart. I chose to ignore it. Abandoning my pride, I succumbed to his obvious ploy. A low moment but justifiable: deprived of food, the beast could get ugly. "Are those your mom's coconut oatmeal?"

"And they're great." He spewed a few crumbs, then wiped them into his palm and tossed them in the sink. "Bet you can't eat just one."

"I bet you're right."

I dove in as Teddie hid his gloat pouring me three fingers of Wild Turkey. The man could read me like a book, putting me at a disadvantage considering I never had a clue exactly what he was up to. I straddled a stool, easing closer to the cookies—culinary crack. "Tell me about Dig Me O'Dell and Smooth Sound Downtown Records."

The question clearly hit him from left field. In that fraction of a second before he regained his equilibrium, I could tell he was hiding something. "What do you want to know?" He easily modulated his voice, piece of cake for a crooner.

"Anything off about them. Any sour notes?"

"Why?"

Yep, hiding something. "They're sponsoring a scavenger hunt. Got a bunch of crazies running around town looking for music memorabilia. Seems odd for a player the caliber of Dig Me O'Dell."

"First I've heard of it. Sounds a bit out of character for O'Dell. Are you sure?"

I thought about Johnny Pismo. He reeked of desperation. Desperation made normal men do interesting things, and Pismo was far from normal. "No. And I can't figure what's in it for O'Dell and the record label."

Teddie pursed his lips as his eyes slid from mine. "Couldn't say."

"Couldn't say or don't know?"

"It's a strange time in the music business. Solid ground is

shifting like quicksand. Digital threw the old paradigm out the window. Songs are selling for pennies a download. Music producers used to bundle some pretty bad songs with the popular ones on an album and make the listeners buy the whole thing to get the tracks they wanted. Not anymore. Every song has to be a winner, or it doesn't gain any traction."

"So why'd you really come back?"

A pained expression rippled across his perfect features. "I told you. I came back for you. You're not going to believe it, and the timing of all of this certainly undermines my story. But, in the interest of all cards on the table, they cancelled the tour. Bookings weren't good enough. Sell-through a bit down. And somebody in the middle ran off with the take."

"Interesting."

He reached a hand across, capturing mine and breaking a perfectly stellar cookie. "That has nothing to do with us. I swear I came back because I love you."

I could tell he believed what he said. Too bad I couldn't. "You came back because you needed a job. I'm just a side bet." I snagged another cookie and popped it into my mouth. Teddie's mom might not have been able to raise a good man, but, damn, she could bake one hell of a cookie. In the balance of the universe, that pretty much evened things out. "Go home, Teddie."

"Side bets have the worst odds but the biggest payoffs." He gathered up the tin, pressing the lid on.

"Leave the cookies."

He gave me a long stare, then did as I asked.

No matter how much I mistrusted Teddie, no matter how much he'd hurt me, the room always felt smaller, colder when he left. Why did loving the wrong man feel so right sometimes?

God, I was just a bad country song.

I took the cookies and headed for the bathroom. A good long soak was in order.

And maybe a good cry.

～

DESPITE MY SOUR MOOD AND SUGAR HANGOVER, THE SUN INSISTED on shining as I made my way to the Babylon. Although I didn't feel like walking, considering my serious cookie consumption last night, some form of physical penance was in order. My father told me that if you enjoyed it, then it didn't count as exercise, so sex was out. The thought dawned that perhaps I'd caved a bit too soon on that one. Just because my father wasn't getting any, or I assumed he wasn't considering he'd recently become the father of twins, didn't mean he had to ruin it for the rest of us.

My father was spit-and-polished in grey slacks with a knife-edge crease, pink socks, Gucci loafers, a starched Egyptian cotton shirt in subtle pink, his collar open meaning today was casual day. When I wandered into the kitchen in his apartment on the top floor of the Babylon, he greeted me with a frown.

"We need to do something about your mother," he said.

This was not news. Nor was it my responsibility. "Good morning to you, too." I took a stool at the kitchen counter. "What in God's name is that?"

We both peered at a mixture of green goo in a glass in front of him.

"I've been told it's breakfast."

"For the twins?" Less than a month ago my mother had given birth to twins. She and my father had yet to give them names, which, considering she'd slapped me with Lucky, I was all for a bit of restraint. But Mona seemed determined to carry the whole naming thing to a dramatic crescendo. Drama queen to the last.

"No. She's decided I need to clean up my diet. I was hoping we could do it in steps."

"Like two double single-malts instead of three?"

"Yeah, like that." He actually looked hopeful. Poor man. He didn't really know his wife; he just thought he did.

"Mona has always been an all-or-nothing kind of gal. But I

wouldn't drink that on a bet. I couldn't get it close enough to my nose to throw it down my gullet. What is it?"

"Wheat grass, cucumber, radish, celery, and I forget what else."

"That's enough."

He poured the gunk down the drain and then flushed it with a healthy stream of water.

"Give it a good shot. You want to totally eliminate the evidence."

"What evidence would that be?" Mona shuffled into the room looking rather un-Mona-like. Her hair disheveled, a crease marring one pale cheek, shadows under her eyes. Her robe looked old; her slippers didn't match.

My father and I both snapped to. Neither of us wanted to get caught in the middle of a culinary crime; Mona's bite was far worse than her bark.

"Motherhood seems to be agreeing with you," I lied.

She stuck her tongue out at me but didn't follow it with her normal verbal barb. Her brain was offline. For a moment I was safe. "First one, then the other. I got no sleep at all last night." She eyed her husband. "Where were you?"

"Right beside you, dear. When you had one, I had the other. Don't you remember?"

"No. How can two very small humans cause so much pain?"

I was going to say something about karmic punishment, but I thought better of it.

Mona glared at her husband. "I think I'm mad at you."

He rinsed his glass and put it in the dishwasher. "Whatever for?" When Mona looked the other way, he gave me a wink.

"This is all your fault."

"Yes, dear."

Cooing sounds filtered from the baby monitor on the counter. "The babies are asleep. Go back to bed." He framed her face in his hands and gave her a sweet, lingering kiss.

Theirs was a grand love story spanning decades of separation and longing. I for one didn't begrudge them their happiness, even though I loved to see just a bit of discomfort visited on my mother. Often I found myself on the receiving end and Mona doing the dishing out. Shallow, I know, and nothing to be proud of, but I could live with it.

"The nurse will be here any minute," my father assured her. "I'll wait until she arrives." He glanced at me. "Lucky and I have something to discuss."

I took the hint. "Yes, we need to go over some contracts. Nothing important but it needs to be done."

Mona waved weakly. "I'll leave the boring stuff to you. Night all." She shuffled out.

I gave my father a sympathetic smile. "You've certainly found a way to keep her out of our business."

"But will we all survive?"

"You're the first line of defense." I slapped him on the back. "Don't weaken. Life as we know it depends on you."

A retort lingered on his lips when the nurse peeked her head in the door. "The babies, they are asleep, Mr. Rothstein?"

"Yes, thank you. My wife had a rough night. She's gone to bed."

"I will see that she is not disturbed." The nurse disappeared.

"Life is safe for one more day." My father sighed. "But God help us if that nurse ever leaves."

"Has Mother put her political ambitions on hold?" I asked, thinking this a safe topic. I was wrong.

My father's face snapped into a glower. "Not in the least. Don't let her poor-pitiful-me act fool you. Under that tired façade lives a barracuda. She's running on a sympathy platform now—twins are such a burden, you know. And if she can handle them and rise to perform her civic duty, well, that's worthy of election to the County Commission."

"I sort of agree with her."

My father brightened a bit. "I do, too. She's a human tornado, that woman, but she keeps life interesting."

He was only beginning to understand the truth of that statement, but I didn't think I should wise him up. With time, Mona would do that herself. I just hoped she brought him along gently.

"You're here about Pismo, right?" my father asked. "You're not heading toward the bar, so it couldn't be bad news. Our ring is safe, right?"

"In a manner of speaking. Why don't I cook you a proper breakfast as we talk about music, crooners, and memorabilia."

He eyed me.

I knew that look.

He was trying to figure out why I was really in his apartment willing to put my paltry kitchen skills on display. "Feeding me a feast before making me drink the poison."

"The sentence must suit the crime." Regaling him with benign stories from the hotel trenches, I let him eat his crisp bacon, soft-scrambled eggs, and buttered toast in peace.

Pushing back from the table, he gave a satisfied sigh. "Nectar of the Gods."

"Compared to pulverized weeds, I should say so."

"So what is it you want to know?"

"First, come clean about Teddie." Yes, I admit it, my personal life is more important than my professional life, and not nearly as under control. My parents also feel it is their God-given right to meddle. I was pretty sure their string pulling would amount to justification for homicide, but, since with my coloring, orange was not on my color wheel, I decided not to test the theory.

"He called me, wanted his old job back. At first I told him no. But then I figured he'd learned his lesson, paid the price, so maybe a second chance was in order."

A thinly veiled ploy.

"Why do all man stick up for each other?"

"It's our only chance to win."

"In some games, winning is overrated."

His face softened. I could see the love in his eyes. "True."

"I thought we were a team, playing on the same side."

"In business. But in life, I'm your father."

I didn't hold a trump card. "But you did all of this without checking with me."

"You would've said no."

"Damn straight."

"But that would've been your head talking and not your heart."

"Now you sound like Mother."

"Honey, you just need to get it all straight. Get him out of your system if that is what you want. But that takes facing him." He mopped up the dregs of eggs with a corner of toast and popped it into his mouth. "You mentioned music memorabilia. Did you find Johnny Pismo?"

He had to mop the tears in his eyes when I got toward the end of last night's adventures, but I'd saved the punch line.

"Yep. And he told you the truth. He really did have the real Liberace ring. At least, I'm assuming her did. We need to get it authenticated."

That wiped the smile off his face. "The ring downstairs, the one in the case. I have already made a call to my guy to test the thing, but he hasn't gotten to it. I just talked to Pismo yesterday afternoon."

"I can save you the trouble. I'm pretty sure it's a fake."

"And that song and dance about a scavenger hunt?" My father's voice hit his lowest register, a threatening growl.

"He's lying." I couldn't prove it, but it made no sense. What I couldn't figure out was why. Why did Johnny Pismo make up such a stupid story that would be so easy to check out? Was he really trying to put us off his trail with a whole lot of stupid?

Or was he giving us a clue?

CHAPTER FIVE

FLASH

*M*ORNING FOR me hit about noon at the earliest, but it came when it came. I rolled over and stretched. I had no idea what time it was, and I didn't care. Yesterday had been a twenty-hour day on the job, nothing unusual. So, given my life, easing into the day was usually wise.

"Ah, you're awake." An unexpected voice. Male. Friendly. Familiar.

Dane?

I didn't remember taking anyone to bed last night, but especially not him. Surely I didn't. I couldn't. Could I? I eased an eye open.

"Dane." I pushed myself up on an elbow and raked my hair out of my eyes.

Lounging in my doorway, fully clothed (which I was ambivalent about), he grinned. His smile held a hint of insecurity I didn't remember seeing there. With good reason, too. Maybe he'd found some smarts back in Texas. Paxton Dane had cut a wide swath

414

through town working security at the Babylon, then throwing his lot in with the Beautiful Jeremy Whitlock, forming the private investigative agency every woman in town salivated to hire. When Teddie took a powder, Dane made a huge play for Lucky. Then his wife none of us knew about had died, and he'd run off to lick his wounds back home amid the tumbleweeds and oil wells. Despite his tall, broad, and beautiful outside, his inside had been a bit of a disappointment, and we were all glad to see him go. Especially Lucky.

And now he was back.

In my bedroom.

Green eyes sparkled at me while he waited for me to get up to speed.

Processing this early in the morning was next to impossible without copious amounts of coffee. "It really is you."

"In the flesh." A smile lifted the corner of his mouth.

I followed his eyes down. "I sleep in the nude, sue me." I didn't bother to cover myself.

"Legal action isn't the kind that springs to mind."

I glanced around just to make sure. Yep, my room, my house. "I don't remember inviting you in."

"You didn't answer the bell. Your keys were in the door." He waved my keys at me, the skull and crossbones hanging from the keychain winking in the morning light.

"It was a late night."

"Must've been a doozy."

I let him think what he wanted. "Man, I'm hungry. Is it time for breakfast yet?"

"Breakfast? A bit late for that."

"Lunch?"

"Late for that, too."

"Champagne?"

"Always the right time for Champagne."

"Then be a good boy and get me some while I try to pull

myself together. Then, when I'm ready, you can tell me why you're really here."

~

Seated at the counter in my kitchen, wrapped in Turkish terrycloth, my belly comfortably warm with Schramsberg Brut Rosé, I felt fortified enough to deal with the man leaning in the corner with his arms crossed, his legs one over the other, his butt on my counter and his eyes on me.

"So what's your story, Tumbleweed?"

"I don't belong in Texas anymore."

"Another square peg. Lucky tells me all the time that's what we all are here, square pegs. She also told me once you live in Vegas, you can leave, but you always come back. It's like some Indian legend or something." I squinted at him. "You talked to Lucky? She know you're back in town?"

"No."

"Chicken."

"I've got some explaining to do. To everybody."

"Especially to her. Even if she wasn't going to give you a tumble, she always had your back. Until you stuck a knife in hers."

Some men are just so damn clueless there ought to be a charity to take them in and train them in the ways of women and the world. A lot of women would love that, but I doubted anyone would be up to the training task—like roping sea lions or something. Dane was a prime candidate, that arrogant yet lost look on his perfect face, hiding the hurt in his emerald green eyes. If I was just a smidge less principled, I'd press that perfect face to my bosom, run my fingers through his thick wavy hair, and just plain make him feel better.

Damn principles. "Well, Cowboy, I'm bettin' you don't have any idea where to take your Vegas reentry from here." His eyes shifted from mine. "I knew it. You pretty boys think just 'cause you show up the world will grovel at your feet, at least the slightly more than fifty percent who are female."

"This is an unusual situation for me."

"Ding. Ding. You earn the prize for the biggest understatement of the year. Give that man a stuffed bear."

The superb sparkling wine lit an idea, probably not a good one, but, with alcohol coursing into my bloodstream rushed in on tiny bubbles of bliss, I didn't care. "Speakin' of bears, if you're planning on holing up in my cave, you gotta earn your keep." I tried not to cringe at the unintended innuendo.

Thankfully, Dane didn't take the bait. His eyes narrowed and his shoulders got all hunched. "What's that got to do with bears?"

"Nothing. That was metaphorical." I waited to make sure he knew what the word meant. With men, especially pretty ones, you never knew. "I need to talk to Busta' Blue, and to get his attention I need to bring my own muscle. He got winged last night, then chased by a tiger. Spent the rest of the evening sucking down bottles of Cristal like they were cheap pop at a primo table at Babel." I glanced at the clock. It read 4:00. Another glance out the window—afternoon. With my life I really needed a twenty-four-hour clock. "Right now, I suspect he's holed up like a bear in hibernation nursing one serious hangover. And he'll be about as mean and angry as a bear prodded from a long slumber."

"Why would we do that?"

"Two reasons. Lucky needs us to, and we need him at a disadvantage if we hope to live."

WORD HAD IT THAT BUSTA' BLUE WAS HANGIN' AT DIG ME O'Dell's place on the Strip—the top two floors of one of those glitzy condo buildings stuck in among the casinos. I'm guessing Dig Me was pretty happy his place wasn't one of the ones that had been constructed out of substandard materials and now sat empty awaiting the wrecking ball. Scratch that. I'm thinking the developer of one of the bad buildings was glad Dig Me wasn't one of the clients he stiffed. As much as Vegas gave the appearance of having left the old ways behind, scratch just under the surface and you'll find the old game—new players, but the same rules.

The place was as quiet as a mausoleum when we stepped off the elevator. Dane looked like a cowboy who'd wandered off a movie set. He should have a Colt revolver in side holster strapped to his leg instead of a neat little Glock tucked under his arm in a shoulder sling. When the odds were against me, I always opted for a big show of force. I'd traded yesterdays' Day-Glo orange for hot pink, my power color. I carried a Derringer in my purse—playing to men's typical under-appreciation for female ingenuity and cunning often worked to my advantage.

"Did you notify next of kin as to our plans?" Dane leaned down and whispered in my ear.

"Don't throw in the white towel before the battle is even begun."

As I raised my fist to knock, the door opened. A well-dressed young woman eyed me stonily and then stepped back. Toothpick thin, mocha skin, flat stare, and a sneer. "Come in. He's expecting you."

"Said the spider to the fly," I said out of the corner of my mouth as Dane motioned me to go first.

Busta' Blue, swathed in layers of silk with some tribal motif, sat at the kitchen table shoveling cereal into his mouth. He paused to give us a look and then growled, "I figured one of you two would show. Thought maybe it'd be the tall one." He didn't pause in his feeding, cereal dribbling back into the bowl when he talked. He gave Dane the once-over, then dismissed him, but he didn't fire back with the insult I saw in his eyes.

"They gotta find you first," I said. "I had the inside skinny."

"You always did keep it on the down and dirty."

Ah, there was the insult. "Worked so far." I pulled out a chair opposite him. Elbows on the table, I leaned closer. "You need to tell me about Liberace's ring."

"Bought that sucker fair and square." He shrugged, a mountain of flesh undulating. "I was a fan." He gave me a glance, looking for derision, I thought. Image was everything with these guys, posturing badasses, but musicians... Well, some of them. All of them could appreciate the showmanship of Liberace. That man was Madonna before she even had a glint of how to work it.

"Who'd you score it off of?"

He hemmed and hawed. You woulda thought I'd asked him for his dealer. "Man, that kind of shit will get me nowhere good."

"If you don't tell me, I call the cops. Then I'll send Lucky." I wasn't above calling in the wrath of God when I needed her.

His eyes widened. "Okay, but don't you go sayin' I said, right? You, bein' a journalist and all, can hide your sources behind one of the Amendments, right?"

"Right." In theory, but I didn't add that part. Busta' Blue wasn't worth my kind of protection, but he didn't need to know that.

"I scored it off Dig Me O'Dell. He said I could keep it here for a while, for safekeeping. I don't know what's going on with the dude. First, I notice all his good stuff is gone. Then he lets me rent this place. Before he wouldn't let hardly anyone in here, and you had to take you shoes off and shit."

"What good stuff?" I asked.

Too late he realized he'd said way more than was good for his health.

"Does he have a secret room here?" Dane asked.

I flinched. I'd forgotten about him.

"Yeah."

Dane stared down Busta'.

The big man caved. "I can show you where the door is, but I don't got the combination." He lumbered through the main room, folds of silk wafting behind him like sails luffing in the wind.

As I trailed after the two men, I tried not to drool at the view up the Strip. Every major property was visible as the Strip tracked north and then made a jog after Sahara, downtown in the distance. The whole glorious tackiness of it all unfurled at my feet. God, how I loved this place. A place where I could be me and still be somebody. That was the real treasure of Vegas.

Pressing a spot on the wall at the far end of the hall, Busta' opened a secret door, so well hidden I never would've known it was there. The door behind it looked to be solid steel, a combination lock in the middle. Dane pulled out his gun and leveled it at Busta Blue's chest. "Open it."

Busta' gave him a narrow-eyed look. "I told you I don't have it."

"I know what you said." Dane pulled back the slide.

Movement behind me made me turn. Dane didn't flinch. A guy rushed at us. I stepped back as if cowering. Cocking my elbow the way Lucky had showed me, I waited. As the guy moved to brush by me, I threw a roundhouse, leading with my elbow. Bone hit soft cartilage. The guy dropped, clutching his nose. On his knees, his hands cupping the blood that poured out, he narrowed his eyes. Coiling his body. I kicked him, connecting under his jaw. The light in his eyes blinked out as he toppled over, blood spilling onto the perfect carpet.

Busta' and Dane, still hiding the gun pointed at Busta's chest, looked at me, their eyes wide. Busta's held disbelief. Dane's held respect.

I dusted my hands together. "Now, where were we?"

Busta' Blue had the next move. He vacillated for a moment, shooting me a murderous look, and then bent over the lock. The door whooshed open, an air lock.

I took a peek inside. "No way I'm going in there." We all have our little paranoias. Mine was being locked in a soundproof vault and nobody knew where I was or could hear me scream—that and too many men and too little time, but that's not really possible. I always had the time.

"Fine, you stay out here and make sure this guy doesn't lock me in." Dane passed me his gun. "Keep it pointed at his chest. If he so much as flinches, shoot him."

"Oh, just the thought of that makes me go all warm and gooey." Dane rolled his eyes.

I handed him my iPhone. "Pictures."

Busta' started to object. I silenced him with a waggle of the Glock. I was liking this upper-hand thing.

"You," Dane nodded at Busta', "over there." He waited for Busta' to do as he said, then spoke to me. "Don't let anyone near this door." Then he disappeared inside. I heard him whistle. A few minutes later, while I was contemplating what it would be like to shoot Busta' Blue, Dane stepped out and handed me my phone. "Hell of a treasure chest. Nameplates are still there, but the stuff is missing."

"You're saying the stuff in there was real?"

Busta' shifted, clearly uneasy. "Man, that ring Pismo had came from there, and it's as real as you and me. I got it tested."

"By whom?"

"My insurance guy."

I tried not to roll my eyes. "A name."

"Livermore. Nelson Livermore. Pansy-ass name. He works out of his house in the Naked City. Pismo put me onto him."

CHAPTER SIX

LUCKY

*L*IBERACE'S RING still glimmered from its case in the mini-museum in the Bazaar, the marketplace at the Babylon where purveyors of every kind of extravagance competed for real estate. From Ferraris to Jimmy Choos, baubles of epic size, designer duds in Lilliputian sizes, graceful original art to gourmet burgers, the Bazaar tempted all shapes, sizes, and tastes. The Babylon Museum was tucked in a tasteful corner near Samson's, the women's grooming salon that boasted a cadre of Samson look-alikes offering limitless flutes of Champagne. Women travelled half the world to spend their entire Vegas trip there. A blue door, standing open, and a tasteful, reverent sign marked my destination.

The dusty blue walls, thick carpet, and focused lighting stood in stark contrast to the rest of the rather bold accents of the hotel. The whole place made me want to whisper as if I was in a place of worship and reverence, which I guess I was. Music played in the background—a loop of the oldies but goodies I'd helped the Big Boss compile. Fun times. Curiously, Liberace crooned *I'll Be Seeing*

You as I staked out my place, holding up the wall, waiting for my father.

Elvis's sequined jacket from his last concert in Vegas hung on the wall above the case holding the ring, next to a signed guitar from B. B. King and sheet music to *My Way* signed by Sinatra. These were my favorite things in what I referred to as the Big Boss's music corner.

Leaning against the wall, I watched tourists wander the room partaking of bits of Vegas's heritage. Music had been almost as important as gambling in the heyday, luring visitors to make the long hot drive through the Mojave from L A. Of course, the Mob and a possible brush-up against bad was a lure as well, but I tried not to focus on that. Although I was born into that world, it wasn't my Vegas.

As if hearing his cue, the Big Boss strolled through the door acting like he owned the place, which stood to reason. Casually, he cased the room, checking every detail, every nuance for the perfection he demanded. His eyes paused and then moved on as they brushed over me. Working his way in my direction, he graciously greeted those who stopped him, spending time and attention on each. Since I'd left him, he'd added a suit jacket and his diamond tie-bar—just enough bling to fit with Vegas expectations. Matching diamond cufflinks flashed where they peeked out of his coat sleeve when he reached to shake someone's hand.

The personification of Vegas, someone had described him in an article recently. Smart, savvy, good, with just a hint of bad. He'd thought the description perfect. "If I was all good, what would they talk about?" he'd said with a grin.

Finally, he made stood in front of the case. When he found me looking at him, he gestured to the bauble resting inside the case. "I told you it was still there."

I shouldered in next to him. "I had no doubt."

"The real one is in Detective Romeo's custody, you say?"

"I'll need to have it authenticated, but I'd stand by that."

"You don't need to. Not unless there's more than one fake floating around. While we were visiting upstairs, my guy tested this one. Jerry had a whole team of security down here." He lifted his chin toward the shiny bauble nestled in velvet under glass.

"So this one's glue, or whatever they're making the fakes out of these days." It wasn't a question. I glanced at his face, red with anger. "I know mother has you on the brink of homicide, but don't do anything stupid. If you want to kill somebody, at least give me the time to figure out who."

He didn't agree, but I saw a bit of rational trickle back into his posture.

"How did you end up dealing with Johnny Pismo?" I asked.

"He came to me with his cock-and-bull story. I didn't believe him."

As I thought. I blew at some hair that tickled my forehead. "Who would? That guy has more angles than a geometry test. But don't worry. Acute or obtuse, I can straighten him out."

THE BAZAAR HUMMED WITH ACTIVITY AS I PAUSED IN THE DOORWAY. This close to dinnertime I felt a burger was in order, or at least a hug from the chef. I had gone too long without and was feeling the pangs. I dove into the sea of humanity and went with the flow, fighting my way to the side when I arrived in front of the Burger Palais. Yes, I am on the record as having opposed that name. I lost. I wasn't broken up about it—Jean-Charles seemed happy, so I was content in defeat.

A few of the folks waiting in line gave me a dirty look as the hostess waved me through. The energy didn't drop by much when I stepped into the welcoming confines of the restaurant. Jean-Charles's transformation of the prior tenant's garish pizza joint still surprised me. Brick walls with drippy mortar, green leather banquets and chairs, white tablecloths, and the soft illumination of brass sconces created an elegant, yet welcoming, environment. A bar in warm wood imported from Scotland and fronted by green leather barstools circled from the right-hand wall. The kitchen worked behind a wall of glass on the left-hand side. I paused to watch my chef. Resplendent in his chef's whites, he toiled, his back to me, over a grill full of rounds of meat sizzling over glowing coals. Jean-Charles put an ahi burger on the menu, which I thought was an insult to all the meat-lovers everywhere, but it's been a big seller. Again, I was gracious in defeat, although he did like to rub it in a bit too often.

He didn't break stride as I eased in behind him, circling his waist, then planting a light kiss on my favorite spot just behind his right ear where his hair curled seductively over his collar. "I have missed you last night. Christophe wanted you to read him the *Very Bad Bunny* story again. He was most ... how do you say it?"

"Put out?" I nibbled on his ear because it was there. Christophe was Jean-Charles's five-year-old son who both charmed and terrified me.

A shiver chased through my chef. "You must stop that. I cannot concentrate. Yes, put out, this is it. He tells me I do not get the voices right." He muttered a curse as he flipped one of the patties into the waste trough and then tossed a fresh one on the grill. "You see?"

I wasn't feeling the least bit sorry. "I'll read it to him tonight, if I'm invited."

Jean-Charles leaned to the side and turned to get a look at me with those baby blues. "Ah, this is a joke."

I tried not to stare at his lush lips. So, to avoid any awkwardness, I did the only thing I could—I kissed them. Long and deep, tasting, savoring. Another shiver, this time mine. "Mmmmm, I do love the taste of hamburgers."

"So I am just another meat on the hoof for you?" Jean-Charles loved American idioms, even if most of the time he got them charmingly mixed up. "This is how you say it, *non?*"

"Innuendo. I love it when you do that. Sexy as hell." Which, of course, he always was, but no need to stoke his already healthy ego.

Rinaldo, Jean-Charles's executive chef, elbowed us aside. A mountain of a man with thick black curls, three chins, and a ready smile, shot us one. "You two, go find a room. The meat requires delicate handling and undivided attention."

A smile ticked up the corner of Jean-Charles's mouth, his eyes still glued to mine. "Special handling, indeed."

"Me first." I grabbed his hand and pulled him to the bar. "Pour me a glass of Schramsberg Brut Rosé and talk dirty to me."

I watched him as he released the cork with a mouth-watering pop; then, with a thumb in the bottom of the bottle, he cradled it in his hand as he poured a frothy flute for me. A French chef who thinks I'm the tastiest dish and a flute full of bubbles, nothing better. "How's the restaurant coming?" I asked. "I haven't made it over there today."

"We will be ready for the opening December 21st. A Christmas party to remember." He leaned casually on the bar. He preferred that to sitting next to me. Easier to look at me that way, he'd told me.

I relaxed into his recitation of the progress that had been made, what still needed to be done, and what needed my particular brand of attention, making a mental note of those items. Despite my very real misgivings, Jean-Charles had crawled into my heart and stayed there. Our relationship had grown and matured. We enjoyed business, good food, his son, and each other. So why did I have this niggling worry that once he decided to shift the spotlight of his focus elsewhere, once he decided I was a bird in the hand, so to speak, that he would put his energy and charm to other uses, leaving me in the shadows? He was a man of intense passions and driving ambition. His son first, then his restaurants and me. Could I be happy with that?

Jean-Charles fell quiet and raised an eyebrow. "Where did you go?"

"I'm sorry. What did you ask?"

"Have you reviewed the guest list for the opening?"

"Not yet."

"Invitations need to go out in a few days. We only have three weeks."

"I'll do it when I get to the office. The calligrapher is waiting for them."

He refilled my flute, which I hadn't been aware of draining. "I do have something to tell you."

Something in his tone made me pause. I really hate it when people do that to me. It's like they're priming me for good news, only to cut my legs out from under me. When she's not felled by twins, my mother was a master. "Okay."

"Why do you say it that way? Like you are holding a shield."

"If you have good news, why don't you just tell me? When you set me up like that I think it's only to deliver bad news."

Jean-Charles shook his head. "Sometimes I do not understand you."

"Yeah, me either." I took a sip of bubbles, holding it in my mouth, trapping the air, feeling it expand, then drinking it down like cotton candy.

"Holt Box is going to be my guest sous chef."

"Whoa! You mean the hottest former star in the country music scene that, if the rumor mill is correct, is considering ending his retirement? *That* Holt Box is going to be *cooking* for the party?"

"And serving."

I gave him the slanty eye. "And what's the downside?"

My chef gave me his patented Gallic shrug, the one I found almost irresistible. "He likes to cook. He likes my food. There is no downside, as you say."

"He asked?" I didn't try to hide my skepticism.

"It is this simple."

DEBORAH COONTS

"No money?"

"*Oui.*"

"Wow."

"Yes, this. Wow."

We were staring at each other, my thoughts wandering from the conversation to something even more delicious when I felt someone elbow me. "I knew you'd be here." Romeo slid onto the stool next to me. "May I have a Wild Turkey and tonic, hold the tonic," he asked the bartender.

I pretended to be happy to see him. I wanted no part of his investigation. What I wanted was a piece of my chef, for the weekend, which technically I had off. "No detective points for you—I'm not hard to find."

"True." Romeo took a sip of his drink. He pretended to like it, but his eyes watered, exposing him.

Jean-Charles gave me a wink as he handed the brave detective a glass of water. "Wait until you are a hard man before you go for the hard stuff," he said.

Romeo gave me a wide-eyed look, managing to keep a straight face.

"Nope, I'm not going to hit that one out of the park," I said. "Be my guest."

"Not touching it."

Jean-Charles looked first at me, then Romeo. He wanted an explanation. I wasn't going to give him one. Not when I couldn't have a hands-on demonstration.

"So apparently you have a reason that you are looking for me?" I asked Romeo, ignoring the quizzical look on Jean-Charles's face.

"I'd sure like to find out if that ring has been out of the case lately. Maybe on loan or something?"

"I know just the person who can help." I chugged my remaining Champagne, making Jean-Charles grimace at the disrespect. "What'd you do with Johnny Pismo?"

"A friend bailed him out."

"Really? Johnny Pismo has a friend? Who?"

Romeo fixed me with an unreadable stare. "Busta' Blue."

"You let him take him?"

This time Romeo's look was pure innocence. "Who was I to say no?"

THE WARMTH OF JEAN-CHARLES'S KISS STILL LINGERED AS I PUSHED through the office door, the young detective in tow. The Babylon was just gathering strength as day headed into night, and the energy from the lobby below pulsed through the walls. Brandy, my youngest assistant, manned the outer desk, which made the young detective blush and stutter. They'd been seeing each other, but I stayed out of it—although, I approved. Romeo paused to talk to his gal while I sailed right on through to my old office. Miss P, her feet on the desk drawer, leaned back in my old chair just as I used to do.

"Be careful, you might end up like me."

"There are worse things." Miss P, all spiky golden hair, bright eyes, stylish attire, and an undercurrent of sarcasm was more me than I used to be.

I brushed the Beautiful Jeremy Whitlock from his perch, one butt cheek on the corner of her desk. The gorgeous Australian was Miss P's boy-toy and fiancé. Over six feet, chiseled, with brown hair, golden eyes, and dimples... he was total swoon material. The fact that he was also a true-blue guy and Vegas's primo private investigator just sweetened the pot. Dane had worked with him. A momentary cloud dimmed my unusually sunny disposition.

Dane.

Now there was a disappointment—the proof to my rule that all men are pigs. Of course, as with any rule, there are exceptions, but, sadly, he was not one of them.

Still unused to seeing Miss P behind my former desk, I looked for a chair in which to alight. Promotions had launched us both one notch up the corporate ladder, which created this office musical chairs game and actually changed nothing other than our take-home pay. "I need your help." I flopped onto the couch against the wall.

Miss P grabbed a pen and paper. Brandy with Romeo in trail stepped into the office. Searching the desk for my cockroach paperweight, a gift from the employees when I'd done battle with a particularly odious guest who'd decided to scam the hotel by letting loose thousands of the beasts. Playing with it while I talked had become a comforting habit. Too late I realized once again this wasn't my desk. My eyes on Romeo, inviting him to participate in the retelling, I regaled the group with my tale of Johnny Pismo and Liberace's ring.

"So the bloke had the real ring when it was supposed to be in the case in the museum," Jeremy summed it up rather succinctly. "Did he say where and how he got it?"

Romeo shifted, pulling his notepad out of his pocket. He'd been holding Brandy's hand, which put a smile on my heart. She sidled into him as he scanned his notes. "Pismo says he pinched it from a guy named Livermore."

Livermore. Miss P's eyes narrowed as her gaze caught mine. She turned to her computer and started hitting keys. "The diamond ring went out for cleaning and reappraisal last week. It was only out for two days." She looked at me, her cheaters slipping to the end of her nose, her eyes pinpoints above them. "The insurance agent who requested the reappraisal was a man named Pressman." She squinted as she read further; then her face cleared, and she looked up.

I held up my hand. "Let me guess. Livermore showed up as an associate of Mr. Pressman's." Livermore, a sleazy PI when our paths had last crossed, apparently was branching out. I motioned to Jeremy. "Let's go pay Mr. Livermore a visit. You know the way."

Romeo rose to follow us.

I put a hand out to stop him. "You know the drill. Give us ten minutes or so before you rush in with lights and sirens. Our hands aren't tied by procedural constraints."

"Got it." He gave Brandy a sweet kiss and then followed us out.

I made a detour thorough my new office to grab my Glock from my desk drawer. First time I visited Mr. Livermore, I'd been shot at. This time, I intended to do the shooting.

CHAPTER SEVEN

FLASH

*L*IVERMORE. WHERE had I heard that name?

"The PI?" Dane asked, filling in that blank.

The tumblers fell into place; my brain lock opened. Lucky had tangled with the dude. Shots had been fired. Lucky on the receiving end. I'd wager a year's salary she aimed to even the score. I backhanded Dane in the stomach. "We gotta go."

"Your wish is my—"

"Yeah, right. Cut the bullshit. Let's boogie."

I sacrificed my dignity once again as I climbed into Dane's jacked-up F-250 with a shotgun hanging in the rear window. "Does every guy in Texas lust for a pickup?"

He cranked the thing, which started with a low growl, settling into a respectable diesel grumble. Bug guts from his long drive across Texas and the desert still smeared the windscreen. I thought I smelled wet dog, but I could've been mistaken. The dealership probably had wet-dog air freshener to add authenticity and play to the rednecks. "The Dallas pansy-asses all drive Lexuses," he said.

"Good to know. Stay away from men driving Lexes," I said, my high school Latin coming in handy as I scooted back in the seat, my feet barely touching the floorboard. "You know where you're going?"

"Unfortunately."

"This ought to be fun."

As promised, Livermore's house hunkered in a beaten-down neighborhood in the Naked City, so named because show girls back in the day who populated the long-gone apartment houses had a penchant for soaking up the sun *au naturel* on the decks atop their buildings. Sidewalks of uneven slabs of concrete, trees thinned through time and inattention, houses with bars on the windows and locked gates securing the doors, Naked City was not a place that inspired confidence. Livermore's house was one of the nicer ones. The roof looked new, a fresh coat of paint brightened the clapboards, with clean windows behind new bars. It looked like Mr. Livermore had recently come into some money.

The Beautiful Jeremy Whitlock's Hummer parked at the curb added a touch of class.

"Showtime, Cowboy."

Dane swallowed hard.

"From the look on your face I take it this will be a home-coming of sorts for you. Should be interesting."

He shot me a look as he grabbed the shotgun from its rest.

"That's really going to help."

"I played by your rules last time; now it's my turn."

Shoulder to shoulder we stalked up the path. As I raised my hand to knock, the door flew open and a human missile launched himself at us. He hit me square in the stomach. I fell backwards, the air rushing out of me. If I hadn't been so angry, I might've just lay there basking in a rare sympathy-garnering moment. Instead, as the guy scrambled off of me and regained his footing, I stuck out a foot and tripped him. Dane whacked the guy with the butt-end of his shotgun, one tap to the temple, and he fell like a rag doll with all the stuffing gone.

Nelson Livermore.

After the last case Lucky and I worked involving Jean-Charles and several murders, I'd spent hours in a small room grilling Mr. Livermore. This time, when he barreled into me, I didn't need to see his face. His cheap cologne made identification easy the olfactory way. Dane tugged me to my feet as Lucky skidded to a stop in the doorway with Jeremy on her heels, both of them with guns drawn.

Lucky took in everyone at a glance. "Well," she addressed Dane. "Somehow finding you here doesn't surprise me."

Dane threw a pleading look for help over Lucky's shoulder to Jeremy, who ignored it. At a loss, he grabbed Livermore, who writhed at our feet, and jerked him to his feet.

A thin, rat-faced man with a bad comb-over, he eyed us all, looking a bit put out. "Why did you hit me?" he asked Dane.

"Why did you run?"

Holding the side of his head, he angled it gingerly toward Lucky and Jeremy. "Those two burst through the back with guns drawn. While I don't have much, I do have a strong sense of self-preservation. Running seemed like a good thing at the time."

Speaking of self-preservation, mine kicked in. Lucky had taught me the best defense is a quick offense, so I jumped in before she could take a bite out of my ass. "Dane showed up at my house this afternoon. He was there when I woke up. I had no idea."

"And bringing him into this mess seemed like a good idea because?"

"Because I wasn't going to visit Busta' Blue unarmed and without my own muscle. You think I'm crazy?"

"Yes, but not that crazy." She gave Livermore a long look. "We got men coming out the wazoo, none of them worth a plug nickel."

As if on cue, Romeo's unmarked screamed around the corner, a rotating red light struck to the roof as the siren wailed. He skidded in behind Jeremy's Hummer and killed the cavalry call. Blissful silence. The neighborhood remained curiously quiet. Sirens were so common in this neighborhood that nobody bothered to react anymore.

Romeo strolled up looking nonplussed. "Shoot anybody?" he asked Lucky.

"Not yet." She pulled the slide back on her Glock to clear the gun and then tucked it back in her purse.

"You're Livermore, right?" he asked the man brushing down his jacket and looking a bit incensed but knowing the odds didn't favor fighting back.

He stood up straighter. "I am."

"We are all here looking for enlightenment. Care to indulge us?"

Considering he'd been chased by two people bursting into his kitchen guns drawn, then clocked with the butt of a shotgun, Livermore looked remarkably unfazed. "If you could provide some context, detective, I'd be grateful."

Romeo gave Lucky a look—those two could communicate sentences in a glance. "Let's start with your interest in Liberace's ring."

"The one in the Babylon?"

"And its copies."

If Livermore was surprised we knew, he hid it well. "I've been hired by the insurance company to investigate several cases of suspected insurance fraud." He named the company.

Lucky nodded once to Romeo. "So how'd the company get wind of the fraud?"

"A robbery in St. Louis. A big collector. Legitimate. The cops found his collection intact and arrested the would-be thieves. Of course, being a legitimate collector and having serious money invested, the guy had everything re-authenticated."

"Let me guess," Lucky said. "He'd just insured his collection."

Livermore nodded. "And the company had requested several of the items be authenticated prior to the theft."

"By whom?"

"An outfit named Memorabilia Rarities. They said everything was copacetic."

"Did he choose another authentication place after his collection was returned?"

"Yes. He had a personal relationship with another group in Los Angeles."

"And some of the items came back as fakes?" Lucky asked, but I could tell she was three steps ahead.

Livermore nodded. "We're trying to get a line on black-market sales to see if any of the stolen pieces had found new owners, but the information is quite difficult to come by."

A bit of an understatement, I felt sure. I could see Lucky thought the same.

"So the authenticators the insurance company requested?" Lucky pressed. "Memorabilia Rarities? I'd be willing to bet they're a Vegas outfit."

"You'd win that bet." Livermore nodded. "I was just in the process of figuring out how to approach them."

Lucky rubbed her hands together as she looked around the group. I knew that look in her eye—it meant action of the most fun kind. "I think it's time we had some music memorabilia authenticated, don't you?" She stuck out her hand. "Flash, let me see those photos you took of Dig Me O'Dell's collection." She handed my phone to Livermore. "Recognize any of these?"

Livermore pulled a list out of his pocket. "Some of these items have gone up for sale recently. Three I know for sure."

"And O'Dell had acquired them from the rightful owners?"

"Apparently so. The sales were through reputable firms, and none have been reported as fakes."

"But the ring was stolen. I wonder who he bought the stolen

ring from." Lucky tapped her fingers on her thigh. "I think I need to pay Mr. O'Dell a visit." She looked around the group. "What else do we know? What about the insurance company? I assume they hired you?" She continued questioning Livermore.

"Yes."

"Did they give you any names of agents handling the accounts?"

"All of them are handled by a local man named Otis Pressman."

"And we come full circle," Lucky said, but didn't provide any context.

"What do you mean full circle?"

"His name came up before. He requested the recent re-appraisal of Liberace's ring. It was out of our care for two days."

"What do you know about him?" Romeo asked Livermore. "Have you paid him a visit?"

"Not yet. I didn't want to put him onto the fact someone might be overly interested in his activities. I figured I'd try to get to him through the back door."

"He's the link," Jeremy agreed. "We don't want to flush him just yet."

"He and Dig Me O'Dell hold the keys right now," Lucky said as she took charge. "Okay," she pointed to Jeremy. "You and Flash, I have a plan for you. I'd do it myself, but I'm a little high-profile to pull this off."

"Down and dirty we can do," I assured her and gave Jeremy a wink, which he fielded with good humor. I knew he was spoken for. So did he. But a bit of harmless banter was always good fun. "What's the plan?"

"I have something I'd like you to insure." Next she turned her eyes on Romeo. "I'm assuming you have Johnny Pismo on a short leash?"

"Got a tail on him."

"Were you able to get a list of the items on the scavenger hunt?"

"After we left you, he changed his story. He said he didn't have one."

"Curious." Lucky looked at me. "Didn't he tell us he had one?"

"Someplace where no one would find it," I confirmed.

"That strikes me as a bunch of bullshit. He's been trying to send us down the wrong path with that whole load. I'd be willing to bet there is no scavenger hunt." She cocked an eyebrow at me.

"You and me are on the same page. I couldn't find anyone who knew anything about it other than Ralph, who had heard a whisper. The whisper came from Pismo himself, but then nothing. Ralph thinks it's bullshit, too."

Lucky turned back to Romeo. "Okay, I want to know where Pismo goes and who he's with or who he sees."

"I hope you have a couple of guys on him. He's a slippery dude," I added, thinking Romeo and Lucky just might underestimate Johnny Pismo. It was easy to do. The guy cultivated an air of ineptitude, but in my experience he was far from it.

"Metro can handle it," Romeo said, but he didn't sound positive.

Lucky gave me an eye roll.

"Where are you going?" I asked her.

"To find Dig Me O'Dell." Her face settled into an expression I couldn't read, her eyes cold. "But first, you," she nodded at me, "and Jeremy come by the office. I have a bauble or two for you to have insured."

OTIS PRESSMAN WORKED HARD TO CULTIVATE THE SHYSTER VIBE, and he succeeded, from the shiny suit with the pimp pinstripe to the gaudy cufflinks to the pink shirt and loud tie, the greased-back hair, and the insincere smile. Of course, he was an insurance agent, one notch above an attorney on the lowest-life-form ladder. Ignoring me, he motioned Jeremy to a chair. "What can I do for you, Mr. Bartholomew?"

Jeremy motioned to me. "This is Ms. Tate, a gemologist I keep in my employ. She's here as a second set of eyes, if you will."

Pressman didn't seem put off. "I guarantee you don't need a witness. We employ the utmost discretion and care with the priceless artifacts entrusted to our care."

Jeremy reached back for the velvet-lined valise I held. One by one he unwrapped the items from their protective covering of cloth around a form mold. He displayed each exquisite item, placing them on the edge of Mr. Pressman's desk—some of Teddie's personal collection Lucky had managed to convince him to part with for the moment. Of course, the poor sucker would do anything for her at this point.

"I'm newly arrived from Australia, and, as you can see, I have some lovely things I'd like to insure." He lifted his eyes to Mr. Pressman's. "I've heard this country can be rather lawless. I'd like to protect against that."

Pressman practically had to wipe away the drool. "These are lovely. I've not seen anything like them come to market. Quite unique."

"Yes, two of those come from a three-part set owned by Liberace." Jeremy pointed to gem-encrusted figurines.

"Where is the third?"

"In the Liberace Museum's collection. I've been trying to get them to sell it for years. The three together would be worth many multiples of these two alone. The museum is placing their collection as we speak in Liberace's former mansion. The complete set used to be in his boudoir. The whole place has been totally restored by an Englishman—he wants to get it as close to the original as possible. As if Liberace himself never left. I'm thinking of putting my two on loan with them so the three may be together again. A nice touch, don't you think?"

Pressman nodded. I could almost see dollar signs whirling in his eyes like cherries on a slot machine.

"The house opens tomorrow to limited groups, private parties. The neighbors objected to the home being opened to the public."

"Can't say I blame them." Pressman held his hand over one of the figurines. "May I?"

Jeremy nodded. "Of course."

Holding it up to the light, Pressman rotated the figurine. Multicolored hues played like a rainbow on the wall as the gems fractured the light. "Exquisite." Pressman sighed as he carefully placed it back next to its mate.

"I bought them from a musician friend of mine who knew Liberace personally. He was quite a fan. Devastated when he passed."

"We'll need them valued so that we can insure them properly. Surely you understand."

"Of course." Jeremy gazed reverently at the items for a moment. "They've never been out of my control. I thought you might need to keep them for a bit, so I made photographs of them before I came." He lifted his eyes. "Surely you understand?"

I stifled a snicker. I had a hard time keeping quiet—not the best undercover operative, at least in this context. Frankly, I was feeling a bit antsy, and guilty. Leaving Dane standing on the curb hadn't seemed right. But, in a fight, I was always in Lucky's corner, so Dane had come out on the short end. But then it had never been his fight. He was just the hired help.

"Of course." Pressman didn't miss a beat. The guy was good, very good.

"You yourself are bonded and insured as well as the valuation firm?" Jeremy asked.

"Memorabilia Rarities, yes, we both are."

"Good then." Jeremy handed over the valise and watched without a hint of emotion as Pressman re-swathed each item and tucked them inside.

"Wonderful." Pressman's lust oozed out of him. Of course, I was looking for it. "Let me make you an inventory so you have a record of what you left with us, and we'll get the process started." He left the room.

"Are you comfortable with this? Lucky—"

Jeremy shot me a warning look and then glanced up at the corners where cameras looked down on us, their red eyes blinking.

"Lucky Mr. Pressman seems to know his stuff, but I know how you hate to let these out of your sight."

"I'm sure it will be fine, thank you."

Pressman returned. Jeremy and he did business while I tried to look inconsequential.

And when we departed, we left Teddie's wonderful treasures with the shyster.

"I hope Lucky knows what she's doing," I whispered once we were in the car.

"Lucky always knows what she's doing." But he looked slightly sick—like we'd tossed Teddie's treasures from the top of the Stratosphere.

I knew how he felt.

CHAPTER EIGHT

LUCKY

*T*EDDIE AND Romeo sat across from me, Teddie looking tense, Romeo looking remarkably relaxed given that we'd just handed over a million dollars' worth of music history to a guy we were almost certain would steal at least some of it. My phone dinged a text. "We're good to go. Pressman took the bait."

Now it was Romeo's turn. He glanced down at the device he held in his hand. "GPS is tracking."

"All of them?"

"I count seven blips, all together."

Teddie relaxed a little.

"Thank you," I said.

He levered himself out of the chair. "For a good cause."

As he ambled out, I tried not to stare at his ass.

Romeo waited until Teddie had disappeared. "You and him. Totally sucks, huh?"

I glanced over to see him watching me. "Lingering disappointment. Folks can't be who we think they should be."

"Like I said, sucks, huh?"

That made me smile. "You still got a team on Pismo?"

"Yeah."

"Can you give me an update?" My insides in a turmoil, my head spinning, I couldn't sit still for another moment. I rose and strode for the door. "Text it to me. I've got to see a friend about finding Dig Me O'Dell."

Teddie was gone when I reached the hall. But I knew where he'd go. Sure enough, when I reached Delilah's, he was perched on the bench at the white baby grand, his eyes closed. Set on a raised platform, Delilah's served as our main bar in the casino. Stools fronted a long bar that was backed by bottles on the sides of a center waterfall. Bougainvillea climbed trellises, giving the area a safe and secret vibe, cut off from the rowdiness of the main-floor gaming operations. Club tables ringed by four chairs each clustered at the far end, the baby grand nestling opposite them. When he'd been gone, every time I walked by I could picture him there. And now that he was, I didn't know how I felt about it.

As I climbed the stairs, Teddie started in on the first few bars of *Lucky For Me*. Ignoring the squeeze in my heart, I joined him on the piano bench. "I couldn't use anything in the Big Boss's collection. Too visible and well-known. But you didn't have to help me."

He tilted his head as he played, losing himself to the music. I'd always been jealous of his passion. What would that be like, to have something so pleasurable, so consuming, that no matter what you could retreat there and regain yourself?

"Unfortunately I need your help with something else." I hadn't asked him before because I didn't want Romeo as a witness if Teddie made me grovel.

He smiled a soft smile as if he knew.

"Can you tell me where Dig Me O'Dell holes up when he's pissed?"

Teddie's eyes flew open. "Why?"

"I need to find him," I said, I thought unnecessarily. "You know him well. You are one of his recording stars. I bet he'd take a call from you." I held out my phone. "Get me a meeting. Please."

He took my phone and began dialing. As he held it to his ear, his eyes found mine. "How long are you planning on punishing me?"

"As long as it takes for the hurt to go away."

～

O'DELL HAD SAID HE'D MEET ME AT BAKER'S BLUE NOTE, A HOLE-in-the-wall in an old stucco building near Atomic Liquors downtown. In the heyday, this had been a happening place, but the mega-casinos sprouting on the south end of the Strip had sucked almost all the air out of the neighborhood. The Blue Note, a haven for musicians longing for appreciation and camaraderie after nights spent toiling in a backup band, had kept the club not only afloat but thriving. It had anchored a strip mall next to a motor lodge when I was young. The club remained, but now everything else was gone.

The door lurked under so many layers of bright red paint it felt spongy as I pushed on it. Stale cigarette smoke, aged whiskey, and the lonesome tones of a sax welcomed me into the dim interior. A guy stood behind the bar, wiping glasses, his eyes on the stage. In the beam of one overhead spot, propping himself on a three-legged stool, Dig Me O'Dell caressed the sax, coaxing the pure plaintive notes of *Body and Soul.*

He was smaller than I'd thought he'd be, thin, balding, without a hint of badass. Crossing my arms, I leaned against the wall. The guy was a master. Who knew? Underneath the surface of the gangsta music mogul lurked the soul of a jazzman. I'd always wondered why he signed Teddie, who preferred old-school crooning to rock.

His eyes flicked up. He knew I was there. We both enjoyed the rest of the song. When done, he rested the sax across his knee, but he didn't move. "What can I do for you?"

"I want to talk to you about a piece in your memorabilia collection."

He looked surprised. "Sure. Which piece? You in the market?"

"Liberace's ring." I watched him for some sign of nervousness, subterfuge, self-protection, something, but I didn't see a hint. "And, no, not in the market. I already own it."

His face closed down. "Busta' Blue sell it to you?"

"Why would you think that?"

"He loaned me some money to make payroll. I used the ring as collateral. I wasn't ever going to sell it. He promised not to."

"So you didn't know the ring was stolen?"

He jumped off the stool like someone had hit him with a cattle prod. "Busta' let someone grab it? That was my favorite piece. He said he'd keep it safe, let me buy it back when things turn around. I'll have his ass."

I held out my hands, palms out. "Calm down. No, he didn't let it get stolen. Well, he did, but we have it. It's safe."

His eyes settled on me in a fierce, feral look. "So if he didn't sell it, how come you think you own it?"

"Someone stole it from my father before you bought it."

He sank back on his stool as the light dawned. "That's a bad piece of business."

"You're telling me. Want to tell me who you bought it from?"

He gave me a slanty-eyed look, his lips pressed into a thin line.

"That wasn't a question. I was just soft-selling my normal pushy self."

"You're Teddie's gal, aren't you?"

"Was."

Dig Me shook his head slowly. "Boy messed it up, man, I know that. First time on tour, man... all those pretty things throwing themselves at you. Young and fresh, too. Only a saint could resist."

"Are you pleading his case? If so, I'd rethink your strategy. Right now, I'm thinking the electric chair would be too humane."

"Ah, it's an explanation, not an excuse. Each man's responsible for keepin' his zipped, know what I mean? We all been there. Sometimes the best learnin' is by doin'. Whether you cut him a break, that's up to you." He put his hand over his heart. "The answer's in here."

He sounded like my father. I was beginning to resent all this advice. "I'd really like to know where you got Liberace's rock."

"Busta' Blue. I didn't buy it; he gave it to me."

I was ready for many different answers, but not that. Don't know why. So Pismo shooting Busta' was just a lover's spat, so to speak. Interesting. I didn't say anything for a bit as I worked out a scenario. Dig Me let me think, playing around with a couple of riffs. Finally, I thought I had it, just as O'Dell's riffs meshed. "I'm thinking that ring was an ace in the hole and Busta' was waiting for the right time to play it."

"How do you mean?"

"Teddie tells me somebody stole a take recently, from his tour. The proceeds from some large sold-out venues."

"Yeah, that's right. I was barely hanging on, and that put me and Smooth Sound on the ropes."

"Where'd the take go missing?"

"Frankfurt. Dealing with the police over there has been a nightmare."

I grabbed my phone. Jeremy answered on the first ring. "Hey."

"Are you at a computer?"

"At your office."

"Can you work your magic from there and tell me if either Busta' Blue or Johnny Pismo left the country recently. If so, where'd they go?"

"Sure. Take me a few."

"I'll wait. And do not lead NSA or the FBI or whoever back to my computer."

"Might be fun."

"Not if you want to live to see your wedding day." He and Miss P were set to tie the knot right before Christmas, so my threat held a bit of intended immediacy.

"You win." He wanted to marry Miss P in the worst way—his most redeeming quality of the thousands that I knew of.

I tried to keep my brain from running away while I waited.

Sooner than few, Jeremy was back. "Looks like Pismo made a quick turn to Europe."

"Where?"

"London."

My stomach clenched. Dang. I was so sure. And I wanted to wring Pismo's neck in the worst way. Unfulfilled homicidal tendencies were the worst to swallow.

"Oh, wait," Jeremy said. "He connected through London. Ended up in Frankfurt."

"You are brilliant."

"Can I quote you on that?"

"Of course." I pocketed my phone and turned to Dig Me O'Dell. "You got a fox in the hen house." Dang, I couldn't curb my cliché tendencies to save my soul. So much expression in so few words. How could I resist?

After securing O'Dell's promise to not do anything stupid—he still had the stolen property issue hanging over his head, and he sure didn't need a homicide one to go with it—I bolted to the Ferrari and sped back to the hotel.

Dane caught me as I came in the front door. "We need to talk."

I didn't even slow down. "Not now, Cowboy."

He fell into stride. "I need to say I'm sorry."

"Not now, Cowboy."

"At least let me help."

I skidded to a stop taking him by surprise. "You mean help like you did last time?"

He turned around in front of me. "I can explain."

I started motoring again, hitting the door to the stairs so hard it slammed against the wall and bounced back.

Dane put out a hand, barely saving his nose.

"Look." I tossed the word over my shoulder as I took the stairs two at a time. "I know how it went down. I've seen that chauvinistic Texas redneck side of you, and I don't like it."

At the Mezzanine level I stopped and turned. "Didn't you learn anything?"

He stared up at me from three steps down. "Do I get to talk now?"

"Not now, Cowboy." I turned and bolted for my office.

He didn't follow me.

When I slammed through the office door, no one moved. Jeremy, Teddie, Flash, and Romeo were glued to the GPS tracker.

"Romeo!" I barked which finally made him snap to. "I didn't get an update on Busta' Blue and Pismo. Where the hell are they?"

He made a quick phone call. From the look on his face he didn't like the information.

My heart sank. "You lost them."

"I told you," Flash added.

I shot her a shut-up glance. She wasn't helping. "And Livermore, he's on Pressman, right?"

"Right," Flash said. "Pressman took the goods to a warehouse in Henderson."

"Okay, Jeremy, you follow Teddie's stuff. I really need all of it back as he gave it to me. Understood?"

He gave me a quick nod, gathered his things, and headed toward the door.

"Wait." Flash blocked his path. "I'm going, too."

Jeremy shook his head at me. "Flash, this is where things get down and dirty."

"I'm a down-and-dirty kind of gal," she said, shooting a warning look across my bow. "I chased Pismo down, remember. Risked bodily harm. You owe me this story."

Over the top of her head, I gave Jeremy a pleading look. He shrugged.

"Okay. But do what Jeremy says. And stay out of trouble." Why I even bothered saying that, I didn't know. If there was trouble, Flash would find it. It's what she would do with it that had me worried.

Flash gathered her things and hustled after Jeremy.

Romeo frowned. "The police ought to handle this."

"For evidence to hold up, you guys need a warrant. I'm not sure we have enough evidence to convince even the most inclined judge, and not enough time to try."

He shrugged in agreement, but the look on his face told me he didn't like it.

"Let them do their thing, then they can call it in as a crime in progress and your guys can charge right in."

"Okay. I'll set it up. I'll need my radio. It's in the trunk of my car."

"You can deal with that as we head across town."

"Where are we going?" he asked, but I thought I saw a glimmer. He knew.

"Hunting." I gave him my best evil grin.

"I thought you'd never ask. We're heading to the Liberace Museum installation, aren't we?"

"My, detective, your powers are impressive." Although I sounded like it, I wasn't kidding. Color rose in his cheeks. The kid never could take a compliment.

"Hope you're up for a little breaking and entering."

LIBERACE'S MANSION NESTLED ON A QUIET RESIDENTIAL STREET ON the east side of town. Formerly one of the most prestigious, the neighborhood now looked old and faded, defeated by heat, time, and the changing of the guard. Wayne Newton's massive home wasn't far—he'd recently lost it to bankruptcy, hanging onto faded glory too long. I thought of my own life. Of Teddie. And I wondered what my heart would say if I listened.

The house, a long, lean brick rambler with a French roof, was quiet. The workday over, daylight was thinning toward night. Fifteen thousand square feet of over-the-top kitsch, restored to its former glory.

"Come with me," I motioned to Romeo as I let myself in the low wrought iron gate in the decorative fence fronting the street. "I know a secret way in."

"You think anybody's here?" he modulated his voice to match my hushed tones.

"We dangled the carrot. The thickening cover of darkness. I don't think they can resist. Hopefully we beat them here."

Moonlight lit our path as we padded down the drive around to the back. The awnings over the windows had been replaced; large potted palms squatted by the pool, which sparkled, catching the light. Everything looked fresh, new, cared for, as if Liberace had never left.

I wiggled one of the frames around the center pane of glass in the door to the grand ballroom, opening a secret panel. "I hope your guys killed the security system alert."

"Would I let you down? The new owner is going along with this. He was very happy to know of this secret way in."

"I'm sure. Glad they didn't change out the doors." I stepped inside and took a deep breath as memories assaulted me. Mona dancing with the Big Boss, hidden from those who would try to stop them. Liberace in his mink-lined cape playing the part he loved so much, then settling in at the white baby grand to play the music that filled his soul. The first true Vegas showman.

"How did you know that was here?" Romeo asked, then whispered into the mic on his shoulder telling his guys we were inside. He had three unmarkeds placed strategically around the neighborhood, the officers inside on the alert.

There was enough light on the horizon and from the moon to drink in what Vegas used to be. I let my gaze travel around the room. "Came here as a kid. Liberace himself showed me that. He was rather proud of it."

"Seriously?"

"I was really young, but some things you remember." I tugged on his coat. "This way. The figurine will be in his bedroom if they put it back where Liberace always kept them."

I pulled him through the front hall, up the stairs, taking a detour through his bathroom and boudoir because, well, it had to be seen. The bedroom, all ornate carved wood moldings, four-poster bed with thick quilted brocade, antiques stuffed in every corner, was fit for a fourteenth-century French queen, which somehow seemed appropriate.

"This is a guy's bedroom?" Romeo clearly knew as little about Liberace as his fellow twenty-somethings.

"In a manner of speaking."

The theme of the bedroom carried into the bathroom. With every surface covered in white marble, gilded fixtures, strategically placed mirrors, the room had been restored as I remembered it. I could picture the man himself in the round tub under mountains of bubbles. Where that image came from, I don't know, but I had a dim memory of him entertaining guests while bathing.

"The figurine is on the second shelf above the tub." Using the light on my iPhone, I confirmed that it was indeed where I'd thought it would be.

"Look at this stuff," Romeo said, his voice holding a childlike awe. He pressed a hand to his ear, seating the earpiece as he listened. "Car coming this way down the alley; lights are off."

I stepped to the window, holding the curtain open only as far as I needed to get a clear view. A black shape eased to a stop behind the house.

Romeo whispered into his mic. "I told my guys to turn the

system back on. Thieves get kind of twitchy when things aren't as they expect."

Doors opened, but the interior of the car remained dark. Shadowy forms met at the hood of the car and then turned toward the house. Flashlights darted and poked the darkness. There were two of them, at least two that I could see. "Let's find a place to hide."

CHAPTER NINE

FLASH

JEREMY'S HUMMER, black on black with dark tinted windows, hid us well as we idled through the warehouse district, a few weak bulbs over doors casting meager circles of light. We clung to the shadows as we closed on the dots on the GPS tracker I held in my hand. "A right at the next corner. We'll be one turn and two blocks away. Building will be second one on the left after a left turn at the next stop."

Jeremy pulled the big truck into the curb, using a construction dumpster to hide it from view. "The rest of the way on foot."

I slid out of the truck, landing on both feet, then shut the door, pressing it closed until I heard an almost inaudible click. Meeting at the front of the truck, Jeremy gave me the once-over. "You didn't exactly dress for this."

I glanced down at my Day-Glo pink. "What self-respecting woman dresses to blend with the background?"

"Different jobs require different uniforms."

"Find me a phone booth and I can change into my superhero tights and cape."

"You sound like Lucky," he whispered, then held up a finger for quiet.

Just like a man to get the last quip in and then end the battle. I took his comment as a good thing, and I only hoped I had her moxie when the proverbial shit hit the fan.

He turned and walked down the street, keeping close to the buildings and out of the light.

I stopped him, pulling his ear close so I could whisper. "What exactly are we looking for?"

He slowed only a little. "A crime in progress."

"Cool." I got that fluttery feeling in my stomach as I followed, practically stepping on his heels. My last encounter in a dark alley had left me with a simmering case of unresolved red-ass. Regardless, I clung to Jeremy—a man with a gun was a nice accessory when walking in on a crime.

A light shone from a single small window in the back of the large warehouse. I could see the triangle splash on the alley from my vantage point crouched behind the dumpster to the side of the building near the street. The bulb over the side door was burned out or gone, leaving a welcoming black hole. In the weak moonlight I could see the name MEMORABILIA RARITIES painted in faded white block letters above the loading docks on the street side of the building. The docks were quiet, empty of activity, the doors pulled down and presumably locked.

"The side door," Jeremy whispered, giving voice to my opinion as well.

We crab-walked, scurrying from one shadow to another. We stopped to take stock around the corner of the building from the door.

Jeremy pulled a set of picks out of his breast pocket. "Stay here until I motion you to join me." Then he was gone.

Leaning away from the building, I could just make out his

outline as he hunched over the lock. A few moments that were probably seconds but seemed like hours, and he waved me on.

I'd just stepped out of the darkness when a hand clamped over my mouth. A body pressed close to mine from behind. A menacing voice whispered, "You move, your friend is dead."

CHAPTER TEN

LUCKY

TWO OF them. Two of us.

Romeo shot me a glance as he unholstered his weapon. I shook my head, then looked around at all the beautiful marble and glass. He gave me a "seriously?" look.

"Can't replace some of this stuff," I whispered, thinking he needed a bit more convincing.

He put the gun away. I grabbed two stone obelisks, handing him one, keeping the other.

From my vantage point tucked back into the closet, I kept my eye on the red light of the alarm control panel on the bathroom wall by the door. Romeo hid himself in the thick brocade drapes next to the largest window in the bedroom and closest to the hall door.

The red light blinked, then changed to green. They were in.

Footfalls sounded downstairs. I cocked my head to listen. A wood floor. The ballroom. They fell quiet. The front hall—marble didn't echo. Then quieter still. The carpeted staircase. They knew exactly what they were looking for and where to find it. *Good job, Jeremy.*

~

FLASH

The clammy hand. The cheap cologne.

I stepped back into the guy, throwing my weight behind an elbow to his stomach. Grunting in pain, he doubled over. I gave him a backhand to the nose, which dropped him to his knees.

"Pismo, you dirty, double-crossing ass." My hands fisted in the fabric of his jacket, I yanked him to his feet.

He cupped his nose as blood leaked through his fingers. His eyes wide with hurt, he looked at me. "Shit, couldn't you save the rough stuff for later? I'm trying to help is all."

"Later?" His arrogance set my blood to simmering. I glanced at the side door. The door stood ajar. Jeremy had disappeared. "You're here to help, are you?" I said, keeping my voice to a low hiss. "You can start by telling me what's going down inside." I let loose of Pismo, but stayed close in case he needed more convincing.

"They got a guy. You'd be surprised at how good his forgeries are. And how fast he can make them. Little dude, covered in tats, a face that looks like adolescence wasn't much fun. He's got skills though."

I felt a frisson of recognition. I lived in the alleys—that's where the stories usually were, the good ones anyway. "He got a name?"

"The guys call him Worm."

"I know the guy. He's a genius. Started in street art. Heard he'd taken a ride on the meth train. Pretty strung out."

"Makes sense." Pismo showed a hint of concern—tiny, but it was there. "I always thought the dude was on the right side. I'm not sure he's doin' this making fakes thing because he wants to."

We both crouched down and peered at the side door. I was

hoping for a sign from Jeremy, but he'd disappeared. That gave me a hollow feeling in my chest. This had the stench of a setup. "The question is what are we going to do?"

"I got an answer," a voice growled behind us. "You two love birds, inside." Pressman.

I leaned around Johnny Pismo, using his body as a shield and found myself staring into the deadly black hole of a short barrel. The insurance weenie waggled the gun—nothing worse than a weenie with a gun and an axe to grind. "Over there. Follow your friend. We've been expecting you."

"A bunch of losers," I growled. "Clowns jumping out of boxes. I can hardly wait to see who's behind door number two."

Pressman stepped in and threw an elbow, catching me across the temple.

I crumpled as my world went dark.

I thought I heard Johnny Pismo scream.

LUCKY

I lost the guys coming up the stairs—one of the downsides to extra-plush carpeting—but I thought they'd slowed, were being careful. The dim light leaking in through the windows helped, but it was still hard to see. I squinted, focusing, watching for movement, afraid to breathe.

The fact that I'd done this sort of thing before made it worse rather than better. I knew what was coming, what needed to be done, what could go wrong. The obelisk weighed heavy in my hand. Sweat slicked my palm. My grip slipped. I wiped my hand on the leg of my pants and then regripped the stone.

"They'll be waiting in here." A dark form drifted across the doorway.

Waiting? So they weren't as dumb as we'd hoped.

A flash made me recoil. Then a pop. A chunk of marble shattered, splinters of stone zinging through the air. Close, but not close enough to make me move. Sweat? Yes. Darn near pass out? Yes. Move? No.

Another silenced shot. This time closer. I felt the trickle of something warm on my cheek where a shard of stone had hit me. This time I jumped.

Another shot. Closer still. Several pinpricks of pain on exposed skin. The next one would get me.

I hefted the stone in my hand. Not much against a gun.

Where the hell was Romeo?

∿

FLASH

When I came to, I was lying flat on my back in a puddle of something gag-worthy. My head thumped; I couldn't see out of my right eye—something had gummed it up good. I was alone. Pressman and Pismo had disappeared. I tried pushing myself up, but my right hand wouldn't move.

Blinking, I lay back for a moment, gathering myself, waiting for the world to stop spinning. Finally, things settled. I pulled on my right hand.

Handcuffed. To the railing on the staircase.

Seriously?

I pulled out one of the pins holding my hair. Ten seconds, maybe less, I was free. Gingerly, I rolled over onto my knees. The world stayed level. Using the railing I got my legs under me. Wobbly, but they held. With the back of my hand, I swiped at my right eye to clear it. Blood. Gingerly I felt my temple—a goose egg, the hair matted with sticky goo.

One of the loading bay doors shrieked open. I tucked myself into the shadow between the stairs and the wall and waited.

"Put those two idiots in the Suburban." A voice, mean, ugly.

Busta' Blue. "We don't have time to get rid of them and the other one."

The other one? They must be referring to Livermore—I remember something about him trailing Pressman.

"And the stuff?" That voice fired every homicidal tendency I had. Pressman. He held his gun at his side.

"We gotta move it tonight. Freddy Mac is waiting."

I peeked around the corner, keeping low. Jeremy, nursing his own bloody face, and Pismo, with a big wet splotch on the front of his pants, waited, cuffed together. I could see Jeremy's wheels turning but his options were few.

So were mine. I tucked back against the wall. What should I do? There were at least three bad guys and my knights were shackled. They were carting boxes, putting everything in the back of the SUV. Moving shop.

"And the bitch?" Pressman asked.

"Take care of her." Busta' seemed fine with everyone else doing his killing for him. Swell guy.

As steps approached, I cast about for something, anything I could use as a weapon. A two-foot section of a two-by-four supporting one of the stairs.

Perfect.

LUCKY

Making myself as small as I could, I cringed against the next shot. Romeo was somewhere behind the two thugs. My finger found the trigger of my Glock, but I wouldn't risk putting the kid in the line of fire.

Romeo had to make the first move. I had to know where he was exactly before I risked a shot.

I curled in on myself, squinting one eye, anticipating the pain.

But it didn't come.

Silence.

Then a meaty thunk. A grunt. The second guy, the one in back, fell.

The first guy turned, gun at the ready. He steadied his gun, pointing into the darkness. A silhouetted figure moved behind him. Romeo.

Holding my breath, I steadied my aim. I squeezed the trigger.

A bang loud enough to shatter glass reverberated around the small room. No silencer for this gal. When I shot somebody, I wanted the world to know it.

With a shout of surprise, the thug clutched his left butt cheek. His leg folded.

Romeo swung the obelisk, landing a bone-crushing blow to the guy's head.

I cringed. The guy's body went limp. He dropped to his knees, the gun slipping from his grip. Frozen for a moment, he then toppled over on his face at Romeo's feet.

Romeo raised his eyebrows at me as he kicked the guy's gun out of reach, then shook his head once, as he spoke rapidly into his mic. Sirens split the silence, so close they could've been in the back yard. Lights knifed through the darkness outside, painting across the walls.

"Two down," I said with more bravado than I felt, although adrenaline made me fearless. "Let's see how Flash and Jeremy are faring."

I stepped over the two inert forms and then stayed out of the way as Romeo and his men tidied up.

Miss P answered on the first ring. "Jeremy doesn't answer his phone. And the GPS trackers have been disabled."

The thrill of victory evaporated. "And Flash?"

"Can't reach her either." While her voice was matter-of-fact, panic frayed the edges. "Should the police be alerted? They're waiting close by."

"Romeo can make that call. We're five minutes away."

I grabbed the kid and filled him in on the way. I was wrong—in the Ferrari we were only three minutes away.

I eased down the street. At the corner I killed the engine—nothing subtle about 500 horses ready to run. Jeremy had done the same thing—I noticed his Hummer pulled off the road into a darker spot by a dumpster. A square of light lit the pavement in front of an open loading bay door. No movement. No cars. I didn't like it.

Guns drawn, the kid and I approached on foot. Everything was quiet... too quiet...as if abandoned in a hurry. With me taking the lead, we were just approaching the front of the building, using the shadows to hide, when a figure jumped out in front of me brandishing a bat.

I skidded to a stop and leveled my gun.

At the same time recognition dawned on both of us. Flash.

I lowered my gun. "Shit. You scared the hell out of me. You're lucky I didn't shoot you."

"*You* are lucky you didn't shoot me." She didn't smile. "They've taken Jeremy and Pismo. I know where they've gone."

I finally got a good look at her. "Are you okay?"

"I'll be better after I shoot Johnny Pismo."

She was fine.

Three in a Ferrari is a very tight squeeze, and under other circumstances I would've taken delight at Romeo's discomfort with Flash in his lap.

"Head downtown. They're headed to a pawnshop. Someone named Freddy Mac is waiting."

"I know where to go." The Ferrari leapt forward.

Flash didn't try to hold on—there wasn't anything to grab—so she let Romeo handle her weight and centrifugal force. "Oh, Romeo, tell your guys when they go in and search the place, I left them a present handcuffed to the metal railing on the stairs to the side door. And Livermore should be somewhere inside. I didn't have a chance to find him."

Romeo, hidden underneath her, tried to throw me a look, but then his face contorted as he took the weight of a two-G turn. "I can see why you're friends," he managed when he once again could breathe. Then he relayed the information to someone one the other end of his radio.

Five hundred horses made short work of the fifteen; then we barreled off the freeway onto the five-fifteen and then dropped quickly down into downtown. The lights of the Fremont Street Experience danced in exploding colors like electric fireworks a few blocks in front of us. I made a hard left before I got there, and then angled the car into a space reserved for Metro.

"We go the rest of the way on foot." Leading the way I plowed through the crowds, opening a lane for Romeo and Flash behind me. I still hadn't gotten used to the new downtown. With Zappos and Tony Hsieh moving in, bringing boatloads of money and a hipster vibe, the neighborhoods had been transformed practically overnight. The down-and-out, the has-beens, the faded glory was long gone, replaced by new buildings, lofts, refurbished hotels and casinos with a young and trendy vibe. I liked it and I didn't.

I carved a path toward the east edge of cool. Freddy Mac's shop was the only tenant in a ramshackle strip center still waiting for gentrification or at least refurbishment. We parked off to the side so we could see the front and the back. The storefronts were all dark, but a soft glow leaked from the backroom at Downtown Pawn, a large space on the end of the building.

Flash tugged on my shirt. "The black SUV in back. Looks like the one they all left in."

"How many are there?"

"Four is all I saw. But, while I was dealing with Pressman, they loaded the car and headed out. What I can't figure is Pismo's role in all of this. He acted like he was going to help me, then Pressman showed up and cracked my head open."

"Pismo is one of the bottom-feeders," I said. "They've got finely honed survival skills. I'm betting he can change teams mid-game."

"So you're thinking he got caught in the middle?"

"Maybe. Pismo's a small fish, always has been. Maybe he's gotten eaten by someone higher up the food chain." I thought about Dig Me O'Dell and Busta' Blue. "Might be interesting to know what's the bad blood between Busta' Blue and his recording label." I looked at the other two. "We've got two guns and three badasses to their four or more. They don't stand a chance."

"How about you take the back door?" Romeo asked me. "Flash and I can go in the front. I don't know what game Pismo is playing, but I have a feeling once we get inside, he's going to grab the loot and make a break for it."

Flash nodded. "Pismo's a runner, for sure."

"Okay. But, Flash, you hang back. If Pismo runs, you stop him, but nothing else. You got it?"

"Sure." She gave me her best go-to-hell look.

Why I ever pretended to be in control was beyond me. That woman would risk life and limb to get a good story, and this one looked to be a doozy. "Just be careful. And aim first. Jeremy's in there." That reminder was for Romeo.

We parted ways as I eased around the back, gun at the ready. The back door stood slightly ajar. Either they underestimated us in their arrogance, or they were vying for a spot on the Stupid Criminal show. Either way worked for me—being a female in a male-dominated world, I'd learned to use people's underestimation to my advantage.

Keeping my back to the wall, with two fingers I opened the door enough to peer inside. Five guys clustered around a table. Busta' Blue, three of his sidekicks, Worm, the forger. He looked unhappy and strung-out.

Freddy Mac, one of Vegas's low-level fences, sat at the table, a jeweler's eyepiece in one eye, as he held one of Teddie's treasures to the light. "Man, these are amazing." He glanced at Busta' Blue with his non-eyepieced eye. "I've heard about these for years—the stuff of Vegas legend. Never thought I'd see them. And never thought I'd have them all together."

"You got us a buyer in mind?" Busta' Blue asked as he carefully placed each figurine back in the valise.

I scanned the room looking for Jeremy and Pismo. I didn't see them. I didn't like it. Throwing caution to the wind, I eased through the door, using some open shelving to hide.

"Several. But these are going to be hot, real hot. It's gotta be a buyer who wants them only for himself. I got a guy in Hong Kong who might be the best." He angled a look at Worm who stood off to the side, rubbing his arms, looking like he was heading for a crash. "You work your magic on these?"

"Man, you got my stuff? I can't do it without my stuff."

Busta' nodded to one of his guys, who pulled a syringe out of his pocket. Worm held out his arm. Everyone seemed fascinated, onlookers at a train wreck.

While they were mesmerized, I slipped around to my right toward a doorway. I had no idea where it led, but I needed to find Jeremy and Pismo before the bullets started flying. Knowing Flash, I didn't have long.

My eyes adjusted to the darkness. I found myself in a storeroom, shipping supplies on shelving, wooden crates, pallets, and, in the middle, two guys tied in chairs. Jeremy's eyes followed me as I moved closer. He nodded, one side of his face covered in blood. After glancing back through the doorway, I crouched and ran, then skidded to a stop on my knees, using the two men to hide.

Pismo started to turn around to watch me behind him.

"Straight ahead, Pismo. You let them know I'm here, and you're the first one I shoot."

His head snapped forward.

Jeremy had almost gotten himself loose, so it didn't take me long to free him from the ropes. I hesitated behind Pismo. Should I, or shouldn't I? No doubt he'd be better tied up—at least then I'd know where he was and what he was going to do. But leaving him a sitting duck when the bullets flew didn't seem charitable.

The crack of a bullet being fired. Glass shattering. I was out of time. I tossed my gun to Jeremy and went to work on Pismo's ropes. "You mess with me, I swear I'll hunt you down and your death will be painful," I whispered in his ear. I felt his shiver as his ropes fell away.

Gunshots sounded as I joined Jeremy by the door, one of us on either side. Crouching low, I took a peek. Worm had slithered down the wall into a heap in the corner. Freddy Mac dove under the table and stayed there, his arms over his head. Romeo had made it inside and was driving Busta' and his men back toward us. He'd picked one of the men off—he held his knee as he writhed on the floor. I didn't see his gun. Now three against one, the advantage was turning Busta' Blue's way. They had Romeo pinned down behind the front counter.

I gave Jeremy a shrug, then launched myself into the fray, hoping Romeo didn't shoot me. Grabbing a chair, I swung it, using my considerable weight. It broke over the head of the nearest bad guy. He crumpled. The guy next to him spun my direction, his gun pointed at my chest. Jeremy took him out with a shot to the shoulder. He fell, and I finished him off with a kick to the head.

That left Busta' Blue. He shot at Romeo but missed wide. Then he swung the gun toward me.

"This one's mine." Flash shouted. A human torpedo in Day-Glo Pink, she launched herself at his chest.

The air left him with a grunt as he went down hard on his back, Flash riding him all the way down. I handed her the piece of chair leg I still held. She hit him once across the temple, then another time just because. I knew how she felt.

Romeo, breathing hard, his gun trained on Freddy Mac, loomed over her. His eyes caught mine. "I ought to arrest you both."

I played along. "For what?"

"Stupidity. What did you guys think you were doing launching into a gun fight with no guns?"

"Ah, kid." I nudged him with an elbow. "I knew you had my back."

Flash nodded. "Me, too. Never a doubt."

Romeo tried to glare at us, failing miserably. "I don't know whether to shoot you both or hug you."

"We have that effect on people, men especially," I said.

Flash nodded, her face flushed with victory as she crawled off of the inert form of Busta' Blue. "He's not such a badass now, is he?"

Romeo motioned to Freddy Mac. "Get out of there."

I grabbed the ropes from the storeroom, and Jeremy, Flash, and I tied up the bad guys while Romeo called the situation in.

We'd forgotten about Pismo.

A flash of mismatched colors. A whiff of bad cologne. The hint of nicotine. He dashed by me, grabbed the valise with Teddie's treasures and ran out the front door.

I stopped Flash as she turned to run after him. "No. This one's mine," I said as I bolted after him.

The night held an eerie glow from Fremont Street as we pounded down 10th Street. I closed the gap. I could hear his labored breathing. Three packs a day took its toll. With each stride, the valise banged against his thigh. The mental image of Teddie's figurines banging around in there spurred me on faster. My long strides ate up the distance between us. Almost within reach, I made a lunge for him. He planted a foot and careened around the corner onto Carson.

I staggered, but didn't fall. Head down, I pushed off and ran after him. The crowd in this neighborhood was thin, but up ahead I could see the lights of the Container Park. At this time of night the central area would be packed with people eating, strolling, shopping. Pismo would try to lose himself in the crowd.

The valise pounded against his leg. He switched hands as he ran, throwing a look over his shoulder.

Measuring the distance as I ran, I lowered my head and reached down for another gear. It wasn't there. The tank was low. My legs churned, running on fumes.

I couldn't let Teddie down. Failure looming spurred me on. My breath came in ragged gasps now. My heart pounded in my ears. I focused only on the valise and wringing Pismo's scrawny neck. Three strides behind, I was just short when he angled into the Container Park, heading straight for the tall slide in the middle. The crowd slowed him down. As he jumped on the ladder, I grabbed his foot. He kicked off his shoe and me with it.

I watched him scramble up the ladder, holding tight to the valise with one hand, using the other to grab the rungs. Following him would've been a fool's game, probably bait he hoped I would take. He had nowhere to go.

Hands on my knees, I watched him as I gulped air. He elbowed kids out of the way. Parents circled the slide below, yelling at him. A particularly irate father elbowed in next to me, bellowing threats at Johnny Pismo.

When he'd made the top platform, he stopped and turned, looking down at me.

"Finally, you figured out how to draw a crowd," I shouted up to him as I motioned to the gathering throng. "You've got nowhere to go. Get down from there. I'll see the police go easy."

He held the valise in both hands and gave me a smile I didn't like. With a big windup, he coiled his body.

"No!" I shouted, every nerve in my body firing, adrenaline flooding my system. The world came into focus. My vision cleared. Thoughts of homicide slowed the action down powering my reflexes. Keeping my eye on the valise, I grabbed the father's arm. "He's yours. Kill him if you have to, but don't let him get away."

"You got it."

Johnny uncoiled, stepping into the throw. In slow motion the valise arced over the crowd. Knifing through the gathering, I followed it. Elbowing people aside, I stumbled, staggered, righted myself, following the valise as it arced over my head. A kid stepped in front of me, a small girl. I tripped.

A hand grabbed my arm, steadying me.

Jeremy.

"Get Pismo," I wheezed as I ran, my eyes glued to the valise.

The valise started down. Three strides as it fell. I launched myself. With a dive, I caught it, then rolled, cushioning it with my body. My breath left me. My vision swam. I clung tight to Teddie's treasures.

I didn't lie there long. I gathered myself. A kind gentleman helped me to my feet. People stepped out of my way as I stalked back through the crowd.

Jeremy held Pismo by the elbow, his shoulders slumped in defeat.

The valise in one hand, I barely slowed in front of him.

With an elbow to his temple, I dropped Pismo like a rock.

CHAPTER ELEVEN

FLASH

*S*LUMPED DOWN in the chair in the interrogation room at the Detention Facility, Johnny Pismo looked like the loser he was. He'd wanted to see me. Romeo watched through the one-way mirror.

Pismo didn't look up when I pulled out the chair across from him and sat. His hands clasped on the table, his head down, he looked like a whipped puppy, which actually was an insult to puppies everywhere.

"You were never meant for the big time, Pismo."

His head snapped up, but acceptance slackened his features. Lucky had given him quite a shiner, various shades of dark purple. Personally, I thought she'd gone easy on him, but I was more the vindictive type.

"Want to tell me how all this went down?"

He shot a glance at the mirrored glass. "You and your boyfriend there go easy on me?"

"It's no fun hurting a guy when he's already down, although for you I might make an exception. I can't promise anything for the cops, but I do know if you come clean, make this easy for them, give them some dirt on Busta' Blue or whomever, they'll try to return the favor."

Staring at his hands, his knuckles white, he weighed his options for a moment. When he looked up, he'd made a decision. "Okay. But look, Worm, he's a victim here. I got him in. We were working it small time. I kept him clean. But Busta' Blue, when he..." Pismo trailed off, an angry flush creeping up his cheeks. "He knew how to hurt Worm. I'm feeling real bad about that. Got in too deep to get him out. You'll help with that?"

I nodded, and I could almost feel Romeo do the same.

"I started small, stealing stuff out of vaults. Stuff nobody'd notice was missing. Worm would do the fake and I'd put that one back in the vaults. The gig was working fine."

"Until Freddy Mac got greedy."

"How'd you know?"

"Good guess."

"He was my pipeline into the black market. Can't really take the hot stuff to Christie's, you know. Then Busta' Blue offered a ton of money for Liberace's ring."

"Wonder why?"

"Why does anybody want that shit? Man, it's addictive." Passion infused his voice as he cupped his hands. "Holding a piece of Vegas history. Man, it's a high like no other."

"Addictive?"

"It's heroin on crack, man."

I felt sorry for Pismo, I really did. This was the closest he'd ever get to greatness. To the adulation of the crowds. To being a part of Vegas and its history. And that was all he had ever wanted, to be part of the story. I was pretty sure the part he played wasn't the part he had in mind. But, oddly, I wasn't sure he really cared about that. "The police need a list of what you stole, and they'll want you to write out your statement."

"I know."

I reached over and squeezed his hand. "This show is closing, Johnny. You've had your run."

LUCKY

I found Teddie at the piano in Delilah's. Clearly worried but trying not to show it, he played around with some Sinatra arrangements while the crowd half-listened. When he caught sight of me he flashed a smile, one lacking its normal wattage. I held up the valise, and he brightened.

"I chased this thing through downtown, but I got it." I wasn't going to tell him about the toss from the top of the slide as I set the case next to him. "I haven't been able to look at them. Will you check to make sure they're okay? They took a bit of a rough ride."

"I was more worried about you." He undid the latch on the valise.

I didn't know what to say.

He sensed that. "What's that on your sweater?"

I pulled the back of it around so I could see what he was talking about. "Strawberry ice cream. I landed in some. Don't ask."

"So who was doing what to whom? Dig Me O'Dell? Did you figure what part he played?"

"The patsy."

Teddie raised his eyebrows. "Not a part he'd take kindly to. What went down?"

"Busta' Blue. I'm guessing he wanted to sit at the top of the food chain. I can't prove it yet, but I'm pretty sure he arranged for Pismo to steal the take from your tour. Then, with O'Dell's back to the wall, Busta' Blue figured Dig Me would start unloading his treasures to come up with enough cash to save his empire."

"And when someone bought Liberace's ring and discovered it was stolen?" Teddie formulated the thought as a question.

"With Dig Me's past record, man, they'd lock him up forever.

And with him out of the way, Busta' Blue would be sitting pretty in the catbird seat."

"So Busta' Blue set him up nice and tidy." Teddie looked impressed. "Pretty slick."

"Pismo was the wildcard. As long as the ring stayed in O'Dell's collection, nobody would be the wiser."

"But once he started liquidating..." Teddie was following.

"Then Pismo would be exposed. Busta' could point the finger at him, and he'd take the fall for everything. But Busta' Blue didn't count on Johnny Pismo's ability for self-preservation. That ring is the only piece we can trace to Pismo. If he could put it back in the case at the Babylon, a reverse switch, before anyone was the wiser..."

"He'd be in the clear." Teddie finished the thought. "I'm guessing Dig Me will be back in business."

"Your tour awaits you, I'm sure."

He shrugged, looking a bit torn. Stardom was an addictive drug.

I gestured to the valise sitting next to him. "Don't keep me in suspense. Check them out, okay?"

He smiled and did as I asked. He looked at the minor treasures, then, one by one, he pulled the figurines out of their foam shells in the valise and held them up to the light. "Look perfect." He nestled them back and closed the lid. "Did you get to see the three together?"

"No. But I did see the one in Liberace's boudoir. It looked lonely."

"I've agreed to lend my two to the collection. I never understood why people buy stuff like this and then keep it all to themselves. It's part of our history and should be shared."

"I know they'll be thrilled." I shifted from foot to foot, an awkward silence stretching between us. Something new. We used to be so comfortable with each other.

"Buy you a drink?"

My phone chirped at my hip, saving me from indecision for a moment and giving me a chance to consider how I felt about a drink with Teddie. I glanced at the caller ID and my heart soared. "Hey, how's the night going?"

"Busy, so many people want hamburgers." Jean-Charles sounded beat. "How's yours?"

"Successful."

"Good. I'm very tired. How does Champagne in bed sound while we share news of our day?"

I flicked a glance at Teddie who watched me, his face impassive, his eyes dark, hopeful. "Perfect. I'll meet you there."

The hope faded.

I reholstered my phone as I looked at Teddie. I wanted to trust him again. I wanted us to be friends. I'd told him being lovers would ruin the friendship. One of the few times I hated being right. "Another time perhaps.

The light in his eyes blinked out.

"Teddie, can we go back to being friends?"

"Sure. I'd like that."

And I could tell that he did.

As I walked away, down the steps, he launched into the opening bars of *Lucky For Me.*

This time, at least for now, my heart stayed strong.

Jean-Charles was debating over several bottles of bubbly in his bar off the TV room in the back of his house.

"I let myself in." I flung my purse onto the couch. "Hope you don't mind."

"It is your home," he said as he moved toward me, capturing me in a hug. He held me tight, savoring. "I've missed you. Life is not right when you are not close to me."

"I know." Home, he'd said. I drew into myself. Yes, in his arms I felt at home.

"You smell like strawberries."

"Ice cream. Long story."

"You must tell me."

"I will." Most of it, I thought. Not the Teddie part. "Over Champagne when you are... more casually attired."

"The anticipation is killing me." He nuzzled my neck as he held me close, so close our hearts syncopated to the same rhythm.

"Where's Christophe and Chantal?" Christophe, Jean-Charles's five-year-old son, had captured my heart. I missed him. Chantal was Jean-Charles's niece, studying at the Culinary Institute to follow in her uncle's footsteps. After an interesting start, our relationship had settled into comfortable and warm.

"Desiree is in town, staying at Cielo even though it is not open." Desiree was his twin sister. He tightened his grip at my unvoiced protest. "They are happy. Chantal is cooking in my kitchen there, and your lovely rooms are finished. They don't need much. Consider them, how do you say it? Alpha testers."

"Close." I chuckled as I eased out of his embrace, stealing a languorous kiss before disengaging completely. "Beta testers."

"This is it." He stepped back around the bar, popped the cork, then nestled the bottle in a bucket and started scooping ice around it. "Why don't you take a shower or whatever you would like to do to relax. I will finish this, then put together a plate of fruit and cheese. It won't take me long, then I will join you. I have something I must ask you."

"Really?" I didn't want to talk about business, not now, but if it was important to him, I would... a little. "Okay. Don't take too long." Knowing we were alone in the big house, I started shucking clothes as I padded through the kitchen, dining room, front foyer and through the double doors leading to the master suite. His bedroom was a lovely room with French doors opening on a beautiful backyard anchored by a stunning pool with a rock waterfall, lush vegetation, and a hidden hot tub to one side. Stepping out of my pants, then my bikini briefs, and unwinding from my bra, I reached into the shower and turned the water on high and hot. It jetted out of the walls as well as from a rainfall showerhead above. If there was one thing I loved, it was a great bathroom. And if it came with a sexy, kind man with a French accent, so much the better.

Teddie and I had almost killed ourselves having sex in a shower.

I closed my mind to the memory.

This was different. Jean-Charles was different. I was different.

The soap was whittled to a shred, so I went in search of another bar as the water heated. Humming a tune, I pawed through drawers and cabinets. In the far cabinet, a box lumped under a stack of towels, a corner poking out. I chewed on my lip as I contemplated looking inside or not.

Curiosity won out.

I eased the box out. Small, square, intimidating.

I opened the top and gasped.

A ring. With one large square-cut diamond.

THE END

Thank you so much for going on a Lucky adventure with me. I hope you enjoyed the ride.

As you may know, reviews are SUPER helpful. They not only help potential readers make a choice, but they also help me win coveted spots on various advertising platforms.

So, if you would please, do me the favor of leaving a review at the outlet of your choice.

ALSO BY DEBORAH COONTS

The Lucky O'Toole Vegas Adventure Series

Wanna Get Lucky? (Book 1)

Lucky Stiff (Book 2)

So Damn Lucky (Book 3)

Lucky Bastard (Book 4)

Lucky Catch (Book 5)

Lucky Break (Book 6)

Lucky the Hard Way (Book 7)

Lucky Ride (Book 8)

Lucky Score (Book 9)

Lucky Ce Soir (Book 10)

Other Lucky O'Toole Books

The Housewife Assassin Gets Lucky

(Co-written with Josie Brown, author of the Housewife Assassin series)

Lucky O'Toole Original Novellas

Lucky in Love (Novella 1)

Lucky Bang (Novella 2)

Lucky Now and Then (Novella 3)

Lucky Flash (Novella 4)

Other Novels

After Me (psychological medical thriller)

Deep Water (romantic suspense)

Crushed (contemporary romance)

ABOUT THE AUTHOR

Deborah Coonts swears she was switched at birth. Coming from a family of homebodies, Deborah is the odd woman out, happiest with a passport, a high-limit credit card, her computer, and changing scenery outside her window. Goaded by an insatiable curiosity, she flies airplanes, rides motorcycles, travels the world, and pretends to be more of a badass than she probably is. Deborah is the author of the Lucky O'Toole Vegas Adventure series, a romantic mystery romp through Sin City. *Wanna Get Lucky?*, the first in the series, was a *New York Times* Notable Crime Novel and a double RITA™ Award Finalist. She has also penned a few standalone novels; *After Me*, a medical thriller, *Deep Water*, a romantic suspense, and *Crushed*, a contemporary romance set in Napa. Although rarely there, Deborah calls Houston home. You can always track her down at:

www.deborahcoonts.com
deborah@deborahcoonts.com

[facebook icon] facebook.com/deborahcoonts
[twitter icon] twitter.com/DeborahCoonts
[instagram icon] instagram.com/deborahcoonts

Published by Chestnut Street Press

eBook ISBN: 978-1-944831-79-0
Paperback ISBN: 978-1-944831-60-8
Hardcover ISBN: 978-1-944831-61-5

Cover design by Streetlight Graphics
(www.streetlightgraphics.com)

Formatting by Austin Brown (www.cheapebookformatting.com)

CPSIA information can be obtained
at www.ICGtesting.com
Printed in the USA
FSHW010508020819
60646FS